CRITICS RAV

MORE PRAISE FOR JADE LEE!

DEVIL'S BARGAIN

"Jade Lee has written a dark and smoldering story...full of sensuality and heart-pounding sex scenes."

—*Affaire de Coeur*

"[An] exciting erotic romance...."

—*Harriet's Book Reviews*

"A luscious bonbon of a sensual read—the education of an innocent: hot, sensual, romantic, and fun!"

—Thea Devine, *USA Today* Bestselling Author

"A spicy new debut...."

—*RT BOOKclub*

"Highly charged and erotic.... You won't be able to put it down."

—Roundtable Reviews

"*Devil's Bargain* is a definite page-turner...a must read this summer."

—*Romance Reviews Today*

WHAT MUST BE DONE

Xiao Fei came back to herself slowly. She lay on something soft, and she smelled herbs. Not the scents she was used to, they had a definite Western meaning in her mind, but no real understanding formed. Someone was chanting nearby, his voice the low drone so reminiscent of the temple of her childhood.

She was in a hotel room. Even in the dim candlelight that dotted the walls, she recognized an innocuous floral painting hanging above a generic chair with sturdy, lime-green fabric. Shifting her head a bit, she saw a utilitarian dresser with a TV on a rotating pedestal. On top of that were candles and simmering potpourri. That explained the incense-like scent.

Next came the tall mirror in which she saw… Was that her? Tied spread-eagle and naked to a bed? She jerked upright, only to feel the bite of rope around her arms and legs. Only now did she feel the sudden chill on her skin, though in truth, the room was quite warm. "What the…?"

The chanting continued without interruption. She was now awake enough to locate the sound, which was to her right, by the second bed. A man in a white bathrobe knelt on the floor, his back to her, reciting a chant from a small book. She could see more candles, ceremonial knives, and a flowering plant's petals scattered in some pattern around him. It was Patrick.

SEDUCED BY CRIMSON

JADE LEE

LOVE SPELL NEW YORK CITY

LOVE SPELL®

March 2006

Published by

Dorchester Publishing Co., Inc.
200 Madison Avenue
New York, NY 10016

ISBN 0-505-52672-7

To Elisabeth for helping when I was spazzing.
To Liz, Chris, and the rest of the Crimson City
team for including me in this fabulous world,
and to my kids who went to camp
so I could get the book written.
From the bottom of my heart:
THANK YOU!

SEDUCED BY
CRIMSON

Prologue

A man can get tunnel vision during battle. He fixates on the sight of blood spurting from a white throat or the smell of charred flesh. If he's trained, he can still fight the demons, the blackhearted Bak-Faru he's likely seen only in a book, but a large part of his mind still fixates on one hideous thing. For Patrick Lewis, it was the taste in the air: blood and bile. Metallic and bitter, it made his throat close and his chest heave. But he had enough training to fight even if he was coming late to the battle.

The screams reached him first. He was in the San Bernardino Botanical Garden, so the sound could travel far, especially at night. He was running full-tilt for the grove when the smell hit him, the smell and that taste in the air.

He didn't even stumble: that was how well trained he was. But his mind was so caught up in not retching that he almost missed the sight of his first live Bak-Faru. The thing was humanlike. Large and dark haired, it had eyes that glowed bright lavender in the night. Patrick's mother had told him the demon gate was being used, and indeed, attuned as he was to nature, he'd felt each and every tremor as something passed through. Still, he hadn't actually believed such disaster was possible until now, seeing one, two . . . no, make that four of the creatures walking away. Two sported wounds—jagged flesh that bled dark down their naked torsos. But the demons didn't seem to be slowed.

Patrick didn't think. He had seven ceremonial knives with him and began throwing. Score. The closest demon clutched his neck and stumbled, but didn't fall. The monster's companions barely glanced around, even when Patrick's second knife lodged in one of their shoulder blades. They were intent on escape.

Patrick wanted to pursue. He even took a step forward, but the need to find his parents burned hotter. He had to get to the grove. Especially since his mother's screams were growing weaker. Yet he had to go slowly. Much though it burned his gut, Patrick shifted from battle mode to stealth; it wouldn't help his parents if he stumbled blindly into more of these creatures.

He slipped around a redwood and peered into the grove, where his tunnel vision returned with full force. His mind registered each sensation as a disparate element: the taste of bile in the air, the smell of death, and the clenching of his gut. He refused to look for long, searching the bodies on the ground with as much speed as he could manage.

He found his father first, with only one shoulder and half a chest; the rest was burned to oblivion, as if a rocket had burst through him. Numbness seeped into Patrick's spirit. At least his dad hadn't felt any pain.

Patrick stumbled, scanning the rest of the bodies. He found his mother. She wasn't as lucky as his father. She'd been gutted by a short blade, or more likely, by long claws. Blood and bile poured relentlessly from her into the ground where she lay. She was still alive.

Patrick skidded to a halt in the dirt beside her, but there was nothing for him to do; too much of her was spilled across the ground. His hands hovered uselessly above her torn belly. What could he do? He dialed 911 and stammered out details. The operator was speaking to him, but he didn't hear her because his mother opened her eyes. The phone left his ear as he leaned forward. He opened his mouth to reassure her. He was going to lie, to say that she'd be just fine, but all that came out was a single word:

"Mom?"

She focused on him and her expression softened. She struggled to speak, her voice a bare whisper, and Patrick lowered his head as close to her mouth as he dared.

"Run," she said.

He straightened enough to look into her eyes. "They're gone. The . . ." He couldn't bring himself to name the monsters, the creatures of nightmare that had at last returned to his world. "They've left."

His mother swallowed, and he was sure he saw relief in her gaze. He grabbed her hands, his mind scrambling for something to do. "Hang on," he said.

"Find her," she replied. "Close . . . the gate." She was fading; he could see it. Her eyes were growing more distant, and her hands were like ice. He wanted to strip off

Chapter One

Xiao Fei Finney didn't like to hunt vampires. It was too dangerous, and she was too vulnerable. But she liked illegal fang activity in Chinatown even less.

The area residents had reported the crimes to the police, of course. They'd told the authorities about the drug addicts sucked dry and dumped between the ginger market and the dumpling palace. Xiao Fei's boss, Mrs. Wang, had even made a big stink about a pair of lovers who'd disappeared under mysterious circumstances. But B-Ops in Los Angeles—the government agency set up to handle illegal paranormals and discord between the species—had bigger problems than a rogue vamp or two, even if all of Chinatown was afraid to go out at night. Truth was—according to the news reports—vamp and werewolf tension was ratched up all through the rechristened "Crimson City," and everybody was afraid to go out day or night.

Everybody, of course, but several too-cocky fangs and the vigilantes who hunted them.

This particular rogue vamp's name was Stan, and he was systematically buying out an entire block of Gin Ling Way. His plan was to corner the local gambling, racketeering, and whoring market. His method was whatever worked: intimidation, seduction, vamp conversion. . . .

The last, of course, had been the final straw. When one of Chinatown's young sons showed up with fangs, the remaining sons and daughters had to act. Xiao Fei hadn't planned the trap—that was Pei Ling's job. He was young—nineteen to be exact—but he was smart, methodical, and well-liked. In short, people followed him, whereas they simply thought Xiao Fei was weird. They were right, of course, but that didn't make her any less lonely.

In any event, they all knew where Stan and his thugs would show up next: Chen's China Emporium. Old Mr. Chen wouldn't sell his little slice of America to anyone at any price, so all they had to do was hide up and down the block, guns at the ready, until Stan's fellow fangs tried to make a move.

Xiao Fei had her favorite weapon—a Glock 27—strapped to her ankle. She'd carried a pistol since leaving Cambodia. Still, as the best marksman in the group, she had a tranq rifle in her hands and had put herself in a good sniping position.

Showtime.

Stan's crew walked like petty royalty—or the newest Hollywood celebs—straight down the center of the street. There was poor Donny Li Chen. Only two weeks a vamp, and he already looked just like the others.

If it were up to her, Xiao Fei would have waited until they did something illegal—threw a brick at a window, threatened an old lady, hell, even kicked a dog. But she wasn't in charge, and Pei Ling wasn't like her, a refugee from harder lands; he had the impatience of an American-born Chinese. He waited only long enough for the fangs to make it past the first two shooters; then he hit the signal: an air horn loud enough to startle anyone who wasn't expecting it. Hell, Xiao Fei was expecting it, and still she jerked.

The vamps flew straight up into the air, just as predicted. Then the shooting began. The others in Xiao Fei's team had basic guns: single barrel, normal bullets. The plan was to make vampire Swiss cheese of the henchmen, knock them out of the sky and finish them off. Donny and Stan were Xiao Fei's responsibility.

All vamps were strong, but some were less so than others. Especially the newly turned. Donny went down first, real easy, her dart in his midsection. Xiao Fei executed a practiced wrist flip, and another dart dropped into her gun. Then she sighted . . . Where the hell was the leader? Where was Stan?

There. He'd already been shot a few times. It didn't seem to be slowing him down, but the bullets had knocked him against a building, and he'd tumbled afoul of a string of New Year's lanterns.

Gung Ho Fat Choy. Happy New Year, vamp, she thought with a smile. *You get to be cured.* She pulled the trigger and a dart blossomed from his neck. *Flip-swish.* Sight and squeeze. Another dart appeared just below his collarbone. *Flip-swish* one more time, and he was down, snoozing on the pavement, right next to Donny and bits of vamp cheese that would never bite anything again.

Xiao Fei put her sights back on Donny. She was pretty sure Stan would stay down; three darts would take care of Dracula himself. As for the other vamps . . . She would just have to trust Pei Ling's crew had done their jobs. Meanwhile, she prayed that Stan's legion of girl-friends were busy doing their nails and not about to drop down as reinforcements.

She bit her lip, abruptly lifting her gun to scan the skies. She loved Pei Ling like a brother, and he could make a damn fine ha gow, but this was her life on the line. Forget watching the sleeping Donny; she was going to look for vamp reinforcements.

The air horn blared again. All clear. Apparently no other fangs were coming. She scanned the skies one more time, weapon at the ready. Her peripheral vision showed all four of her companions moving with no ill ef-fects. Nothing new dropped out of the sky. Nothing erupted from side streets. Everything really was all clear.

She waited another ten seconds, watching without moving as the others grabbed Donny and Stan and dragged them into the acupuncture shop. Pei Ling re-mained in the street to set fire to the bullet-riddled vamp bodies, and to bellow up at her.

"Xiao Fei, hurry up!"

She winced. Did he have to shout her name like that? Did he really think that they were safe just because they'd caught these two vamps? But that was an ABC for you: never enough paranoia to survive in a war zone. Well, her position was given away now. With one last look around, she straightened into a half crouch and skittered down the fire escape. Now came the real work.

"Wow. Awesome playground."

Patrick ignored Hank's reverent tone as he powered up his mother's massive computer. His druid friend stroked the flat screen while behind him Hank's girlfriend Slick fingered a silk jacket his mother had bought in Vietnam for seven dollars.

"Where'd she get all this stuff?" Slick asked.

Patrick didn't answer. He'd long since gotten used to the layers of scrolls, dusty fans, and various Asian paraphernalia that perpetually surrounded his white mother. Still, he couldn't stop himself from reaching out and stroking a carved sandalwood fan that scented the air next to the monitor. Then his eyes drifted to a photo from his tenth Christmas. Even at twelve, his sister been a beauty, and his brother had the geek glasses and pocket protector of the genius accountant he would eventually become. But what Patrick noticed most was his mother's bright Asian scarf knotted about her neck. It had a batik design in brilliant red, the perfect accent to her dark green gown. And yet, despite all that, it was her face that glowed. She was no beauty by even a fond son's standard, but she had a vibrancy inside her that outshone even that brilliant red scarf.

His gaze drifted to his father, Mr. Stern Hard-Ass, as he'd used to call him. Except in this photo, Mr. Hard-Ass wasn't disciplining his children. He wasn't even looking all professorish and serious. He was gazing at his wife with such devotion that Patrick was stunned he hadn't ever noticed before. His father had loved his mother. Passionately, devotedly, and . . .

And it was over now because they were both dead.

The computer trilled—new e-mail for his mom—and Patrick forced himself to focus. Behind him, Slick and Hank had begun to bicker.

"Don't touch that," Slick ordered. "It's like a violation or something. I mean, they're—"

"I know what they are," Hank snapped. "I . . . I know. I saw."

"So don't touch—"

"Find the monk's book," interrupted Patrick. "Hand-written in Chinese characters. It'll have Mom's translation on blue paper folded inside. I think it's over there."

He gestured randomly, pleased that his voice didn't shake. There was precious little time before the authorities showed up. Once the bodies were found, then everything would be frozen for the investigation. He had to be long gone by then. Hopefully, he'd have found the Phoenix Tear and closed the demon gate before anyone brought him in for questioning. Before he had to deal with . . .

He pushed his grief away. As Draig-Uisge, pain had no place in his heart.

"Damn, they're all written in Chinese," grumbled Hank. "How the hell are we supposed to—"

"Let him be," Slick hissed. "Just look for the blue papers—"

"But—"

Patrick bit out an order before the bickering sent him postal. "Hank, I need the file on Phoenix Tears. From that cabinet." He pointed, and Hank immediately hauled open a drawer.

"There's nothing—"

"It's in Celtic, Hank."

His friend growled again. "Jesus. Isn't there anything you need in English?"

Patrick didn't answer. He was too busy typing. Thankfully, he knew his mother's passwords. Her research was too important not to be coded, but her son was the Draig-Uisge and her nearest research partner. He knew her security protocols better than anyone.

"Got nothing in English or Celtic," Hank called.

"Try 'tears.' Phoenix Tears. They're a Cambodian cult," Patrick responded. "Bunch of girls with tattoos."

"Cult?" Slick gasped. "Like a sex cult?"

Patrick shook his head as he scanned his mother's e-mail for anything she hadn't been able to tell him yet. Ever. Because she'd never— Once again, he cut off his thoughts. "They're not sex girls, they're bleeders. Hemophiliacs."

"Got it!" Hank's voice merged with the sound of the file drawer rolling further open. "There's a butt-load of . . . Holy mother, these are adoption papers! Xiao Fei Finney. This girl escapes war-torn Cambodia, gets adopted by an L.A. family, and gets saddled with Finney as a last name? Sometimes life just sucks." He paused. "So, do we want her or the sister? They're both here."

Patrick frowned as he looked up. "Who's got the tat?"

"Xiao Fei."

"She's the one."

"Right."

Slick interrupted from Patrick's side. "This the journal?" She waved a dark slim volume in front of his eyes.

"Yeah." Patrick grabbed it and dropped it into his coat pocket—the same pocket where he kept his ceremonial knives. The same pocket where he should have had a gun, but he'd been too much of a traditionalist to learn modern weaponry. God, what an idiot he was. If only he carried a gun. If only he'd arrived a little earlier. If only Slick and Hank had been there on time. But they hadn't, and now demons had killed . . . everyone.

Hank slammed the file drawer shut. "We taking all this to Pete?" He didn't seem pleased with the thought, but that was the protocol. Demons had just massacred the entire San Bernadino druid circle, save the Draig-Uisge. Peter the Pompous Prick was the leader of Hank's

11

circle, the largest California druid group, the one in L.A. He ought to be notified. And yet, the thought of putting that man in charge of a war against demons turned Patrick's stomach.

Slick set a hand on his shoulder, her small fingers warm and intensely irritating. Patrick shrugged her off, but he couldn't stop her question. "Are you sure it was *demons?*"

"Yes." He bit the word off. They'd known there was movement between the demon world and Earth. His father had felt it. Patrick, with the amulet burning a hole against his chest, had felt it from the very beginning. That's why they'd chosen to meet tonight. That's why they'd asked Hank to come up from L.A. They were going to discuss plans for how to combat . . .

"That's why they hit us tonight," he murmured, slowly realizing what he should have figured out right away. "The demons. They knew we could fight them. We had the knowledge and the . . ."

"The amulet," murmured Hank.

Slick nodded. "They knew. And they took you out."

"But how?" Hank said as he leaned against the dark metal cabinet.

"We knew because we were researching it!" Patrick snapped. "Because Mom . . ." He swallowed his words and set the file to print. His mother was a disastrous housekeeper, but her computer files were meticulous. He'd found all the electronic notes on Miss Xiao Fei Finney, one-time Phoenix Tear, and he knew what he had to do.

"Not how did you know about the demons," Hank growled. "I get the whole feeling-the-energy thing."

"Hank's been practicing too," Slick piped up with clear pride.

Hank acknowledged her with a warm glance, but his words were for Patrick. "I don't understand how the demons knew about us. How did they know where to hit us and how?"

"They feel the amulet . . . ," Patrick began, but then his words faded away. "But they didn't attack me. They didn't even notice me."

"Yeah," Slick chimed in. "They went for the druid circle. Not ours in L.A., but yours out here. How did they know?"

The printer was still spitting out pages, so Patrick spent a moment to clear his thoughts. He had to focus. This was a chance to get information here without police interference. The last chance.

He closed his eyes and breathed deeply, fighting the waves of grief that threatened to drown him. He was the Draig-Uisge. He had a mission: Close the demon gate before all of Earth was overrun. Everything else would have to wait.

And yet, the scent of sandalwood, the whisper of silk, the intelligence that was his mother and the knowledge held by his father . . . He couldn't think. He couldn't breathe. They were dead.

"Patrick. Buddy. Dude, don't fade on us now."

"Leave him alone. He's just lost—"

"Jesus, Slick, I know what he's just lost, but the whole freaking planet is at stake. We got demons on Earth!"

"I'm here," Patrick interrupted, startled by how steady his voice sounded. As if his heart hadn't just died with his parents. As if everything he'd ever known hadn't just been ripped out from under him. "I'm the Draig-Uisge," he finally said. "I will end this."

"Yeah," said his friend with obvious doubt. "But how? I mean, I'm here to help and all—"

"*We're* here," Slick corrected.

Hank nodded. "But what's the plan?"

Patrick shrugged as he bent to retrieve the print-out. He grabbed Xiao Fei's adoption papers with his other hand. He already had the druid book of spells; his father had passed it on to him when he'd become their enforcer. Their Draig-Uisge. His father had . . .

"Pat—"

"You go tell everything to Pete. Let him figure out the whys and wherefores. He's good at that." And Pete was. A born researcher intent on multiplying his little academic kingdom, Mr. Pompous Prick would be great at understanding what happened—afterwards. But in the present . . .

"You're going to find this Finney girl, aren't you?" Slick's voice was nervous. "Do you think she's in danger from the demons?"

Patrick didn't answer. The more important question was whether she was in any danger from him, the Draig-Uisge. He moved toward the office door. He had to get to L.A., but Slick grabbed his arm, holding him back with surprising strength. When he turned to glare at her, she glared right back.

"Why do you need this girl?" she pressed.

How to explain? "I shape energy. I can use it to seal the demon gate."

She brightened. "Awesome. But why do you need—"

"But I need power. I can shape the power, but I can't create it."

Hank stepped up and gently tugged his girlfriend's hand away. "The girl Xiao Fei has the power," he explained.

Slick glanced at the adoption photo. Patrick didn't need to look down to know what she saw: a hollow-eyed Cambodian waif. Even on this printed copy of a copy, Xiao Fei looked lost and dirty and empty of everything except a painful confusion.

"She's just a kid!" Slick exclaimed.

"She's in her twenties now and lives in Chinatown."

"But—"

"But nothing," interrupted Hank. "Demons are here on Earth. If the Draig-Uisge can stop—"

"It's in her blood." Patrick used his words to clarify his purpose. Somehow stating his meaning out loud made it that much clearer exactly what he had to do. "She bleeds and creates power."

Stunned silence. Then Hank cleared his throat. "How much power?"

"How much blood?" asked Slick.

Patrick shrugged. "Enough power to un-turn vamps and werewolves, according to that monk's journal."

"Whoa . . . ," Hank murmured. Patrick didn't stay to respond. Instead, he pushed past them out the door. He knew without looking that the two would fall into flanking positions behind him. They did, but Slick could not keep silent.

"Patrick! How much blood?"

He growled, annoyed with her for the question, annoyed with himself for having to answer. "All of it," he finally spit out. "Unless I can find a different way."

Slick's voice came from just behind his right shoulder, her words a little breathless as she tried to keep up with his rapid pace. "*Is* there a different way?"

"Maybe." He'd studied the texts. Hell, he'd been the one to find the texts. He'd cross-referenced, re-translated, even sent it to other druids around the globe in the hope that he was wrong. But he and his father were the foremost experts in arcane druid spells. They hadn't gotten it wrong.

15

Closing the demon gate required three things. First, an energy source—Xiao Fei's blood. Second, a shaper of energy. That was the Draig-Uisge's special talent, beyond killing people. And lastly, a way for the Draig-Uisge and the power source to sync up. They had to merge their energies such that he could shape her power. How to do that? They had to have sex.

Which meant he had to copulate with a complete stranger, bleed her during the act, and then use her energy to close the demon gate. All before the demons found and killed them both. And if he failed, then Earth would fall to the beasts who had just massacred his dearest friends and family.

Crimson City had better watch out. The Draig-Uisge was off to spill some blood.

They were almost ready for her by the time she made it inside Wang's Health Emporium. The acupuncture tables were not even remotely intended to restrain a vampire, but she worked here and the space was available—her companions had improvised with leather belts and rope. Assuming the two creatures remained unconscious, everything should be fine.

"How this gonna work?" Old Mr. Chen hovered nervously at the edge of the room where Donny lay. *Good question,* Xiao Fei thought with a grimace. Unfortunately, she couldn't say so out loud. This was the man's son after all.

She dredged up a reassuring smile that didn't fool the old man for one second. Then she abandoned it in favor of a shrug and honesty. "I've never done this before. I don't know if it will work at all. There was a monk in Cambodia who thought we could do it—change a vamp back. But we never got a chance to try.

16

We Phoenix Tears never got a chance to try a lot of things."

Mr. Chen nodded. He already knew this. They'd gone over it a million times. "Your blood," he said.

She nodded and crossed to the unconscious boy. And he was a boy, she thought, as she stared at the slack-jawed vampire. His skin was unfed-pasty, and in sleep it sagged a bit and gave him a more childish look. Sad.

Because it was suffocatingly hot in the tiny room, Xiao Fei rolled up the sleeves of her black turtleneck. She rarely revealed her arms to anyone, and certainly not when she was out monster hunting. Still, there was little choice. She stared at Donny's face, moving slowly into position. Mr. Chen craned his neck to watch, his wrinkled eyes wide as he tried to see.

Xiao Fei looked up. "This may not be pretty, Mr. Chen. And it may not—"

"I stay." He was adamant.

Xiao Fei nodded. At least Mrs. Chen wasn't here. Apparently the woman was at home, crying herself to sleep over the loss of her son, blissfully ignorant that something unheard-of was being attempted in Crimson City tonight: unturning a vampire.

Xiao Fei put the razored thimble on her left thumb, then began the chant. She kept it soft, knowing the prayer itself had no effect. She had long since stopped believing in a beneficent deity—Buddha or otherwise. But the words helped focus her thoughts and drowned out the other noises in her head.

As she chanted, she extended her right forearm so that the third-lowest tattooed teardrop hovered just above Donny's mouth. Then, at the appropriate moment, she pressed her left thumb to the tattoo.

The razor cut was quick and sharp, but she'd long

since stopped reacting to pain. Her blood began to flow. Her chant changed to echo the blood-letting. First came a staccato beat to mimic the steady drip, but as her words came faster and more fluid, so too did the stream of blood. Without aid of the razor, the wound widened until it encompassed the whole of that tattooed teardrop. And the red stream poured strong and steady into Donny's mouth.

"Ewww. Gross!"

Xiao Fei didn't stop chanting. But she did slant an annoyed look at Pei Ling, whose large frame filled the doorway. He'd just planned and executed a vampire slaughter, then set fire to the fangs' remains, and he was grossed out by at a little blood? It amused her how squeamish Americans could be.

"Uh, Fei . . ." he said, his skin going a little green. "You're spilling."

Xiao Fei's attention flew back to her arm. Her blood still poured steadily into Donny's mouth—dead center between the fangs—but the stupid phnong wasn't swallowing. What now?

Fortunately, Mr. Chen had the answer. He stroked his son's throat from chin to clavicle, just as if the boy were a dog who needed to swallow a pill. Stroke. Stroke. Stroke—swallow! She saw it. Mr. Chen saw it and praised Buddha. In the doorway, Pei Ling grunted.

A couple more strokes, a few more swallows, and then the convulsions began. Vamps were strong. Incredibly strong. And no leather belts were going to restrain him, especially as his body began violent spasms.

Donny's eyes flew open, and Xiao Fei saw madness inside. A growl began low in his throat that quickly built into a howl both inhuman and piercingly loud.

"Damn," Pei Ling cursed. "He'll bring more fangs!"

Xiao Fei felt the same fear, but she couldn't help. She was a small Cambodian refugee, too small to restrain Donny or muffle his cries. Besides, she had to focus and close her wound or the entire floor would soon be covered with her blood.

Pop! The belt across Donny's chest burst. No way was he going to stay restrained.

Mr. Chen pressed down on his son's shoulders. He spoke a garbled litany of pleas, prayers, and admonitions to behave, but he was old and not very strong. If Donny got his arm free, he might very well kill his father in his confusion.

Then Pei Ling was there, in a headfirst dive on top of Donny. It was a dangerous place to be—neck exposed on a crazed vampire—but Xiao Fei had never questioned her friend's willingness to be foolish in the pursuit of a greater good. That too was very ABC.

She reached out to help, but her hands were slick with her own blood. Xiao Fei had to concentrate. She had to close her wound. She wouldn't be good to anyone otherwise.

Stepping back, she forced herself to close her eyes and concentrate. The sealing chant came difficult and slow. It was hard to block out the grunts and howls of the scuffle, but she did and remained focused. That was her true power, after all. Mental focus. Prayerful attitude.

Her skin sealed. She felt the rush of warmth as health returned to her wrist and palm. She was whole once again. She opened her eyes, only now realizing the other sounds had ended. No feral growls. No frantic pleas. Were they all dead?

The first thing she saw was Pei Ling still atop Donny. His skin was slick with sweat, but his chest rose and lowered with breaths, and his face glowed pink with healthy blood flow. Beneath him Donny lay completely unmoving, but with steadily clearing eyes. Beside them both, Mr. Chen stared hopefully into his son's eyes.

Donny was the first to speak. "What the fuck are you doing?" he growled—but in a completely human way.

Quick as lightning, Mr. Chen flicked him on the temple. "Shut up. We're listening."

"Ow!" Donny complained. "That hurt!"

Pei Ling lifted his head and grinned. "We have a heartbeat!"

"Are you sure?" Xiao Fei leaned forward. She hadn't believed it was really possible. Not until this moment.

Pei Ling rolled off Donny, who grunted in relief. "Listen for yourself."

Mr. Chen was there long before Xiao Fei could make herself move. He pressed his ear to his son's chest. A moment later, his grin told the story. "My son," he gasped, then abruptly began to cry even as he flicked Donny's belly in punishment. "How could scare us so, you stupid boy? Why would you talk to those vampires? What were you thinking? I'll tell you what you were thinking? Foolishness! Stupid, stupid . . ."

The man went on and on, ranting despite his son's protests. It was just another parent-child argument in Chinatown, and Xiao Fei was weak with pleasure at the sound.

"Are you all right?" Pei Ling asked, his large hand warm on her elbow.

She nodded, unable to speak.

"Can you do the other one? You don't have to, you know. We can just kill him. It's all he deserves—"

"No!" she snapped, forcing her knees to straighten.

"You don't punish a patient for what he does from dementia. We won't kill this one either." She didn't like vamps, but rogues . . . if she could save this one, maybe things would change.

Pei Ling sighed, his whole body shifting. He looked her in the eye. "Vampirism isn't the same thing as dementia, Fei."

She pushed his supportive arm away. "It's a disease, nothing more. And I now have a cure."

So saying, she mentally reinforced her spine with steel and made herself walk to the next treatment room. Two more members of the team were there, standing guard over their prisoner. They looked relaxed and happy, flushed with success.

"It's not over yet," she snapped, and was gratified to see them jump to attention. For a moment they even looked like real soldiers. Then she turned her attention to Stan.

This vampire was a lot healthier than Donny. Even with the rapidly healing bullet wounds, his skin was pink in color, and his body looked lean in the way of a fighting dog. His face was handsome, angular and sexy. He looked like a Hollywood bad boy.

"Some woman cried long and hard over this one," she said.

Pei Ling grunted over her right shoulder. "These leather straps won't be enough. I'll get the ones from Donny."

He didn't take long. And yet, Xiao Fei was jittery by the time he was finished.

"Stay close!" Pei Ling ordered the others. "And don't vomit."

Xiao Fei felt her lips curl into a smile. Trust Pei Ling to remind everyone just how young he really was. Still, he deserved the respect the others gave him; he was smart and driven, if a bit squeamish. She began the chant.

This time, she used the second-to-last teardrop above her wrist. Her blood flowed, and amazingly the phnong swallowed on his own. Once. Twice. Five times in total before the convulsions began.

Pei Ling was prepared. The extra straps held in part because he and the two others clutched down whatever they could. That allowed Xiao Fei to pour more blood into the patient's mouth. Which was when the screaming began. Howls, screeches, bellows of agony—all of it came from the phnong. They were bestial sounds, inhuman, and yet they had one of Xiao Fei's helpers in tears. Pei Ling merely grew grimmer as he put all of his weight into holding down the vamp's shoulders.

It took a lot longer this time. And the vampire clearly suffered agonies while the conversion went on. And on. And on. Everyone in the room was shaking by the time it was over. Sweat and fear and blood-smell poisoned the air. Then, finally, Stan surrendered to unconsciousness.

"Heartbeat," Pei Ling said, his voice rough with strain.

"The bullet wounds aren't healing like before either," another team member piped up.

Xiao Fei nodded. "Human frailty returns. We should probably get him to a hospital."

"I'll do it," Pei Ling volunteered, his voice strengthening with purpose. "I'm gonna be up all night anyway." He turned his grimace into a wink. "Archeology exam tomorrow." He was studying to get out of this neighborhood, to better himself. Through education he would take control of his life. She felt a flash of jealousy.

"Really?" Xiao Fei strove to make her voice normal, even casual. "Which region?"

He shook his head. "All of them. Curating."

She nodded as if she understood. Some educational directions were beyond the realm of her experience. But Pei seemed to find his work fascinating, so she pretended interest while they all managed to awkwardly carry the ex-vamp to Pei's car.

The others split up, one to help Pei, the other to help Donny and his dad. A half hour later, they were all gone. Which left Xiao Fei alone to clean up the shop. She wanted to erase all evidence of their activities, so she was extra careful. She even went outside to kick at the vamp ashes in the street.

Which was when she had her first black chill. It was strong enough to drop her to her knees. Her hands were sliced open on the gravel, her vision blacked out and she vomited right there in the street. It couldn't be true, her mind screamed, and yet she knew it was. Her blood burned.

There was a demon nearby. Worse, it felt like a battalion of *gun dan* demons. And they were coming to Chinatown.

From Patrick Lewis's journal.

June 7, 1985
To Patrick—
    Happy thirteenth birthday! May you use this journal to brighten the light that is your most inner neart. (That's Celtic for strength.)
                                    Love, Mom and Dad

    First Entry:
    This is a stupid journal and a stupid present. I asked for a new surfboard and an electric guitar.

No, I get this stupid book where I'm supposed to write my feelings. Well, my feelings are that this is a stupid-ass present!!!!

Like I don't know this is a punishment. And it really bites that they'd give me a punishment for my thirteenth birthday. Plus I have to go to summer school. Might as well be living at juvie.

I hate math. I hate writing. I hate my parents. And it's a perfect day. Good winds. Nice sun. Great waves! Everybody else is out, but no, I have to write in my stupid-ass journal for punishment.

I HATE MY STUPID-ASS PARENTS!

Chapter Two

Demons were in Chinatown. Run! Hide! Xiao Fei turned to do just that. There was an old bomb shelter under the shop. They used it as a storage area, but she could disappear down there.

Except, she couldn't do it. Chinatown was defenseless. She had friends here who would die without her help. But oh, the instinct to disappear was strong enough to make her breath freeze in her lungs.

She turned and headed toward the danger. She wasn't doing anything noble. Deep down, she knew that. Something else drew her, something sick and twisted in her psyche. It was the same part of her that had made her look when she was eight in Cambodia, that had made her watch as everyone she knew was slaughtered. That tortured part of her drew her outside to see the monsters.

She moved silently, all but invisible.

It was a skill she'd perfected as a Phoenix Child in

Cambodia, but which she hadn't had much cause to use in the United States. Not until recently. Not until L.A. started reearning its nickname as Crimson City.

In truth, she wasn't invisible, just really unnoticeable. Psychically, she hunched down inside herself. She surrounded herself with a wall of nothing-interesting-here, and *bam,* no one paid the least bit of attention to her. Not humans, not werewolves or vamps. But... demons? She wasn't sure it would work the same. But it was all the protection she had beyond the Glock now clutched in her sweaty palm.

She slid around a corner and felt nausea choke her. The demons were close, and she couldn't breathe. She slid down a wall to crouch in a shadow. If she didn't move, then she wouldn't need to take deep breaths, which meant—with luck—she wouldn't hurl.

It took some time, but eventually she got her stomach and lungs under control. Just when she was about to start moving again, the demons came around the corner. She counted four of them, plus one male human. The demons looked like she remembered: muscular humanoid bodies, ugly sharp weapons, and strange light-colored eyes. She heard their gutteral language and had to restrain a whimper. Add in the screams of the dying, and she could have been in Cambodia.

Focus! she ordered herself. She was in the U.S., in Los Angeles. The demons hadn't taken over... yet. There was still time to escape. But first she had to know what the phnongs were planning.

They were arguing with the human male, who apparently held some sort of sway with them. He was dressed in stylish leather, had dark hair and a rugged profile. She couldn't be sure, but she thought his eyes were dark, which marked him as definitely not demon.

She raised her gun and sighted the human's temple. There was no way she could kill all five at once, not with her one gun and not before the demons got to her. But the collaborator would die first.

Only one thing to do before pulling the trigger. She had to see if he had the demon tool: an amulet worn like a necklace with a blood-red stone and bright filigree leaves around it. Did he wear one? If so, maybe she could put a bullet through the center and end this nightmare quickly.

Unfortunately, the bastard was in profile. Though his shirt was open, he wasn't turned enough for her to see if he wore any jewelry. Turn! she ordered. Come on, phnong, show me your pretty . . .

"You didn't find it? God damn it!" The collaborator's pale face gained some color with his vehemence.

Xiao Fei shifted her attention slightly. Now that they were within shooting distance, she could see that the demons looked slightly the worse for wear. She saw cuts and orangy-red blood from a variety of different wounds. One even had a carved knife still sticking out of his shoulder. She briefly wondered who had managed to hurt the demons and if they were still alive. She doubted it, and a part of her sent a prayer for the dead to Buddha.

"You have to go back! You have to find—" The collaborator's words were cut off by an adamant gesture from the lead demon and growls from the others. The human visibly restrained his temper. "You're sure you killed them all?" he pressed. "Nobody had it?"

The demons were getting impatient. So was Xiao Fei. The damned man wouldn't turn.

The collaborator grimaced and pointed. "Fine. The demon researcher you want is up the street a half mile.

She was on the initial team that opened the gate, but she wasn't working that night. Blue house. Swingset in back." Then he paused to stare hard at the leader. "But we're not done. We have to get—" He cut off his words, finally twisting toward her. Just a little more and she would see . . .

"There's someone here," he said. "Someone powerful. . . ."

Panic blossomed in her chest. He felt her. He knew she was there. She began scrambling backward without conscious thought. She was halfway down the block before she remembered the Glock still clutched in one hand. She could have shot them. Should have, in fact, but then she'd be dead right now beneath a demon onslaught, and that would make her adoptive parents very sad.

But she could have killed the collaborator. She might never again have the chance.

Damn, she'd screwed up big time. But then that was the story of her life, wasn't it? Too scared to do anything useful. May the ancestors—and Crimson City— forgive her.

She made it into the shop in record time. She waited just inside the door, straining her senses for any signs of pursuit. Nothing. It took another hour before she relaxed enough to slip upstairs. Even so, she couldn't force herself to climb into bed as if this had been a normal night. She slithered beneath the bedframe instead, and held her Glock pointed at the door. She didn't move until her alarm went off. Then she jumped so hard she banged her head against the bed slats and nearly put a bullet through her door.

Glancing out, she saw that it was just past dawn. The demons would be hidden now. Assuming they had a coordinated plan, she figured they would strike all at once when they were ready. They'd probably wait until night for the first attack. That's what they'd done in Cambodia.

She belatedly thought of calling the authorities. After all, L.A. had a police force, right? They were much better prepared for a demon incursion than Cambodia had been.

But what would she say? Americans didn't believe in demons—not even with vamps and werewolves running around. How ludicrous! Some didn't even think real evil existed except the darkness in men's hearts and minds. Hah! Still, she had to try, didn't she?

She crawled out from under her bed long enough to call 911. Then she had the predictable conversation. No matter what she said, the operator thought she was a lunatic. After a fruitless twenty minutes, the operator finally lost her temper.

"Honey," the woman snapped. "There are no such things as demons. Now I'm sorry, but I can't talk to you any more. Not unless you have a real emergency involving blood or fire. No? Then thank you for your time and have a nice day."

The line went dead. Xiao Fei sighed and reluctantly put down her Glock. She had to open the shop. Right after she called her sister and told her to get out of Crimson City. Now. Thankfully, her parents had moved to Arizona some years ago.

She toyed with the idea of leaving too. She could be packed and on her way to her parents in a half hour. But that same twisted part of her psyche that had made her seek out the demons last night kept her in town. She was a Phoenix Tear. It was right that she be where the demons were. Even if she spent the whole time in agonizing terror. She didn't even know what she could possibly do, but she couldn't escape her fate. She belonged in Crimson City.

Which meant she had to get up and open the shop.

It never ceased to amaze her how people could continue on in a war zone. For years life had gone on with vampires and werewolves sharing this city, albeit with periods of violence and instability. Most humans simply pretended rogue vamps weren't ever on the prowl. They chose to believe the laws protecting them were enough. And who cared about werewolves infecting the unwary so long as you could get a good manicure or acupuncture treatment? Adding demons to the mix would have been surreal if it hadn't felt so freaking normal.

It was Tuesday, so there was no need to water the plants. She dragged her sorry butt to the shower and poured caffeine down her throat. Yes, she drank black tea in the shower. It saved time. This way she could be on her second pot by the time she made it downstairs to open the store.

Her first appointment was a no-show. *Thank you for making me get up for no freaking reason.* But there was a steady stream of customers for the shop's high-profit items—garlic, wolfsbane, and make-me-rich charms— so at least she was busy. As far as Xiao Fei could tell, none of the charms worked, but faith and superstition lived on.

The owner sauntered in around eleven. Mrs. Wang wrinkled her nose at the latest potpourri simmering on the decorative brazier, reminded Xiao Fei to dust the good-fortune frogs, then wandered off for her hair appointment while taking the morning receipts with her. Unfortunately, Xiao Fei had no time at all to dust—*gosh darn*—before her second appointment showed.

He arrived late, of course. Chronic digestive problems always did. She tripled the potpourri in the room before he took off his socks. Caucasians had the worst foot odor on the planet.

So progressed her day until four. That was when *he* walked in: a thirty-something surfer with a killer tan, easy manners, and a fat wallet. Xiao Fei's favorite kind of customer. Or he would be if her knuckles hadn't been dragging on the floor from exhaustion.

"Good afternoon," he said, his Hollywood smile brightening the room. Yowza, he was pretty. His green eyes caught the light despite the dim shop illumination. She even liked his thick braid of sun-streaked brown hair, and she usually hated long hair on men.

Suddenly she didn't feel so tired. "How can I help you, sir?" *Please want a treatment. Please want a treatment.* A big tip and a half-naked surfer—what more could a girl want? True, she'd never followed through on such a fantasy, but a girl could dream.

"Well, I'm looking for a plant."

Her smile didn't slip, but the disappointment was crushing. "What kind of plant? We mostly sell herbs." She gestured at the wolfsbane and lucky clover. "We also have decorative bamboo. . . ."

He waved away her suggestions without a second glance. "I'm thinking of a very particular plant. Phoenix persimmon—from Cambodia." He gave the botanical name too, but Xiao Fei didn't hear it over the roaring in her ears.

"Miss? Miss? Are you all right?" he asked. He touched her, and she felt a tingle of hot awareness spear through her.

"Uh, yeah. Sure. Didn't sleep last night. Too much partying, ya know? What were we talking about?" She was babbling, slipping into her valley girl stupid persona because she was freaked out. It wasn't because he was a gorgeous guy that dialed her hormones to "happy." It wasn't even because he'd asked about her super-secret Cambodian magic plant. It was because the world was ending in the next couple days, and she just wasn't capable of rational thought. So she slipped into ditz mode and let her brain go on vacation.

He smiled that dazzling smile again, and Xiao Fei willingly lost herself in it. Much better than those other thoughts. "An herb. Phoenix—"

"Oh, yeah, oh, yeah!" she interrupted. Did he have to bellow the freaking name all over the neighborhood? "Never heard of it. Don't carry it. What made you think we did?" She couldn't afford to give up any fruit now. Not with the demon apocalypse about to begin.

He looked surprised. "I was told you were the girl to talk to. You're Xiao Fei Finney, right?"

She would have denied it, but her stupid name tag declared it loud and clear—in both English and Chinese. "Y-yes," she stammered. "But—"

"Please, let me introduce myself. I'm Professor Patrick Lewis. My mother has been in contact with you."

The damn Internet, seducer of the greedy. It had seemed so simple at the time: sell a few plant cuttings at exorbitant prices, maybe earn enough to get out of her crappy little apartment above the shop. To realize the American dream, even here in Crimson City. Even as a refugee. Who'd have thought those *gun dan* demons would show up, making any mention of the plant highly suspect? How long before they learned how to use the Internet and tracked her down, too?

Better to deny it completely. "So sorry, so sorry. You must have me confused with a different Xiao Fei

Finney." *Yeah, right.* As if that were possible. "But thanks for dropping by. Here, have a free ornamental bamboo for your trouble." She shoved a cheap planter at him, but he resolutely pushed it aside.

"Hey, relax. I'm a perfectly harmless guy doing an errand for his mother." Did his voice break a bit on that last word? "Maria Lewis from San Bernardino." There was definitely a note of strain there. "You told her she could pick it up at the shop. *This* shop."

Xiao Fei blinked. She forced herself to breathe. Truly, when he smiled like that, he didn't seem harmless. She was going to kill that online listing right now. "Sorry," she forced out. "Things have been a little crazy here in Crims—er, Los Angeles. Everyone is a little on edge."

"Yeah. I noticed." He leaned against the counter, looking all sleek and toned and handsome. It was a movie-star pose if she'd ever seen one, and yet on him it just looked casual. Gorgeous casual. Can-I-buy-you-a-latte-and-take-you-to-bed casual.

Normally, Xiao Fei would have tossed him out right then and there. From the moment she developed a figure, Caucasian boys had been hitting on her. Something about Asian girls just made them think they had to try. She'd lost count of the number of guys who had come in for treatments just for the chance to get her in bed.

She wasn't interested, never had been. Sex for a hemophiliac wasn't a casual thing. And besides, she'd spent her life just trying to find a place to feel safe. Boys—and men—were many things. Safe wasn't one of them.

But that was before—before the demons showed up, before she realized the world was about to end. Suddenly she regretted having lived so celibate a life. She found herself thinking, why not? Then she was smiling at him in the weirdest way: with warmth and interest.

"I drove by that house on my way here," he continued.

She frowned, lost. "House?"

He nodded. "A couple of miles away. Completely torn to shreds, straight down to the foundations . . ."

Ah. The demons. Last night.

"Like some monster tore it straight out of the ground . . ."

The house with the swingset. She cringed.

"And then torched it just to be sure."

A memory clicked into place. The demons she'd seen last night were *gun dan* demons. The kind that shot fire and got in your head like flies until you were screaming and screaming and screaming and couldn't ever stop. Xiao Fei knew them well. She remembered how one of their fireballs could cut through three monks leaving nothing but cinders behind. She knew, and she feared.

"Didn't you hear about it?"

Xiao Fei nodded but said, "No. I've had the radio off all day."

He arched a sun-streaked eyebrow at her. "Uh-huh."

She abruptly realized she was bobble-heading and froze.

"Do you need to lie down or something? You're looking awful pale."

She almost started nodding again. Almost. But then she was hit by a wave of paranoid self-preservation that said, *No lying down! No exposing your throat or anything else! No talking any more with this way-too-casual-and-freakishly-handsome stranger!*

"I'll just get the plant, okay? You can leave then. Take it to your mother. Whatever. Just don't tell anyone where you got it. Hell, don't tell anyone about it at all. Not while you're in Crimson City at least. Not ever!" She spun on her heel and headed for the stairs.

34

He followed, a bare inch behind her. Geez, she felt his heat on the back of her neck. She stopped and abruptly spun back.

"What the hell do you think you're doing?"

He flushed and retreated a step. "I . . . uh . . . I was just going to follow you. You know, to get the plant. But I guess . . ." He rubbed a hand through his hair, instantly changing his 'do from sleek chic to rumpled, just-out-of-bed gorgeous. "I guess you probably don't want a strange man in your bedroom, huh?"

She narrowed her eyes. "My bedroom? How did you know I lived here?"

He frowned. "You told my mother. In your e-mails to her. She said so . . ."

Had she? She didn't remember.

"Wow. You really are paranoid," he remarked.

"I'm Cambodian." *Crap!* What the hell had induced her to say that? Geez, the United States was rubbing off on her if she gave out such details so casually. What was wrong with her? Why couldn't she keep her mouth shut, shut, shut?

The man raised his hands and took another step backward. "Look, I'm obviously freaking you out here. I'm really sorry about that. I don't need the plant right away. . . ."

Good. He was leaving.

"And besides, I'd like a session. Acupuncture. I can get the cutting afterward."

She blinked, her brain too befuddled to compute.

"I'm . . . having a little problem lately." He swallowed, and his tan skin seemed to pull a little tighter around his mouth. "Dealing with change, you know. It's been really hard." God help her, his voice cracked on the last sentence. And were those tears in his eyes?

She nodded. "A single acupuncture treatment can do wonders to help the body deal with stress." The words were out before she could stop them; she'd used that sales pitch so many times to so many people, it just popped out automatically.

He smiled and, stupid her, her insides brightened. "That's what my mom used to say."

She frowned. "Used to?"

"Er, yeah. Whenever we talked about acupuncture. She's a regular, you know. In San Bernardino. Where she lives." He looked at her, and it seemed as if she saw his whole heart in his eyes. "I'd like to try it this once. To see if she's right. If you don't mind."

"Of course not." She spoke before her brain engaged. She didn't want him to hang around her anymore. She didn't want to get intimate with his energy flow. She didn't want anything to do with him. And yet here she was, gesturing to the smallest and coziest treatment room. What was wrong with her?

She sighed. She was short-circuited, that was what. No sleep, a quart low on blood, and surrounded by demons who wanted to take over the world. Why wouldn't she loiter about with a gorgeous man who was making her act stupider than she had in years?

At least she'd get to see him naked.

Well, this was a new experience, baring his ass to someone so reputedly dangerous. True, she was supposedly a demon killer, but that didn't make Patrick's clenched buttocks feel any warmer. Not much hand-to-hand you could do with your butt in the breeze and your shriveled privates bellying up to a cold treatment table. At least he was lying facedown; she wouldn't have to see his beet-red expression if she decided to kill him.

It had seemed like a good idea at the time. After all, his goal was to seduce Xiao Fei. What better start than getting completely naked and disdaining the use of a covering drape? But while he'd intended to flirt with her while she touched him, the trick was to make the scene romantic rather than clinical. And he couldn't be aggressive. And he couldn't turn over until he was a bit more . . . impressive. Unfortunately that might be a really, really long time from now.

Her fingertips touched his lower back, rotating slightly as she walked around the table. "No wonder you're having problems," she said. "Your entire body is bottled up. You're shriveling your qi. Relax. Let it flow."

She trailed her hand up his spine to his shoulder blades, then down, way down, to the curve of his buttocks. Her touch was soothing, her strokes both professional and incredibly erotic—though how she managed that, Patrick hadn't the vaguest idea. Well, well. Maybe he could do this after all. At least the shrinkage problem was going away.

He took a deep breath and mentally girded his loins, so to speak. He had a job to do here. A damn important one. His parents had given up their lives, and he was damn well going to see this through. Even if he had to get needles stuck in his ass to do it. He was the Draig-Uisge, after all. He had killed for his cause. How much easier would it be to seduce a beautiful woman?

He closed his eyes and threw all his focus into casting the spell. In truth, he would have no idea if it worked; he'd never used a seduction spell in his life. Women just hadn't been that hard to come by. But he had precious little time to make love to Xiao Fei, and if this ancient love charm helped, he was happy to take advantage.

"That's better," she said, her voice low and husky. "Your body is opening up."

That wasn't all that was opening up, thanks to the love spell. The problem with druidic charms was that they often worked great on the intended target—in this case, sweet little Xiao Fei. But they also worked on the caster—himself. All the mental energy that went into making him more sexually appealing to her made him randy as hell. And at the moment, all Xiao Fei had agreed to do was stick needles in him.

Start with small talk. Ask about her life. Act like this is a normal interaction. "So, how long have you been doing acupuncture?"

"I learned as a little child in the old country," she replied. A canned speech if there ever was one.

"In Cambodia? That old country?" he probed. She'd started to press warm, nimble fingers into the base of his skull, but stopped when he spoke. She made a small noise. He shifted to look at her face. "I'm just trying to make conversation. Are you always so jumpy?"

She visibly inhaled. Her utilitarian white blouse stretched taut across her chest; then she exhaled in a slow release that ended in a smile. "Perhaps I should be the client."

"Sure!" He almost leaped off the table. Then he remembered he was supposed to want this appointment. Her eyes widened in surprise, and he hastily scrambled to cover his gaffe. "Er, but then I wouldn't . . . I mean, I need this treatment, right? So I should probably stay where I am. Right?"

She set her hand gently on his shoulder. "I think we'll keep it like this for the moment."

He felt his face flush again, and he allowed himself to be pushed back down on the table. What was wrong with him? He'd made passes at women before. He'd even seduced a few. His old best friend, Jason, used to call him a lady-killer when they were boys. And yet now, when it was vitally important he be smooth and accomplished, he was practically barfing on his shoes.

Xiao Fei began the treatment again at the base of his skull, her fingers moving in slow, wonderful circles. Patrick closed his eyes, relaxing into the heat, the pleasure of the moment. Then he heard the scrape of a lighter flint and smelled the acrid scent of smoke. She was likely lighting one of the zillion candles set about the room.

"Don't set me on fire, okay?" he joked.

He heard humor in her voice. "I've never lost a patient yet. Their hair, on the other hand . . ."

He almost jerked upright, but she held him down, her small hand a strangely powerful force against his shoulder. "I'm kidding. Your hair is out of the way." As proof, she tugged slightly on his braid. She'd flipped it over the top of the table, well out of harm's way. "Doesn't long hair get in the way of your surfing?"

He frowned. "How do you know I surf?"

"Your body tells me. Good tan, but dry skin from the water." She trailed her hands across his shoulders, down his ribs, and all the way to his tensed buttocks. "The broad shoulders of a swimmer, but a generally lean build," she continued. "A tight bottom." She paused, giving a gentle push to help him unclench. "*Very* tight." Was there a purr in her voice? "And thick, corded legs with calluses around the ankle for the leash. You have to be a surfer."

"Er . . . right." If he blushed any more, he was going to go up in flames. "Good deduction."

"That, and your underwear advertises sex wax."

He glanced over to the corner, at where his briefs had tumbled out of his jeans along with his Chap Stick and car keys complete with a wooden surfboard and mini bikini-clad surfer. Xiao Fei had returned to his shoulders, pressing and kneading the muscles there until his skin tingled with awareness. The tingling expanded as she again trailed her hands down his lower back to his bottom. But instead of a soft pat there, she used both hands and began to knead with a vengeance. He had to admit, it felt really, really nice.

Her voice interrupted his mellowing feelings. "So, how good are you?"

He suffered a full-body clench and squeaked, "Excuse me?"

"Surfing. Remember? We were talking about surfing."

"Oh, right. Sorry." He scrambled for an answer. "A few tournament wins. Nothing too exciting. I was pretty good in my teens when I had nothing else to do. But now . . . I just do it for fun." He abruptly added, "The surfing, I mean. I do the surf—"

She cut him off. "I get it." Then she stopped massaging him and stepped back from the table.

It took a little mental nerve for him to crack an eye at her after his last babble-fest, but Patrick had to know what she was thinking, even if it was that he was a total ass. So he looked at her, and his heart immediately sank to his toes. She had her arms folded across her chest, and her face was tight with stern disapproval.

"Okay, Mr. Professor. Confession time. Why are you really here? It's not acupuncture."

He attempted an innocent look. "What do you mean?" She arched a single well-sculpted eyebrow. Yeah, well, he'd always sucked at lying. He groaned. "What gave me away?" he asked.

"You've obviously never had treatment before, and you really don't want it—your mind isn't on what I'm doing. And you're clearly not just trying to get it on with the stupid Asian chick," she added.

He was startled enough to push up from the treatment bed. "What makes you say that?"

She smiled. "If you've been trying to seduce me, you're doing a really bad job."

Ouch.

She frowned as she continued speaking. "Still, you knew about the plant order. Who are you really?"

He made to swing his legs off the bed, but she stopped him with a sharp look. "Don't move! Those needles are in pretty deep."

Needles? He twisted to look over his shoulder. Sure enough, there were four long spikes sticking out of his butt. He reached up a hand to his neck and shoulders and found four more.

"Careful. They're hot."

They were. The ones on his shoulders had smoldering herb packets attached. "I didn't even feel them go in," he murmured. Turning back to her, he was jolted to see her pulling his wallet out of his back pants pocket. "Hey!"

She glared at him and snapped, "I said, don't move! You tense those muscles and the needles'll break. How're you going to surf with two-inch spikes up your ass?"

He stared back at her. It couldn't be true. It wasn't true. And yet the very thought had him frozen in place. She flipped casually through his wallet.

"Okay, Professor, it seems you have the right credentials," she said at last. Holding his school ID and driver's license up to the light, she slanted him a glance. "Or at least appear to."

He flopped back down on the bed in disgust. "Why would I lie?"

"I dunno. Why would you?"

Because he was out to close a demon gate and doing a really bad job, apparently? He grimaced and decided on the truth. "I don't know, either. I'm a really bad liar."

"You got that right." She smiled and started flipping through his pictures—both of them. "This your family?" she asked.

He nodded without looking up. Xiao Fei referred to a family photo from last Christmas. *The* last, he suddenly realized with a twinge of pain.

"Oh, don't look so tragic," she groused, misreading him. She drop his wallet back on his pants. "The needles won't break. They won't even set your hair on fire." She frowned. "Well, they might, but only at the very beginning."

"Just take them out," he growled. He lay forward and waited.

A moment later, he'd still gotten no response. He turned his head and saw her staring at him. She'd recrossed her arms, but this time her regard was speculative.

"What?" he demanded.

"Nope."

He frowned. Had he missed something?

She clarified: "I'm not taking the needles out until I get a straight answer."

He cursed. Loudly. In Latin. Let her think he wasn't a professor now.

She actually smiled, as if it were all a big joke. "Just give me a straight answer. Why are you here?"

"For a date, goddamnit!"

She blinked. "You're kidding, right?"

"No, I'm not. My mother likes you. She said you were lovely. That's why she sent me to get the plant, and why she'll never give me any peace. Not until I do you."

"Do me?"

"Not do you," he backpedaled. "*Date* you. Dinner. Movie. Putt-Putt golfing. I don't give a good goddamn. I just need proof that we went out."

"I'll get my camera," Xiao Fei suggested. "We can take a picture here." She looked caught between amusement and annoyance.

"No!" He almost vaulted off the table.

"Stop, stop!" she cried, though it sounded like a laugh. "You'll rupture a vein." She put a hand on his back, and Patrick could feel her humor shimmering through the contact. "Relax. You have to relax for me to pull the needles out." She stroked her hand over where his fingers had a death grip on an herb packet. "Take a breath, Romeo. I swear this won't hurt."

"I'm just doing this for my mother," he said sullenly. God, could he sound any worse?

He didn't feel the needles slip out, but he heard them drop onto a tray. Out of his neck first. Then his shoulders. Then a long caress moved lower down and had him growling.

"Okay, okay." She lifted her hand off him. "But I couldn't resist." She leaned down to look him in the eyes. "You're lovely, too." Then she winked, and he heard four more needles hit the tray. "Flip over. We'll do the front."

"Not a chance in hell," he snapped.

She laughed. It was a real, honest-to-goodness laugh and not a mocking one. It was light and airy and sounded like freedom, whatever that meant. It just sounded *right,* and he would have given a whole lot to hear it again.

"Tell you what," she said. "While you get dressed, I'll get my purse. I know a great place for dumplings. It's perfect for surfer dudes who love their mothers."

He'd been staring at her after the laugh. Now he openly gaped.

"That's right, Professor," she added. She spoke really, really slowly, just so he understood. "I'm saying yes. You want a date? Well, yes, I will go out with you."

He nodded, thunderstruck. "Why?"

"Why not?" she shot back. Then she shrugged. "You made me laugh, Professor. And on today of all days, that is no small thing."

He frowned. "I don't understand."

"I've decided that I should go on a date today. What if the world ended tomorrow and I hadn't had any fun? What if the last guy I shared dumplings with was my father eight years ago? I don't want to die that way."

Alarm shot through him. Did she know about the demons? "Do you expect to die tomorrow?"

She looked calm. "I expect to start living, Professor. And if that means going out on a date with you tonight, then so be it. Any objections?"

"No! None at all, but . . ." His words faded away. She had already ducked out of the room. He stared at the closed doorway for a long moment before abruptly pulling on his clothes.

Wow. Who'd have guessed. Druid mojo did work.

From Patrick Lewis's journal.

July 4, 1985
Jason's tutoring me in math. Mom and Dad are paying him, but what the hell? He's my best friend. The butthead is such a money-grub. But it's okay, be-

cause algebra's easier when he explains it. It takes us five minutes, and then we look at magazines.

He wants a little red Corvette, the Prince wanna-be. I told him he could get chicks on a good surf-board. A short fiberglass with a kick-ass tail and short wings. He's such a dork, though, he wouldn't even know how to wax it right.

Hour's up. Arcade time!

Chapter Three

Who'd have thought regular life continued in a war zone? People still went to work, still ate dinner at restaurants, still had a great time munching dumplings with weird, funny professors of botany. Patrick was not only sexy, but he had Xiao Fei laughing at the bizarrest things, like the way the bao chef's eyebrows collected steam when he lifted the dumplings free, and the simple gusto with which a certain nearby toddler attacked his fried rice despite less than perfect chopsticks skills. He was never cruel in his observations, just aware of the details of his surroundings in a way that coaxed her to relax and enjoy. After all, he seemed to see everything around them. She could trust him to watch for danger even if she let her attention lapse.

Her ha gow stilled halfway to her mouth. When had she ever trusted anyone to watch out for her? She'd just met the man, and already she was acting as if he were her protector. The thought was as startling as it was ter-

mouth shut. Babbling wasn't her style—at least not usually. "I was young, and it was a confusing time."

"I'll bet. Civil wars aren't pretty." He reached across the table and touched her hand. His fingers were long and calloused, and they infused her with a soothing peace that she couldn't fight.

She raised her gaze to his. He did understand. Not specifically about her or her past, but about . . . What? She couldn't quite name it.

"So let's change the topic." He looked around. He did that often, scanning the room, placing the people and the exits. She recognized the gesture since she did it as well. "Are you feeling worried with the new anti-vamp campaign?"

She shrugged and started making designs with her chopsticks in the pool of hot sauce on her plate. "I've got no love of vamps. Have another pot sticker—they're best hot."

He shook his head. "I'm stuffed. Have you been having problems with vamps?"

Glancing up, she decided to be honest. "Most of us are barely getting by in Chinatown. The fangs've got money, altitude, and attitude. Haven't seen one yet who wasn't willing to take us for blood, money, or just for kicks."

He drew back, clearly surprised. "Is this personal experience? Or just rumor?"

"We probably see a lot more fangs here than you've got in sanitized San Bernardino," she snapped.

He gave her an odd look. "We've got vamps up north. Nice people, all social levels. They make good laborers 'cause they're strong, good managers 'cause they're experienced, and good academics 'cause they're really old."

"And good eaters 'cause they're hungry."

"They don't do that," he argued.

"The hell they don't."

He sighed, then looked at the elaborate death character she'd drawn in her hot sauce. He probably thought she meant it for vamps—and maybe she did, a little. But her real thoughts were on another species. The one that had torched that house not four blocks from here last night.

"Does your hatred extend to other races? Or just vamps?" he asked. His tone was neutral.

She didn't look up, simply grabbed another tsu mai dumpling and carefully wiped it around her plate to erase her hot sauce art. "Why? You got a special love of demons?"

He glanced up sharply. "Demons? I meant werewolves."

She bit her lip. Oh, yeah. The wolves. Just because it was getting dark and she was feeling hyperaware of every shift and nuance in the night's energy didn't mean he was feeling the same. "The dogs don't bother me. Not unless they get within biting distance."

"Your teeth or theirs?" he asked.

"Either." She grinned and snapped her jaws. A moment later she sighed. "Okay, so my bitterness is showing through. Honest to God, Patrick, I just want to live my life in peace. I want to make enough money to go to grad school; I want to open my own little business. And I don't want to have to worry about vamps forcing out my neighbors to build casinos, or adolescent weres threatening to bite kids on the playground. And I don't want any kind of demon anywhere in the city. Ever."

He stared at her, his expression unreadable. "So, you know."

She blinked, completely lost.

"You know there are demons in the city," he clarified. "You know the gate's been used."

She froze, and in her sudden stillness, an answer

blossomed. She abruptly knew why he understood her, why he attracted her like a moth to a flame: because he knew the truth. He knew that demons existed right here in Crimson City, right now. He might love plants and books and all things professorial, but he'd fought the beasts as well. She could feel it in her bones and in the power the surrounded him like a mantle. He'd fought and lost, just like she had. He was afraid, just like she was. And he was ready for the next moment, aching to strike back, whereas she . . .

She ran. It wasn't a conscious decision, it just happened. Patrick scrambled after her, of course, but she knew Chinatown like no visitor from San Bernardino ever could. She left the restaurant, ducked into a side alley, slid around and behind a garbage bin that reeked of grease and soy sauce, then slipped between a pair of cheap New Year's lanterns into the back of the incense and spice shop.

The shop owner—bone-thin Mrs. Lo—looked up in surprise, but relaxed the moment she saw Xiao Fei. With a smile and a quick wave, she turned back to her portable TV and the latest white-as-Wonderbread sitcom. Which gave Xiao Fei a moment to get her panic under control.

He knew. Patrick knew there were demons in L.A. He knew about the demon gate and, worse, he knew that she knew. What else did he know about her? Did he know her power, her purpose?

The old paranoia came roaring back. It flooded her blood with lead, and she dropped to the floor. She tried to reach for a calming chant, a protective chant—hell, even a chant against indigestion—but nothing came to mind, no prayers, no soothing notes, nothing. She was a rock thrown into the ocean, and was sinking fast.

Okay, this imagery was not helping. She was a normal person, a usual human being who knew nothing at all about demons or unturning vamps or anything of that nature. She was just an average working girl, and she was going home now. She was calm, rational, sedate. And she would lock her doors, crawl under her bed, and suck her thumb. That was what a normal person would do. She forced strength into her legs, pulling her face into a bad semblance of a smile as she stood. Then she tried to saunter out the front door.

"It's okay, Xiao Fei," Mrs. Lo called without looking up. "Things settle down soon enough. They always do." Then she tossed Xiao Fei a dry noodle cake for long life.

Long life . . . Xiao Fei had the wrapper open before she hit the street. And when she ran straight into Patrick, who had just rounded the corner, looking for her, she uttered a big, embarrassing "Oomph!" and sprayed dried bits of noodles all over his shirt.

That didn't stop him from wrapping his arms around her to support her, though. And right there, she understood the lure of every American surfer movie—at least for girls. Surfers had good bodies. They had *great* bodies. Surfers were strong and broad in all the right places. They had all those rippling abs, which were right now pressed against her belly. And when Patrick wrapped her in his arms, Xiao Fei felt as if she'd been surrounded in sunlight and sand, crystal-cool water, and all the seductive beauty of the most peaceful, secluded lagoon.

Unable to stop herself, she relaxed into his embrace and buried her nose in his chest. Lord, he even smelled like sunshine and water.

"I didn't mean to spook you," he murmured into her ear.

"You didn't," she lied. "I just wasn't hungry anymore." She surreptitiously tossed the remains of the noodle cake aside.

"Let's go someplace quiet where we can talk."

She nodded. Anything, so long as he kept his arms wrapped around her.

"My hotel is quiet—," he began.

"My apartment is right around the corner—," she said at the same time.

They both pulled back enough to see each other's eyes. All that expanse of tan, toned body to look at— broad shoulders, muscular chest, strong chin. But what arrested her most were his dark green eyes. They were verdant forest eyes, primal-lust kind of eyes. Xiao Fei's breath caught. Her pulse sped up. Her knees even went so weak that wherever her body hadn't been pressed against him now came into intimate contact. Her legs were too weak to straighten, but not her chest and neck. She stretched taller, higher. Closer to his mouth.

It was a nice mouth, a pretty shape without being too full, and his cheeks were covered by the barest hint of five-o'clock shadow. He had such straight white teeth. "I've never had braces," she blurted, feeling outclassed. "They're not a Cambodian thing." What freaking stupid synapse had made her say that?

He smiled. "I like your teeth."

She blinked. "Why?"

"They're yours."

He kissed her. And that was when she learned what had made Annette Funicello do all those movies: Surfers kissed well, too. Deep, probing, powerful—all the things she most liked in a man, Patrick was. Was it awful to revel in his domination? He was bigger than her, stronger, and he took a masterful command of the kiss. She surrendered to him. Right there in the street, she opened her mouth. It felt like she opened her entire body and soul to him.

God, he had the nicest ass. She'd already managed to squeeze it during his earlier treatment, and hadn't that been great fun? But this was different. This was a full caress of his backside. Open. Admiring. And . . .

What the hell were those two lumps on either side of his hips? Not muscles. Those couldn't be so hard. Not his hips; those were further back. But closer to his belly were two hardened . . . sheaths? One on either side.

"Have a thing for knives, do we?" he asked.

She smiled up at him. "Apparently it's mutual. You're the one wearing them."

He grinned. "Mutual it is. Wanna see my knife collection?"

But then the vamps attacked.

Patrick heard the rush of air as the vamps descended, but more, he felt the shift in energy, that vague dissonance from the Earth that heralded a vamp's arrival. A whole shitload of them.

Geez, just how deeply in lust had he been not to notice four . . . no, five . . . gawd, six foes converging on his position? Two women, four men, all young-looking, the men running to fat. The girls—one blonde with big boobs, the other a brunette with a high ponytail—were skinny enough to be wraiths.

"Oh great," Xiao Fei groaned. "The girlfriends plus reinforcements."

He didn't have time to ask what that meant as he pushed Xiao Fei behind him for protection. Except, with six vamps dropping from the sky all around, there really wasn't a "behind" that was safe. It was time for diplomacy.

He smiled. "Hey there. What's up? Besides you, of course." He received cold stares in response.

Well, Charlie—his surfing vamp friend—had thought it was funny back when they were sixteen. So, maybe it wasn't so funny as lame jokes went, but that was no reason for one of them to lunge at him.

He countered easily. He'd sparred with vamps often enough to be prepared for their faster reflexes and extra strength. There were lots of vamps at the dojo, where there was less of a sun problem than surfing.

He growled, "Guys, you're ruining my date here. What gives?"

"*She* gives. To us. Right now." One vamp lunged for Xiao Fei, but she slid out of the way and gave a quick wrist-breaking kick while she was at it. The vamp pulled back with a howl of pain. Patrick was impressed.

"A little martial arts training, my dear?" he asked as he surreptitiously reached for the wooden knife he carried.

"A little," she answered. "I did grow up in a temple."

He was surprised. "I didn't think there were any fighting temples left."

She shrugged. He couldn't see it because his eyes were still on the vamps, but he felt her pride. "We weren't typical Buddhists."

That was all the time the vamps gave them to chat. Patrick didn't see the signal, but once again, he felt the energy shift. They lunged forward all at once. The vamp nearest Xiao Fei went down, Patrick's wooden knife in his heart. There was no time for him to shudder at his first vampire kill, but he did manage to thank Mother

Earth that he'd practiced obsessively since the last time he'd seen an honest-to-godness fang attack.

Fortunately for him, the vamps were more interested in grabbing Xiao Fei than him. Not so fortunate for her, but at least that gave him room to fight them off. It helped that they didn't seem to want to kill her, just to grab her, and that Xiao Fei wasn't all that easy to grab. In truth, a whirling dervish would be easier to catch.

The vamps fell back in surprise. Obviously they weren't used to such stiff competition from mortals.

"What'd you do?" the brunette demanded. "What'd you do to Stan?"

"Never met him, don't know him," Patrick said. He knew the question was directed at Xiao Fei, but since she wasn't talking, he felt the urge to fill in the gaps. He prayed the vampire girl kept talking. That was better than fighting.

"You!" screamed the other woman—the busty one—as she lunged for Xiao Fei, claws and fangs fully extended. Xiao Fei ducked just in time for the vamp to land on Patrick's fist.

Ow! Those fangs were sharp! His knuckles stung. Fortunately, there was no impairment in function. His hands flexed just fine as he snatched his other wooden knife. "Guys, really. This isn't necessary," he growled.

"She killed Stan!" bellowed the vamp with the broken wrist.

"I did not!" she shouted back. "I cured him!"

Patrick frowned. "Cured him of what?" He'd never heard of a vamp getting sick, but he supposed it could happen. But if Stan was cured . . .

"He's dead, you bitch!" The brunette hissed, and again she and all her friends lunged.

Didn't they know any other method? Surround and grab—that was their whole MO? Unfortunately, it would work. Eventually. Vamps had a lot more stamina than humans, and Patrick and Xiao Fei were outnumbered.

Still, he did what he could. He knocked the nearest arms away, putting his shoulder into a fang as best he could. Both he and the barrel-chested vamp grunted at the heavy impact. Then he pivoted and threw, praying that the vamp landed on his neighbor.

Bingo. Well, sort of. The pair collided but combined their momentum right into Xiao Fei as she was ducking around the vamp girl with the big boobs.

How much longer could they keep this up? Around the vamp's heaving breasts, Patrick could see Xiao Fei breaking free, panting with exertion. She threw a neat kick, but that left her open to another pair of grasping hands. Patrick took care of those with his own power punch—broke the wrist, too—but that left him open to a strong set of hands on his back.

There was too little room to maneuver. Things were starting to look grim. The fight descended into that moment-to-moment flash of total focus, partial under-standing. He saw an attack and countered it—a fist that he beat back. Saw another body encroach and shoved it away, adding a punch for good measure. But he couldn't go on the offensive, and he couldn't compre-hend the strange sounds he was hearing.

"Aie! Aie! Aiyiyiyiyiyi!" A new voice. A Chinese Tarzan?

"Ow! *Ow!* Geez, woman!" That was a vamp.

"Huh? Hey! Yah!" And a middle-aged male grunted.

"Come on!" Xiao Fei tugged on Patrick's arm.

He grabbed the brunette vamp's ponytail and whipped her around by it. She landed—by his design— right in another vamp's arms. Which was when Patrick caught his first flash of what was on the outside of the circle of his attackers: a score of middle-aged Asians attacking the vamps with brooms and . . . trowels? Even a pair of wooden chopsticks. *Wow.*

And just beyond them, at least a dozen more were rushing forward brandishing whatever they had in hand. A backpack. A skateboard. A set of keys shoved between fisted fingers. And the vamps were going down amid the onslaught.

"Patrick! I'm gone!" Xiao Fei ducked and maneuvered out of the melee. The nearest vamp made a lunge for her, straight out from under a dripping mop, but Patrick was able to shove the jerk backward to trip over the mop bucket.

Then Patrick was off and running after Xiao Fei. And damn, she was fast. Plus, she had this way of fading out from sight if he didn't focus really hard on her. It wasn't like earlier, when he had followed her just by concentrating. Her energy was so bright, so powerful that he'd had no trouble finding her when she'd dashed out of the restaurant. But this time . . .

He shook his head. Damn, she was good. If he'd doubted she was the One before, he now knew the truth. It was like she lifted the energy of the Earth right through the concrete. And she could wrap herself in it and become virtually invisible.

"Right here!" she called, reaching out her hand. Good thing, because he'd lost her again.

He grabbed her, and *wham*, Earth-force slammed through him, surrounded him, became an all-consuming power. It was him, and he was it. Earth. Peace. Silence. Ever-present, and yet invisible. Xiao Fei was making him as invisible as she was. *Wow.* She was amazing.

They started moving. One block away. Around the corner. Two blocks . . .

And then the world ripped open. Patrick felt it, but only distantly. He felt a punch in the gut as the air was sucked away. Except it wasn't air; it was energy—Earth energy pouring out of some open wound. He felt it. He knew it. But Xiao Fei was living it.

She cried out in agony. If he hadn't been holding her, she would have dropped right there in the street. As it was, he completely supported her as she curled into herself.

The protective barrier of Earth energy ripped away. They were completely exposed, but Patrick barely noticed as Xiao Fei began moaning.

"No. No, no, no, no."

"Xiao Fei. Come on. We can't sit here in the middle of the street. Xiao Fei!"

She didn't hear him. She was trapped in her head, so it was up to him. He looked up. No one was around. She'd taken them down a back alley, but he thought he saw a larger street ahead.

He looked down at Xiao Fei. She was chanting, her eyes clamped tightly shut. He knew what was going on. He had felt the fluctuations in the demon gate before: momentary flashes when the portal opened and closed. This time was different. It wasn't closing back up. If anything, it was growing larger, splitting wider, and—worst of all—staying open. He kept waiting for the rip to seal, but relief never came.

Whoever had been toying with the portal had screwed up big time. Now the rip was self-sustaining. It would stay open until someone—until *he*—closed it. He looked down at Xiao Fei. Her eyes had rolled back in her head, but her lips kept moving. She was chanting something, but he didn't know what.

It didn't matter. Earth had just run out of time. He and this semicomatose woman were its only hope. Steeling his resolve, he knelt down and wrapped his arms around Xiao Fei. Murmuring softly in her ear, he spouted lies while his stomach churned in disgust. He told her that everything would be fine, that he would take care of her, that nothing bad would ever happen to her again. Then he hoisted her into his arms. She was a slight woman, not much heavier than a long board. So with surprising ease, he began to walk.

No one stopped him. He caught the surprised look of one late-night shopper, but he simply shrugged and said, "Chinese girls can't hold their liquor." And in this way, he carried her into his own private hell.

From Patrick Lewis's journal.

September 5, 1985

My parents are so lame! They won't let me go to L.A. to compete. I went last year and won. But no. 'Cause I didn't take out the stupid garbage.

They're making me do that stupid essay for ugly Mrs. Wormbreath. Like she can read! And I have to pay for my own Sex Wax now, too. Like I can buy anything on five dollars a week for chores.

Jason says I should go anyway. He learned how to drive from that bum Leonardo. We'll ditch school and just go. I can sleep on the beach, and Mom just bought a boatload of Chee·tos.

When I win I can use the prize money for that new surfboard.

From a letter stuffed into Patrick Lewis's journal.

September 10, 1985
Dear son,

I am writing this letter because you are not here. The police have called and are bringing you home. Your father is so angry he's started smoking again and watching Jeopardy. He hasn't turned a single page of Chaucer since we discovered you and the car were missing.

Oh, Patrick. How could you do this? And for what? A surfing competition? We do not tell you no lightly. We have reasons behind our decisions. As your parents, we judged you too irresponsible to go to a competition in Los Angeles. And we were right. Stealing my car to go on your own demonstrated just the lack of foresight and maturity that we feared.

Where would you have stayed? What would you have eaten? Son, did you even think of these things?

It was irresponsible, Patrick, and reckless. You have harmed not only yourself, but Jason as well. By involving him in your scheme, you have put his entire future at risk. You know how disadvantaged he is. A criminal record would be disastrous for that young man. Why would you hurt your best friend's future in that way?

There are dangers in the world, Patrick. Serious dangers that you can only imagine. Not just junkies and gangs. There are other, darker things to fear.

Jason's father knows. As Draig, he daily fights horrors that your young heart cannot even comprehend. Why would you expose yourself to that? Or Jason? Like it or not, both of you boys have knowl-

61

edge that puts you in danger. What would you have done if something magical attacked without us there to defend you?

I have never been more disappointed in my whole life. We love you so much, Patrick. Why would you hurt us this way? Do you know what could have happened?

I cannot write any more. I am too sad.

—Your mother

Chapter Four

It was amazing how fast old habits returned. Twenty years since she'd last felt the sucking drain of a self-sustaining demon gate. Twenty years since she and her Phoenix sisters bled to save the world. And twenty years since they'd all died—every last one of them except her, the youngest and most able to hide. And just like that, old instincts returned. *Hide. Disappear. Be no more.*

Except it wasn't "just like that." It took time to escape the horror of her memory. It took a long time before she had the sanity to focus, and when she did, it was to hear Patrick murmuring into her ear that he would take care of her.

She believed him. She believed him because twenty years ago someone else had said that to a terrified child, and it had been true; she had escaped the slaughter. She had escaped Cambodia. And eventually, she had escaped Asia to be adopted into a lovely Christian family in Los Angeles . . . where another demon gate had just opened and the whole nightmare was beginning again.

She slipped back into madness.

She came back to herself slowly. She lay on something soft, and she smelled herbs. Not the scents she was used to; they had a definite Western meaning in her mind, but no real understanding formed. Someone was chanting nearby, his voice the low drone so reminiscent of the temple of her childhood. And in the background she felt that ever-present horror teasing her consciousness. It was the steady drain of energy from an open demon gate sucking at her spirit, if not her mind. No longer that. She had control of herself again, so she opened her eyes.

She was in a hotel room. Even in the dim candlelight that dotted the walls, she recognized an innocuous floral painting hanging above a generic chair with sturdy, lime-green fabric. Shifting her head a bit, she saw a utilitarian dresser with a TV on a rotating pedestal. On top of that were candles and simmering potpourri. That explained the incenselike scent.

Next came the tall mirror in which she saw . . . Was that her—tied spread-eagle and naked to a bed? She jerked upright, only to feel the bite of rope around her arms and legs. Only now did she feel the sudden chill on her skin, though in truth, the room was quite warm. "What the . . . ?"

The chanting continued without interruption. She was now awake enough to locate the sound, which was to her right, by the second bed. A man in a white bathrobe knelt on the floor, his back to her, reciting from a small book. She could see more candles, ceremonial knives, and green leaves scattered in some pattern around him. It was Patrick. She could tell by the short braid of his sandy-blond hair, the broad set of his shoulders, and the seductive timbre of his voice.

"Patrick Lewis, you get me the hell out of this now!" she snapped.

The chanting stopped. Perversely, she missed its reassuring cadence. But her anger was rising as she focused on her bonds. A few experimental tugs told her she was held fast.

Patrick stood, lithely rising up from the ground. He turned slowly to face her, and she bit her lip to hold back her gasp of horror. Patrick was not a man. Well, he was human, but his spirit was more: a steely, razor-edged, intensely focused weapon. And worse, there was now a touch of madness in his eyes that scared her even more than the open demon gate.

"Don't do this," she said. She didn't even know what "this" was, but it couldn't be good. Not with her naked and a six-inch blade gripped in his right fist.

"I have to," he replied, his voice harsh between clenched teeth. Whatever was going on, he clearly believed what he said.

"You don't! Think! There's a way out." She was babbling to herself as much as him. He was getting awfully close with that dagger. "I'm special. I mean, my blood's special. You know, the last of my line thing. *Patrick!*" She was getting desperate; she had to reach him somehow. The ropes were really strong, and she didn't think she could break them on her own.

He pressed his free hand to her mouth. The intent was to keep her from speaking, but there was so much of a caress in his touch that she was more surprised into silence than muffled.

"Don't call me Patrick right now," he said. "It . . ." He

shook his head a moment, his eyes drifting closed as he struggled with himself. Stupidly, all she could think was that he had really long eyelashes. Quite gorgeous.

His handsome face contorted. "Don't call me Patrick," he repeated more strongly. "It dilutes my purpose. I'm not Patrick right now." Then he opened his eyes to look at her, and she again caught a strong hint of some emotion in his eyes. It wasn't madness, she realized. It was desperation.

" 'Patrick' really likes you, Xiao Fei. Our date was . . ." His eyes softened into a kind of misty green. "It was great, you know?"

She nodded. Yeah, right. Up until the bound-and-naked part, it had been awesome. "Think what you're doing, Patrick. I'm freezing and . . . freezing. Please—"

"But I'm not Patrick right now. I'm Draig-Uisge."

Drayig Ooshey? Great. She'd fallen for the nice half of a split personality. Could she pick 'em or what?

He must have seen the horror on her face, because he was quick to reassure her. "It's my druidic name. And I was charged with a task. A desperately important one. That's why I had to tie you up. I can't fail."

"Patrick—," she began, but he pressed his fingers to her lips.

"Draig-Uisge. I have to close the demon gate, Xiao Fei. I know you feel it's open, so you know it has to be closed. All life on Earth depends on this."

She shook her head enough to dislodge his fingers. "Killing me won't close the gate," she lied. "It'd just be murder."

He frowned at her, then followed her gaze to the dagger in his hand. "Oh!" He gasped, abruptly setting it down on the side table. "Not kill. I just need a bit of your blood. For the spell. There was something about the blood—you know, of a virgin—but I think a simple cut would do." His gaze traveled down her naked body. "Unless you're—"

"Don't go there, Patrick. I mean it. Don't even ask."

His gaze snapped back to her eyes, and she was pleased to see he was blushing. At least that much of the Patrick she'd known was back. "Er," he stammered. "As I said, we can fake that part. I think. We'll probably only need a bit."

"I'm a hemophiliac," she blurted. "I'll bleed and bleed and it won't stop." That last part was a lie, thank heaven, but he didn't—

"I know," he said gently, gingerly sitting down on the bed beside her.

Okay, so maybe he did know.

"How do you think we found you?" he asked.

"Bad luck?"

He shook his head. "No, it was *great* luck. And a lot of time and effort. Many searched." He lifted a shoulder in a half shrug. "Well, actually, they were more computer hacking than anything else, but it took a great deal of time."

"So, you're a hacker," she accused. Anything to keep him talking. The more he talked, the more he was Patrick and not some stupid druidic weirdo.

He shook his head. "Naw. I really am a botany professor, just like I said. It was my mom. She's an Asian studies professor by day. But at night . . ." His expression abruptly darkened and he looked away.

"At night she's a hacker?"

He shook his head. "She's not anything anymore. The demons killed her two nights ago. My father, too."

She lifted her head, straining against her bonds. Absurd that she wanted to hug her captor, but honestly, that was what she felt. He was clearly grieving. Both parents killed by demons? That had to suck. She knew what it was like to feel loss, and to hate demons.

He swallowed and visibly beat back his grief. She saw him put it away as clearly as if he were closing a dresser drawer. Then he turned back to her, focused again like a weapon.

"We knew there was increased activity at the gate," he said.

"We, who?"

"We druids. The best of us can feel the Earth. And the . . ."

"The holes in it."

His eyes widened. "So, you do understand."

"No, I don't understand a damn thing here, Patrick!" she snapped. "Why the hell am I tied up and—" She cut off her words.

"Draig-Uisge. Call me by my druid—"

"Fine. Drag-Shoer, untie these damn ropes now!" She had to stay strong. To take back control.

"Draig-Uisge," he repeated clearly. "And not yet. You need to understand what's about to happen."

His words caused ice to form in her veins, and she clenched her teeth rather than start screaming. "You know," she said, "I've really got a headache right now. The gate . . ."

"It's like mosquitoes on your skin," he said.

"Really big ones. Sucking at . . ."

"Your sanity."

She shook her head. "My blood." She didn't know how to explain it. Just that the longer she stayed near the gate, the less power she felt inside her. She tugged uselessly at her bonds. "I have to get out of Crimson City."

He shook his head. "No. We have to close the gate. Now."

Xiao Fei let her body drop back in defeat. "Cripes, Patrick." At his stern look, she hastily called him by his druidic name. "Okay, Draig-o'shoe. It's time to fish or cut bait. You've got me tied up here. What the hell are you planning to do?"

"I'm going to make love to you."

She blinked. Somehow, she'd known that was coming. I mean, why else would she be naked? But . . . "I'm missing the logic here."

He nodded. In fact, he gave her a look that clearly meant, *I share your skepticism, but I'm loony tunes enough to go through with this anyway.* He shifted awkwardly on the bed. "I know it's tough to understand, but there's this spell. Stuff about a man and a woman merging with all of Earth. And when they become one in the b-biblical sense . . ." His stammer and accompanying blush were almost endearing. Almost. He paused. "You know what that means, right?"

"Yes," she snapped. "I went to school in the U.S. I know what 'biblical' means."

He paused again, cleared his throat, then plunged ahead. "Well, when they do that with the right preparation and stuff . . ." He gestured at the surrounding candles and incense and assorted druidic paraphernalia. "Plus the blood—"

"I got the blood concept." Her whole life had been defined by her unnatural blood.

"It will make the Earth whole again."

"And close the demon gate." It wasn't a question so much as a clarification.

"Yeah."

She stared at him. Truly, he looked completely sane.

Amazing how madness could hide in the hottest-looking guys. She sighed. "Let me get this straight. *Sex* will close the demon gate."

He gave a self-conscious laugh. "It's a lot more complicated than that. I have to be focused. You're the power source—or your blood is. I don't know which, exactly. Anyway, I can shape energy. Your energy." He took a deep breath. "So we have to sync with each other before we merge with the Earth. Then I can take your power and shape it to close the gate."

"And by 'sync up,' you mean have sex."

He nodded.

"So, good sex will close the demon gate."

He shrugged. "It's not just sex. But I suppose from your perspective—"

She cut him off. "Really, really great sex will close the demon gate."

He paused. "Yes."

"Patrick, I doubt your dick is that powerful."

He jerked. His entire body twisted, and he faced her more fully. She thought he might hit her. That was the usual response when a man's ego was threatened, right? She tensed her body for the blow.

Instead, he just stared at her. A split second later, he burst into laughter—deep belly laughs that had him holding on to his sides. His eyes even watered. The sound was so infectious that she found herself giggling right along with him, and it was a relief. She half expected him to grab the dagger off the table and slice through her bonds; then they'd go grab a drink or something while they laughed at his little joke. Ha, ha. Tie up the funny Asian chick. Ooooh, and make sure she's naked.

Except he didn't do that. He took a deep, shuddering breath and calmed himself. His laughter faded, though some merriment still seemed to shimmer in his eyes. "You're an exceptional woman, Xiao Fei." He reached out and stroked the phoenix tattoo on her shoulder. "And not just because of this."

It took her a moment to understand. Her tattoo was so much a part of her that she'd forgotten it was there. She'd had it her whole life. She was no more conscious of it than she was her hand or leg. But normal people didn't have a large Chinese phoenix tattooed on their chests dripping tears down their arms. That tattoo marked her as a Phoenix Tear. It proclaimed to the world exactly what she was.

"That's how we found you, you know," Patrick said, still tracing the elegant bird's outline. "It was listed on your adoption papers."

Her sealed adoption papers. Patrick's mother must have been quite the hacker to find that.

"You had no right—," she began, but he cut her off with his touch. He was stroking the phoenix tattoo. He caressed the bird's head, right at the ball of her shoulder. The beak curled toward her armpit so that the dripping trail of phoenix tears slid one by one down her brachial artery. Each tear perfectly outlined her best bleeding spots.

But he didn't move his hand down her arm. Instead, his fingertips danced over the bird's head and across its shimmering neck and back. The line traced the dip and curve of her collarbone, and to those who knew, each tattooed feather circled more dangerous incision points along her neck. But Patrick didn't stop with those either.

Instead, he stretched out his fingers to touch more and more of the phoenix's body, the tail feathers blossoming and curling around her breast. Objectively speaking, the art was incredible. The monks had taken a great deal of joy in their work. Apparently, Patrick did too. He stroked the red feathers and brought her nipple to a tight, hungry peak.

She hated that she responded to him, but how could she not? His touch was gentle. Reverent even. But . . .

"I'm not your thing!" she snapped, contorting away from his hand. "I'm not a tool or a sacred vessel or any damn religious artifact. I'm just a girl, Patrick. One who doesn't go for bondage."

His hand froze a scant millimeter above her breast. Her traitorous body ached for its return. She had to force herself to breathe normally and not inhale deeply just so her breast would graze him again.

"Have I touched a nerve?" he asked.

She glared at him. "You were touching a whole fat lot of them. Damn it, Patrick, I'm done with this game. If you have to boink some girl, then go get some druid chick. I'm not playing." He straightened, his hand dropping into his lap. Once again, her body betrayed her. She felt disappointment at his withdrawal.

"It has to be you, Xiao Fei." Then he huffed out a breath. "Come on, this can't be a surprise to you. You must have participated in the Cambodian gate closing we read about. How else did you get that tattoo?"

She swallowed, the low burning in her gut spreading heat into her body. "It didn't work," she ground out. "They all died."

"It did work," he argued softly. "The gate closed."

"But they all died!"

He nodded, his green eyes inexpressibly sad. Then: "Not all of them. You survived."

"I was small, and quiet—and damn lucky. The . . . They thought I was dead. And they got disoriented when the gate closed. That's why they overlooked me."

"The demons?" he asked.

She nodded.

"They killed the others, and yet the gate still closed."

She nodded. There was nothing to say.

"But we aren't going to do it that way. This way, you'll be safe."

She blinked. It took a moment for his words to penetrate her thoughts, but when they did, she rolled her eyes in disgust. "The whole druidic sex thing?" she mocked.

"Yeah. The whole druidic sex thing."

"You're delusional. You know that, don't you?"

He shrugged. "Maybe." It wasn't the most reassuring statement she'd ever heard. "But I'll make you a deal," he went on. "I'll know if it's working or not. I'll feel . . ." He shook his head. "I can't describe it, but trust me. I'll know."

"Oh, right," she drawled. "And do I get to see your etchings, too?"

His lips curved in a smile. "No etchings. But if it's not working, if I'm not getting anywhere, I'll stop. I swear."

Xiao Fei jerked at her bonds, slamming forward as hard as she could. It did nothing but bring tears of pain to her eyes. But what else could she do? She wasn't getting through to him.

"Patrick—"

"It'll work. Or I'll stop. I promise."

"It's not going to work!" She was screaming at him. Then, just for good measure, she stretched her wail into a long, loud bellow for help. He let her go at it until she had to stop for breath. Then he spoke—so softly that she had to be silent to hear him.

"Do that again, and I'll have to gag you."

She believed him—there was no compromise in his eyes—so she shut her mouth. But her tears were still there. In fact, she encouraged them. If screams didn't help, maybe tears would reach him.

Apparently they didn't help enough. Patrick stroked them away with his thumb, his touch tender. "I'll make this good," he said. "I promise."

"It can't be good when it's forced," she answered.

His shoulders slumped. "Maybe not," he conceded. "But I have to try." Then he paused, staring hard at her. "You understand why I'm doing this, right—what happens with the gate? It's not just that some demons will kill everything in sight; it's the wound itself. As long as the Earth is open in this way, it pours its life force into that other place. Orcus, it's called, the demon home world. Earth is bleeding into Orcus, and if we don't seal the wound, everything here will die. All the people, the plants, the fish. Even the air will sicken."

Xiao Fei swallowed. She knew this. To be honest, she could feel it happening. She had been feeling it for some time now. And Patrick must have seen the knowledge in her eyes, because he smiled, though the expression was grim. "You do understand. You know I have to do this. We have to do whatever it takes."

"It won't work," she choked out. "You've got to know that. On some level, you know that one person just isn't that powerful."

He shook his head. "Pray that you're wrong, Xiao Fei. Pray that this ancient spell will work, because otherwise, all life is doomed."

He watched her a moment longer. She could feel him silently begging her to understand. He wanted her blessing on this most unholy act, but she shook her head. "We could have been good together, Patrick." she whispered. "But if you do this, we'll never get past it. I'll never forgive you."

Her words scored a hit. She saw his anguish. Then the last shimmer of humanity drained from his face until there was no Patrick left. Only Draig-Uisge. "I've already lost my parents to the cause, Xiao Fei. What more is the love of my life?"

Her breath froze in her chest. He couldn't possibly have said what he just had. He couldn't possibly mean it.

Before she could pose another question, he pushed to his feet. She heard his low chanting begin again, and he slowly walked to the base of the bed.

"What are you doing?" she asked.

He didn't answer. He was too busy chanting and stripping off his robe. Heavens, he was beautiful. All sensuous golden skin and sleek, rippling muscles. His hair was drawn back in a braid, but he took a moment to untie it and shake it out.

She lifted her head up as best she could to see him fully. Narrowed waist. Nice hips. Proud, full sex. So much for the hope that he couldn't get it up. Then his chanting stopped and he carefully knelt down, leaning across the bedspread. He crawled between her legs, his face between her thighs.

"What the hell are you doing?" she asked.

He glanced up in surprise. "I told you. I have to find out if this works. If we . . ."

"Yeah, yeah, I got that part. But what the hell are you doing?"

He frowned and tilted his head slightly. "You have to be into this, Xiao Fei. You have to have at least some semblance of interest or it's a complete no-go."

"I have no interest whatsoever," she snapped. "None. *Nada.* Nothing. Headache, remember?"

He nodded. "I remember."

She twisted in her bonds. "So, untie me. We'll give it a go tomorrow. Maybe I'll—"

"Nice try. But there's no time." He set his hand on her inner thigh. She gasped at the contact, heat washing delightfully over her skin. Then he gave her a surprisingly boyish grin. "Let's see if I can make that headache go away."

Xiao Fei rolled her eyes. "Sex is not a substitute for aspirin." But that was all she got out before the bed dipped between her legs. She felt Patrick's hands—large and strong—spreading her farther open. Then he said, "Try to relax. . . ."

He pressed his mouth to her sex.

From Patrick Lewis's journal.

Dec 22, 1985

Winter solstice celebration yesterday. Like I care. I only went because Jason did. Except he gets into it, the goony. And we get picked. He's beaming like it's some great honor. It's only because we're thirteen, but he doesn't care. He wants to spend more time studying weeds and moon phases and bird shit.

He doesn't fool me. He wants the money for tutoring me. I'd bust him except he lets me read my mags while he does the studying. Then he tells me enough to get by his dad. It's so bogus. Stevie gets guitar lessons, Tom gets to play the bongos. Me, I get to learn the life and times of mushrooms. Like any girl ever got wet talking about fungus.

At least I get to surf again. It's cold as a witch's tit out, but I got a new wet suit for Christmas. Oh, yeah, I mean "for solstice." Like changing the name of a holiday makes it all secret and stuff. I'm sure the FBI really cares what you call the fat guy who climbs down chimneys and leaves stuff.

Of course, Mom and Dad won't let me keep surfing unless I pass the druid tests and keep my grades up. So I'll give Jason an extra buck a week and he'll tell me what happens in the lame-o English book. Too bad he doesn't need any help in science or I'd make it back.

I wish it weren't raining. I wish Sherry Jameson was my girlfriend. But at least my new wet suit is cool.

Chapter Five

Relaxation was not an option for Xiao Fei, because Patrick's tongue did things to her that made her want to sing. Really, really loudly. And in the key of "yes."

And yet, she also felt violated. Sure, he was cute, but he was also loony and this was not, not, *not* what she wanted. And yet, it so was. Her thighs were quivering, her belly doing a strange undulation thing, and it was all she could do to keep her eyes from rolling back in her head.

"Patrick," she gasped, forcing his name out. "Please. Don't."

His response was to slowly—oh, God, and so sweetly—slide a single finger down through her folds and into her. She felt his every movement, and couldn't stop herself from releasing a moan of frustration. She didn't want this, she kept repeating to herself. And yet her back was arching as she pressed her pelvis forward.

She felt him smile against her thigh, and she might

have kicked him right then if she hadn't been restrained. Then again, she probably wouldn't have, because he was using his tongue once more. How could a man be such a master? He was so precise, hitting just the spots he should, though there was no way he could see what he was doing. And yet, he showed no hesitation. He stroked his finger up through her folds. Up, up, up, he stroked to what Pei Ling called a girl's happy point. And wow, was Xiao Fei's happy.

"Give yourself up to it," Patrick said, the vibration of his words against her sex as erotic as everything else he'd done to her. Her legs clenched. Her breath stuttered. Could she do it? Could she surrender to the inevitable?

He began a steady pushing and withdrawal of his finger. Then he was larger. Two fingers? Whatever. It didn't matter. The stretching sensation was just what she wanted. Then she felt his lips again—his tongue all around that grinning, happy spot. And then . . . his full mouth.

God, the man had timing. No normal man had timing like this! He pushed his fingers inside her at the same moment he sucked on that happy spot. And then the steady thrust and withdrawal was accompanied by that tongue. A circle. A push. Her shiver of delight.

There was no fighting this. Her happy spot expanded until it encompassed her whole body, even her brain. She was pushing down, straining toward him. *Again. Oh, please. Again. Oh, yes . . .*

She surrendered and shattered. An orgasm ripped through her; her body clenched and unclenched, rolled, writhed, and quivered. Every muscle, bone, and pore gave off a huge, happy grin. And what was more, Patrick kept going. God bless a man with timing. He stroked, he caressed, he licked—he did everything right so that the rolling waves kept crashing, kept tossing her about on the sea of ecstasy, kept at her until . . .

He stopped. Bit by bit, the waves quieted. Xiao Fei's breath returned, and her entire body melted into the limpid pool named afterglow. Never again would she doubt how very beautiful, how serene, how yummy this place could be.

Until she heard his huff of disgust.

She cracked an eye. It took way too much effort, but there he was, looking rumpled and put out. He was frowning at her as if she'd done something wrong. Then he rubbed a hand across his face and into his hair, clearly upset.

"Patrick?" she said.

He pulled his hand from his head and let it drop. She felt it brush across her ankle right above her bonds, but his face was what held her attention. It was disoriented, tragic, little-boy-lost. She frowned and raised her head. Or at least she tried. Really she could manage it for only about a half second before dropping back, exhausted.

"Talk to me, Patrick. What's going on?"

He shrugged, an apology in his eyes. "It didn't work," he said simply.

She blinked. She'd had the best damn orgasm of her entire life, and he had the nerve to say it hadn't worked? It sure as hell had. It—

His expression abruptly shifted. "No, no. *That* worked. That worked really well." He peered at her. "At least, it seemed to."

Honesty forced her to nod.

He sighed. "But closing the gate . . ." He shook his head.

She rolled her eyes. "I told you *that* wouldn't work."

"But it can," he countered, a plaintive note entering

his voice. "When we kissed, back on the street—I felt it, Xiao Fei. I felt the . . . the whole Earth. It worked then. Why wouldn't it work now?"

She thought back. Yes, that kiss on the street . . . that had been awesome. And yes, she'd felt something then, too—something big and much larger than herself. At the time, she'd thought it was just a really good kiss, but could it have been more? A connection of sorts to . . .

"This is lunacy," she snapped, irritated because she was beginning to believe him.

Suddenly, he snapped his fingers—a loud ripple in the silent room. "No blood," he said.

She raised her head. "What?"

He gestured to the knife that he'd left on the bedside table. "I forgot to cut you. Maybe—"

"There's blood, Patrick. Look at my ankles. There's blood."

He looked down and immediately started cursing. The ropes had indeed chafed her skin. She was bleeding from several points and, given her hemophilia, there was no stopping the flow. Well, he couldn't stop it.

He leaped up from the bed and tripped in his haste to get the knife. Then he scrambled back and immediately began sawing at rope to free her. He looked horrified.

"Slowly, Patrick. You don't want to slice my tendons as you rescue me."

"Why didn't you say something? Why didn't you tell me what was happening?" he hissed.

"Would it have made a difference?"

"Hell, yes!" he snapped. Her right leg was free. Hallelujah. "I just want to close the demon gate. I don't want to—"

"Rape me?" she couldn't help saying.

He froze, her bonds half undone. The look he gave

her held desperation, horror, and even self-loathing. He was a good man. She could see that in his eyes, but even good men committed atrocities given the right motivations. He swallowed. "No." He looked down at the knife in his hands, the blood staining the bedspread, and her swollen, battered legs. "God, no. Not now."

"Because it didn't work?" Her voice was a whisper. She wasn't even sure how she felt about this anymore. It would have been nice, wouldn't it—if a quick roll in the hay and *wham, bam,* the evil-spewing hole in the world shuts? That'd be great.

Except . . .

"It didn't work." He sounded as if his dog had just died. Or his parents. Or twenty-nine Phoenix Tears, plus nearly fifty monks in Cambodia.

Xiao Fei closed her eyes with a moan. "Untie my hands, Patrick."

She heard him shift to free her hands. She wasn't bleeding there, so it took a little longer; the rope wasn't wet, so the knife didn't slide so easily.

"We have to get you to a hospital."

Her eyes popped open and she saw him staring at her. "Why?"

He glanced at her ankles. "You're bleeding."

"Yeah. So?"

"So, we need to stop it. Geez, it's soaking through the bedspread. It looks like you cut an artery or something."

"Finish untying my hands, Patrick," she said.

He blinked, then abruptly nodded. Clearly, he wasn't used to seeing blood. Or at least this much blood. It was a reassuring thought, actually. Nice to know the guy didn't make a habit of abducting and bleeding all his dates.

Her left hand released, she busied herself flexing

feeling back into her extremities while he went to work on her last restraint. He finished in short order, and she swung around, feet on the floor, hands in her lap. He was already bringing over her clothes, all neatly folded.

"Put these on; then I'll take you to a hospital," he said.

He looked depressingly contrite. She almost missed the forceful obsession of Draig-Uisge. Well, not really.

"Actually," she said as she stood, "I think I'll take a shower instead."

"You can't!" he cried. "You'll bleed!"

She grinned. He really did sound panicked. Good. He deserved it for what he'd just put her through. But then she relented. After all, she really had enjoyed what he'd done in a sick sort of way. She'd never thought he would really hurt her, and he had made good. It had been awesome, in fact. And she was technically still a virgin.

She peered at him. "Forcing someone is wrong. You know that, right?"

He stared at her, his cheek turning red.

"Answer the question, Patrick!"

He reared back and there was a flash of anger in his eyes. But it was quickly suffocated. "Of course I know it's wrong." He shook his head. "But I had to do that. I still don't understand. . . . I know you're the one."

"Yeah, yeah, well, maybe *you're* not," she snapped. "Ever think of that?"

His shoulders visibly tightened. "Of course I thought of that. But if I'm not the one, we're royally screwed. I'm the best we've got."

Xiao Fei rolled her eyes. "We're royally screwed either way. I keep trying to tell you that. The demon gate's open, and great sex is not going to change that."

He sighed. "But it was working back on the street. That kiss. That's when I became absolutely sure."

She shrugged. She'd been too busy fighting the vamps to know.

He shook his head and groaned. "Well, let's get you to the hospital."

"No need." She pointed down to her ankles. They were covered in blood, so it was hard for him to see. In the end, she grabbed his hand and walked him to the bathroom.

Odd, that she wasn't in the least bit self-conscious about being naked with him. Not anymore. They maneuvered awkwardly in the small bathroom, but there was still plenty of space for her to sit on the edge of the tub. She pulled on the faucet, knowing that cold water was best. Then she closed her eyes for a moment and did her little prayer chant. It was the one for the closing of wounds.

The words were reassuring, the motions familiar, but focus was hard to find. Her emotions were too unsettled for it to be easy. But in time, she found her center, and just like that, her skin sealed and her heart found a way to forgive. She plunged her feet into the chill water.

"Oh, God," Patrick breathed beside her.

Xiao Fei's eyes opened. Wow. That really looked bad. The blood was swirling around and around in the tub. If this were Cambodia, a monk would be busily bottling the stuff as a cure-all for everything from warts to a toothache. But they were in the United States, and those monks from her childhood were dead. With a quick flick of her wrist, she stopped the faucet and raised her feet.

"Hand me a towel," she said.

Patrick complied in silence. It was a bright white towel, soft and soothing to the skin. Xiao Fei mourned the pink stains she was about to leave on the pristine fabric, but there was no help for it; she carefully dried her legs on the towel, then let the cloth fall open so he could see clearly. Her ankles were raw, but not bleeding anymore.

"I heal quickly when I concentrate."

"When you pray," he clarified.

Xiao Fei shrugged. Prayer, magic, focused thought—to her, they were the same thing. "I don't worship any deity, Patrick. Not like a Christian."

"What about Buddha?"

"He was a man. A very smart and holy man who showed us a way to think and live. I don't deify him, and I don't need him to close my wounds."

"You just . . . chant them closed?" he asked.

She nodded. "Or open."

It took a moment for him to catch her meaning. But when he finally got it, he pulled back and dropped heavily onto a nearby stool. "You faked this."

She shook her head. "The blood was real, Patrick—the wound and pain were all real. But no, they weren't from the rope." She shrugged. "Well, they were, but not because you tied me too tight. I purposely made myself bleed."

"So I would stop."

She nodded.

"But I didn't notice!" he said.

She smiled ruefully. "Well, you were rather occupied at the time."

He dropped his head into his hands and released a long moan. No words, just raw despair. Moved, she touched his shoulder. When he didn't respond, she leaned down, brushed his hair aside, and pressed a kiss to his bare neck.

"I forgive you," she said.

Then the building exploded.

From letters tucked into the journal of Patrick Lewis.

July 4, 1986
Dear loser,

This sucks. You're away at surfer camp and I'm stuck here scooping ice cream for rich snots who laugh at my hat. Like I picked the stupid thing. When I'm the new Draig, I'm going to cast a spell on all of them so they get bad hair. With bugs! And I'll make them all smell like fish fries.

At least your mom lets me come over and play Atari. Still, it's not the same without you. Dick-head. When are you getting home? I can't even call you because my dad didn't pay the phone bill again. You'd never guess he had so much power. You'd think a man who could wield the you-know-what could manage to pay the phone bill. Or at least make the company forget we owe anything. Yet another reason my dad is a schmuck.

Okay, well I'm writing for a special reason. It's not like I'd talk to you otherwise. I want to borrow your books. You know which ones. Your father gave them to you instead of a new board. I know where the key is, so I was just going to take them. It's not like you give two farts what happens to them, but Dad insists I ask.

"Things of power should be respected," quoth my dickhead Dad.

So . . . can I? You gotta write back, because of the phone. Do it soon so I can stop reading under the covers. Yeah, I already took them.

Jason the Amazing

July 7, 1986
Hey, Jason—

Sucks about your phone. Your dad really doesn't remember to pay the bill? Next time just work it out with my mom and call from my room. They think of you as their son, anyway.

Yeah, take the books—on one condition. I get them back with crib notes. Dad's all over me to read them, so this way we both get what we want.

Are you really close to doing spells? Can you feel the energy and stuff?

It's weird. Dad thinks that surfing is taking me away from important stuff, but surfing's the only time I can feel the Earth's energy—when I'm in the water or on the board. And it has to be real ocean water, not some lame pool, you know? That's just dead water in too small a space. But surfing I can hit a rhythm that's peaceful. I thought everyone did, but only some of the really good surfers—the older ones—know what I'm talking about. And maybe even they're just bullshitting me. But I feel it, and it's great.

Did you start with water? Can you really feel energy in other things? Or is this all just crap?

Oh well. Sit-time's over. Back to the water! Don't forget the crib notes.

Patrick, the greatest surfer in the galaxy

Chapter Six

Boom!

Patrick shot to his feet, narrowly missing a head butt to Xiao Fei. Fortunately, she had fast reflexes.

Boom! Boom! There came a rolling kind of thunder. The hotel was shuddering, but not really in the way of an earthquake; more like the building being shelled. But that made no sense.

Gripping Xiao Fei's hand, Patrick dashed out of the bathroom, only to pull up short. There came an orange glow from outside the window. Forcing himself to move, he crossed the room and hauled open the curtains as wide as possible.

LAX was on fire. He leaned forward and peered into the coiling smoke, trying to make sense of what he saw.

Boom! Ba-boom! More explosions, but they were to the left this time. His window wasn't facing that way, so he couldn't see, but he knew in his gut what was happening. "The fighting's started." He pressed his hand to the glass. The building had stabilized. He doubted it had been truly hit, though it sure had felt that way at first. He'd have to go down to the lobby to make sure.

And yet it felt so surreal, as if he were watching a movie or something. Demon invaders in Crimson City. It couldn't be real.

He heard noise from behind him. He turned. Xiao Fei was pulling on her pants with quick, efficient movements. Her face was gray and her hands shook, but she was fully clothed in the time it took him to cross back to her.

"What are you doing?" he asked.

"Where are my shoes?" She was scanning the carpet. *Boom!*

She dropped to her belly. Before the echo could fade, she was flat out on the floor. "Get down!" she screamed at him.

"It's off to the side," he said, struggling to remain rational. "LAX. And the docks, probably. Or the subway." That would make sense. Take out the means of travel— air, water, land. Create as much civilian chaos as possible. "We're probably okay right here for the moment." It was a lie. Nowhere in Crimson City was safe.

Xiao Fei wasn't talking. She'd found her sandals and was pulling them on with quick jerks.

"Xiao Fei . . ." He put a hand on her arm to calm her, but she threw it off. "We're safe here," he told her.

She stared at him for a moment; then her face screwed up in disgust. He thought she would spit at him. Instead, she said just one word. It came out a curse. "Americans!" He pulled back in shock, and she rolled her eyes. Then she began speaking in rapidly degenerating English. Her words were short and punctuated by gestures, but her meaning came across nonetheless. "The airport . . .

boom! The docks . . . boom, boom! Subway, too! And you want to sit in hotel room? On the thirty-seventh floor?"

"Tenth, actually," he corrected. But she had a point.

"Aie!" She gripped his arms and shoved him to the side. Her eyes were wild, but her actions weren't. Those were focused and clear: she was getting out. "Money. Where money?"

Her purse was in the dresser, but he wasn't going to tell her that. He needed to delay her a moment. At least until he got his own clothes on.

Sirens cut through the air outside, and muted explosions followed brief flickers of light. It was hard keeping an eye on Xiao Fei, and what was happening outside, and dress all at the same time, but somehow he managed. Even though Xiao Fei was blowing through the room like a tornado.

She found his luggage and threw it open. She tossed him a pair of jeans, a leather belt, and a T-shirt. Then she found his knives.

The armband sheath for one of his wooden knives was too big on her, so she strapped it to her thigh. Then she pulled out the blade, tested its weight, and slammed it back into its holder.

"Careful!" Patrick said. "Those are specially made. That's really, really thin wood at the tip." He paused a moment and snapped closed his jeans. "And they're mine!"

She gave no indication she'd heard. She was trying to find a way to carry a silver stiletto. He was at her side before she grabbed the obsidian dagger. "This one is for me," he growled, taking it.

He parceled out the weapons after that—even helped her adjust a shoulder harness to hold one between her breasts. "This is a throwing knife," he said. "Do you even know how to use one?"

"I'm Cambodian. We know how to cut things," she replied.

Yeah, right. Because a cleaver and a stiletto worked the same way. "Just stay behind me. I'll protect you," he said.

"American John Wayne." Again she used that spitting, sarcastic tone. She stared hard at him. "Stay low. Hide. Stay alive."

She was about to duck out the room when he grabbed her. He was a good sixty pounds heavier, and a great deal stronger. She stayed in place despite her initial struggles. "Just where do you plan on hiding, Xiao Fei? Where are you going?"

She broke free of him. "Safe place." Then she glared. "Where is my purse?"

Her English was coming back. He took that as a good sign. So he tried to reason with her again. "I don't think this building's hit. We should be fine up here."

She cursed him in Cambodian. "Vampires fly up here." She stabbed a finger at his chest. "You can't."

"Vamps aren't—"

"Demons, too." Her voice was low, barely above a whisper, but he heard her nonetheless.

"What?" The ones that had attacked his parents hadn't been flying. "But . . . they don't have wings."

"Some demons can fly, too," she insisted. "Like vamps. Levitation. It's safer for us underground." Her eyes were haunted, and she turned to stare out the window. "Safer in Canada."

He couldn't disagree, but he still had a job to do. His mother had charged him to end the demon threat. With her dying breath, she had ordered that. He couldn't just run away. He had to try. "We have to close the gate," he said.

Again, Xiao Fei gave a string of Cambodian curses.

Patrick turned toward her, pointing to the closet. "There's a small satchel in the safe." He reeled off the combination and she punched it in. He grabbed socks and shoes and hauled them on. She dug into the safe and tossed him his bag, then pocketed the five hundred dollars cash.

"Your purse is in the dresser," he said. Let her keep the money if it made her feel safer; he figured he owed her at least that much. Besides, he had no intention of leaving her side until his task was done or one of them was dead. Either way, money wasn't going to be the issue.

"We go. Now," she ordered.

He smiled. He couldn't help it. She was so cute, all small and serious, with that knife between her breasts and threat in her voice. She was going to take charge? But she was out of the room before he could laugh, moving with a stealth that stunned him. His smile faded. Perhaps she did know what she was doing.

She avoided the elevator bank and slid into the stairwell. He had to run to keep up. He nearly crashed into her as she crouched just beyond the doorway. "Xiao Fei—"

"Shhhh!" she hissed.

"I told you. There's no reason to expect an attack here. We can probably even take the elevator."

"Always expect an attack!" she snapped. Then she glared hard at him. "Didn't they teach you how to survive in druid school?"

He blinked. "There isn't a druid sch—"

She *tsk*ed in Cambodian. He didn't know how, but it sounded completely Asian. "You're the keepers of your people's ancient knowledge, right?"

"Well, I suppose. We mostly work with plants and earth—"

"Shhh!" She grabbed his hand and started moving quickly down the stairs, all the while speaking in an undertone. "You druids hold the knowledge of how to close the gate to Orcus, right?" She glanced once over her shoulder. "Or at least you think you do."

He nodded. "Yes. My mother was—"

She waved him to silence. "You have ancient scrolls. Texts. That book . . ." She gestured to his satchel where he'd put his Book of Chants.

He nodded. It was rare for the ancient druids to write anything down, but some texts had survived, and he carried one of the rarest. He also carried the amulet.

He stumbled as a light went on in his brain. He hadn't been touching the amulet when he . . . when he'd worked with Xiao Fei. He had felt its presence like a brand from the moment he'd ripped it from Jason's hand, but maybe he needed to hold it to close the gate. Maybe he needed to—

"Hurry up!" Xiao Fei hissed from ahead. She'd rounded a corner and frozen on the fifth-floor landing, obviously listening hard. There was a lot of noise on this level—people milling about, anxious cries, and police and ambulance sirens coming through the walls, muffled but identifiable.

She hurried on, moving even faster. "Demons will search for those with ancient knowledge. They will kill those people first."

"Like the monks who raised you?"

She didn't answer, but he knew it was true. He could read it in the tension between her shoulder blades.

"So, you think they have specific targets," he said. "That I'll be one right away?" He fought hard not to shudder. She obviously thought it was true, and of the two of them, she was the one with real experience.

Then she shot him a look that chilled his blood. It was cold and angry and filled with an empty despair.

"You do not have a tattoo running up your arm," she said.

Then he understood what she was saying. He knew the truth and damned himself for being self-involved. The demons knew about *her*. They could feel her. Hell, he could feel her, and he was merely an adept. She was the one in the legend, the female warrior whose blood could heal the Earth. And just to make sure everyone knew who she was, the monks had tattooed the truth all over her body.

"Geez, why the hell would they do that to you? Could they be more obvious—"

She cut him off with a quick slash of her hand. "The demons can feel my difference, and we Phoenix Tears are obvious even without the ink." She paused on the last landing before the main lobby. Pulling up the cuff of her blouse, she grabbed hold of his hand. Extending his finger, she allowed Patrick to rub the inside of her wrist.

He felt her pulse leap beneath his touch, but more he noticed the steady bumps of scar tissue. In the light, he could see that each scar was circled by a tattooed line—a "tear." But she was right; anyone who understood the pattern's meaning would know what she was.

She shrugged and released his hand. "Everyone knows who I am anyway. Might as well make my scars pretty. At least, that's what the monks thought."

Though she had released his hand, he did not release her. He traced the lines on her wrist until he was stopped by her blouse. "So they know who you are. They know your blood will close the gate."

She shook her head. "One person cannot do it. I am not enough." She straightened. "It is more important that I live and . . ." She swallowed.

"And?"

"And have lots of babies. I am the last living Phoenix Tear. If I die, there is no hope to ever close the gate."

The theme from *Jaws* echoed loudly in the stairwell. Xiao Fei jumped. Patrick cursed and scrambled for his cell phone to cut off the ringer, then cursed again when he read the caller ID. One glance at Xiao Fei and he knew she was about to bolt. He grabbed her arm and held her close. "Stay here. Let me get a situation report."

She frowned and looked up at him, her entire body going abruptly still. "A situation report? That sounds very military," she said in a low voice.

He shook his head. "Don't get your hopes up. I'm not B-Ops or anything. I just associate with people who like to pretend."

She sighed and leaned against the wall. "American toy soldiers."

"Worse," he admitted. "This guy's a balding academic who plays paintball and reads military suspense."

She shook her head. "No wonder you think sex will cure the Earth. Paintball and girls. What else is there?"

Patrick understood her frustration. Coming from someone like that, he wouldn't believe it either. But Peter the Pompous Prick still had to be dealt with. "Yes?" he said into the phone.

"Report!" snapped L.A.'s head druid.

"You first," Patrick snapped back. "What the hell's going on out there?"

"World War Three," Peter said. "Can't you hear?"

"That's not specific enough—"

"No, goddamnit. You're the Draig-Uisge. What are you doing to fix this disaster?"

"Everything I can. Now, what's happening out there?"

"Demons are everywhere. Killing people. Blowing things up. We were caught with our pants down, and—"

"That much I already know. Details, Peter."

"Don't use my name!" the head druid squeaked. "This isn't a secure line."

Patrick would have said something scathing just then, but he truly didn't want to spare the breath. "Look, Be-ach." He used Peter's druidic name, hoping to focus the man. "I'm trying to do my job here. Do yours, all right? Give me the details." He couldn't help but fix on the appropriateness of Peter's druidic name. Be-ach was a bee, for God's sake. A fat little insect. Wasn't that Peter to a T?

"We haven't got any details, damn it!" the older man said. "That's what I'm trying to tell you—"

The line went dead. After trying to reestablish the connection, Patrick switched the phone to vibrate. The last thing he wanted was another *Jaws* interlude at a lousy time.

When Xiao Fei raised her eyebrows in question, he simply shrugged. "I was cut off. Reports are confused and disorganized," he explained.

"I'm shocked," she replied.

"Look, he'll get it together," he countered, stunned that he was defending Peter. "That's what academics do."

"But never in a useful time frame," she retorted.

Patrick grimaced. "Maybe he'll surprise us."

Xiao Fei didn't answer; she'd already moved on to the stairwell door. She and Patrick were on the lobby level, but not in the main area; the door opened up on a side alcove. Sliding out into the tiny area, they peered around and saw exactly the chaos Patrick expected. People milled about the lobby in various states of dress and a variety of levels of hysteria. The lobby television was on loud, broadcasting news reports of explosions, screaming people, and general devastation, all to dramatic theme music. In big letters across the bottom of the screen he read: *Los Angeles Under Attack*. Then it switched to hospital shots and a caption that read: *Crimson City Bleeds Again*.

Patrick sighed. Xiao Fei just shook her head and stared at a shot of confused, milling people. She didn't have to say a word for him to know what she was thinking; Didn't Americans know anything about war? Rushing aimlessly about the streets did nothing but add to the confusion. Which, of course, would be exactly what the enemy wanted.

Fortunately, she didn't say a word. He wrapped an arm around her shoulders and whispered, "At least we'll blend in. What're two more frightened people in a mass of hysteria?"

She answered in Cambodian. When he raised an eyebrow in question, she gave a rough translation: "More cannon fodder." Then she laughed.

He stared at her a moment, then abruptly grinned. Was this battlefield humor? If so, he liked it. She abruptly grabbed his hand and they were moving again, out through the side doors and into the chaos of Crimson City.

Downtown was aflame. The streets had a ghoulish red glow from the fire, and people were everywhere—many with camcorders.

Xiao Fei cut sideways, weaving easily between people and buildings. Patrick struggled to keep up with his larger, less agile body. Fortunately, he knew where she was heading—back toward Chinatown, which fortunately wasn't too far. In fact, that had been the whole point in booking the room here.

The chaos grew as they left downtown. The more residential the area, the more people and cars choked the streets. But Xiao Fei always found a way through, and they were soon moving at a good clip following the edge of Highway 101. When the sound of gunfire buffeted their ears, Xiao Fei slowed down, and Patrick watched her chew her bottom lip in consternation.

"Isn't there a subway near here?" he asked. This might be her city, but he hadn't come unprepared. He'd memorized as much of an L.A. map as he could manage, including most subway access points.

She shook her head. "That's wolf territory."

He frowned. "So? Wolves aren't demons."

She glared at him. "They're werewolves," she repeated more firmly. From the tone of her voice, she obviously considered all nonhumans in the same category.

"This way," she said, abruptly tugging on his arm. "A safe place in Chinatown." Slipping between a warehouse and the freeway, she skirted another fence . . . only to land them smack-dab on the edge of a firefight.

She dropped to the ground. He landed beside her. A hasty glance told him she wasn't hurt, so he occupied himself with peering around the dubious shelter of a large personal storage shed. That was when he saw them.

Demons.

From a note card stuffed in the journal of Patrick Lewis.

COME SEE THE GREATEST DRUID OF OUR TIME
JASON, LORD OF BLACK MAGIC, DESCENDED FROM
GENERATIONS OF DRUIDS

SEDUCED BY CRIMSON

HIS SKILLS WILL AMAZE AND DELIGHT YOU
NECROMANCY, AURA CLEANSING, HYPNOTISM, HEALING, AND MOST
ESPECIALLY FUTURE CASTINGS
YES, HE CAN CREATE THE FUTURE YOU WANT!
COME SEE IT! BELIEVE IT!

Call for appointment. Special group rates. Available for parties.

Chapter Seven

If it hadn't been for the adrenaline rush from the gun-fire, Patrick would likely have felt them long before now. He saw the demons clearly huddled beneath an overpass. Even if there hadn't been loads of streetlights, the police had spots trained on the small band of five.

A wash of hate temporarily suffocated him. They looked and felt just like the ones who had killed his parents: muscular men with naked torsos and strange breeches over equally strange shoes. They bristled with a variety of knives, but what occupied Patrick's thoughts most was what they were attaching to the free-way supports. He imagined that the gray substance wasn't benign.

Below his stomach where he lay, the ground rum-bled as the subway rolled past. They were at a junction then. Freeway above, subway below. An attack here would seriously compromise transportation in and out of the city.

Which obviously was the point. Just as clearly, the demons had been caught. Patrick heard a police officer—or perhaps it was a B-Ops-officer—bellowing through a megaphone: "You're surrounded. There's no hope. We won't hurt you if you . . ." The voice went on, but Patrick tuned it out, especially as the demons hauled out guns and began firing.

Or at least they tried. Obviously, the demons weren't all that skilled with firearms. He'd seen children with better aim. Of course, in a situation like this, accuracy didn't really matter. No human—even an armored one—was going to storm a position with bullets flying.

Ping. Patrick hunched his shoulders and slid backward an inch. Xiao Fei did too, her face pale. To reassure her, he squeezed her arm.

"Good news for us. Demons are really bad shots," he pointed out.

"Bad news for us. Explosives don't require much accuracy."

So, she'd seen it too. All the demons were doing was buying time to carry out their plan. Which apparently was almost set, as all but one of the demons began bellowing back at the officers. Patrick couldn't understand their language, but then again, he didn't need to. The words were a war cry, the final whoop before the attack.

"They're about to detonate!" he shouted, lifting Xiao Fei and hauling her back. If that gray stuff they were using really was C5, it was going to be one hell of a boom.

Apparently, the officers saw the danger too. They attacked. A sudden barrage of gunfire permanently silenced two of the demons who had stepped out from cover. The other three were still protected by the overhang—but not from the sudden descent of two vampires. Like the demons, Patrick had been blinded by the spotlights. He hadn't seen the dark figures descend until they were on top of the demons.

Three against two in hand-to-hand. If either side were human, the result would be clear. Vamps and demons both had superhuman strength, so mortals would be toast. But demon against vamp? Patrick wasn't sure who would come out on top. Apparently, neither were the officers.

The gunfire fell silent as everyone watched. Would the vamps be in time? Would they succeed where mortal man had floundered?

It didn't matter. The demons had the explosives rigged to blow, but the vamps had the element of surprise, and that was enough. While one vamp held off the demons in an ugly one-on-three battle, the other ripped the C5 off the support column and took off. Two demons went after him, but the third simply grinned and pressed a switch somewhere.

The resulting explosion knocked everyone to the ground.

Dead vamp hero. Dead pursuing demons. Dead detonator-demon too, as the remaining vamp got in a few lethal blows and a kick, effectively smashing the demon into a grease spot along the column. But the freeway remained. And the subway, presumably, hadn't been touched. Score one for the good guys. And one too for the demons, with the death of that one heroic vampire.

"One survived!" Patrick said, gesturing to the vamp. The fang was bleeding from a number of wounds and would need to feed soon, but he still lived. So that was good news.

Or maybe not, because Xiao Fei just grunted and turned away. From her expression, she'd clearly wanted everyone in the group to wipe themselves out, leaving only humans.

"We really are going to have to work on your ability to embrace all forms of life," Patrick said as she began to move past the battleground.

"Vamps aren't alive," she shot back. "That's why they're called the undead."

"*Un* means not," he countered. "Undead. Not dead. Ergo, alive."

She rolled her eyes. "Trust an academic to split hairs."

He had a retort ready, something really clever about the uneducated confusing categories and obscuring facts, but he never got a chance to voice it. An unholy cry split the air.

In truth, the shrieking must have been going on for a while, but the high-pitched wail of the child had been drowned out by the megaphone and battle cry, gunfire and explosion. But now Patrick and Xiao Fei both heard it clearly, especially as they rounded another corner and came upon the source: a child half-buried under his mother's body, screaming bloody murder. Which was exactly what had happened; his mother had been murdered by a stray bullet, or perhaps by more than one. The whole area had been right in the firing line, and pockmarks were everywhere.

"Where was she going?" Patrick asked, his eyes scanning the deserted block. He didn't want to draw fire if there was a demon lurking nearby.

Xiao Fei shrugged, but in a stiff way. In fact, her hand where he gripped it was ice-cold. She moved like one divorced from reality, and she was turning away from the child. He tugged her back toward the alley. He felt no demon energy, and so he moved quickly to the child.

"Leave it," Xiao Fei said. "The police will hear the wails. They'll take care of it."

He glanced toward the freeway. The noise from the passing cars roared through this particular area, and the child was growing hoarse. "They'll never hear him," he said, gingerly feeling the mother's neck.

She was a werewolf. She'd half-changed in death. The child was still wailing. Patrick shifted the body off the boy, but the toddler wouldn't let go of his mother even when his legs were free.

"Hush now," he crooned. Not that it had any effect. Patrick forced the child to let go, lifting the tiny thing easily into his arms. "Here. Take him while I search for identification." He offered Xiao Fei the child, but she remained out of reach.

"It's a werewolf," she said. She didn't seem to object to the child; she was only stating the obvious.

He frowned at her. "Come on. We shouldn't stay long."

"We shouldn't be here at all," Xiao Fei snapped, her large eyes still pinned to the child.

"Then help me finish this quickly." He was beginning to lose patience. Again he offered her the boy, who was straining toward his mother, wailing like the very devil and kicking his legs hard now that the blood had returned to his limbs. Xiao Fei stepped forward reluctantly. Patrick didn't wait for her to second-guess herself. He shoved the child at her.

"Don't let him wriggle free," he warned.

The prick to her pride worked. She lifted her chin and tucked the child close to her belly. "I know how to hold a kid!" she snapped.

Patrick began searching the mother. No ID. Little money. Nothing to give them a clue as to her identity or that of her child. And then another explosion boomed.

His head snapped up. He'd felt the explosion all through him. It had come from the direction of downtown—the Harbor Freeway, if he had to guess. Whatever had happened, they had to get moving. Xiao Fei apparently agreed, as she was already shifting toward Chinatown. He was at her side in a moment, and they started moving in unison.

Their progress was just like before: hugging buildings, skirting fences, keeping low. Xiao Fei led, since she knew where she was going, but this time she held the sobbing child in her arms. She shifted the toddler. The child wrapped his arms around her neck and buried his face against her cheek, his sobs slowly softening into tragic hiccups.

"I can hold him now if you like," Patrick offered. Xiao Fei was so small, he feared she'd have trouble with the boy's weight.

She just shook her head. "He looks like a real boy," she commented.

"He *is* a real boy," Patrick snapped.

She didn't answer. Instead, she picked up speed.

He didn't know if it was his imagination or not, but Patrick was sure he heard another battle nearby: sirens, screams, and the roar of fear like that of an angry ocean. The sounds beat at him, muddling all his senses and wearing away his rationality.

"Is this what every war zone is like?" he wondered aloud as they paused to scan a dark street.

Xiao Fei shifted her gaze to him, and he could see fathoms of horror in her dark eyes. "Every moment, every day, and for long after the fighting stops," she answered. Then she tilted her head against the child, unconsciously stroking her forehead against the boy's hair. "You taste the fear in the air, smell it in the stale sweat. You merge with it to survive so you don't stand out, but then you become part of the problem." Her voice trailed off into a shudder that rocked her whole body, though he could see that she tried to suppress it.

He reached out and stroked his finger across her dirt-stained cheek. "So be part of the solution," he said.

She raised her chin. "Right now, I only want to survive." And with that, she turned and made the last dash into Chinatown.

Unlike downtown, there was no chaos here; all was battened down and silent. And yet Xiao Fei was right; fear was a palpable force here, a sour taste that permeated the air and numbed the mind. The residents of Chinatown had already settled into bunkers well-stocked with old, ugly memories.

"This way," she whispered.

Patrick followed easily. He guessed correctly about where she was heading: back to the acupuncture shop. She had supplies of her own to collect.

He followed her to the shop door, where she fumbled with the key. The boy wouldn't surrender her now, so she ended up passing Patrick her purse. He opened the door with her key as she called out softly in Cantonese. He didn't understand the words except when she said her name and maybe his. She was calling a warning to whoever might be inside. Then they slipped in and quickly shut the door.

The shop was dark, and Xiao Fei left it that way. It also felt deserted.

"I'm going upstairs," she murmured. "To get . . ." Her voice trailed away. She apparently didn't want to say exactly what she was getting. Too bad. He wasn't leaving her side. He moved as silently as he could, but he still felt like a lumbering ox next to her. He didn't know the store like she did and kept running afoul of herbs and tables of ointments.

"Shhh!" she hissed, when he banged his shin and cursed under his breath.

He didn't bother to respond. They'd made more noise in the street, where no walls muffled the sounds. Still, the tomblike feel of the store accentuated every sound and every imagined terror. He pressed his lips together and doggedly followed her up the stairs to her home.

"Home" was of course an exaggeration. It was one room and an attached bath. A microwave and hot pot rested on a card table right above a tiny refrigerator. A single plastic cup and bowl were stacked nearby. On the opposite side, a sleeping bag was spread open in the corner next to a stack of books, all of the how-to variety. He saw *Beginning Plumbing, Basic Accounting*, even a standard *Care For Your Plants book*.

Which brought him to the thing she coveted. The item that had brought her to her bedroom in the first place was the phoenix persimmon and three small cuttings. They sat in a place of honor right beneath an expensive grow light. The leaves were dark, the tiny flowers dark red bloodstains bursting out right beside long, sharp thorns.

It was too early for the plant's pale white fruit, but apparently Xiao Fei knew how to store those for long keeping. Without releasing the child, she grabbed a small plastic container of the dried fruit and pushed it awkwardly into her purse. A Glock went in next. Then she gestured to Patrick, to the cuttings and the light. "We need those. Can you carry them?"

He nodded and did what he could to efficiently store the plants. From his research, he had a good idea how important they were to Xiao Fei's physiology. But he didn't have exact details. "How often do you need the fruit?" he asked.

She glanced sharply at him. "I don't," she said. Then she shrugged. "I'll live just fine without it. I'll just wish I were dead."

"Pain?" he pressed.

She nodded, then gestured to her purse. "One a week can keep me happy. Fewer if they're fresh."

Patrick frowned as he remembered how few she had in her small container. "You're cutting it awfully close," he said.

"Growing season is right around the corner."

He nodded. Assuming, of course, that the plants survived this war. "So . . . this accents your blood connection to the Earth, right?"

She was turning toward the door, but stopped to stare at him. "My what?"

"It makes your blood more . . . earthy." Then he frowned, gesturing vaguely. "I don't know how to explain it. The text my mother found wasn't very clear. It said the fruit strengthened your connection to the Earth through your blood."

"There are texts on me? On Phoenix Tears?" She sounded horrified.

"Only one, as far as I know. Written by an old monk named Wang."

"Wang Bun Rong?" Her eyes widened.

Patrick nodded. "Sounds right."

"I know him. Knew him. At the temple. He was the keeper of secrets." She frowned. "He wrote about us?"

"Pseudoscience stuff. Mostly guesses and simple observations."

"And you have it?"

He nodded. "Mom found it on her last trip to Cambodia. Bought it for ten dollars U.S."

Xiao Fei rolled her eyes. "So much for our national treasures and most closely guarded secrets."

"Mom said they didn't know what they were selling."

Xiao Fei shook her head. "And now it's here."

"Right when the information is most needed. Kinda makes you think she was meant to find it. And that I was meant to find you," he added.

Her gaze hardened. "Don't flatter yourself. No great God is guiding your destiny." She readjusted the sleeping toddler's weight on her hip. "Unless you want to claim his mother was meant to die, too."

Patrick kept silent. He didn't pretend to understand the workings of the higher powers—God or Mother Earth or even Buddha. But that didn't shake his faith that there was something out there helping him.

"Let's go," Xiao Fei said, her face set in hard, angry lines.

He nodded, and then they were moving again. Down through the shop and out the back where another set of narrow stairs clung tightly to the building. She was down them in an instant and tapping on the door in a clear rhythm. There came an answering series of taps. And a third set from her.

"How can you remember all that?" Patrick asked.

She glanced back at him. "Popular Chinese lullaby."

Not a bad idea. And one that clearly worked, for the door cracked open. Xiao Fei slid through before he could draw breath. Patrick had to duck and twist his large frame to squeeze into the narrow opening, but he got through. He felt more than saw the door shut. It was heavy wood that sealed with a deep, satisfying thud. Then he had to wait a few moments for his eyes to adjust.

It was still full night outside, but the lights of Crimson City kept everything in a perpetual neon-accented gloom. Not in here. A single candle flame flickered, but did little to relieve the darkness, so Patrick quieted his mind and expanded his senses as only an adept druid could. Mentally, he felt the earth, the air, even the water and metal that surrounded him.

A basement cellar. He felt the nearly dead energy of poured concrete around the variety of herbs and spices that he could taste on the air. But mostly he felt the fear that enveloped Chinatown, magnified once by the surrounding building, then again by the even smaller space inside this room, given off by the people who huddled inside in terror.

They were all silent. Now that his eyes had adjusted, he saw their faces—all Asian—but of different ages and sexes. Nine in all.

"Who is he?" hissed a woman with dark shadows beneath her smeared eye makeup.

"A friend," Xiao Fei answered in a respectful tone.

"And the child?" asked another woman.

"An orphan." Xiao Fei pushed her way inside, forcing her presence on people who watched her with narrowed, suspicious eyes. She was stopped by the woman with smeared makeup, who grabbed her arm.

"We don't have room," the woman hissed.

Without a word, Xiao Fei handed over her Glock. There was a moment's consideration and then the woman nodded in grudging acceptance. Patrick pushed forward. "What are you doing?" he whispered into her ear.

"Payment for the three of us. Nobody gets safety

110

space for free." Xiao Fei took a deep breath, then waved toward the back. "Put the plants and the light there."

"Plants?" snapped a young man. "What the hell do we need—"

"Shh!" came the immediate response from the others.

The teen subsided into an angry whisper. "Why do we need some stupid plant?"

"Because *she* needs it." The statement came from an old man with a quavering voice, but his words were cold and clearly final.

Patrick worked his way to Xiao Fei's side. "So they know who you are?"

She twisted, and he felt more than saw her face him. "They do not know for sure. But they guess."

"I was right. You are the one."

She sighed. "I am only one."

"*The* one," he pressed.

"The only one alive." She gripped his arms, the fierceness in her body easily transmitted to him. "I am not enough."

"You don't know that," he said.

She didn't answer. She busied herself with gently setting the child down on a makeshift bed. The boy fussed as she did, but she shushed him and soon he settled into a fitful sleep.

Patrick surreptitiously slipped the amulet out of his satchel and dropped it around his neck. It burned, the cold stone and intricate metalwork quickly heating as it settled against his skin. He knew from experience that he wouldn't actually sear. He'd become used to the feel, though the heat seemed stronger than usual. He endured the pain because it seemed clear he would have to be touching the thing the next time he made any attempt to close the gate.

He glanced around, acutely aware of the hostile stares of the others in the cramped room. Fortunately, he and Xiao Fei were behind a shelving unit and thus hidden from just about everyone's line of sight. Or so he hoped.

Xiao Fei straightened right into his arms; he'd designed it that way. She gasped and tried to pull away, but he didn't let her. This was too important.

"You are the one," he repeated.

"Stop it—"

"And so am I," he stressed.

"Patr—"

He kissed her. He didn't want to hear her denials or excuses or anything else. In truth, he didn't want to hear at all because then he would remember they were in a cramped cellar with nine other people—and that somehow, some way, right now he had to make love to her.

From Patrick Lewis's journal.

June 1, 1988

I think I can do it—become a pro surfer. I'll get a cool line of clothes, too. Lisa's got loads of ideas on that stuff. She says it'll make lots of money. She's already sketched some. As soon as Dad signs the Hang Ten sponsorship papers, I'm going to show it to the rep. But I've got to win the classic first.

So it all works out. Lisa's working on her fashion design. I get the time to practice. At least we're teaching surf school together. I still get to see her in a bikini, and there's no interruption in the waves.

I even like teaching the sand rats now. They're always oohing and ahhing. One kid asked for my autograph! That started this whole thing, but I have to admit: it's cool being a celebrity.

Guess now I know why Jason likes it so much. Except, he's getting money for what he does. It's weird that he's rich now. I can't believe how much money people are giving him. Obscene amounts. My prize money goes right back into my stuff. Even with the sponsorship, I still have to work as an instructor. Especially since Dad won't pay for any of it anymore.

But Jason's got a car and girls, too. Lisa says it's weird how all the cool girls just fall all over themselves for him. Even girls who are smarter than that, girls who don't give a shit for anybody are suddenly all ga-ga over Jason.

Still, I'm happy for him. And it's cool that I don't have to be all worried about our money differences anymore. Hell, I've had to bum a loan from him a couple times—even with interest.

Actually . . . I'm worried about him. It's summer now, and he's really pushing his powers. He's tired all the time. He says that bugged-out eyes and saggy skin really draw chicks. It's that dark-lord image. They all want to mother him. Lisa says that's bullshit, but whatever. He's got the girls.

It's just about time to meet him at the movie. Lisa's cough is keeping her home again. Seems like she always gets worse on weekends, which leaves me at loose ends. Again. Jason always brings a girl for me, but it's not the same. He just wants to show off his powers anyway. But it's freaky what the girls do for him. He's always happy to share, but it's too weird, and I'm with Lisa now even though she's home sick. Which is always.

Maybe I should read some of those druid books. Maybe I could figure out how to heal with a touch! like Jason does. That'd be cool.

Chapter Eight

Xiao Fei understood what he was doing. In a war zone with dead bodies and lots of adrenaline—what else would a man do but go for sex? It was a primal need, the reestablishment of the species. And besides, he likely hadn't given up on his strange druidic sex rite being the key to closing the gates. So when Patrick abruptly backed her against a pile of twenty-five-pound rice sacks, she wasn't in the least bit surprised.

Until she returned his kiss.

Put simply, she was not the horny type. Her life had been about survival, about education and trying to get ahead, about living as something other than a refugee. Therefore her first reaction to anything was to be inconspicuous. Her second was to think, then plan. Making connections that led to sex was somewhere around ten thousandth on the list. She'd only gone out with him because the world was going to end. She hadn't wanted to spend her last night alone eating Chee·tos.

And yet, here she was kissing him back. In full view of her boss and her boss's relatives, the people who had generously allowed her to hide out here in return for her favorite weapon. It made no sense. But he felt so damn good.

She clung to him. Like a monkey on a branch, she wrapped herself around him. She breathed in his masculine scent, gripped his taut muscles, and fused her mouth to his. His body was so large. She loved the way his biceps bunched against her arms. His mouth tasted so hot, and wow, did she want him. She wanted him with her, around her, inside her—his tongue, his sex, his entire soul.

He was saying something. He spoke low and sexy in her ear, and tongued her jaw. She didn't understand the words, and didn't care. The low vibration set her belly to quivering. Besides, he gave her other sensations to focus on. His hands were on her breasts—so large, so gentle.

"Harder," she said in a half moan.

He complied. He spread his fingers until he covered the whole of each breast. Then he lifted and squeezed. She arched into his hands. She pressed her groin up against him and gloried in his strangled gasp. Then he narrowed his fingers and pinched her nipples. But he didn't pinch both at the same time. First one, then the other. Wow. Who knew rhythm could short-circuit a woman's brain?

He found her mouth again. His lips moved over hers, and she opened to him—her mouth and her thighs. He was pressing her backward onto the rice sacks, so it was easy to do. It was easier still to grip his hips with her legs and draw him down onto her.

He was tall and heavy. She ought to have felt suffocated by his size, but she didn't. She felt safe and hot and hungry.

He was muttering again. She could feel his lips moving, and the sensation was as frustrating as it was erotic. She wanted more of him. He was fumbling with the buttons of her blouse, but she wanted more kisses. Her hands were on his back, slipping under the soft fabric of his tee. His skin was hot and silky smooth, but she abandoned that. Instead, she slid her hands toward his head, quickly grazing the contours of his back, the chain at his neck, and finally burrowing her hands into his hair. She turned his face to hers and thrust her tongue into his mouth.

He growled low in his throat. It was the sound of masculine possession, dark and primitive. She answered with a sound of her own, a high warble that was as much purr as demand. And then she thrust her tongue out again as he pushed rough and hard against her. God, she was on fire.

He drew back so they could breathe. He pulled back so that he could look in her eyes and she into his while he thrust, thrust, thrust against her. He wasn't inside her, though; they were fully clothed. He'd at least gotten her blouse unbuttoned. Her bra was still a tight, restrictive band about her body, but she felt him nonetheless, and the steady grinding was making her body arch and her eyes drift shut.

"Look at me!" he ordered.

She did. Her eyes popped open, and she stared into his mesmerizing green irises. How she could see in the darkness, she didn't know, but she did. She felt his body, and she knew—she *knew*—that he was more than just a man. There were whole forests in his eyes, dark jungles, and black fertile Earth. She felt the roar of the animals rumbling through his chest, and the surging, pulsing ocean in his steady strength between her thighs.

She saw blue sky as well: open sunlit expanses and wide star-studded nights. That was the place where she soared. Her spirit plunged deep within him. She spread wings that had never stretched so wide, and she began to fly upon currents that he encompassed or created or simply represented. She didn't know. She didn't care. She was flying, and her heart had never felt so free.

"Drui-en," he said. Without asking, she knew he was naming her. And perhaps he was giving voice to what she felt. The word echoed through the sky and shuddered through both the Earth and Xiao Fei.

"Draig-Uisge," she said, and as she spoke, there he was: a sleek, golden water dragon, cutting through the waves until—with a burst of power and a shimmering splash of liquid color—he leaped from the water into the sky.

"Xiao Fei! Have you lost your mind? Xiao Fei!"

Her happy world was abruptly ripped away. She lost her connection to Patrick's eyes, and she dropped with a painful thud onto a dirty stack of rice sacks. Above her, Patrick lost the struggle to stay balanced—Mrs. Wang was shoving him sideways. He was too heavy for the woman to lift, but what she'd begun, gravity finished. Patrick rolled off of Xiao Fei to tumble into a basket of ginger, a single cry torn raw and furious from his throat.

Mrs. Wang ignored him, saving her fury for Xiao Fei. "I thought you had more sense! Bringing a *wei guo ren* here." She called Patrick a white man, but her tone implied much worse. "And shut up that squalling baby!"

Xiao Fei blinked, only now realizing the child was sobbing. She reached over without thought, cradling the screaming child in her arms. He quieted, but not entirely. In fact, part of her mind registered that he felt hot and fretful. But the primary part of her brain, the majority of her thoughts and feelings, was trained on Patrick as he sprawled on the floor beside her. His head was in his hands and his entire demeanor was frustrated and angry.

He looked up and met her gaze. Again she saw him clearly despite the gloom, and again she felt that echo of Earth and sky. It was distant now, but still present, as much a part of her awareness as the steady drain from the demon gate. Two opposites—the gate was emptiness, while Patrick was a fullness, a warm center of being whole.

"You were using magic," she whispered. Then her voice and anger got stronger. "First you tie me up; then you bespell me!" She didn't know why she was so angry; she'd known what he was doing from that first kiss. She'd known and yet she still felt betrayed.

He didn't say anything. His eyes remained on her, but they were both very aware of the Wang family staring at them and the squalling, squirming toddler in her arms.

At last he said, "I've never lied to you, Xiao Fei."

She blinked. No, he never had. So why did she feel betrayed?

"Shut that child up!" Mrs. Wang screeched.

Xiao Fei looked down at the kid. She thought he'd been hot because it was hot in the room, because he'd had a bad dream, because of a hundred unimportant reasons. But she saw now how foolish she'd been. The boy was feverish. His skin was mottled and his eyes glassy. Was that why his mother had been out on the street in the middle of a battle? Had she been taking her child to a doctor?

Xiao Fei looked at Patrick. "He's got a fever. I think he may be sick."

"Then get out!" screeched Mrs. Wang. "We can't—"

"You can't throw a sick child out on the street!" Xiao Fei shot back. "His mother is dead. Shot through the head."

Mrs. Wang blanched. In truth, the woman wasn't evil, but family came first, and Xiao Fei wasn't related. "I paid you," Xiao Fei reminded her in low tones.

"Not enough," the woman spat. "Not for what you bring."

Patrick's cell went off. He'd turned off the ringer, but on vibrate it still made a low noise audible in the stiflingly silent room. He grabbed at his hip. Everyone watched him look at the caller ID.

"It's Peter," he said to no one in particular. "Maybe he can tell us what's going on out there." He stood and walked to the opposite side of the room. Xiao Fei could still hear his conversation, though he tried to keep his words soft. Unfortunately, his side was comprised of single unhelpful words. "What? No. Can't. Military? Damn."

In short, things weren't going well on the outside. Not so good on the inside, either—the toddler was becoming more fretful.

"You can help him," a voice said. "Why don't you help him?"

Xiao Fei looked up to see the drawn face of a preteen boy. She frowned as she searched her memory. "You're Sam," she remembered. "Pei Ling's cousin's friend."

The boy nodded and gestured to Mrs. Wang. "My mother's sister."

Xiao Fei immediately clicked him into place in the Wang family structure. The toddler let out another cranky wail.

"Cure him," Sam pressed. "We know you cured Donny, and he was a vampire. So you can fix this kid."

She bit her lip. "It's not that simple. My blood isn't some magic elixir. I don't know if it'll work."

"It can't hurt, can it?"

She shook her head. "I don't know."

"But it's just blood, right?" he pressed. "I mean, I know it has medicine in it, but if it doesn't work, it's just like—you know—drinking blood. It can't be *that* bad."

She cradled the squirming child closer. His fever seemed to be climbing, especially in this overheated space. His skin was mottled, and he'd started coughing when he wasn't crying. He looked so small in her arms, so vulnerable.

"We should get him to a doctor," she said. She looked up at Mrs. Wang. The woman was more than ready to throw them out the door.

"Hospitals are overloaded," said old Mr. Wang. Xiao Fei only now noticed that he cradled a receiver in his arthritic hands. He must have been listening to a radio report. "Power's out in whole sections of the city. The One-ten was blown up. Surface streets are clogged." He shook his head. "You won't get help for a simple fever at any hospital."

Xiao Fei glanced at Patrick. He was still on the phone, his face pulled into grim lines. That was all the confirmation she needed. If someone were going to help the child, it would have to be her. Besides, she knew her blood could reverse lycanthropy, and it would be ten times easier getting the boy medical attention if he were fully human. Some health professionals were understandably reluctant to treat were-patients. The risk of infection was always there.

She acted quickly, before she could change her

mind. Sam helped. He knelt beside her and held the boy still as she raised her wrist. It took little time to focus her thoughts. The chant came easily. She didn't even need a knife; her fingernail was sharp enough to rip the scab away. Her blood flowed quickly and easily into the boy's mouth.

The child drank. He grimaced at the taste, but then Sam wasn't giving him much choice, holding the kid's head steady so Xiao Fei could trail the stream of blood across his lips. And as she watched the boy swallow, she decided to name him. He couldn't stay "the orphaned ex-werewolf" for the rest of his life.

"You will be called Jimmy by Americans," she intoned, "but for me . . . I name you Jian Ying, because you will be both vigorous and healthy. You will grow strong and proud and be well loved by all."

To one side, Mrs. Wang grunted. "A good name," she admitted.

Xiao Fei smiled. At last she'd done something right. Then she closed her eyes and softly chanted. She didn't have to watch to know when her wrist wound clotted and closed. She'd have a scab for a day or so, and would have to be careful that she didn't reopen the cut, but beyond that she would be fine. She began her final prayer, only to have the child begin jerking in her lap. She cut off her words as she tried to hold the suddenly bucking child.

Convulsions?

She bit her lip, doing her best to keep little Jian Ying from hurting himself. Sam helped as well, pinning down a shoulder and arm. Even Mrs. Wang added her strength to the boy's legs.

"What's happening? Why is he doing this?" Mrs. Wang gasped.

"I don't know," Xiao Fei answered, fear cutting off her breath. "Sometimes the conversion back to humanity is hard."

"*This* hard?"

She didn't know. She'd done it only once before on a werewolf—a freshly bitten human—and it hadn't been anything like this. But the unvampiring of Donny had been violent. Still, it was excruciating to restrain this tiny contorting body and not be able to help. She was almost in tears by the time Patrick returned.

"My God, what happened?" he asked.

The toddler's convulsions were getting weaker, but not because they were easing. Little Jian Ying was losing strength.

"She gave him the human medicine," Sam said. He was sweating, and his eyes looked huge. His face was drawn.

"Human medicine?" Patrick knelt down and placed a hand on the toddler's forehead. "His energy is all over the place. What did you do to him?" he asked Xiao Fei.

"Chinese medicine," Mrs. Wang snapped. She tried to edge him back and away with her hip. Patrick didn't move. If anything, he leaned closer to the boy.

"What did you do, Xiao Fei?"

"We need to get him to a hospital," she answered. But even as she said it, she knew it was hopeless.

"It's too far away," he said, confirming her fear. "He won't make it."

Tears splashed her hands, and Xiao Fei looked up sharply to see if they were Mrs. Wang's. Nope. Xiao Fei brushed at her own cheeks. When was the last time she'd cried? Not since . . . Well, it had been a long time.

"He's just a boy," she whispered. "We have to do something."

Jian Ying's struggles were fading, his spasms weakening. He had only a few more minutes. A half hour at most. Patrick whipped out his cell phone again and dialed 911. "What did you give him?" he asked.

It shamed her that she thought twice about answering. The boy's life meant more than her secret. Still, old habits died hard, and Patrick was a foreigner. Well, he was a foreigner to her.

"Xiao Fei," he began.

"My blood!" she gasped before she could stop herself. "It's cured lycanthropy before. I've done it before."

"To whom?"

"A teen. One who was bitten—"

He cursed and snapped his phone shut. "You cured an infected human, not a natural-born lycanthrope."

She frowned, tears blurring her vision. "What?"

Mrs. Wang abruptly pulled away. "He's a wolf?" Even Sam jerked backward.

"He's a boy!" Xiao Fei snapped. She understood their reaction, though. In truth, she would share their fear if her blood hadn't made her immune. No one wanted to become a werewolf, to exist hand-to-mouth in the tunnels, and live by the phase of the moon. She stroked a finger across Jian Ying's pasty cheek. He was still twitching, but so weakly it made her chest hurt. "He's just a boy," she repeated. "He'll have more options as a human."

Patrick's fingers met hers across the boy's forehead. "He was born a werewolf. That's who he is. Trying to change him into a human is like trying to change a dog into a cat—it's unnatural and wrong."

It took a moment for his words to penetrate her fear for Jian Ying, but when they did, Xiao Fei's fingers stilled and her eyes jerked back to his face. She swallowed, trying to erase the bitter taste in her mouth, but it wouldn't go as the horror of what he was saying sank in.

"You mean . . . I did this? My blood . . ."

"Poisoned him."

"No . . ." But she knew it was true. It made sense. "I-I was trying to help. I—"

Mrs. Wang's voice interrupted as she touched Sam's shoulder and drew him backward. "It's better this way," she said. "Better to die than live as a dog. Sad, of course," she added. "But better."

Anger flashed hot and hard inside Xiao Fei. "No, it is not! He's a child." She tucked the toddler close to her heart. Even with her limited ability, she could feel the boy's energy weakening. He was dying. She looked to Patrick. "We will go to the hospital."

She struggled to stand without jostling the boy. Patrick stopped her with a single touch of her shoulder. "We'll never make it," he said.

"We have to try!"

"There's another way," he said, his voice grim. "He needs to be stronger. To fight the poison."

She blinked back her guilt. "To fight what I did to him."

Patrick shrugged, then glanced significantly around him to the Wangs, who were watching as avidly as if this were the latest hot TV show. "His werewolf physiology is strong," he said. She frowned, not following. "Wolf DNA usually doesn't assert until adolescence."

She nodded. "That's why he looks normal."

"He *is* normal!" he snapped. Then he took a deep breath and moderated his tone, putting his other hand on the boy's belly. "I'm going to make him stronger. I'm going to accentuate his wolf energy." He glanced nervously around. "That's what I do. That's my druid skill. I shape energy." When Xiao Fei frowned, not following, he explained further. "I can amplify energy signatures. Of the Earth, of life, of . . ."

"A wolf."

He nodded.

"But that will make him into a wolf, won't it?"

He nodded. "He'll change. Into a puppy, probably, so you have to be prepared. You'll have to control him. Don't let him bite anyone. At least, don't let him break skin."

Xiao Fei nodded. She understood. "It's the only way, isn't it? To save his life?"

Patrick nodded.

"Do it," she agreed.

Mrs. Wang finally understood. She leaped to her feet in horror. "You'll make him a wolf! Here? No! *No!* He'll bite us."

It was too late; Patrick had already begun. He closed his eyes and began to pray. Xiao Fei didn't hear the words, but she saw his lips move, felt the shift in his energy. It was strange; as an acupuncturist, she daily felt for the shift and flow of a body's energy, but never had she met anyone who could consciously change himself the way Patrick was now doing.

She felt his energy grow stronger. She felt him merge his rhythm with the child's. She pulled back slightly to give him more room. The beat of his power was that overwhelming—and yet it was amazingly subtle, too, gentle and tender as he slid into the child's life force. How could anyone be so sensitive as to find the weakened pulse of Jian Ying's wolf essence? Xiao Fei was in awe.

She looked into Patrick's face and thought she could see the shift: a slight yellowing of his eyes, a tiny elongation in his bones. For a moment she saw the wolf in his body—an echo of the child. Energetically, he and the boy were one. Then Patrick's power began to grow stronger and stronger, bringing the child with him.

In Xiao Fei's lap, the boy began to change. He grunted, and his bones began to shift.

"No!" Mrs. Wang screeched. She leaped forward to drag Patrick back.

"Don't touch him!" Xiao Fei shouted. "You'll kill us all!" It was a lie. There was no danger to anyone but Jian Ying and Patrick. Their energies were linked, and so if the child died, Patrick was also at risk. But Mrs. Wang didn't know that, and the fear was enough to pull her back.

Meanwhile, the boy continued to change. His body was stretching. Xiao Fei felt the prick of fur begin on his pale skin. He released a moan of pain, and she bit her lip. Was the shift to wolf always painful? Or just the first time?

She heard Patrick grunt with effort, and her gaze leaped to his face. He was sweating and his hands were beginning to tremble where they rested on the boy's belly. Looking down, she watched half in terror, half in awe as his hands elongated beside Jian Ying's. She saw paws, claws, and heard a grunt of pain. Patrick's teeth were clenched, and she began to realize just what he was risking to save the child. He was not a natural were-wolf; this shift was not normal to him, and had to be hugely painful if not downright dangerous.

"Patrick," she whispered, not knowing what to say.

Suddenly Jian Ying leaped in her arms. The move was so startling that she was unprepared. Suddenly she had a twisting, snarling wolf cub in her arms. Thank goodness he was still weak, or she would have lost him altogether. As it was, the boy-wolf half jumped, half fell to the floor.

Xiao Fei was quick to recover. Even if she weren't, Mrs. Wang's squeals would have startled her into focus. Xiao Fei grabbed the snarling cub and held it back. Meanwhile, Patrick had obviously exhausted himself. He fell backward, his eyes glazing over. His body trembled as his natural energy signature began to reestablish itself. She watched him shudder, heard his moan as he curled into himself. Then she felt his body energy return to what she'd felt before: that of a sleek, toned, fully human man. His skin remained slick with sweat.

How much had it cost him to heal Jian Ying? Xiao Fei glanced down at the cub. It too had exhausted itself. The surge of power as the wolf asserted itself had faded. It wasn't struggling as much as before. In fact, as she turned her attention to his soft, furry body, the cub shuddered and half fell, half cuddled into her body.

"Aw," Sam murmured from the side. "He's so cute."

And he was. Brown liquid eyes, big dark paws, and really big ears. He nipped lightly at her hand, licking even as he mouthed her skin. It tickled, and she couldn't help but smile. Jian Ying would live.

"He's biting! Get out! Get out!" Mrs. Wang screamed in terror, and Xiao Fei looked up in shock even as she tucked the cub tighter against her chest.

"He's not biting . . ." She began, but Mrs. Wang wasn't having any of it. She hauled on Xiao Fei's arm—the arm at Jian Ying's feet—and dragged her toward the door.

"Out! Out!"

Xiao Fei looked to the other Wangs, and she saw fear in a variety of degrees. But the thought was so different from what she herself was feeling, she could barely comprehend it. How could these people be afraid of a little puppy?

Sam was helping Patrick stand. Patrick's face was taut with exhaustion, but his legs were clearly strengthening; he stood with some semblance of his former grace.

"Are you all right?" she called to him.

He nodded, but didn't bother trying to speak over Mrs. Wang, who continued to screech and shove. Xiao Fei didn't try to fight her either—there was no way she could both protect little Jian Ying and defend her place in the basement shelter. "All right, all right!" she finally said. "We'll go, but he's just a little boy. There's no danger to you."

This last attempt to sway them had no effect. Xiao Fei could see it now: the bigotry caused by terror of infection. She sighed, knowing that a day ago she had felt the same, even with her immunity. But after feeling the energy, the power, the *life* that pulsed within the cub, she couldn't revile him. Jian Ying was a living creature, and that was a wonderful thing. Didn't these others understand that?

Of course they didn't. They couldn't feel it as she had. They couldn't live it as Patrick had. They were merely afraid. And so Xiao Fei sighed and allowed them to push her and Patrick out the door.

"I'll be back for my plants," she said firmly to old Mr. Wang. Of all the Wang family, he alone could guess the significance of those fragile leaves.

"They will be safe, Phoenix Tear," the old man answered. She thought about demanding her Glock back, but decided against it. She'd rather it remained as payment for her return here after she dealt with the boy and Patrick. Besides, she could hide herself from just about anything; it was more important that her plants have a safe place to rest.

So the Glock stayed behind while Mrs. Wang shoved

them out. A second later, Xiao Fei was hunching over the puppy while gunfire rattled through the air.

From a card found in Patrick Lewis's journal.

Sept. 18, 1989
BIRTHDAY PARTY!!!

Come celebrate Patrick's seventeenth with a day at the beach! Surfers get breakfast at ten A.M. All the rest get dinner, cake, and entertainment from Jason the Dark Lord at the bonfire beginning at 7 P.M.

Chapter Nine

Patrick took a deep breath of soy sauce and ginger. Though the connection to Jian Ying was fading fast, he still retained enough wolf senses to smell and taste Chinatown with incredible clarity. What an amazing thing it must be to live as a werewolf, to sense life in all its glory. He licked his lips as the last of the ability faded. He was fully human again—and appallingly weak—and they were once again outside in the middle of a war.

"Where to next?" he asked.

Xiao Fei sighed. "I don't know."

"The werewolves," he suggested.

Xiao Fei looked down at the cub in her arms. She held it tightly, then ducked her head to rub a cheek against its fur. "He's stronger now," she said.

"He'll live," Patrick concurred. But they couldn't wander around LA with a were-child in their arms, not with gunfire every few blocks. They needed a place to regroup. Somewhere private where he could try again with Xiao Fei. "We have to get to the tunnels. We have to give him back—"

"To his own people," she finished. "I know."

He smiled at the reluctance in her voice. She'd obviously bonded with the boy. Her love flowed clear and strong to the child. Indeed, Patrick suspected that was half the reason the boy had survived.

Did Xiao Fei know how much the energy of her love had healed? Did anyone know how much power the simple act of loving created? Patrick doubted it. Few could understand; fewer still could see. If only they knew, if only the world could feel the power of an all-accepting love like he could . . . Well, it would be a different world.

"There's a subway station a couple blocks over," she suggested. "We'll go there."

They began moving at a depressingly ponderous pace. Patrick knew Xiao Fei was slowing up for him, and he tried to move quicker, but damn, he was tired. And the gate was still open, draining him more.

"We have to try again," he said, as much to himself as to her. "It was working. Back there on the rice sacks. *It was working.*"

She glanced at him and didn't answer. She was avoiding the topic, but he couldn't let her. Too much was at stake.

"When we kissed," he pressed. "It was working." He spoke in short bursts when they paused at corners and before crossing streets.

She frowned at him. "You're too weak to try again."

"Every moment we wait, more demons can pour into our world. And Earth loses—"

"I know, I know."

They came to the subway tunnel. He touched her

arm before she could dash inside. She pulled back, a question in her eyes. He gestured to the side, where a werewolf lurked in the shadows of a dumpster. It was clearly a sentry. The werewolves were on full alert.

"We've got one of their children," she whispered. "They shouldn't harm us."

He agreed. "But let's take it slow, okay? Wouldn't want to scare anyone."

They walked quickly—but not too quickly—down the steps. Jian Ying had settled into a fitful doze against Xiao Fei's chest, but who knew how long his quietness would last. Becoming one with a wolf had required enormous amounts of energy, and Patrick's stomach was already cramping with hunger. The cub wouldn't be far behind.

They made it to the bottom of the stairs, only to have their way blocked by two more large werewolves. The first sentry had shifted to block their retreat.

"We don't mean any harm," Patrick began, but the largest sentry cut him off.

"The tunnels are full. No room . . ." His voice trailed away as the cub shifted irritably in Xiao Fei's arms.

"We found him near the One-oh-one," Patrick said. "His mother was killed. Shot." He shook his head. "Many times. I'm sorry."

"He's Lysander clan," said the smallest sentry. He reached out a dirty hand to touch the cub's cheek. "But he shouldn't be able to change until adolescence." There was awe in his voice.

Patrick sighed. In for a penny, in for a pound. "He was sick. I had to activate his wolf DNA to survive."

Xiao Fei lifted her chin, clearly being forced to confess by her conscience. "He was poisoned. It was a mistake, but he's better now. I didn't know."

"And hungry," Patrick added. He was hoping to distract the sentries into dealing with the immediate problem and not dwelling on—

"*You* poisoned him," snarled the original sentry. "And now you bring him to us and pretend to be friends?"

"No—" Xiao Fei began, but the two others took up the charge.

"You want safety in our tunnels after you poisoned one of our children?"

"She gave him human medicine," Patrick cut in. "She didn't know it was poison to werewolves."

"And he risked his life to save the cub," Xiao Fei put in. "Do you know how hard it is to activate a wolf's DNA? It's not something just anyone can do."

The cub twisted so that two of his paws poked out from beneath the blanket—two blood-red paws that were quite clear in the tunnel's light. All three sentries gasped and took a step back. It took a moment for Patrick to understand, but the sentries were all focused on those paws, which clearly meant something to them. He just wished he knew what, and whether it was good or bad news.

"Shut up! Shut up!" growled the largest sentry, though no one had spoken.

They remained silent, all but the cub who had been woken by the argument. He squirmed harder in Xiao Fei's arms; then, when she didn't release him, he began to howl.

"Shut him up!" bellowed the angry sentry.

Xiao Fei was trying, but the cub was hungry. He wasn't going to quiet until his belly was full. And Patrick was watching where the cub's claws were digging at Xiao Fei's chest. If she were to start bleeding . . .

"Down. *Down*," snapped the first sentry. "Take 'em to Keeli."

Patrick had just enough time to take one last deep breath; then one of the sentries led the way into the black maze of the werewolf domain. It started in the back of the subway station, off a tunnel where the lights had long since been broken. Werewolves had keen vision and didn't need more than a fraction of the light that a regular human did.

Patrick immediately calmed his thoughts and expanded his senses. He touched his chest, reaching through the fabric to grip his amulet. He was nowhere close to seeing in the dark—such was not his skill—but with the amulet's help, he could sense more of the energy that surrounded him: concrete, iron grate, werewolves, and Xiao Fei. She was the easiest of all, a beacon to his senses, growing brighter to him with every moment they remained in each other's company.

Right now, he could sense her sidling closer to him in nervousness. He touched her lightly with one hand, then reached into his bag with the other. He withdrew a small flashlight the size of a credit card. When he pushed down on the switch, the slick concrete was illuminated. Her sigh of relief made him smile.

Silly as it was, it gave him a warm feeling to protect her in this small way. She was not nearly as tough as she pretended. He touched her back with his fingertips, and hovered near her.

"Get back," she practically growled. "You're standing on top of me."

So much for the warm feeling. "Sorry," he muttered.

She flushed and shook her head. "No. I'm sorry." He could barely hear her over the howling cub. "I don't like being underground," she admitted.

He thought he understood. She had probably spent far too much time hiding underground from the demons in Cambodia. "Why don't you carry the light? I'll hold Jian Ying," he suggested.

"No, I've got him."

He could see that her hold was tenuous at best. Especially as . . . He narrowed his gaze on one of those squirming red paws. "Has he cut you? Are you bleeding?"

She didn't answer, which suggested exactly what he feared—she was bleeding and couldn't stop it, not while they were bumping along in dark tunnels behind an angry and nervous werewolf.

Patrick reached down and gathered up the cub. Xiao Fei started to protest, but he spoke over her objections. "Can you stop the bleeding? Do we need to get you to a doctor?"

"I'm fine." Again, she gave a half growl that told him she was anything but. She touched his arm. "I'll manage."

They stopped moving. The sentry was in a whispered conversation at a grate-covered doorway of sorts. Even the cub had temporarily stopped howling to sniff the air. Clearly he smelled his people nearby. And when he wasn't sniffing in curiosity, he was extending his claws to play with Patrick's amulet through the fabric of the T-shirt. Patrick tried to stop him, but the cub was extraordinarily curious. In the end, he had to shift the puppy around, specifically turning its eyes and paws away, which only made the creature yap in frustration.

Suddenly, Xiao Fei's energy flared before Patrick's heightened senses. There was no visible light, only a quick surge of power that faded almost as soon as it appeared. Patrick waited a moment, then asked, "Were you healing yourself?"

Xiao Fei spoke, her words shaky, but they quickly evened out. "It was harder than usual. The gate is draining my strength."

"Then we'd best get it closed soon," he said.

She didn't answer. She hadn't yet accepted that they could close it—or how. In truth, he had trouble believing that himself, but then he remembered what it had been like in the storage room. Kissing her had been like kissing the wind and the sky. She was a flesh-and-blood woman, yet she had also been clear summer days and hot, sultry nights.

"We can do it," he said firmly. "We must." Then there was no more time for talk as they passed into another tunnel, and then more tunnels, and then . . .

Werewolf central. Patrick had no idea if that was the area's real name. It was obviously the central gathering place of the Crimson City werewolves. They were everywhere—dashing about or knotted in tiny, worried clumps. The air was ripe with all sorts of smells, but overriding all was a quiet sense of terror.

Fear was the slowest energy vibration, and Patrick felt it permeate everything—depressing all sounds, movement, even the sense of life. Fear deadened the living, and no more so than right here where the wolves congregated.

Except, as he walked, he began feeling flashes of hope. It came from the clusters where they passed, where the wolves turned to stare at them and whispered. Two words were repeated: *blood claw*. Patrick looked at the cub. Just how significant was that bloodred fur? And how could a mere child bring such faith to the frightened?

"He's just a child," Xiao Fei whispered as she tucked the boy close.

"They think he's more," Patrick replied.

Jian Ying let out a howl of hunger. Xiao Fei looked around. "We have to get him some food," she said. "He's starving."

And just like that, food was provided. A nearby woman pulled a small bottle of milk from a bag at her feet. She had two little children holding on to her skirts, but she passed the milk to them.

"For the blood claw," she said.

Patrick wanted to refuse the gift. Xiao Fei apparently did, too. The woman would need the milk for her own children, but there was no refusing. Jian Ying was in sore need. Except, how did one use a milk bottle with a large puppy?

A saucer appeared, and many hands helped to clear space on the ground. The milk was poured into the dish and Patrick set Jian Ying down near it.

Two saucers full of milk disappeared in moments, while a crowd gathered to watch. Patrick's own stomach rumbled. He didn't say anything, but apparently the wolves heard. Within moments both he and Xiao Fei were given food: fruit, bread, someone's cold french fries. He ate it all and bowed his head in thanks. And when the cub was on its third saucer of milk, Patrick at last found breath to ask the question burning in his thoughts.

"What do the red paws signify?"

No answer. For all that they welcomed the bringers of this strange cub, the werewolves were obviously not prone to sharing secrets with outsiders.

Xiao Fei straightened. "He's just a boy. Nothing special. Don't make him feel like he's a symbol. He's just a boy." She kept repeating that, and Patrick heard an echo of desperation in her words. Jian Ying was just a boy in the way that she was just a girl. Except that her blood made her the possible savior of her entire people, and this boy's red paws made him . . . what?

"The beginning of great change," came a woman's voice.

The crowd parted, and Patrick saw . . . a vampire? In these wolf tunnels? Such was unheard-of, and yet here he was: a tall man with an energy that felt sharp and deadly. The vampire frowned in curiosity and studied Patrick and Xiao Fei. Then a young woman stepped up beside him.

She was obviously the werewolf leader. The crowd had parted for her, not the vampire—and yet the two of them were obviously together. Wolf and vampire intertwined their fingers even as the vampire looked away, over his shoulder toward the exit.

"I have to go," he said to the woman, his voice low and intimate. "Tell me everything later." He glanced significantly at the cub.

The crowd let him pass as he moved away, but it was an uneasy parting. Then the woman spoke to the group at large. "He goes to help those trapped beneath the Harbor Freeway—wolf, human, and vampire alike."

Patrick spoke without thought. "You have formed an alliance? Against the demons? That's great news."

The woman grimaced. "That's premature. The alliance is tentative at best," she said cautiously. "But Crimson City is under attack. Only a fool argues with his brother while the house is on fire." She turned as she spoke, looking into the eyes of every person who would meet her gaze. Most did. A few slunk away. She finally looked down at the cub. "So it's true," she said.

Xiao Fei was sitting on the ground beside the wolf-boy, but her eyes were filled with a dark challenge as she looked up at this female leader of the wolves. They were about the same age, these two, and Patrick could sense the unspoken clash of power between them.

"He's just a boy," Xiao Fei said clearly. "Don't make him a symbol."

"She poisoned him!" growled the sentry from one side. Patrick had almost forgotten him, but now the man was stirring the crowd against them.

"It was an accident," Patrick said. "We gave him human medicine. We didn't know. . . ."

"*I* didn't know," asserted Xiao Fei. "But—"

The werewolf leader silenced all with a quick slash of her hand. "We'll go to my chamber."

A loud bang and then a rumble filled the tunnel. It was a distant sound, muffled by many concrete walls, but it still roared in Patrick's head and echoed for a long time in the large room. Instinctively, Patrick reached for his amulet, gripping it with his right hand—whatever came, he would be stronger if he wielded it. But then the sound faded, and he realized he'd overreacted. He released the amulet, feeling foolish for giving away its presence. Still, he doubted anyone noticed. Like his, their gazes had sought out the source of sound, somewhere deep in a nearby tunnel. Even so, it had been a foolish gesture.

The werewolf leader blanched but retained control. "Go to my rooms," she repeated firmly. "I'll be there in . . ." She bit her lip. "I'll be there as soon as I can. You can tell me everything there."

Xiao Fei nodded and bent to gather Jian Ying. The wolf leader stopped her. "He will go to his kin," she said.

Xiao Fei looked up sharply, fear tightening her face. Then she shoved past the woman and picked up the cub. "I won't let you hurt him."

The woman drew back in shock. "He is one of our own young! How dare you think—"

"She speaks from experience," Patrick interrupted in a low tone. "Symbols are feared as much as they are revered. Her own kind did not always treat her well." He was mostly guessing, but it wasn't such a great leap. Her blood cured all manner of ills. He wondered how many times as a child she had been bled just to cure some disease. And had there been any consideration for her as a girl?

One look at Xiao Fei's face told him he had guessed correctly. Her childhood had been anything but easy.

The wolf leader paused a moment, her eyes narrow as she studied both Patrick and Xiao Fei. Then she dropped to one knee beside the cub.

"I am alpha here. I lead all the werewolves. And as Alpha Keeli, I say to you, this child will not be harmed." She lifted her voice as she spoke so that all could hear her. Looking around, Patrick saw most faces on the crowd nod in agreement. "He is one of our own," Keeli continued, "and every child is precious to us." Then Keeli gestured, and the woman who had given up her milk stepped forward, her two children still tugging at her legs. "This is Arweena. The cub—"

"Jian Ying," Xiao Fei said. "I named him Jian Ying. Jimmy to the whites."

Keeli nodded. "We will add that name to his real one. Meanwhile, Jian Ying is of Arweana's clan. She will find out the truth of his family, and we will care for him."

Patrick could see that Xiao Fei was not convinced. Or perhaps she did not want to be convinced. She cuddled the cub as if it were her own.

"You cannot keep him, Xiao Fei," he said softly. "I know you love him, but we have a great deal to do. He would not be safe with us." She bit her lip. He saw tears tremble on her lashes, and he guessed again at her thoughts. "Do you love him for himself, Xiao Fei? Or because he represents the childhood you never had? The life you would give him if you could?"

She looked up, and he saw surprise flash through her expression. "He's just a boy," she repeated fiercely.

The werewolf leader reached out her hands. "And he will be loved. You cannot doubt that." She glanced significantly around to where the crowd was clearly ready to go to battle for the child. Whatever this red-claw prophecy meant, it was important to them. They would not hurt the boy.

"Xiao Fei . . ." Patrick began.

"Okay, okay." She dipped her head and pressed a tender kiss to the cub's furry face. He was growing sleepy now, his belly well filled. He licked her face, then closed his eyes. She passed him to Alpha Keeli, who handed her to the waiting woman.

"Now . . ." Keeli began, but the distant sound of howls rumbled into the room. Everyone lifted their heads to listen. "I have to go. Wait in my chambers. I'll be there as soon as I can." As she turned and rushed off, the crowd parted quickly and respectfully for her.

The sentry who'd led them here turned to lead them away. For a moment Patrick didn't think Xiao Fei would follow; her eyes were still on the young cub. But in the end, good sense returned. She straightened and looked at their guide. "Let's go."

He nodded. They began to move through the tunnels again. The people gave way before them, and Patrick could hear the whispers as they passed. All were telling the story of the were-cub with the bloodred paws. He extended his hand to caress Xiao Fei's shoulder. The stroke was meant to be supportive—loving, even—but she shoved him away.

"You think you know me," she practically spat. "But you don't understand."

He let his hand fall away, strangely hurt by her words.

The pain was leagues out of proportion to the situation, and he could not fathom the reason. Still, his hurt made him lash out. "Then explain it to me, Xiao Fei. Tell me what you're thinking."

They were wending their way down a deserted corridor, so there was ample room for her to turn and glare at him. "I'm thinking that you're a demon—and that perhaps I ought to have this nice sentry here kill you."

Patrick stared, his mind freezing up. What the hell was she thinking?

Unfortunately, the werewolf sentry felt no such confusion. He made a neat spin and shifted to wolf form; then he attacked.

From the San Bernardino Gazette—*September 25, 1989.*

BIRTHDAY MURDER
By Sam Smith
A local teen's birthday party turned to disaster last night when a werewolf lost control and attacked partygoers, killing Lisa Wilson, sixteen. The werewolf in question, Thomas Ericson, seventeen, was also killed when struck repeatedly with a shovel and beheaded.

"I always thought there was something strange about Tommy," said entertainer Jason the Dark Lord, who killed the rampaging wolf. "I had to do it. He was eating Lisa."

All the surviving teens have been tested for lycanthropy. Currently, there is no sign of infection.

According to witnesses, Jason the Dark Lord was just starting his grand finale when Ericson began howling.

"We just thought it was funny at first," a partygoer said. "Part of the show. But then he really changed and started attacking. Then he was on top of Lisa. She didn't even have the chance to scream, and Jason was swinging that shovel. We were all really freaked out."

Doctors say that adolescence is when many natural-born werewolves first experience the change. "It's not unusual for a teenager to lose control of the wolf," said expert Dr. Stephen Wauters. "That puts regular teens in danger—especially at parties where drugs or alcohol sometimes weaken normal controls."

Police found no evidence of illegal substances, but are still investigating.

"We've never seen an unprovoked werewolf attack weeks away from a full moon before," said Police Chief Stanley Goldberg. "But rest assured, we are doing everything to keep our children safe."

Such measures include a new list of proposed restrictions on all werewolves. See "City Council" sidebar, page two.

Chapter Ten

"Don't fight, Patrick! Surrender!" Xiao Fei couldn't contain her alarm. She hadn't expected the sentry to react like this. But he had, and now Patrick was on his back beneath the onslaught. Xiao Fei bit her lip, wondering if she should interfere. Patrick was a demon, or possessed by one—she was sure of that—but he was also a nice guy.

No wonder people were seduced into trafficking with demons. She'd never understood before exactly why anyone would open a gate to the demon realm. Why would anyone bargain with total evil?

Well, now she understood. Because demons could be gorgeous and seductive and have really great smiles. They could touch one with reverence. They could kiss with skill. And a huge part of her was already seduced.

Thank God she'd noticed him clutch that necklace in the tunnel. Thank heaven she'd recognized the shape outlined by his T-shirt. And thank Buddha she'd seen the evil one in Cambodia wielding the very same artifact. She knew how destructive the amulet was, how it could corrupt the weilder and terrify an entire country. *She knew.* So she had to gather the strength to destroy it, even if her heart was already in agony at risking Patrick's life. If only he would stay still, so she could get the amulet off of him. Then she could destroy it without hurting him.

But Patrick wouldn't lie still. He was struggling with the werewolf, who'd immediately gone for his throat. And worse, other werewolves were coming, drawn by the sound of the commotion. The sentry was on top, half-changed, snarling muzzle directly above Patrick's face. Patrick held him off with his arms, but his strength was failing. The werewolf's front claws dug into Patrick's shoulders.

Patrick kicked, knocking his attacker off, but not far enough. The werewolf had amazing reflexes. He landed on his feet and immediately sprang back. Patrick didn't have enough time to recover. Soon they were both rolling on the floor again.

Xiao Fei closed her eyes. The grunts, the cries—hell, the smells of blood and sweat—were too much, too familiar. Memory and reality began to merge. Her sisters were dying! The demons were attacking! The gate was moving—shrinking or growing or simply pulsing, she didn't know. It was all so confusing. She felt something impact her knees: the hard floor. She'd fallen to her knees. She was losing her sanity big-time. She had to stay here, in the present. She was in the United States, not Cambodia. She was an adult in Crimson City, not a terrified child half-buried in blood and mud. And if she didn't want a repeat of what had happened in her home country, then she had damn well better get a grip.

She opened her eyes and glared at the snarling mass of rolling fur and man. She counted two werewolves now on Patrick, more all around. She needed to gain control of the situation, and fast.

"Your alpha will want to question him," she cried. "Don't kill him." Then Xiao Fei forced herself to rise. "Don't kill him!"

The werewolves didn't seem to hear. Blood and fear poisoned the air. Xiao Fei waded into the melee, kicking at the werewolves. She hauled them back. One turned its dripping, snarling muzzle her way and she beat it aside. Or she tried. Instead, it locked its jaws on her right arm. Right over the tattooed tears.

"Xiao Fei!" Patrick screamed, but not nearly as loud as she herself. The pain and the werewolf's weight knocked her to the floor. And then there came another loud howl. From her attacker. He ripped his jaws away. Her blood sprayed over everything.

"Stop!" she screamed. "Don't kill him! Your alpha needs to question him." She had enough presence of mind to see one of the nearby wolves nod. He understood the importance of interrogation. Then she closed her eyes and focused on breathing. She had to calm herself or she'd bleed out from her wound. The gashes were deep, and her blood flowed too easily. Some of her sisters had died from less.

Breathe. Calm. Close the wound. She managed it, despite the continued howling. The growls and grunts of the fight. Even a muffled thud next to her.

Her blood clotted. Her wounds closed. She opened her eyes.

Patrick was facedown on the floor. His clothing was torn and bloody, and his jaw was bleeding from a deep slash. Two werewolves in human form pinned him to the floor, one of whom seemed to take great pleasure in wrenching Patrick's arm behind his back. But what Xiao Fei saw most was the burning accusation in Patrick's unblacked eye. He focused on her, and the hurt she saw there chilled her blood with guilt.

Everyone else, however, was staring at the werewolf who had bitten her. He'd turned more human as he rolled on the floor, foaming spittle coming from his twisted mouth. Someone jerked Xiao Fei around. It was one of the other sentries from before. "What did you do to him?" he demanded.

She had no answer, her mind still too full to formulate words. Her eyes were on the writhing half wolf as he finally shifted fully into an agonized young man clutching his face.

"What did you do?" the sentry growled again. He shook her a bit to get her attention.

She sighed. "My blood. It's poisonous to your kind."

A murmur of horror ran through the crowd. The sentry tightened his grip on Xiao Fei's arm. "Is he going to die?"

She shook her head. "I don't know."

"No," came a muffled voice from the floor. Patrick. "He didn't get enough—"

"Shut up, demon!" growled one of the werewolves, grinding a heel into Patrick's back.

"Not . . . demon." Patrick's voice was a half grunt, but everyone understood.

"Let him speak!" ordered the sentry.

Patrick's captor eased off enough for him to speak. "I'm not a demon." He glared at Xiao Fei. "And your werewolf friend isn't going to die from that blood. He didn't get enough. He'll probably just feel weak for a while." Sure enough, the young wolf on the floor was quieting. His body still trembled, but the spasms were easing, and he was able to roll into a tight, whimpering ball. "Use your senses," Patrick continued from the floor. "All of you! Do I feel like a demon to you?"

Confused murmurs ran through the crowd. Xiao Fei needed to speak. She had to explain. If nothing else, she had to get the amulet from Patrick. But the words didn't form. He was right; he didn't feel like a demon. But then, she knew there were different types of demons. Maybe some of them felt normal. And he did have the amulet, which meant he had to be a demon. But . . .

"Take 'em inside," the sentry growled. "Keeli will know what to do."

Patrick was roughly hauled to his feet. Xiao Fei was jerked forward too, and she winced at the pull on her arm. Fortunately there wasn't any bleeding below or above her skin. For her, unattended bruises could be just as deadly. So she hurried forward to ease the pressure on her arm and quickly stepped into Alpha Keeli's official rooms.

"Tie 'em up," her captor snapped.

"What?" Xiao Fei jerked sideways, but he didn't release her. "I'm the one who—"

"Shut up!" he growled. Clearly the man had lost patience. "I don't know who's what here. My job is to keep everything safe and then get Keeli."

"But I'm no threat to you! I'm . . ." Her words faded away as his growl became lower, more threatening. It would do no good to argue.

He sat her in a hardwood chair. Someone brought rope, and all too soon she was bound tight—hands behind her back, legs strapped down. After he stood, she surreptitiously tested the knots. She was held fast. Once glance to the right and she saw Patrick was in a similar state.

"His bag," Xiao Fei said. "Get it away from him. And that thing around his neck."

Patrick's head snapped up, and she fully saw his battered face. Damn, he looked awful. Blood seeped down his chin. The cut would need stitches. One eye was swollen shut, and yet she still saw the beauty underneath. Good-looking men shouldn't be demons—it just wasn't fair to the female gender.

Patrick's bag was pulled from his shoulder and dumped on a nearby table. The amulet was ripped from his neck and dropped beside it. The head werewolf made to inspect them both, but Xiao Fei rushed to stop him.

"Don't touch the stone. It's deadly!" She'd watched a monk become engulfed in flame when he touched the amulet in Cambodia.

The wolf dropped both the bag and the amulet, and scrambled backward. He looked nervously at the other two werewolves. One looked much too happy—from restraining Patrick. In fact, he had remained in half-changed form and had his claws at the ready. The other wolf had shifted back to human form, and he just looked jumpy. Really, really jumpy.

Apparently, the leader noticed it too. "Outside," he ordered. "Guard the door."

Both wolves obeyed, but sullenly. Xiao Fei didn't breathe until they'd left. Then she turned back to the sentry-leader. Perhaps he was in a more reasonable frame of mind. "Thank you," she began. "I—"

"Save it for Keeli," he snapped. Spinning on his heel he exited, shutting the door behind him with a ponderous thud. Which left Xiao Fei staring at Patrick's battered profile. She gulped and decided to look elsewhere.

She took in what she could of Alpha Keeli's rooms. They were large, comfortable, and clearly where she met officially with . . . whomever the leader of the Crimson City werewolves would officially meet. Xiao Fei saw a large table on one side, and a large desk on the other. In between was a couch, chairs, and papers and books everywhere. If nothing else, Keeli obviously was a working werewolf, literate and half-buried under the details of governing her people. The open demon gate probably hadn't helped any.

"Why, Xiao Fei? Why would you lie like that?"

She'd known Patrick would talk to her, try to turn her to his side. But he didn't sound sneaky right then, not even seductive or threatening. He sounded hurt and confused.

She looked at him and immediately regretted it. That had been her one saving grace in Cambodia: she could look into the demons' eyes and read burning hatred there. They weren't really very good at hiding it. Any sympathy she might have had for them had disappeared right then and there. But Patrick's green eyes held honesty and pain. She looked away.

"You owe me an explanation, Xiao Fei. Why would you—"

"You're a demon!" she practically bellowed. "I don't owe you anything!"

"I'm not a goddamned demon! Geez, what the hell would make you think I am?"

She straightened her spine—at least as much as she could, given her restraints. Then she mentally strengthened her resolve and turned to look evil in the eye. "You *are* a demon," she said, forcing her voice to remain calm. "There's no use denying it. I know what that amulet is, and I know who can wield it." When he frowned at her, she almost rolled her eyes. "Demons, you idiot. Only demons can wield it."

"So, since I have this amulet, I'm a demon?"

She nodded. "Since you wield that amulet."

At his confused frown, she explained. "You haven't ever seen what happens to a human who touches its stone, have you?"

"I am human," he protested.

She shook her head, her heart breaking. "You can't be."

He sighed and tossed aside the ropes on his hands. As she gaped at him, he flexed his fingers and rolled his wrists. Then he leaned down and began work on the bonds at his ankles.

"How'd you do that?" she gasped.

His words were spoken toward his feet as he worked. "How *can't* you? They weren't very good knots."

She jerked on her bonds. Yes, they were good knots—at least, good enough to hold her. And he was seconds away from releasing his legs. Then he'd be free. And she'd still be strung up like a rotisserie chicken. *Oh, hell.* She'd just revealed that she knew he was a demon. She knew about the amulet. Which meant she was seconds away from being killed.

She took a breath to scream. Too late. He was across the floor with his hand pressing hard into her throat.

"Don't. I'm not going to hurt you unless you force me. I'm not a demon. I'm not here to hurt you. I want to close the gate. End of story. Don't scream." He took a breath. "Please."

It was that last word that got her. In truth, he looked very fierce and very scary with his battered face right up in hers, but that one word—*please*—cut at her. It sounded so vulnerable. So . . . innocent.

She shouldn't believe him. She *didn't* believe him.

But she couldn't scream with his hand on her throat. She couldn't even breathe.

"Tell me you agree, Xiao Fei. Tell me you won't scream. Promise."

She nodded. What else could she do? She was starting to see stars instead of his intense green eyes.

He released his hand a fraction. She drew a shaky, painful breath.

"You're right," he said, his hand still on her throat. But he wasn't hurting her, just holding it there in case. "The amulet is of demonic origin."

She closed her eyes. She didn't want to look into the face of her enemy.

"And there was a . . . a ceremony. To make it easier to wield." His voice shook slightly, and her eyes popped open. Something about that ceremony had obviously been difficult. "But I'm not a demon. We druids have kept this amulet for hundreds of generations to guard against just this type of event." He took a deep breath. "The amulet opens gates, Xiao Fei. It can also be used to close them."

She didn't answer. Everything was happening so fast. She didn't know what to believe.

"What about your blood?" he asked. She frowned and didn't answer, so he continued, "The book I read on you says something about your blood burning demons." He abruptly stood and crossed to his satchel. He pulled out the Cambodian journal and rapidly flipped through the pages.

" 'The Phoenix's blood is of Earth. Purified by prayer, strengthened by devotion, her blood will burn the unholy. It will close the doorway to hell and destroy all of the unclean who poison the earth.' " He looked up from the book. "Is that true?"

She bit her lip and looked away.

"Xiao Fei—"

"I don't know. I . . ." She swallowed. "I think it is. When . . . Before . . ." Tears blurred her vision. She didn't want to think, didn't want to remember that time.

"When you closed the other gate," he prompted. "Did your blood burn the demons? Like acid?"

She shook her head. "Not mine. I . . . Not mine." She'd been struck and fell down. Then she'd crawled underneath something and hidden. She'd hidden while the rest of her sisters had fought and died.

Patrick's voice softened even as he continued to press her. "But others did. You saw your sisters' blood—"

"Yes. It burned the demons."

He nodded and tucked the monk's journal away. Then, while she struggled to overcome the nausea, he knelt beside her. "How old were you? When you closed—"

"Eight. I was eight." She spoke over him, not wanting to think about that time again.

"Very young. Too young to understand everything."

"I knew enough."

He nodded. "I'm sure you did. But another gate's opened here in this place where you felt safe. It must be really hard for you."

She didn't answer. Sure, it sucked. But she was handling it.

"I'm sure that other experience was highly traumatic. You were eight. Everyone was dying. Demons were attacking—"

"Stop!" She jerked at her bonds and succeeded only in wrenching her wrists. "I know what happened. I don't need your psychoanalysis." He paused, his expression both startled and sympathetic. She preferred anger.

"Just do it, okay?" she suddenly snapped. "Kill me and be done with it."

He frowned, but it was his sigh that startled her. His breath was warm where it caressed her cheek. "I told you. I'm not going to hurt you." Then he pulled a switchblade out of his bag. The sharp blade extended with a snick that made her gasp. "I'm just trying to make you understand," he said clearly. "You're confused. Traumatized by the other event. In pain from the current gate. Things have got to be muddled in your head. I'm just trying to make things clear."

"They're very clear," she whispered. Nothing confusing about the blade; he was about to slit her throat.

"Your blood burns demons." He leaned down and pressed the blade to her forearm—right at a tattooed phoenix tear, right where the wolf had bitten her, right where the skin was thin because she had just closed the wound. As always, the blood flowed warm and steady.

He paused. "No chance of lycanthropy, is there?"

She glared at him. "You're about to kill me, and I'm supposed to worry about infecting you with lycanthropy?"

He smiled. "You get really snappy when you're scared, you know that? It's kinda cute."

She glared at him, and he sobered.

"I'm not going to hurt you. I'm proving that I'm not a demon."

She felt the cool edge of his blade—the blunt side now—against her wrist. The sharp side cut the rope. Then, before she could react, he twisted her arm back to him. Her blood trailed down her palm in a thin stream. He pressed his mouth to her wound.

From Patrick Lewis's journal.

September 25, 1989
   The funeral was today. It was awful. Everybody cried, except for those who just stared. Mom keeps asking me how I feel. Dad keeps asking what happened. I can't tell him. I can't say that I just stood there. Tommy was my friend. I knew he'd been through the change. He told me, and besides I could feel it. That's why we had the party so early before my birthday. Before the full moon. And now he's dead. Jason's a hero, and Lisa . . .

September 26, 1989
   I put away her pictures. I can't look at them anymore. Mom didn't say anything, but she noticed. Dad, too. It makes him feel better when he knows I'm writing in this journal. He thinks I'm getting my feelings out. Maybe I am. Maybe I just don't know what to do with myself.

September 27, 1989
   I'm sick. I threw up all day. Mom says it's the flu but I know it's not.
   Jason stopped by. He offered to heal me, but I told him to fuck off. I'm not sick. And if I were, I could damn well heal myself.

September 28, 1989
   Why wouldn't she scream? I keep asking myself that. Why didn't Lisa scream? We all saw Tommy change. We all saw him stand there fighting the wolf. Then he leaped up and knocked her down.

She could have thrown him off, kicked or some-thing. But she just lay there like she couldn't move. Like she was frozen. Why didn't she scream?

Why didn't I stop him?

Why didn't I stop Jason?

Where the hell did he get that shovel, and why the hell didn't I stop him when he lifted it up in the air? He was working the energy. I felt it. It was so strong . . . But I can't believe Jason would activate the wolf in Tommy. Not for kicks and certainly not to kill Lisa. It's not possible. It's not, and I don't be-lieve it.

The truth is that it's my fault. I was too slow. I work energy, too. I could have shifted Tommy back to human. I could have; I know it. Why didn't I? I just stood there like an idiot. I thought Tommy would get ahold of himself. I thought . . .

It's all my fault.

Chapter Eleven

Heat. Wet heat caressed Xiao Fei's skin, and she tried to move away. This was too intimate, too close to who she was. But Patrick wouldn't let her escape. He held her fast and sucked on her wrist, his tongue swirling around and across her skin. His teeth nipped slightly at the wound, and she shivered in reaction.

Then he drew her inside him. She was so attuned to his essence that she imagined her blood sliding into his system; she felt the energy leave her and slip drop by drop into him. She closed her eyes. She thought of him and his dark green irises. She saw pristine blue water, soaring waves, and all the life that surged in the ocean. And she saw herself playing on his shores, swimming in his depths, immersing herself in all that was him.

It was a silly fantasy, and yet she couldn't deny the rightness of the image. When they touched—when they kissed—she felt the echo of all of Earth in him.

"Are all druids so . . ." She had no word for what she meant to describe. Persistent? All-embracing? "Large?"

She felt his lips purse in a kiss of her wrist. His tongue swirled one last time; then he pulled away. "Have I drunk enough blood?"

"Not for a vampire."

His eyes flashed with surprise, then humor. "Am I suspected of that, too?"

She shook her head. "How do you feel?"

She saw him hesitate a moment; then he bent to the ropes at her feet. "I won't lie to you. Your blood burns a bit." He flashed her a quick grin. "Kinda like a fine, dark brandy."

"Intoxicating?" She meant it as a joke. She drawled the word and smiled as she spoke, but his eyes grew serious. His pupils expanded and the tight lines of his face softened.

"Yes, I think it is. I feel drunk. I've never told anyone as much as I've told you."

She almost laughed, but he was too serious for her to mock. "You haven't told me anything substantial."

"You know I am Draig-Uisge. That I am not a demon, but that I wield their tool."

She sobered immediately, her eyes drifting to his satchel and the amulet nearby.

"That burns, too," Patrick said softly. "Every time I touch it." He sighed. "It is the reminder that with power comes pain and responsibility."

She bit her lip. "The amulet is evil. If you have it, if you use it—"

"Then I must be evil too?"

She nodded, knowing her logic was sound. But he didn't feel evil, and more important, he wasn't acting evil.

He sat back on his heels and looked directly at her.

"It's a tool, Xiao Fei. Like a knife or a gun, it can be used for good or ill."

"It was made by demons. It's energy is demonic." She swallowed and came to the real point. "It corrupts. Even if you are good now, you won't be for long."

He looked at her and she saw a soul-deep sadness in his eyes. "Give me a chance to prove that's not true. I've held the amulet for over a decade now. My purpose is still strong."

"Your purpose?" she challenged.

"I defend Earth. That's what a Draig does. He defends Earth from evil."

She folded her arms across her chest. "You tied me to a bed. And you cast a spell on me in the storeroom."

He sighed. "It was a charm spell, and I cast it when we first met."

"And that makes it different, how? Manipulation. Force. These are the tools of evil men and horrific demons."

A shadow crossed his face. She couldn't identify its meaning—remorse, frustration, maybe anger. But then it passed, and his expression cleared. "Remember back in the hotel room? I told you I'd lost my parents to the cause."

She remembered. He'd said something else too, something that she'd blocked from her thoughts.

"I also said you were the love of my life."

She winced. "Don't lie to me, Patrick. I'll know you're evil then, and I'll kill you." She didn't know where such murderous fury came from, but it beat in her words and in her blood.

"I'm not lying. I think you might be." He grimaced and looked so totally unhappy that her anger began to fade. If he tried to touch her—seduce her—then she would know it was an act. But his body was bunched tight with frustration, and his expression remained fierce. "It's not the charm," he said. "That just makes people interested sexually."

"Horny."

He shrugged. "Yes. But what I feel is stronger. It's much more than lust." He looked into her eyes. "My *soul* aches for you. I can't say why, but you are so completely important to me that I can't begin to describe it. When I touch you, it's like . . ."

"The whole earth is there with us." The words were out before she could stop them.

"Yes! You're you, and you're the Earth as well. Nothing like that has ever happened before, Xiao Fei. I need you. I love you!" He cut off his words, obviously struggling with what he'd said. "Well . . . is that love, Xiao Fei? Are you the love of my life?"

He was asking her? She'd spent her life running from anything resembling emotion—good, bad, or otherwise. She'd lived in fear and looked for safety. She had just started to hope for a better life, and then the demons invaded. Now he said he loved her? It was ludicrous! Except, she believed him.

She groaned. "Everything is moving so fast. I can't keep up."

"Tell me about it," he groused. When she didn't comment more, he sighed and bent over to untie the rope around her legs.

She lifted her hand to touch him, but it was covered in blood. Her wrist was still bleeding. She would need to close the wound soon, but she couldn't stop watching Patrick. His hair was that indeterminate blond that was part brunette, part white-blond, part everything else. His shoulders were broad, his hands strong and capable, and he had the oddest habit of ducking his head slightly when he was being funny. His skin was tan without looking leathery. If he had freckles, they were long since lost in the lines that came from long hours of squinting into the sun or laughing with a wide open spirit.

Unable to stop herself, Xiao Fei reached forward and touched his head. Was his hair thinning, or had it always been this delicate? He lifted his face. Was his mouth just now becoming sensual and seductive, or had he always been a lure for girls?

"Tell me how you came to use the amulet," she said.

His reaction wasn't obvious. In fact, he covered it well, but she was watching him closely. His jaw tightened slightly, pulling at the bleeding cut there, and his eyes misted with pain.

"Not now," he murmured. "Can you heal your arm? Or do we go to a doctor?"

"Both." At his surprised look, she gestured to his chin. "Your jaw."

He frowned, then put his hand to his face. She watched his long fingers gingerly explore the slash on his cheek. "Oh, yeah," he said on a half laugh. "I'd forgotten in the overall agony."

She stood and walked over to him, looking closely. Unlike her, his blood clotted easily. The wound looked ugly, but not mortal. "How much does my blood burn?" she asked.

He smiled, though she could tell the movement pained him somewhat. "Like a fine brandy."

She snorted and gently pushed him back into his chair. She had been watching him closely, waiting for the effects, which she saw now. The discoloration around his temple was moving from black to green. His swollen lip was slimming. "My blood is healing you."

His eyes widened. "Really? That little bit?"

"I'm tiny but strong," she quipped. Then she used her hands to tilt his head back and more fully expose his jaw. "Only a plastic surgeon could make this look good again."

Patrick shrugged and muttered, "Jason always said I was too pretty."

She raised an eyebrow in query.

His eyes cooled, and he shrugged. "An old friend. He died a few years ago."

There was more of a story there, but he obviously wasn't willing to share it, so Xiao Fei focused on her task instead. She raised her wrist and angled it just right. Then she began to chant. She didn't know exactly what about this process made her blood more effective, how one chant could substantially increase a healing effect, how another thickened and closed her skin, she only knew that it worked. So she dripped blood onto his face, and when enough had coated his skin, she pushed the jagged edges of his wound together.

After two more minutes, his skin held together. She switched chants, and her own flesh knitted. "There will be a scar," she warned.

He nodded as he gently touched his face. "Does it always work so fast?"

She stepped backward. "No. Rarely. Some people just seem to . . . Your energies and mine seem to . . ."

"Our energies align, right? That's what you're trying to say. You and I work well together."

She swallowed, unwilling to admit anything of the kind, even if it was true. "I don't fully trust you," she said. "You still carry a demon amulet." But her blood had healed him, and that would never happen if he were a demon.

He smiled. "I don't trust you either. Not after siccing those werewolves on me."

She couldn't fault him for that. So she leaned against the arm of the couch and sighed. "Please. Tell me how you came to carry the amulet."

He shrugged, and his gaze became unfocused. "The previous Draig misused it. He was a Draig-Teine, a fire dragon. I . . ." His eyes returned to hers. "I fought him for it and won. There was blood—his and mine. And the damn thing burns, Xiao Fei. It really hurts to hold, but I had to. He was . . ." He shook his head. "The Draig-Teine was working on opening the gate to Orcus. He had to be stopped, so I did it."

She doubted it was anything so simple. "You killed him?"

"Yes. There was no other choice." Patrick pushed up to stand over her, his shoulders slightly hunched, then spun away. "After that it was obvious I was the next draig. Only, I'm a Draig-Uisge. A—"

"A water dragon."

He frowned as he turned back to her. "I didn't tell you that, did I?"

She shook her head. "But I know. I saw it. Back when . . ."

"Back in the storage room. When we kissed."

"Yeah." It was her turn to look away. She didn't really like that she synced with him so well. On the other hand, in some ways it was wonderful. It *felt* wonderful. She made an effort to redirect her thoughts to the task at hand. "So, what do we do now?"

Patrick's gaze steadied, holding hers with a strength that weakened her knees. She knew what he was going to say before the words left his mouth. "We have to try again. We have to close the gate."

"It won't work."

His lips compressed, as if he were disappointed by her response. "It will work. Denying it won't change the facts."

She scratched lightly at one tattooed scar—the tear she had opened to cure Stan the vampire. Was that only yesterday? The hours had blurred. She didn't know how much time had passed, and in these werewolf tunnels, she couldn't even tell if it was day or night.

"I'm so tired," she murmured. "And I stink." Silly how attached she'd become to American showers. In Cambodia, she'd sometimes gone weeks without bathing. But now . . .

"There's a shower here. Why don't we use that?"

She narrowed her gaze on his too-innocent face. *"We?"*

He grinned. "Water is precious. They say you should always shower with a friend."

She shook her head, knowing what he intended. "I'm too tired to try that again."

"No, you're not." He pulled her bag of dried persimmon out of his satchel. "This will perk you right up."

It would. And it would stoke the fire in her blood, her ability to bleed, and her sense of . . . everything. Her awareness of energy was part of her blood's ability, and the fruit accentuated it. Which meant she would also be hyperaware of Patrick.

"You need it," he said as he brought the bag over. "You've been bleeding all over the place."

"Messy me," she joked.

He reached out with his free hand to touch her face, but she avoided him. She ducked away, but as she moved, she grabbed the bag. He was right. She had been extending herself in the last day or so. She'd known she would have to eat some persimmon after healing the vampires.

"Why are you so reluctant to take care of yourself?" he asked.

She flinched slightly at his perception. "I do take care of myself," she said.

"Sparingly. You push yourself to the edge."

"Conservation. I've barely got enough of this stuff to last until harvest."

He stepped closer to her, looked her in the eye. "There's more to it than that. I think you're punishing yourself for surviving when your sisters died. Back in Cambodia, when—"

"I know when and where they died!" she snapped, then immediately regretted it. What better way to tell him he'd struck home than to lash out at him?

"It's disconcerting, isn't it? I feel you, Xiao Fei. Your feelings. Your—"

"Thoughts?" The idea was horrifying.

He shook his head. "No. Not what you think, what you *are*." He lifted his hands in a gesture of confusion. "I don't even understand what I'm saying, but I know it's true. I know it's getting stronger too, the longer we're together—our bond."

"Then we'd better separate right now."

He laughed, but there was little humor in the sound. "No. We'd better get closer right now." He fitted words to action, stepping right up to her side, close enough to cup her right elbow in one large palm. "This bond tells me we were destined to meet. That we can—"

"Fuck?" she sneered.

He flinched at her crude word, but didn't shy away from it. "To bond physically, to heal the Earth."

"Mystic mumbo jumbo," she muttered.

"Yeah," he agreed. "Because blood that can heal wounds and cure vampirism is so not."

She shot him a hard look. "How did you know about the vampirism? I didn't tell you that."

He smiled. "I wasn't asleep during that vampire attack, you know. Besides, weren't there vampires in Cambodia?"

Her suspicion abruptly deflated. "The monk's journal says so, doesn't it?"

"It raises the possibility."

Xiao Fei sighed and planted the heels of her palms in her eyes. Everything was happening so fast. She felt him lift the bag from her fingers. Moments later she smelled the bitter fruit and her mouth watered reflexively. She let her hands drop away from her eyes just as he brought the small bloodred food to her lips.

"Eat," he urged.

She opened her mouth, and he pushed the fruit inside. He was right: she needed it. And perhaps he was right about her guilt. Every time she tasted one of these damned things, she remembered the ritual in Cambodia.

Food was scarce, this fruit even more so. Which made the time of eating precious, shrouded in ritual, and viewed as sacred. Each Phoenix Tear was given a small, ripe globe the size of a plum while the monks chanted a prayer in the background. They ate one bite with every beat of the gong. Three bites and the persimmon had to be consumed. Then three sips of tea, and three hours of prayer.

Sacred. Holy. And now she popped one into her mouth like it was a large cheezy curl. There was no ritual because there was no one to share it with. All her fellow Phoenix Tears were gone, all dead in a horrible way.

Patrick wrapped his arms around her. She wanted to

fight him, but she didn't. Instead, she buried her face in his shoulder and took solace from his warmth.

"I don't know what you're thinking about, but I can feel your sadness and your guilt." He tucked her closer beneath his chin. "It wasn't your fault that they died."

She breathed deeply of his scent. She held it close to her heart, but not so close as his words. It *wasn't* her fault. She'd been eight years old. There was nothing she could do to save anyone. Or so she kept telling herself. "It wasn't my fault," she murmured.

"That's right. But it will be if more people die here, Xiao Fei. You have to help me."

His words were a dousing of cold water, and she shoved him away with all her strength. He allowed her to. He stepped backward to give her room, but he didn't go far.

"Xiao Fei—" he began, but she cut him off.

"Is there anything you wouldn't do if you thought it would close the gate?" she demanded. "I already know you'd commit rape."

He blanched at that, but his expression remained stern. "People are dying, Xiao Fei. Earth is dying."

"Would you kill for it, Patrick? Would you kill me if you thought that would close the gate?"

He didn't even hesitate. "You know I would."

"Well, bully for you. I ought to—"

He moved so fast, she didn't have time to react. She had training: martial arts, self-defense. She didn't even have time to draw breath, and suddenly he was gripping her arms, drawing her right up to his face.

"I've never lied to you, Xiao Fei. The demons are invading. People are dying every moment that passes. Earth is dying. You can't be so selfish as to leave the gate open just to preserve your purity."

She was cringing beneath his onslaught, not on the outside, but inside where her heart was breaking and her soul was shattering. "It's not true!" she said, stunned to hear her words break on a sob.

"Isn't it?" he challenged. She shoved him away, but he wouldn't let go. "Isn't it?" he demanded again.

"No!" she bellowed. "Your plan won't work!"

"You don't know that."

"Yes, I do!" Then she drew up her knee as hard as she could right into his privates—or so she planned. She missed. He was quick to avoid the impact, but not so quick as to move his foot away from the downstroke. She might not have nailed his privates, but she slammed down hard on his instep, and he howled in reaction. He also slackened his grip.

She was away from him in a moment, but there was nowhere for her to go. The werewolf sentries outside wouldn't let her go anywhere. And even if she escaped the tunnels, Patrick would chase her. She knew that. He believed in his druidic solution. He believed it would work.

"Tell me what you know," he gasped.

She brushed the hair out of her eyes, only slightly surprised to realize her face was wet with tears. When she spoke, the words were wrenched out of her memories, her voice thick with remembered pain and the smell of death. "I felt it before. I feel it now: the hole in the Earth, the gaping wound."

Patrick nodded. "The demon gate."

"In Cambodia. In Crimson City. Wherever. I feel them."

"So do I."

"But I've felt this before. In Cambodia. The closing started out so beautiful. We reached out to the Earth, all of us. I felt the sky and the sun, the moon, though it was on the other side of the world—even the stars in the heavens. There was stone and earth and water, too. I felt all of it."

She had his full attention. The pain in his foot must be fading, because he straightened and moved toward her. She held him off with a single raised hand. He had to understand. "I felt it all, Patrick. The monks were chanting, but I barely heard. Earth. Sky. Alive—so alive." God, she had never felt more awed or more perfect. Everything about the ceremony had been so perfect.

"Like when we kissed," he suggested.

She nodded. "Exactly like that."

"That's good! That means we can do it," he said.

"No! No, it doesn't. Listen to me." It was so hard to get the words out, so hard to explain.

"I'm listening. Keep going."

"The demons found out what we were doing. They must have felt it."

He nodded, and when she didn't speak any more, he prompted her. "They attacked?"

She nodded. "They attacked. Demons and monks, everybody was screaming. There was so much blood. And I felt the Earth surging with life."

He frowned. "You mean death. Everyone was dying."

"Yes! No!" She pressed her fists to her head, trying to remember clearly, trying to make sense of something incomprehensible. "They were dying, but the Earth was living. Because of our blood."

"Because your blood was closing the gate."

"No." Her hands dropped heavily to her lap. "Because we gave our life to it, the gate . . . I don't know why the gate closed. It wasn't our ceremony. The demon with the amulet was killed. The blood circle was smashed, and everywhere was life and death." She bit her lip, remembering, reliving, feeling. "Life—so strong. And death." She raised her gaze to his, willing him to understand. "It was a massacre."

He stepped forward again, but she held out her arm. She held him away as long as she could while he just looked at her. He stood there and watched until her arm grew weary. Still, she held him away. But eventually her strength gave out and her arm dropped.

Patrick was with her in a moment. He tucked her close to his heart and wrapped his arms around her so tight that she could barely breathe. She felt his biceps bulging as he pulled her near. She felt his breath stir the hair that teased her forehead. And she breathed in his scent, his warmth, his life.

She felt him all the way down to the core of her being. She sighed. He was right: they were becoming very attuned to another.

"So you don't know," he murmured. "You don't know what closed the gate."

"I'm just one person. Even with your druidic power, that's only two. In Cambodia there were twenty Phoenix Tears and forty monks. Sixty people, and still they all died."

"The gate closed. Earth healed," Patrick said.

Xiao Fei shuddered. "If I die, there will be no more Phoenix Tears. No more children who bear my blood talents. The ability to close the gate will be lost forever."

Patrick pulled back slightly and pressed a kiss to her forehead. "Then we'll just have to make sure that you don't die."

Why didn't he understand? "Our *lives* are what closed the gate."

Patrick looked taken aback. He shook his head. "No.

Your blood was just an essential ingredient. It doesn't have to involve death."

"You don't know that." She shook her head.

He smiled and touched her chin. "That's my point: we don't know that. Not for sure. For the moment, I'm going with the good sex theory."

She laughed wryly, done in by his stubbornness. "It would have to be really, really good sex."

"I'm okay with that." He grinned.

Suddenly the door burst open, and Alpha Keeli pushed in, flanked by three guards. She looked haggard, dirty, and exhausted, but her eyes were keen as she stared at the two of them. "All right," she half growled. "Which one of you is the demon? Or do we just kill you both?"

From Patrick Lewis's journal.

November 1, 1989

I can't surf. I can't even go to the beach without throwing up. I told Dad not to sign the new sponsorship agreement. I won't be going to any more tournaments.

Mom tries to help, but she just makes me nervous. She watches everything I do like I'm a freak. Dad told me to find a job, one far away from the water. He got me hooked up with the nursery. I'm building water gardens for people, but that's okay. It's water. Dead water that I bring to life with plants and stuff.

It's okay.

Chapter Twelve

Patrick stepped in front of Xiao Fei, protecting her as best he could. Just as she, apparently, decided to do the same. They ended up colliding shoulders and presenting open targets to the werewolves.

"I was wrong," Xiao Fei said.

"We're not demons," began Patrick.

Keeli waved them to silence. "I know you're not demons; I was just messing with you. You make too damn much noise to be demons." She pointed to her ears. "Werewolves have really good hearing. I've been listening at the door. Plus, you smell human."

Patrick took a moment to absorb this information, and with that knowledge came embarrassment. Just how much had she heard?

Keeli crossed wearily into the room. "Do you really think you can close the gate?"

"No," answered Xiao Fei.

At the same moment, Patrick said, "Yes."

Keeli stared at them. "What do you need from me to attempt it?"

Patrick shook his head. "Nothing. Except maybe a room where we can be undisturbed."

"Druid mojo?" Keeli asked.

Patrick nodded, ignoring the glint in her eye.

"Any danger to the tunnels or my people?"

"None."

"Except for having pissed-off demons come storming the door," said Xiao Fei. "They'll come for us." She swallowed. "They'll come for me."

Keeli sighed. "We've already got pissed-off demons storming our door. Not to mention frightened humans and a few vamps." She dropped down into a chair, and Patrick noticed a deep scrape along her arm.

"How bad is it out there?" he asked.

She looked at him, her eyes hollow. "The demons knew what to hit and where. LAX is in flames. B-Ops is under attack; I know that much. They had problems with infiltrators. The One-ten is blown near downtown, and one of our subway stations is impassable." She lifted her chin. "But we're strong and resilient. The demons won't get a foothold in wolf territory."

"And the human population?" Xiao Fei asked, her voice subdued. "The regular people?"

"We're helping as best we can, but we've got limited resources. There's no doubt the demons are a threat to all of us, so whatever you can do, druid, do it fast."

Patrick nodded. Here it was: the weight of yet another race descending on his shoulders. He didn't need the werewolf alpha pressuring him to do his job, but he felt the keener responsibility nonetheless. "I'm working as fast as I can."

"Good." She gestured to the sentries. "Take them

to Riley's old room. Get them whatever they need."

Xiao Fei stepped forward. "I don't know what you heard outside the door, but don't pin any hopes on this. It's a silly dream that . . ."

Her voice faded away as Keeli waved her to silence. "I don't care. We're going to shut it one way or another. Luckily, the humans started this disaster and they're the ones taking the brunt of the damage. I have to believe they're also the ones who have the best tools to fix it. If that means druids or B-Ops or whatever, my job is to keep my people safe and help as best I can."

Patrick nodded in respect. This one small woman was already showing herself to be a great leader. "Thank you. We won't fail you."

The werewolf rubbed a weary hand over her face. "Whatever. Go do it."

Riley's old room was spare, small, and had the stale scent of disuse. Patrick could smell the faint odor of wolf permeating the room, but didn't care once he saw the blessing of a shower. Another bathroom with running water. In the werewolf tunnels. Hallelujah!

The guards left with barely an acknowledgment. One thought to ask if they needed any food, but both Patrick and Xiao Fei shook their heads. Privacy was what they wanted. The other guard glared hard at them, his wolf fangs bared in anger. He clearly didn't want them there, but was bowing to his Alpha's orders. Patrick waited in tense silence, wondering just how many wolves felt the same. Were any of them reckless enough to disobey Keeli? There wasn't time to find out. And thankfully, the guards soon left.

"Don't even think of touching me," Xiao Fei said

when the door closed. "Not until I've showered. I hate feeling like this."

"Dirty?" Patrick asked.

She shook her head. "Stinky. Everything in a war smells: the fear, the death, the rot." She shuddered. "That's what I remember most about coming to the United States. My first hot shower. The smell of soap and cleanliness."

"How old were you?"

"Ten. My mother gave me French vanilla bath wash and herbal shampoo. I didn't even know what vanilla was, but how I loved that smell."

Patrick pushed open the bathroom door and sniffed—unscented Dial soap and indeterminate shampoo, both from some hotel chain. It was a good bet that Riley worked in housekeeping. "I swear that, when this whole thing is over, I'll buy you the most expensive shampoo and soap money can buy."

She shrugged and joined him in the bathroom. "Clean is all I care about." Then she pushed him out the door.

He left the bathroom willingly. He'd already seen there wasn't a lock. Let her get clean while he made his other preparations: candle, rowan leaf, flint. She'd already be running water; he'd heard her turn on the tap. The amulet was heating up on his chest. All that was left were his prayer and the belief that this time it would work.

He was the Earth. His blood flowed like the rivers and pulsed like the oceans. His flesh was the ground: dark, rich dirt all the way down to the planet's molten core. The strength of his bones was of the rocks and metals, the hardened exterior of the planet. And his mind encompassed all life: insect, plant, bird, and human, plus vampire and werewolf. They were all one. He was one with them. Together they would heal the world's open wound.

He stepped into the bathroom, the creak of the door muffled by the shower noise. His bare feet absorbed the chill of the concrete floor. The steam merged in his mind with the mist of a primordial forest, an image from the past. Xiao Fei represented the future.

He didn't take the time or focus to analyze his thought. To him, Xiao Fei was simply a beautiful, unsullied, awe-inspiring future. When he merged with her, he would have it all: Earth in past, present, and future.

She stood inside the shower stall facing the stream, her face raised to the needle-thin trails of water. The light was stark, but also diffused because of the steam. Still, he could see her pearly white skin, as luminescent as the moon, and the long, sensual curve of her back, her buttocks, her legs. He also saw the full extent of her phoenix tattoo. The art was stunning, even more so because it adorned a fabulous body. Beautiful plumage outlined sensual curves. He knew the monks had tattooed her when she was a child, but clearly they'd known the woman she would become.

The face of the phoenix covered her right shoulder. Its bright red rooster neck arched erotically over her right breast, swelling into a full and glorious chest that brought wondrous attention to the dusky nipple. Huge wings soared upward over her left torso, outling her left breast in golden highlights. Lower down, the phoenix's bright tail feathers seemed to ripple and dance around her left hip, while sharp talons extended down her right thigh. In between was her sex—dark, wet, and so alluring. He felt the surge of his blood along with his desire. He wanted to feast his eyes longer, but he couldn't wait. He pushed open the fiberglass door and stepped in behind her.

She must have heard him coming. She didn't move,

didn't even gasp. And when he slipped his hands around her waist, she released a sound that might have been a purr of delight or perhaps simply acceptance.

"Are you okay with this?" he asked as he pressed his lips to her wet shoulder. Indeed, he traced his tongue around the arch of a curling feather. "There are no spells this time, no ropes, no coercion. I shouldn't have done any of that." He paused, needing her to choose this of her own free will. "Will you let me make love to you?"

"Yes," she answered. Then she looked over her shoulder at him. "We're saving the Earth, right? With really good sex."

He smiled. "Right."

"Then why not?" He caught a flash of something new in her eyes. "You up to the task?" she asked.

In answer, he allowed his hips to drift closer, letting his male organ glide sensuously along the crease between her buttocks. His fingers slid upward to cup her firm breasts. "I'll do my best." When she stiffened in his arms, he gentled his caress. "Lean back into me. Relax. Let me do the work."

"So . . . this is your job, huh?" Her voice was tight, betraying her anxiety, but she leaned back into him. He felt her heat all the way from his shoulders down to his swollen organ.

"No harm in enjoying one's work," he said, pushing a knee forward between her thighs. He liked watching the flex of her thigh as it extended and retracted the phoenix's talons. She resisted at first, but in time she opened her thighs, and he felt more of her settle on his leg. God, she felt good. Especially as she slowly— finally—allowed her head to lean back against his shoulder.

Abruptly, she flinched and jerked away. It took him a moment to understand what happened, but when he did, he cursed himself for his stupidity. She'd leaned back against the amulet. How well he remembered that first agonizing bite of pain. With a quick flick, he tossed the amulet over his shoulder so that it hung down his back. His shoulder blades twitched at the impact, and he took a moment to absorb the burning heat in that unaccustomed place. Meanwhile, Xiao Fei was pulling away from him.

"Give me a moment," he ground out, mentally accepting the burning energy against his back. He felt it, accepted it, then relegated it to a distant part of his mind. There was always pain on Earth, he told himself; that was part of living. And so he folded the sensation into his thoughts on Earth just as Xiao Fei was in front of him representing not only a blissful future, but also pleasure, joy, and all things beautiful.

She stepped forward and tried to straighten off his leg. He held her by her hips, but she fought him. "Do you have to wear that thing? Does it have to be part of what we do?" she asked.

"Yes. I have to touch it. It accentuates my ability to shape energy. That's what it does."

She ducked her head so the water stream hit him full in the face. "It's evil. It's a demon—"

"It's a *tool*." He adjusted his position and hers; then he took a deep breath and began reciting what he remembered from Jason's notes and his own studies. "Aeons ago, back before recorded time, the demons used these amulets to travel between Earth and Orcus. They were like mad gods to the humans. They had superior strength and magical powers, but their understanding of the gates was flawed."

Xiao Fei stilled as he spoke, so he allowed himself to caress the tattooed tail feathers along her wet hip, massaging the muscles there as he spoke.

"There was a disaster. I don't know what, but something happened to the gate. The veil started to close, demons went nuts, and the humans took advantage of it to kill as many of the monsters as possible. Most everything demonic was destroyed—but some things survived."

"That amulet."

He nodded. "There are other things too, I'm sure, but eventually this amulet came to be guarded by us druids. We know it for the tool it is: a way to shape energy, a way to open or close a gate to Orcus."

"And after this is all over?" She looked at him with a clear hope in her eyes. He hated to disappoint her.

"I can't destroy it, Xiao Fei. It's my job as the current Draig to protect it." He leaned down and pressed a kiss to her shoulder. "It's what allowed me to bring out Jian Ying's wolf DNA. It can heal as well as harm."

She didn't respond, and he spent long moments under the rapidly cooling water wondering whether she would even accept what he'd just told her. Her experience when she'd seen the Cambodian amulet had left her deeply scarred. Who could blame her for hating everything it represented and anyone who wielded it?

Fortunately, Xiao Fei was a practical woman. She understood the difficulties with managing energy. Her blood was at least as powerful as his amulet. So she eventually sighed and settled back on his thigh. "I'm so tired," she murmured. "I don't want the fate of the world to rest in my hands. I never did."

"Then relax your grip, Xiao Fei," he said. He slid his hands forward to rest against her belly, right at the base of her trailing wing feathers. "I'm a strong man. I can hold things up for a while."

"There's a fine line between strong and delusional, you know," she said, but there was no heat in her words. And then—to his shock—she lifted his hands to her mouth and pressed a kiss into each palm. He was more moved by that simple act of faith than anything he'd ever done or felt in his entire life. It rocked him to his core, and choked off any words he might have said. In the end, all he could do was press his cheek to her forehead as he pulled her back into his embrace.

"I suppose we had better get on with it," she said.

He still had no words, so he tried to put his thanks into his touch, his awe into a worshipful caress. Holding her steady with one hand, he grabbed soap with the other and lathered her up as best he could. She wanted to be clean? He would make her skin shine. She wanted this to be good and he would make it the best experience of her life.

He slid his soaped hand over her belly, letting the suds hide and reveal the glorious art. But then the colors of the tattoo faded from his thoughts as other sensations pushed to the fore. He felt the sharp jut of her hips, the softer trembling flesh of her abdomen, and he even played with the tiny indent of her belly button. She stretched against him, lengthening her rib cage, sucking in her stomach and flexing her bottom around his straining organ. He licked water off her shoulder in response. Wet and nourishing, she tasted like life to him, and in this way he was recalled to his purpose.

"Your body is the Earth," he said as he caressed his hands up over her stomach and ribs. "It has soft hollows and hard mountains." He caressed even higher. His palms encircled her breasts, narrowing in a slow, sensuous slide to her taut nipples. "You nourish your young and bring life to all who touch you."

"How very erotic," she drawled. "My boobs are milk jugs."

She was nervous, defusing her tension with humor. He smiled and kissed her neck. "That's not how I see them at all." He settled her more firmly on his thigh. "Do you know why men are fascinated with breasts?"

"Why?"

He paused. "Uh . . . I have no idea, we just are. But they're round and firm and they peak when I touch them." To prove his point, he narrowed his fingers until he pinched her nipples, then had to grin when she gasped in response. Warming to his theme, he continued. "They're soft and squishy. They jiggle when you walk. And, er, I don't know, I just love playing with them." And it was true; he did. He lifted them with both hands. He squeezed slightly and twisted. He flicked her nipples with his thumb, then pulled her breasts taut by their tightened peaks. "Ever play with Play-Doh?"

She frowned as she looked over her shoulder at him. "You mean what you flatten down on the comics to pull up an image of Snoopy? Then distort him into a weird shape, like a bad dinosaur?"

He shook his head and laughed. "That's Silly Putty."

"Really?"

"Really." He pinched her nipple again and she arched back in delight. "I was thinking about the way I kinda just had to feel it, to move it, knead it. You know—do stuff to it."

"Play-Doh?"

"Yeah, but only till I was about thirteen. Then I found these." He kept toying with her breasts, loving the slide of her flesh in his hands, the weight and her heat. Most especially he loved the way her breath seemed to catch and stutter with his every movement.

"So . . . my boobs are an adult form of Play-Doh?"

He twisted her on his thigh so that she half sat on his leg, half reclined across his arm. "Ever eat it?" he asked.

"Eww! You ate that stuff?"

"Nope. But I definitely have the urge now." He pressed his lips to her body. Water splashed past, but he found that sensation incredibly erotic, especially as he felt the rapid beat of her heart. It seemed to tremble beneath his lips even as he lapped at her right nipple. He liked the differing textures of skin and nipple. He loved the sensations of water and hot skin. And he loved sucking her pointed breast into his mouth and rolling his tongue around and around the nipple. His free hand continued to play with one breast as he sucked and kissed his way over the other. "Breasts are just awesome," he murmured directly above her heart.

"How poetic."

He grinned at her dry tone, then lifted his head to look into her flushed face. "Don't try to distance yourself, Xiao Fei. Allow yourself to feel every moment of this. You need to enjoy this, to *be* this. Every inch." She frowned at him, but he reached up and trailed his finger across her lips. "Don't speak. Don't analyze; just live. Let go."

"Just *you* don't let go," she said around his finger. She was balanced precariously on his leg, her arms gripping his neck with surprising strength.

"Do you trust me?" he asked, knowing there were multiple layers to his question.

She sobered. He quieted as well, waiting nervously for her answer. "Yes," she finally said, though the word sounded rushed, as if she had to force herself to say it.

"Yes?" he pressed.

She took a deep breath. "I think you're completely loony. I think this whole concept is messed up. It's some old druid's weird sex fantasy, and it has nothing to do with reality. So I think it's a waste of time." His blood cooled and his breath froze in his chest. Then she shrugged, and her breast slid up and down his palm. "But that's my head. For whatever reason, my stupid heart trusts you."

He blinked, trying to absorb what she'd said. "Your heart?" he echoed dumbly.

"You can't think of ifs and whys during a war. There's no reason, no logic to what happens. You just have to accept, to shut down your brain and act on instinct. Like a beast."

He blinked again. He had no free hand to brush the drips from his eyes, just as he had no way to escape the confusion that came from her words. "You're allowing yourself to become completely bestial?" The thought was so alien to him, and somewhat repulsive, even though it was exactly what he needed. What the *world* needed. But he was a druid and a Ph.D. He lived in his head, even when he was merging with all that was natural.

She smiled, obviously unashamed. "You are so American."

He pulled back. She hadn't said it like it was a compliment.

"I am not becoming an animal," she clarified. "I am allowing all that is instinctive to surface and rule. How else can one survive madness?"

"War is madness," he agreed, as much to himself as to her.

"Especially this demon war."

He nodded. "Total madness." So he surrendered to it. Following her example, he allowed his instincts to rule. He didn't struggle to hold the image of Earth in his head; he trusted that together he and Xiao Fei represented all of Earth. He simply worshiped her as a man worshiped a woman, as Earth embraced the moon, as the sky loved the sun. Images slipped in and out of his consciousness, few making sense.

This was Xiao Fei. And he was going to make her his.

He bent his head to her breast and took the nipple again in his mouth. He sucked on it, teased the peak with his tongue, drew her essence into himself and feasted on it. She gasped, and soon she was writhing beneath his onslaught. Her hands gripped his shoulders, tightening and releasing in a clear rhythm. Her clenching increased his desire.

He broke away to take her other breast. When that made her balance unstable, he braced her feet against the fiberglass wall. Her back rested against the tile, while his hand moved down her belly. He extended his middle finger and slid it between the folds of her sex. She arched against him. Surrendering to the beat in his head, he widened his grip on her and pushed his finger deeper and deeper in. He cupped her entire sex, his middle finger continuing to probe.

Wet and slick. Soft and hot. A molten core. Her heavenly body. Inside . . . inside. He wanted to split her wide open, to push inside her. The words slipped through his thoughts. Images. Sensations replaced meaning.

He felt her hands fluttering against his back, near the amulet. He felt himself surge forward, the need to join with her trumping all other impulses.

His mind tried to gain a foothold. This was supposed to be a holy merging, a worshipful act, a spell that would heal the Earth. He was descending to the level of simple sex, of the primal need to possess, to join, to procreate.

She was gasping against him, his finger buried deep inside her. She was so tight, so firm. Her inner muscles gripped him in a way that fired his darkest hunger. He pushed his finger deep, then pulled it out, reveling in the wet slide of flesh. He drew his finger up between her folds, up and under the hood. She arched against him, pushing hard against his hand.

She made a sound of hunger. He growled in response. Circling his finger around the center of her pleasure, he plunged two others inside of her. God, she was tight.

Her belly began to tremble. He felt it both inside and out: a clenching, a tensing, a need.

Again he drew his fingers free, using the moisture of her desire to slick her folds, to caress the nub, to open her wider as he rolled his hips against her.

He wanted to be in front. He needed his cock to be where his hand was. "Wider," he murmured, and he used his hands and knees to spread her thighs. "Open for me." As his body moved, so did his fingers. They rotated around her opening, touching, feeling, stroking whatever he could find. Giving pleasure wherever, however he could.

She was crying out—gasps, sobs, even nervous laughter. The sound was what he needed, a female pulse of desire. His mouth descended onto hers. He wanted to own those birdlike sounds. He needed to draw them into himself. He had to have her—now.

His hands shifted and wrapped around her thighs. His tongue was inside her mouth, pushing, plundering, loving. He lifted her legs so he could step between her thighs. And as he did it, she opened as never before—willingly, wantonly, wondrously. She was at her most vulnerable, and he arched his hips. He thrust inside her, as hard and fast and powerful as any beast. And she screamed, but not in ecstasy—in pain. Her back arched away from him, her hands became claws. She tore her mouth from his.

His concentration shattered. He was abruptly Patrick, his swollen sex embedded within a suddenly stilled woman. Xiao Fei's eyes were huge, and she stared at him in shock.

From Patrick Lewis's journal.

September 24, 1991

I went to the beach today. I owed it to Lisa. She died three years ago today. Mom and Dad offered to go with me, but I said no. Jason was there. I knew he would be.

He's not doing the Dark Lord gig anymore. He says he hasn't since that year. We talked about college. I told him I actually like plants now. Go figure.

He's working as an assistant in Hollywood to some big agent, dines on caviar and helps work megamillion-dollar deals. He says he picks up clients that way, so I guess he's still doing the healer tricks. He's on the fast track with the druids, too. In line to be the next Draig.

I knew his dad was sick—Mom and Dad told me—but I didn't realize he was going to give up as Draig-Athar. Jason's going to be the Draig-Teine. A fire dragon. That suits him, and he's really excited about it.

He said he was sorry about Lisa, that he thinks

about her a lot, that everything was out of control that year. It's better now, he says. And he's going to be the Draig-Teine, so life is good for him.

I said okay. Lisa wouldn't want me to hate him. What happened was just one of those things. It wasn't anybody's fault. The police ruled it accidental right away.

All those things I imagined before were just grief; I see that now. Crazy teenage stuff plus grief. It was an accident—a terrible, horrible accident. And Lisa wouldn't want me to hate anybody anyway. Especially not the guy who used to be my best friend.

I think I'm going to try surfing again tomorrow.

Chapter Thirteen

Xiao Fei lifted her face to the shower—chilly now—as it streamed sideways across her face. She licked her lips, tasting, drinking. She breathed slowly and felt him. Right there. Really, really big. Right *there*.

He felt painfully huge. Humongous. And yet, with her legs wrapped around him, her weight settled upon his hips and his sex thrust into her, she didn't dare move. She wondered how long he could hold her up like this.

"Xiao Fei?" His voice was tight, breathless, even. He clearly had himself under rigid control. He wasn't moving either, thank God. "What's wrong?"

She shook her head. "Nothing."

"Don't lie to me!"

His anger startled her, and she canted her eyes away. He gently stroked her cheek with his thumb, exerting steady pressure to bring her gaze back to him. She complied slowly, but didn't speak. She was too embarrassed.

"What happened?" he asked again.

"I just wasn't prepared," she murmured. "You're . . . you're a big guy. But it's okay now."

He closed his eyes with a muffled groan, and his forehead tilted forward to meet hers. She felt him breathe—their chests were pressed tightly together—and she was immediately swamped with guilt. She'd ruined it for him. She'd ruined it for the world.

"It's okay," she said. "Keep going."

"You were a virgin, weren't you?"

"It's okay. It was working."

He made a rumbling low in his throat, kind of like a growl. "Xiao Fei, were you a virgin?"

She didn't know why she was ashamed to admit it. Stupid, really. Her virginity was a good thing, but she couldn't help feeling like she'd betrayed him.

His hands tightened on her arms. "Xiao—"

"Yes. Yes, I was. Which is all to the good for the spell, right? *Which was working*." She wanted him to know that she believed.

He lifted his face, turning his head slightly so the water hit more of his hair than his right ear and eye. "Was it? Was it working?" He leaned forward, readjusting her weight, and she gasped at the increased pressure inside her.

"Sorry," he murmured.

"No. Keep going. We have to close the gate."

"My concentration's shot. I wasn't sure before . . ." He grimaced. "I lost myself in the . . . in you."

Xiao Fei tensed her legs, lifting herself slightly. But then her strength failed, and she slid back down him. She felt her buttocks on his thighs. The pain was more of a vague discomfort now.

He shifted his hands to brace her hips. "Don't move, Xiao Fei. I'm not . . . I'm not part of the Earth anymore, and I . . . I've only got so much control."

She nodded. She understood. Part of her shimmered with hunger, wanted to feel him push against her in just the right place, in just the right way. But the rest of her was burning like a scraped knee. It was as vulnerable as she had ever felt.

She frowned, realizing she was distancing herself. And that was not what was called for. Not if they wanted to do what was necessary. "Patrick," she said. "It was working. I felt the gate. I felt all of Earth." She swallowed. "And now I feel her wound—the demon gate." Just like she felt her own wound. "There's blood. . . ." He flinched at that, but she kept speaking. "We have water. I ate the fruit. There's . . ."

"Fire in the candle, stone and iron in the bathroom. But . . ."

She pressed her mouth to his, absorbing his objection. She had meant the kiss to be quick, but his mouth was strong and wet and just right. She teased him with her tongue, running it along his bottom lip, foraging inside to tickle his teeth and challenge his tongue.

He groaned. Then he began to kiss her back. Soon he was invading her mouth with his tongue. She felt his legs flexing beneath hers. But a moment later he broke the kiss. "I don't feel the Earth, Xiao Fei. I don't feel it."

She kissed him again, trying to renew the passion, doing her best not to feel the pain.

He broke away. "Xiao Fei. I don't know that this will work."

She shook her head. "It will. It *was* working. And we can't sit here like this all day." She arched slightly, deepening the angle of her pelvis and thrusting her breasts harder against him. "Finish it."

"I don't want it to hurt."

"It doesn't," she lied.

"I—"

"Oh, for God's sake!" she snapped. "Quit whining and do me!"

He pulled back in surprise, but quickly recovered. "Yes, ma'am," he joked. Sweet heaven, he made her smile.

He braced her more firmly against the cold tile, enough that he could free one hand. "I . . . cannot connect with the gate," he murmured. He began to caress her breast.

She closed her eyes. "I feel it." And she did. More than ever she sensed a wound, an opening where something other invaded. She felt the hole from which Earth poured its life force. She felt that, and she felt Patrick's hand lifting and stroking her nipple. Odd how both could be in her head, both overwhelming, both amazing.

Patrick's hand slid down her belly; his thumb burrowed between their joined bodies. He had to shift her weight. She gripped her thighs tight, lifting herself higher. But then he stopped. "The water's cold. The angle . . ."

She nodded, agreeing. With one hand, he shut off the now-freezing shower. She leaned forward, popped open the shower stall, and then pulled a towel from the rack to wrap around them.

"Hold tight," he gasped. She did. And then she was jostled in the most delightful way as he half walked, half stumbled to the bed. It had a small mattress, but large enough for their purpose. Patrick dropped her on it and followed her down. He probably didn't have much choice, given how joined they were. She giggled at the thought.

"I'm sorry this isn't great," he said.

She grinned at him. "Are you kidding? It's what every girl wants: memorable."

His expression stilled, and she caught a flash of sadness in his eyes. "No, it's not."

She would have responded; she would have said something witty or charming or whatever, but words deserted her. His thumb was doing its work again. And while it slid up and down between their bodies, his hips began to shift.

There was still a little pain, enough for her to remember Earth's wound. Enough to feel both Patrick and the hole. The tension built. There came a wonderful sensation: the stillness before the storm, the gathering of clouds before the thunder.

Xiao Fei's belly quivered. Her breasts seemed to tingle. Her legs lifted to wrap around Patrick again. He was moving slowly in and out of her. But he was too weak, his thrusts too gentle for her growing sense of . . . something.

So she gripped his back with his next push. She pulled him in with the all the strength she had, and the impact against her—inside her—was just what she wanted. Except there was more. She knew it. She just had to get it.

On his next withdrawal, she arched her hips to follow him. That made his next impact all the more delightful. Heat. Power. They were building in her belly and lower. Just a little more . . .

Another thrust. Another caress. Again. Again!

Implosion!

Xiao Fei's belly contracted. Her body convulsed. Everything she was contracted and tightened and rippled.

She heard Patrick cry out, a guttural grunt that was oh, so male. And then he was pouring himself into her. She knew, though she couldn't feel it. It didn't matter. She still felt his presence, his strength, and a boneless sense of eternity.

Patrick was gasping above her, his body quivering. He strained. Xiao Fei smiled.

Eventually, the power receded. The contractions fluttered, then stopped. Eternity faded.

She looked up at his drawn face. His hair was still wet from the shower, his skin flushed a rosy gold. From this angle, his shoulders looked broad enough to carry the world.

"Did it work?" he asked. "I can't feel . . ."

She swallowed and tried to expand her awareness. It wasn't all that hard. The world had been with her during the entire experience; she merely had to direct her attention to it, concentrate until she had the answer.

"Xiao Fei? Did it work?"

"Yes," she finally said. Then the full truth hit her. "Yes! The gate's smaller."

"Smaller?" he asked.

She opened her eyes and realized that they hadn't succeeded after all. "Smaller. Not closed."

"It wasn't enough?"

She shook her head. "We failed."

Patrick tried to sleep. He was bone-weary. Lord, he could barely even lift his head, but he couldn't sleep. Every time he closed his eyes, he replayed in his mind what had just happened. He had been so focused. All the components for the spell had been in place. Most important, his concentration had never been stronger. With everything at stake, he had allowed no deviation in intent, no wavering of purpose.

Until he'd touched her. Then he had shifted from the Draig-Uisge, working with a woman to close the gate, to Patrick losing himself in Xiao Fei's body. Worse, as their lovemaking continued, he had descended from man to beast. He had taken her like a bull takes a heifer—whether she willed it or not. He'd been bestial. He'd been brutal. He'd been—

"Go to sleep, Patrick. It wasn't that bad," Xiao Fei said, reading his mind. She snuggled deeper into his arms. "In fact, it was pretty good."

He lifted his head to look at the petite body cuddled up against him. Damn, she was gorgeous. In any other situation, he would be all over her again, horny as a teenager. But he'd just taken her virginity. And he'd forced her . . .

"Stop it, Patrick," she said to his chest. "Geez, stop thinking. You Americans get lost so easily in your heads."

He frowned. "I'm not lost."

"Are you tired?" she asked.

"Yes."

"Are you sleeping?"

"Uh, no."

"Then you're lost in your head. We need to sleep before we can do anything else. Before we can plan on what to do next, we need to sleep. So shut up and sleep already." She sounded half-amused and half-annoyed.

He protested. "I wasn't talking."

"You were groaning and sighing and . . . Just stop, already. I'm tired."

He dropped a kiss on top of her head. There was no reason for him to do it, except that she was there. And she made sense. "Okay. I'll sleep."

"Good," she replied.

And he did.

The fruit tastes bitter but familiar. Even at eight years old, Xiao Fei finds comfort in the ritual, and excitement in the difference.

It is just before dawn in a torn and broken ancient garden. Her mature mind recognizes the place, remembered in this dream. She understands that this was once a holy place, an ancient site of worship and reverence. Her eight-year-old mind merely curls her lip at the rocky stones, the broken trees, the trash that litters the ground. Yes, even in war-torn Cambodia, there is trash: broken cups, useless bits of plastic.

Her group surrounds a large tree. It is one of the few standing, and there is little life left in it. Dead branches have been stripped away for fuel, even the ones that should have towered well above the heads of men. What is left is a lumpy stick of a tree, jagged and ugly. Xiao Fei's eight-year-old self thinks of a badly made chopstick and laughs disrespectfully.

She is rapidly silenced by a monk's hard smack to the back of her head. They all kneel in circles around the ugly tree—Phoenix Tears in the smaller circle, monks in a larger one behind them, and then a third circle of branches and fruit. Xiao Fei's younger self doesn't notice, but the adult recognizes an echo in the placement. They are forming the same pattern as on Patrick's amulet, only theirs is made of living flesh.

This is when they eat the fruit again. A second taste, unheard-of in her short life. And even more surprising, *all* of them eat, including the monks.

They begin the chant. Both the eight-year-old and the adult Xiao Fei relax into the sound, the surge and flow of power. They both frown at the outflow of strength that pours from the Earth into the demon gate, which they can feel though it isn't here. The adult remembers that the gate is about a mile away, guarded by demons. This ancient garden was as close as they could get, but in a closing ritual, close proximity to the wound isn't a requirement. They are on Earth, and all of Earth needs the healing.

Xiao Fei's adult mind screams. Over and over she rails at the group to stop, but no one hears. This is a memory replayed in a dream. At eight, she simply closes her eyes and lets the power pour over her. She is doing her part to feel the gate and then, with the power of her mind and blood, to close it.

The abbot walks to the center of the circle, making small nicks one by one in the women's veins at the wrist. There is a tattooed tear there, and all are well used to this process. Young Xiao Fei is toward the end of the line. She barely even notices the pain as her life blood begins to pour. Somewhere in the distance, she feels Earth's energy shimmer. She knows the planet's wound is beginning to close.

She doesn't hear the sound at first—screaming, some in fury, some in pain. It is a noise of the ears, not the spirit, and so it doesn't penetrate her consciousness, except as something not to notice.

Until a monk falls on top of her. She crashes forward, pressed hard into the ground, and she must break her concentration or breathe dirt. Then she begins to notice other things. She knows there are demons everywhere. She watches in stunned horror as one uses a short curved sword and slices Brother Kiman's head right off his shoulders. The gory object lands on the ground with a dull thud, then is kicked aside as the demon steps forward to kill again.

There is noise behind her. Xiao Fei turns in slow degrees, but she is restricted by the weight pinning her. She struggles, pushing ineffectively at it. She focuses on the open, lifeless eyes of Brother Solvann. He is the one weighing her down. He is the monk who played ball games with her and loved to braid her hair. His blood is thick and sticky on her belly.

She has lost all connection with the chanting. She looks to the abbot for help. She doesn't act with intention; she simply hears his bellow and responds as she was trained. She looks up to see him face the pink-eyed demon. In a country of dark hair and dark eyes, those irises frighten.

She barely notices the amulet clutched in demon's hand, but the abbot sees it and attacks with enough speed to stun. He uses a sharpened ax to chop off the pink-eyed one's hand, amulet and all. Then he buries his sharp blade through the center of the jewel. Xiao Fei sees it happen because the hand and amulet rest on a thick root of the ugly tree—and when the blade lands, she sees it severs fingers and metal, all the way through the gnarled root.

The tree won't live through that, she thinks, and neither does the abbot. The pink-eyed demon uses his remaining arm to punch straight through the cleric's chest.

The adult Xiao Fei screams. She's buried in bloody mud and she is screaming until her head bursts, but not the eight-year-old. Young Xiao Fei's head is swelling. Her body is bloating like a waterskin. She doesn't understand, and can't think through it.

Stop!

That is the word that soars through her spirit and shapes the power in the air. There are other words too, thoughts and shapes that she can't identify.

Stop! Stop! Stop!

Demons roar. Monks scream. The Phoenix Tears die.

The power is too much. She curls into herself and dies, too.

"Xiao Fei! It's a dream! Xiao Fei!"

She can't move. She can't breathe. She's dead. She knows it. She's dead.

"Wake up! Xiao Fei!"

She feels his hands on her shoulders, the press of his body against hers. She knows her mouth is open in a silent scream. It is always silent; the sound is never released. That's because she is dead, buried in the blood and the mud and the bodies.

She's dead. She can't wake. Except, she does.

"Xiao Fei!"

Her eyes fly open and a vision floods her swollen mind. Patrick, his blond hair shoved up on one side and flattened on the other. Patrick, with his golden tan and rich green eyes. Patrick, with a voice that booms like thunder.

"Xiao Fei!"

She can't breathe. She's buried in this black room underground. She can't think. She can't live. She has to get outside.

She shoves Patrick away, but he won't move. He's just like the other bodies—a heavy weight suffocating her. *Move!*

She shoves as hard as she can and he tumbles backward.

"Xiao Fei! Stop!"

They're chasing her. The bad ones. *Demons! Run!*

She hauls open the door but doesn't know where she is. At least there's some light, but it's not the moon; it's not the sun. She still can't breathe!

Someone is coming down the hall. Some part of her brain recognizes what he is: a werewolf. She draws back in alarm, but then reason kicks in, albeit sluggishly. Werewolves aren't the danger; demons are. She hesitates.

Boom! The dull sound trembles in the air, echoes in the stone walls. *Boom!*

She cowers. *Hide! Run! Outside!* The different urges clamor in her brain and freeze her muscles. A man comes up behind her and she pivots, hands raised to attack. He holds up fabric—clothing?—and talks to her, but she can't understand his words.

The werewolf speaks in words she understands. "This way. Outside."

The sounds of fighting continues. It lives in these tunnel walls. It surrounds her as she runs after the werewolf. She keeps her head low and her hands clutched over her ears. *Hide. Run. Outside. Away.*

Patrick is following her, and she cringes from him even as part of her mind wants his companionship. He is both pursuer and safety to her, part of the ugliness that was and is, and the wonder that could be. It makes no sense, and so she runs from him, but not so fast that he cannot follow.

"Up here."

The werewolf climbs up a ladder, punches buttons on an electronic keypad, then shoves off a manhole cover. Xiao Fei can smell the air, the tang of exhaust, the whisper of mist, and the brutal scent of sweat. But it is fresher up there than down here, so she scrambles up the ladder. Then she is outside.

Weak dawn. She can breathe. She closes her eyes and focuses on just that fact. She can breathe.

Then Patrick is beside her, pulling clothes over her head, coaxing her into pants. She does not fight him now. She is beginning to think again, beginning to separate dream from reality. He is real. The demon, the monks, and the deaths were a dream.

She zips her jeans shut. Has she been naked all this

time? Behind her she hears the werewolf step around them. Where is he going? She doesn't really care. She is outside again. She can breathe.

"Demons!" the werewolf bellows around the corner. "Look over here! The ones you want are over here. Now leave the rest of us the hell alone!"

From the records of the druids of San Bernardino.

March 7, 1992—For health reasons, Draig-Athar relinquished his position. With prayer and blood, he passed the token of power to his son, who has chosen the title Draig-Teine. The proofs of power went according to ritual. The Draig-Teine can indeed wield the token of power. He now bears the burden for all of us.

Chapter Fourteen

Patrick spun around, his mind flailing as he tried to keep up. Xiao Fei had had a nightmare that left her so freaked out that she'd scrambled naked for the front door. She'd followed a grizzled old werewolf up a manhole, outside, to an alleyway somewhere near downtown. The distant sounds of demon rampage weren't so distant up here. In fact, they were downright close, but the alleyway was a deserted dead end, so he took the time to regroup. Or it was more to dress, because, hallelujah, Xiao Fei began to recover once the gray morning light hit her face. She allowed him to put some clothes on her gorgeous body.

But then grizzled old guy betrayed them. Patrick hadn't even realized they were in a trap until he heard the demons roar.

"What the hell?" he sputtered.

"Sorry," the werewolf replied, dashing for the manhole. "We can't hold out against them, not forever. If it's you or us, I pick us." Then he disappeared back into the tunnels.

Patrick ran after him. He made it to the manhole a second after the Judas, but it was too late; the werewolves security coded their entrances, and this one was shut fast. Patrick spun around, too out of breath even to curse effectively. He'd just woken up, for God's sake. And now . . .

Oh, geez. Four, no, eight, maybe nine demons were trying to cram themselves into the mouth of the little alleyway. All of them had a sharp weapon of some sort, though no guns. None of them looked particularly friendly, and damn it, none of them was even wounded. These were the bad guys.

The good guys—himself and Xiao Fei—had clothes and that was it. No weapons, no anything—though the amulet still dangled down Patrick's chest. Hell, he wasn't even wearing shoes.

He looked for an escape route as he yanked Xiao Fei behind him. There were three huge Dumpsters a couple yards away, two of which were painted green for recycling. Apparently they were on the garbage side of a large copy store. Behind him was a brick wall, probably the side of a condo complex, if he had to guess. It was completely useless for his purposes; there wasn't even a fire escape. And in the back . . . more brick. The condos apparently took a right turn and butted up against the copy shop. In short . . .

"Trapped," Xiao Fei muttered.

"Yeah," he agreed, though he was relieved to hear full lucidity in her voice. At least they would die fully aware.

Think! he ordered himself. "They don't know who we are . . ." he began.

"They do," she rebutted, her voice grim. Damn, she sounded fatalistic, as if she'd already accepted the outcome.

"They can't—," he said.

"They know. And if they didn't, your amulet isn't exactly subtle."

Patrick glanced down, cursing himself for not putting on a shirt. All he'd had time to do was grab his pants and bag, then dash out after Xiao Fei. She was lucky he'd remembered her clothes.

His cell phone went off. Out of the tunnels, he had reception again and a dozen messages, probably all from Peter. Unfortunately the electronic noise was like a signal to the demons; they surged forward as one, their battle cry filling the air.

Patrick tensed, then did the only thing he could do: he grabbed Xiao Fei and threw her between two of the Dumpsters. Then he dove into the tiny space that was left. At a minimum, this would reduce the number of demons that could come at him at once. If he was really lucky, he'd find an Uzi in the trash.

No such luck. The demons charged with all the coordination of a ravaging horde—a really-skillful-with-a-sword ravaging horde. Their wicked blades cut through the air, and Patrick could hear the singing metal. Still, he wasn't sliced or diced. He flexed his muscles and prepared to fight.

He maneuvered as best he could in the narrow space, trying to get into a good position. For the moment, the demons were hampering one another. In fact, one demon howled as he received the brunt of another's attack. Patrick watched in pleased amusement as the two monsters clearly lost their tempers and started attacking each other.

Which gave him a moment to think. Adrenaline worked just as well as coffee. *Think!*

"Okay, druid. Do your stuff." Xiao Fei's tone was dry, but he also caught a lighter note of hope. She clearly wanted to believe he had some great druid magic. Too bad—he could do only one thing. And that one thing was pretty useless.

"I can increase Earth's energy. Demons aren't from Earth, so it will give them a good case of nausea." But would a tummy ache really stop any of them?

"Shut up and do it while you still can," was Xiao Fei's response.

"Right." He gripped the amulet where it hung from his neck. Pain lanced through his palm and up his wrist, but he was used to that. He'd been the Draig-Usige for a while now; the aching burn was almost welcome. He glanced back at Xiao Fei. "I can't fight while I'm doing this," he told her.

"Already on it." She'd been digging in the Dumpsters and hauled out an old metal folding chair.

"That won't—"

"Shut up. We'll do what we can."

He nodded. She was a fighter. It was up to him to make sure the demons were incapacitated. He had to give them one hell of a tummy ache.

He closed his eyes and focused. He funneled his thoughts into the amulet, merging with it. And then he let the amulet filter and color his senses. His mind expanded, surfing on the waves of energy and power. He felt the tight, high vibration of Xiao Fei behind him. He recognized the lower vibrations of the metal and stone that surrounded them. He even felt the dissonance farther away of werewolf below and vampire above, and the really strong clang of the rampaging demons: a completely alien energy from everything else. But beneath it all was the steady beat, the all-embracing power of Mother Earth. He found it as quickly as he could; then he dove in, submerging himself in her energy.

She surrounded him, and he became an echo of her. Earth's energy resonated in him. Her vibration built, stronger and stronger. He was the Draig-Usige, with the power to strengthen all that was Earth and thereby dampen all that was not of her holy creation.

That was what he did. Right there, in that location between two Dumpsters with himself as the focal point, he strengthened Earth's vibration, magnified and concentrated it. He did it with one hundred percent of his body, mind, and spirit. And, he did it with one thousand percent of his will.

He opened his eyes. He saw Xiao Fei before him, wielding her chair like an avenging angel. He saw Earth's energy magnify in her, giving power and unusual strength to her body. She smashed a demon over the head with the chair, and he went down like a rock.

There were other demons all around. Two had jumped on top of the Dumpsters and were already swinging their weapons—axlike blades—down toward Xiao Fei and himself. Patrick increased the Earth's resonance in their direction. One lost his footing and tumbled to the ground. The other remained upright, but his eyes rolled strangely in his head. His ax dropped from nerveless fingers. He stumbled and vomited on one of his compatriots.

But there were still more demons coming, pushing through, and though all were slowed, not all were stopped. Another slashed with a sword at Xiao Fei, catching the back of the folding chair in her hands. She tried to hold on, but the force of the blow was too much; the chair was ripped from her grasp. She and Patrick were now defenseless.

Patrick strengthened the Earth's force directly in front of them, but this particular demon was hardy. He grimaced, exposing sharp, crooked teeth, and kept advancing. Xiao Fei backed up into Patrick.

"Jesus, I'm going to be sick," someone growled. "Tone it down, will you?"

Patrick could not identify the voice, but he could see Xiao Fei look up. His own attention was still directing Earth's energy, but it was not enough. The demon kept coming, with two more behind him.

"I got her," came another voice. "Can you . . ."

"Got him. Upsy-daisy."

Strong arms gripped him around the waist. He would have fought, but his attention remained focused through the amulet. He could do nothing with his body without abandoning his attack on the demons.

He had enough focus to recognize vampires behind him, lifting him up in the air. Xiao Fei too, looking sick as she went airborne, clutched in a male vampire's arms. The demons followed as well, levitating just like the vamps. But the Earth's power weakened them too much. They couldn't fly here. Not while he . . .

His strength ran out. His focus faded, his hand lost its grip, and he gave a moan that came out more as a sigh. He was not Earth. He was not Draig-Uisge. He was Patrick, who was going to be violently ill, except that he lost consciousness first.

The bastard demons were still following. As Patrick blacked out, they recovered their ability to fly and made a beeline straight for their prey.

"I need a gun!" Xiao Fei cursed.

"Right hip. Can you reach it?"

She'd done her best to forget she was being hauled off by a vampire. She knew they were rescuing her, but she couldn't keep Stan and his merry band from her thoughts. Would her rescuers drop her and Patrick from the stratosphere if they knew what she'd done to one of their kind? She didn't want to think about it, especially when there were more immediate problems.

She twisted and got her hands on a pistol. Sweet—another Glock. It took a moment to adjust in the vamp's grip, but then she was all about trying to shoot the pursuing demons out of the sky.

The vamps who carried her and Patrick were hovering low to the ground, zipping in and around buildings at speeds that left her reeling, but not so dizzy that she couldn't aim. Around a corner, and *bam!* A demon spun out of control. She didn't see where he landed, only that he wasn't following anymore.

"Nice shot."

Was there admiration in the vamp's voice? Xiao Fei didn't answer; she was busy sighting another one. *Bam, bam!* Scratch another demon. Hell, this was fun!

Until a group of four demons suddenly launched from under a freeway overpass. She heard her vamp rescuer curse and swerve scarily close to a very pointy cell tower. She glanced sideways to see that Patrick and the other vamps were still with them, still okay. Or at least she prayed Patrick was okay; his skin seemed abnormally gray. But then there was no more time for thought as she began shooting more demons. She emptied the Glock.

"Got any more bullets?" she asked.

"Not on me." Then her rescuer made some sort of gesture to his companion, and abruptly the bottom fell out of her stomach. They soared into the sky.

She screamed. Like a damn baby, Xiao Fei screeched in terror. It was only sheer luck that she didn't drop her pistol. When she ran out of breath she began to hyperventilate. But at least that gave her a moment to marshal her thoughts. Very soon she would make a reasoned and passionate argument to return to terra firma.

"Stop! Stop! Where are you going?" she cried.

"Home," the vamp answered calmly. "Strata Plus One. I've got more bullets there."

She nodded. Bullets were good, especially as additional demons were likely to start appearing at any moment. Even better, there seemed to be more vampires appearing around them, sort of a scary, pale-looking escort.

She frowned. "Don't you guys burn up in sunlight?"

"We've got lots of sunscreen," he replied.

She blinked. She would not get distracted by trivialities. There was something very wrong with the idea of going to Strata Plus One. Something . . .

She glanced at Patrick. He was looking more ill the higher they went. And then suddenly it clicked. He drew his strength from the Earth. Sure, there was Earth energy in the sky, even in that temple of high-rises that was Strata Plus One. But it was stronger below.

"Take us back down!" she ordered. "To a beach or the woods. To something earthy."

"We won't bite. I swear." There was humor in the vamp's voice that sounded . . . wholesome somehow. And that thought seriously gave her the willies.

"You don't understand," she said, focusing on her worry for Patrick rather than her bizarre rescuer. "He's a druid. He's attuned to the land. He needs water, green things, trees and stuff."

"A druid?"

"Just take us, damn it!" She was losing her calm. Hell, she'd lost her control a long time ago, but Patrick's skin was looking worse than that of the vampire holding him. That couldn't be good.

"What about the demons?" Mr. Vamp asked.

She scanned the skies. "They're gone."

The vamp sounded grim. "Not for long. While we're at it, why are they after you?"

"Just lucky, I think," she lied. She twisted as far as she could and tried to change the topic. "How'd you guys find us?"

"We were looking for a way to help out the wolves; then suddenly, all those demons just turned and went for you." The vamp paused long enough for Xiao Fei to start to squirm. "Now, what do you two have that they want?" She could feel his intense regard.

"Nothing anymore," she groused. And it was true. She already felt a quart low on blood, and Patrick . . . "Just get us down, okay? He doesn't look so good."

The vampire took a moment to stare at Patrick, who didn't appear to be recovering at all, then nodded. He gave a signal to the four vamps with them, and abruptly their angle shifted. They were going down.

"Thank you," Xiao Fei breathed.

"We'll take you to Redondo Beach. There hasn't been any demon activity there yet, but you never know."

She nodded, already regretting her choice. Wherever they went now, the demons would find them. After what they'd done to the gate, she and Patrick were the demons' greatest threat. So, why did she want to be dropped right back in the pathway of danger? She sighed. Because she didn't want Patrick to die, that was why. And because she didn't like vampires.

She bit her lip in frustration. Intelligent, logical thinking had never been her forte. The monks had taught her to bleed, nothing else. Just bleed, they said, for the good of the people.

"You're that Chinese girl, aren't you?" the vamp said.

She frowned, doing her best not to watch the fast-approaching street. "Cambodian, but that doesn't mean anything to you, does it?"

She felt him shrug. "I know it's a different country." Then he cleared his throat, as if he were feeling awkward. A nervous vamp? The thought boggled her mind. "You're the one who changed Stan back, aren't you?"

She didn't want to react. In fact, she had feared that this was where he was going, so she kept herself very still. But she still had the impression that this keen-eyed vampire saw right through her. "I don't know what you're talking about," she said. "Who's Stan?"

"Mmhmm. See, here's the thing . . ." He kept talking in the most casual way while they careened down streets, barely missing light poles and satellite dishes. It was scary as hell—as he no doubt intended—but all the while, he kept talking as if it were no big deal. "Your energy feels really strange to me, good and bad. I can't really explain it."

She could. Good, in that she was of Earth. Bad, in that he was not. Or he was just off enough that she felt strange to him.

"And Stan was screaming about Chinatown and stuff. About this woman with short hair and a crazy-ass tattoo."

Geez, Stan had seen her tattoo? He couldn't have. He'd been unconscious—or so she'd thought. But then again . . . She swallowed. She would have tugged the sleeves of her blouse down, but the vamp who held her had already seen enough. Maneuvering behind that Dumpster had put some telltale rips in her attire.

"And then these demons show up," continued Mr. Vamp, "and they're gunning for you. So, I wonder exactly how this all fits in."

He stopped. They were hovering a good twenty feet above a deserted beach.

"What are you doing?" Xiao Fei cried, obviously failing to keep the panic from her voice. "Put us down."

"All in good time," the vamp answered. "I just want some answers, that's all. What did you do to Stan?" The threat was clear: if she didn't talk, he would drop her. She might survive a drop from this height, but she sure as hell couldn't risk Patrick. She bit back a sob of frustration. What the hell was she supposed to do?

"I don't know anything!" she snapped.

"Lies make my hands really slippery," he warned.

"I just cured him, that's all! I unturned him. Now put us down!"

The vamp didn't move. "You *un*turned him? How?"

"My blood. That's what feels different to you. It . . ." She glanced desperately at Patrick. He didn't look so bad right then, but then again, most everyone looked good in crisp morning sunlight. Everyone but damned vamps, that is.

"It what?" he prompted.

"Patrick says it accentuates the Earth's vibrations. It brings out the Earth in people. Problem is, vamps aren't from the Earth."

"Yes, we are. We're born here. We live here."

She shrugged. "Okay, you're from Earth, but . . . different." In truth, it was the demons who felt really different, really alien. Vamps just felt like a different key of the whole Earth song, not a completely different instrument.

"So, what did you do to Stan?" the vamp asked again.

"I brought out the Earth energy in him, I think. Enough to overcome the vamp." Of course, the werewolf cub was strong in her mind. He hadn't been naturally human enough for her blood to work, which meant her blood probably wouldn't work on natural-born vamps either. She closed her eyes. She didn't really care. Not right now, not with Patrick hanging there like a dead dog. "I don't know how I do it; I just do." She twisted to look closer at her rescuer-turned-captor. She had to know. "Is Stan really dead?"

The vampire sighed. "Yeah. Couldn't stand not being a vamp. He fell off the highest tower of Strata Plus One." They started descending toward the ground. "Could be he forgot he couldn't fly—he was completely plastered. Could be he just didn't want to live."

Xiao Fei didn't answer. She didn't know what to think.

The vamp said, "You thought you were curing him, didn't you?"

She nodded.

He set her feet on solid sand. She'd never felt more pleased to feel grit between her toes.

"Look. I think it's great that you exist, that there's an option for those who change their minds."

She frowned as she looked at him. The vamp's back was to the sun, but she could still see warmth in his brown eyes. Reassurance in his tired face. And then she felt it: the Earth in him. He wasn't a natural-born vampire. He'd been turned.

"I could heal you," she said, stunned by the impulsiveness of her action. "Not right now; I'm too weak. But later . . ." She would never have offered just like that, but the words were out before she could stop them, and this man invited confidences. Especially when he smiled, slow and sweet like that.

"That's my point, Cambodian woman. I am cured. This is exactly how I want to be."

She didn't doubt him. There was so much joy in the statement, so much passion in his words, that there was no room for doubt. Whatever the reason, he absolutely wanted to remain a vampire.

She nodded. "Okay." What else could she say?

"So, no more unturning people who don't ask."

Xiao Fei felt her face tighten with anger. "Stan turned Donny Chen against his will. And Stan tried to take over Chinatown. I just stopped him, that's all. I wouldn't have touched him if he hadn't taken Donny."

The vampire arched a single brow. "I know, and believe me, I've got no love of Stan. But next time, come to me. Let us vamps take care of it."

She gave him the look, the one that said: *I'll trust you when hell freezes over. Or when I'm trapped behind a Dumpster with a horde of angry demons attacking, and not a second before.*

He sighed. "I'm Dain Reston. I used to be with B-Ops. I'm trustworthy."

She didn't even bother giving him the look for that statement, but he understood.

He shrugged. "So, is that why the demons are after you? Because your blood accentuates Earth energy? What about that pretty little necklace around your boyfriend's neck?"

She shrugged right back at him. "If it is, they're too late. I've burned everything I got. And my power works only in conjunction with that pretty little necklace, so don't get any ideas there either."

"But you'll recover," he pressed. "Perhaps we should protect—"

"Ungh . . ." came a voice. *Patrick!*

Xiao Fei pushed away from Dain, the strangely nice vampire, and dropped to her knees beside Patrick. He was lying in the sand, his skin tone looking better by the second, and he was coming around. His eyes fluttered, and she leaned down to press a kiss to his lips.

"Hey, baby," she said. "How's it going?" Part of her was

stunned by her words. She'd never called anyone *baby* in her life, much less in that cooing, goo-goo-eyed tone. And yet she couldn't stop it. When his gaze finally steadied and she saw his moss-green eyes, her heart started beating and beating like it hadn't been working at all before.

"Hey," he murmured, and her heart flopped in joy. Then he looked around at the surrounding vamps, at the sky, at the ocean. "Is this Redondo?" Trust him to recognize the beach.

Dain's cell phone chirped. The vampire pulled it out in one motion, withdrew a few paces, and began talking earnestly into the receiver. Xiao Fei couldn't have cared less. Her eyes were all on Patrick, who seemed to be growing stronger by the second.

"Too bad the demons attacked," he was saying. "It'd be a nice day to surf." Okay, so maybe his brain wasn't all back yet. . . . "How about you? Any cuts or anything I should know about?"

His eyes were intense, his meaning crystal clear. She smiled, relieved that his mental facilities weren't really in question. Well, no more than usual. "I'm fine. You're the one who passed out."

He sighed. "I take it the vamps rescued us?"

"Well, after you rescued us, they did some taxiing."

He reached out and stroked her cheek. "You're the one who beat them off with a folding chair."

"You're the one who—"

"I know," he interrupted. "But I'm done now. No juice left."

Okay, so he didn't want her talking about his powers in front of strangers. It was a wise precaution, and one she would have thought of herself if she hadn't been so ga-ga over one too-pale druid.

Dain snapped his cell phone shut and quickly returned to their side. "Something's happened. The demons are reorganizing. They've laid off the were-wolves and are massing again at the main gate." He looked pointedly down at Patrick. "Something you'd care to share about that?"

Patrick pushed himself upright so that he was sitting, and he faced Dain. "The gate's shrunk but not closed."

"Yeah, we noticed." The vampire said nothing else, but his eyes showed keen interest in exactly how a druid and some Cambodian bleeder fit into all this.

Patrick shrugged. "We can't do anything more. We're both spent."

"But—"

"We won't recover. At least not fast enough to help you. We're out of the game."

Dain shifted uncomfortably. "Still, if there's a chance that you can do more . . . You need to be protected."

"We are," answered Patrick with surprising vehe-mence. "And I'll recover faster on the ground." He ges-tured to the other vamps, who were obviously anxious. "You need to get back into the fight."

"But—"

"My name's Patrick Lewis. And you're Dain, Fleur's guy." The vamp nodded, so he continued, "You'll be the first to know if I can help any more. Honest. Right now, I've got people I can call. We're just going to hide for a while until things get better." He stared pointedly at the vamp. "Until you make things better."

Dain nodded, and for a moment it looked like an ac-knowledgment between warriors. "We'll keep things un-der control. We live here, too."

"I know," Patrick said.

Dain looked at Xiao Fei. "And no more—"

"Bleeding on vamps. Yeah, I got that," she said.

He grinned. "Not unless they ask, and I can watch." He held out his hand. Xiao Fei looked at him, not understanding. "The Glock," he explained.

"Oh!" She gave it back to him. No use keeping it if she didn't have ammo.

Dain waved good-bye with the gun; then he and his vamps launched straight up into the air. Xiao Fei watched them go—up, up, and up, straight into the clouds. And just like that, she and Patrick were very alone and very exposed.

From The Hollywood Reporter.

MIRACLE OPENING!

December 1, 1992
By Howard Berns
Hollywood's elite celebrated in style yesterday in a most unusual gala opening. Miracles by Jason, another health spa for the rich and famous, opened its doors with glittering fanfare. With a client list that includes the most powerful in a city of power brokers, Jason charges equally astronomical prices.

But what exactly are his services? That, apparently, is a mystery to all but those who pay.

"We offer health and energy miracles," claimed Jason, who declined to give his last name. "My customers are very satisfied."

And indeed they are, if the turnout is anything to judge by. But only time will tell if Miracles by Jason survives past the initial faddish nature of Hollywood or passes into obscurity like yesterday's glitter.

Chapter Fifteen

Xiao Fei hadn't felt vulnerable with all those vampires around, but now she had to repress a shudder.

"You really don't like vamps, do you?" Patrick's voice was soft, more intimate than a moment before. Xiao Fei happily returned her gaze to his golden freckles and sparkling green eyes.

"I've never met one who—"

"Was nice? Was a decent guy?"

"They feel . . . off."

"That's just the vampirism. Their energy is different, that's all. They're still a part of the Earth. They're natural in their own way."

"Can you walk?" She didn't want to sit here in the sun like ducks waiting for the hunter. She also didn't want to pursue this line of thought, but Patrick was insistent.

"So, when we tried to close the gate, you felt it? The gate? The world?"

"Mother Earth in all her vibratory glory." Xiao Fei

spoke in a mocking drawl, but only because she felt strange speaking of things like vibrations and Earth energy. She believed in them, knew such things were real from her time as a Phoenix Tear, but she'd never actually discussed it in the open. Not like he did, and certainly not in English.

But he would not let her off the hook. "Xiao Fei, did you feel it?"

She nodded. "Yes."

"You're the reason it worked as much as it did. You're very powerful. You closed it."

"I didn't close it!" she snapped. "I just made us a demon target, that's all. A half-open portal is still open. Now let's go. The demons haven't stopped looking for us, you know. They'll never stop now. So can you get up off your lazy ass and walk?"

He grinned. "Yes, ma'am," he said. Then he smoothly rolled to his feet—something only a druid surfer could ever do on the dry, powdery sand.

"You were only pretending to be wiped out, weren't you?" she accused.

He grinned and held out his hand. "Never know what you might hear when people think you're unconscious."

"But you were sick." She took his hand and started to stand. "I saw—"

"Yes," he said as he jerked her into his arms. "Yes," he repeated right next to her lips. "I was . . . I *am* pretty damn tired, but I'm not completely useless. Yet."

"I never said—mmph."

Wow, he was a good kisser. And it was even better that he was alive, she was alive, and no demon was roaring down the beach at them. His mouth was warm, his tongue was playful, and his chest was very, very solid where she pressed against him. A girl could feel pretty safe against a chest like his. A girl could get pretty warm, too, and not just because it was hot in the sun.

Then his hip began to vibrate. His cell phone. She pulled away as he groaned. He twisted so that he could keep one arm looped casually around her, and the other hauled out his phone.

Xiao Fei gestured to a nearby bench. "You want me to step away?"

He shook his head. "I just have to report in to Mr. Pete the Pompous. Geez, why did the demons have to invade on *his* watch?" With an exaggerated eye roll, he flipped open his phone. "Yeah?"

Xiao Fei couldn't hear the other half of the conversation, but then again, she didn't need to. Patrick's body language gave it all away. It told her quite clearly that he was tired, both physically and mentally. So she led Patrick to the bench, clearing off the sand and grit as best she could before they sat down.

Patrick said, "Redondo Beach, and yeah, I know. That was us." There was a long pause. "Yeah, I know." He let his head drop to the back of the bench and stared sightlessly up at the sky. "Yeah," he repeated, louder this time. "I know. We failed."

Xiao Fei curled tight to his side. She knew she ought to watch for demons or werewolves or all things deadly on this deserted beach, but it was early morning, the area felt deserted, and Patrick seemed to need her closeness more than he needed a sentry. Or was it that she needed to feel him around her more than she needed to protect herself from danger?

She frowned. This surfer druid had become much too important to her in a very short time. Especially considering how they'd begun.

"I know," Patrick said into his phone, a clear edge to

his voice. "Damn it, Peter, I know, but what the hell do you want me to do about it?" Tension was pouring off him in waves. He'd stiffened in his seat. Then he straightened, dislodging Xiao Fei from where she was tucked against him. When she made to draw away, he abruptly pulled her back.

"No. Peter, no. I need some time to figure things—I know. Goddamnit, Peter!" Then Patrick abruptly pulled the phone away from his ear and snapped it shut. "Oops," he drawled at the device. "I think we got cut off. Boy, cell phone service sure is flaky right now."

"He'll call back in a minute," Xiao Fei guessed.

"He can try." Patrick held down a button and his phone chirped a cheerful good-bye.

"You told him we were here."

He frowned. "Yeah, I guess I did, but he lives in Malibu. It'll take him a while to get here."

"He wasn't so happy."

Patrick glanced wryly at her. "Nobody's happy right now—not even the demons."

She couldn't disagree with that. She looked out at the waves. Patrick was right. If it weren't for the demons, it would be a great day for surfing.

"You gonna tell me what happened?" Patrick's question broke awkwardly into her thoughts.

"What?"

"Why did we run out of a nice cozy bed into a demon attack?"

She flushed and pushed off the bench. "Oh, *that* what."

He stood as well. "Yeah, that what."

She didn't answer. Instead, they both began walking. She hadn't a clue to where, except that he was aiming her off the beach, up a concrete flight of stairs to the street above. "Xiao Fei—"

"It was just a nightmare," she said.

"Yeah, maybe, but I think you were dreaming about Cambodia. I think you were remembering the gate closing there."

She jerked sideways against the handrail. Not the most subtle of reactions, but she wasn't controlling herself as much as usual. "What makes you say that?"

"Because I dreamed it, too."

She stared at him, her mouth ajar. She just couldn't fathom that this man—this damn stranger—could possibly be so far into her head. "You're a freak," she said. "You know that, don't you?"

He laughed. "You kill things by bleeding on them—how freaky is that?"

"Only bad things!" she argued.

"Werewolves aren't bad, necessarily. Neither are vamps."

She rolled her eyes. "You're still a freak." She turned back to climbing the steps. "And stay out of my head."

"Tell me about the dream, Xiao Fei," he demanded.

"You were there. You tell me about it." She didn't understand why she was being so irritable. Lack of sleep, psychic druid, demon gate—any or all of those could be the reason, she supposed. Or maybe it was a simple lack of caffeine. "You think there's a coffee shop open anywhere?"

He shrugged. She could feel the motion because he grabbed hold of her arm and held her still. "It's weirding me out too, Xiao Fei. I've never shared anyone's thoughts or dreams before. Not like this."

"Lucky me," she drawled, and tried to pull away. He held her fast.

"It makes sense, you know. We're trying to merge with—"

"We did merge," she snapped.

"—the world, each other, and the gate too. Mix in certain strong feelings, and it makes sense that everything would bleed from you into me."

She shoved away. "It doesn't make sense. Nothing makes sense."

"Now you're being petulant."

"And you're being a know-it-all!"

His step hitched. "A what?"

"I don't know what petulant means!" she bellowed at him. "It wasn't in my ESL class." He frowned and she growled, "English as a Second Language."

"Oh. Right."

She turned and started stomping away. There had to be a coffee shop somewhere around here. She was damn well going to get some caffeinated tea if she had to break in to get it.

"Stop, Xiao Fei! Just stop. Too much is at stake for you to run away like this," Patrick called.

"I'm not running." She was, in fact, *stomping* away.

He caught up easily. And with his long legs he made it seem like a casual morning stroll. "You're running from the question. You're making up something to be pissed off—"

"I don't have to make up stuff to be pissed about."

"You're picking a fight; you're stomping off. You're doing everything but talking about the one thing we need to discuss."

She knew he was right, but that didn't erase the burning anger that gripped her heart.

"Step outside of yourself, Xiao Fei. Step away from the fear and the hurt and the trauma. I know it's hard, but you've got to. *We've* got to."

222

"Don't psychoanalyze me," she snapped. But then, to her horror, her vision blurred with tears. Tears? God-damned tears *now?* What the hell was she crying for? They'd tried to close the gate and they'd failed, end of story. Except, of course, for the hordes of demons who were no doubt scouring the city for her. She swiped angrily at her cheeks and started walking away. "It's over, Patrick. We failed. Now go away."

"No."

She thought she'd left him behind. She hadn't heard him move, didn't think he had followed her, but she should have known better. She suddenly felt his arms enfold her from behind. He was the one who was weak; he'd just fought a demon horde and lost consciousness. He should have been easy for her to brush off.

Instead, he wrapped her in his strength, and she found herself falling backward into him. On some level, she knew he was right. He was smart; he knew things. If he said they had to think about what had happened, he was probably right. But damn it, it was so hard. Everything, right then, was so damn hard.

He pressed his lips against her temple. "It'll be okay, Xiao Fei. I won't abandon you. I'm right here. We'll figure it out together. It'll be okay." His words went on, the same sentences repeated with such feeling that she couldn't help but believe. He murmured his support, and she absorbed his strength. That was no small thing for her when she felt so alone, so lost.

She turned into his arms and gripped him back, sobbing, though where the hell all those tears came from, she'd never know. She wasn't a crier, never had been. But he'd folded her in his arms and she'd just lost it.

As her grief poured out of her, so too did some of the

pain and a great deal of fear. And in the hole left by all those tears, she felt something else grow, something from him: strength, power, maybe even a little determination.

"Don't let the bastards win, Xiao Fei. Let's end this demon war before it really begins. We can still do it. Together."

"American idealist crap," she muttered against his now-wet shirt. "John Wayne was an idiot."

"Afraid to believe in a happily-ever-after?"

"Cambodians know what comes 'ever after.' We believe in death, in struggling to survive and failing in this ugly, ugly world."

"And yet you're alive. I'm alive. And we're living in the wealthiest country on the planet."

"That's now under attack by demon hordes."

He shrugged. "Can't have everything."

She took a deep breath and absorbed his scent, his comfort, and his hope. "But we're gonna try, aren't we?"

He tightened his hold on her, just for a moment, then drew back. "Yes. We'll find breakfast, we'll get some coffee, and we'll figure this out together."

She shrugged. Still, there was hope in the gesture—hope she'd gathered from him. "I suppose I can pretend to be a flaky, idealistic American for a little while."

"That's my girl."

"But only if you feed me waffles and black tea."

"Breakfast of champions," he said.

"With strawberries and whipped cream."

He grinned. "Is there any other way?"

And so they would create the Great Plan to Save the World. Assuming, of course, that they could find an open IHOP.

* * *

Some things could be counted on, even during a great demon offensive. The sun always rose, the guys with money had all the power, and Americans loved their breakfast foods. Not only was the International House of Pancakes open; it was hopping—so to speak. And since this was Redondo and right on the beach, no one commented on their lack of shoes.

Xiao Fei smiled and shoveled in cholesterol-filled yumminess. She had to admit, a possible life under demon control didn't seem so bad as long as the syrup kept flowing. The tea wasn't her special brand; it wasn't even Chinese tea, but it contained caffeine, so it satisfied her craving.

Patrick grinned back. He seemed to be enjoying his omelet with a side of blueberry pancakes and the bottomless cup of coffee.

But then Patrick ended their little idyll. When he set down his fork, she knew it was time to talk. Mr. Ph.D. wanted to sort things out, to analyze the facts and come up with a plan. That was right, of course, but it didn't make the coming discussion any more appealing to Xiao Fei. So she delayed by eating more, though she already felt stuffed. She even ordered a refill on her tea, but the end was still the same.

"Tell me about your dream," Patrick said.

She sighed and tried to stall. "What do you remember?"

He shook his head. "Feelings mostly: fear, death, being buried." He shuddered. "That was the worst part—being buried."

She set down her mug, nauseated. Patrick glanced up, his eyes widening in comprehension. "You lived that. Oh, God. No wonder you have nightmares. Oh, Xiao Fei, I'm so sorry."

She lifted her shoulders. It wasn't really a shrug, more

a shift to push the weight away, to release the memories. It never worked, but she did it a lot anyway. "I survived," she muttered.

He took a breath. "Yeah. How, exactly?"

"I . . . I was small and young. I think they overlooked me."

He frowned. She almost laughed at how funny he looked, glaring down at his coffee cup. Clearly he was trying to piece things together. "Let's start from the beginning. The monks took you to that place with the tree."

"An ancient holy place, I think. As a druid, you must understand the power in a location—"

"Yeah, I get that," he interrupted. "I'm trying to remember the ritual."

"Oh." She closed her eyes and tried to recall. She already did, but the smell, the hurt—the whole experience was just too much. She couldn't face it.

"You surrounded the tree," Patrick prompted.

Xiao Fei picked up the syrup. She couldn't speak about it, but she could still communicate. She had to. She poured the syrup onto her empty plate without thinking too deeply about what she was drawing: a dot in the center of three expanding circles.

He looked at her plate, then began pointing. "Tree in center. Phoenix Tears next. Monks around them. So, what's the largest circle?"

She grabbed a sprig of parsley off his plate and set it in the outside circle.

"Greenery. A special plant? The Phoenix persimmon?" Patrick guessed.

She shook her head. Definitely not the last.

"You don't really know, do you?"

"Sorry," she croaked, startled at how tight her throat felt, but pleased she could still speak.

"That's okay." He glanced up, and she felt his hand surround hers on the table. "I know this is hard. You're doing great."

Don't cry. Don't cry, she told herself.

"Okay," he continued. "You began chanting then."

She shook her head. "We ate."

"The phoenix fruit?"

She nodded.

"But you were chanting already. I remember the taste of it. . . ." He frowned even as he nodded. "I remember you tasting the fruit, and the chanting. . . ." His voice slid into awe. "I *really* remember that." Then he abruptly grinned. "This is so cool."

She rolled her eyes, glad he was having fun.

"Okay," he said, sobering. "There was something before that, something before you ate the fruit."

She closed her eyes, focused on just her breath, then on the memory before the ugly. *Not on of the ugly; stay with the excitement.* The naive, stupid, childish excitement before everyone in her entire life was brutally slaughtered. Her throat tightened. She smelled the blood and mud. She heard the screams. She . . .

"Stay with me, Xiao Fei. Stay right here. With syrup and strawberry pancakes, in L.A."

She swallowed. "They were waffles, not pancakes."

"See, you knew that. That's because you're okay. It's all over." As he spoke, the waitress walked by, pausing long enough to reach in and grab their dirty dishes. She had long fingers and an even longer reach. She snatched up the syrupy plate.

Xiao Fei's hand wrapped in a death grip around the waitress's wrist. She didn't even remember moving, but she heard the woman's squeak of alarm as they both froze, plate suspended in the air. Fortunately, Patrick was there to reassure the waitress that Xiao Fei wasn't a psycho.

"Uh, we'd like to keep that plate, please." The server nodded, her overly mascaraed eyes still trained on Xiao Fei. "You can let go of her wrist now, sweetie," he added.

Xiao Fei hoped she could. Taking a deep breath, she forced her fingers open. Index finger, middle finger, last two fingers, thumb . . . The plate returned to the table with a loud clatter.

"Iheldthetree," Xiao Fei said.

Patrick's gaze was on the retreating waitress, but it abruptly snapped back to her. "What?"

She didn't wholly remember. She could feel the root in her hand, the rough scrape of the wood, the dirt that wedged under her nails as she gripped it—even the slickness around the edge of her palm as her blood soaked everything. Brother Solvann was on top of her, his shoulder an unbearable pressure against her spine, the roll of his heavy head against her side. But when she hit the dirt, her hands had grabbed . . . whatever was there. Her nails had dug into the dirt and one hand gripped mud, the other a root—a large, pulsing root of the lumpy tree.

"It wasn't on the surface, not on top of the ground," she murmured. "I had to dig to it. I was trying to get out from underneath. I had to claw . . . and the root was there—solid, strong." She glanced up at Patrick, needing the steadiness in his calm green eyes. "Alive. It was alive. Brother Solvann . . ." She shook her head. "Wasn't."

Patrick extended his hands toward her on the table. Her left hand remained slack, welcoming his touch, allowing him to surround her in his presence. But her right hand came alive.

Just as she'd done with the waitress, Xiao Fei latched

onto his wrist with her left hand. She knew she'd probably given the waitress bruises, but not Patrick. His arm
was hard, the bone solid, the sinews strong. He didn't
even flinch, but held her gaze with a power that en-
abled her to go on.

"Alive," she repeated in a whisper.

"It was an old tree," he encouraged. "There's power in
trees, especially ancient ones that protect holy ground."

She bit her lip. "It kept me alive." She struggled with
her thoughts, struggled even more with her words. "I
don't understand how, but it shielded me. It taught me.
I knew things were happening because I held on to it."

"The amulet." He was clearly remembering her
dream. "The monk chopped off the demon's hand, and
then he chopped the amulet with his ax, right?"

"Yes," she whispered. The abbot had swung the ax.
The blade went through that amulet, through the demon's severed hand and . . .

"Straight into the tree," he said. "You understood what
happened because you were clutching the tree root.
You bonded with the tree."

She nodded. That made sense. Well, actually, it didn't,
but it made as much sense as anything else.

"All that power—from the amulet, from the demon,
from your sisters—surged through the tree and came
to you."

"No." It hadn't come to her.

"You were linked to it. You were part of it," he argued.

"I survived. I was right there. There were bodies
everywhere . . ." Her throat closed up, but she forced
herself to continue. "They walked right by. The demons
didn't see me."

"You were part of the tree then—your energy and its
intertwined. It protected you." Patrick smiled. "We

druids believe in great tree spirits, in their power to love and protect. You have been richly blessed."

Xiao Fei swallowed and saw a drop of water splash on their intertwined hands. She stared at it, and another splash fell a few inches away. It took her a moment before she realized she was crying—and that she had pulled his hand tight to her chest. She'd drawn him all the way across the table so that his hand was pressed against her heart. Thank goodness he had long arms.

"Xiao Fei?" he asked.

"It died." Another drop fell: a cool kiss on her overheated hand. "The tree. I felt it die. All that power and energy. It couldn't handle it all."

"Did it use its last energy to shield you? To protect you?"

Maybe. She didn't know.

Liar! She did know. The tree had died protecting her. Tears continued to drip on her hands. She was traumatized by the death of a tree. "I need therapy, big-time," she said.

"Yeah, probably. Though it seems to me you're doing a good job of handling your bizarro life."

She took a breath, then another. Bit by bit she unclenched her hands. She untucked her hand, his hand—*their* hands—from between her breasts and released his wrist. She unclenched everything about her body.

He slid back into a more normal position across the table from her, but he kept hold of her left hand. Then he touched her right with the gentlest of caresses. "We'll get through this," he promised.

She released a laugh. It was short and pitiful, and sounded like a chair squeaking across a linoleum floor, and yet it felt good. "How? We don't have any new answers, except maybe that I'm a twisted shell of a woman."

"You're a beautiful, amazingly strong woman."

She snorted in derision. He couldn't possibly mean that, even if he looked like he was serious.

"Besides," he added after a moment. "I've figured out what we did wrong with the gate. We'll get it right tonight."

She stared at him, her mind completely paralyzed. He couldn't possibly think they could do that again. "We're both exhausted. We haven't got the power."

"We'll close the gate tonight, Xiao Fei," he said firmly. "But we have to do it in a sacred grove."

"Do . . . *it?*"

His skin flushed slightly, red flooding his lean face. "Yeah. In a sacred grove with . . . um . . . with druids chanting around us. For . . . um . . . protection." He arched his brows as he twisted awkwardly in his seat. "There are demons still after us, you know."

"Sex in a grove with druids watching," she repeated.

"Chanting. And yes, uh, watching. But not us. For demons."

She laughed. It was a real laugh this time, though it might have been tinged with hysteria. And when she could finally draw breath, she patted his free hand with hers. "And here I thought I was the only one who needed therapy."

May 30, 1992
Patrick—

I write to you in desperation, as a father writes to his son's best friend, but also as the old and faded man of the world sends a plea to a young, new hope.

As Jason's father, I watched you grow and mature. I know you think I saw nothing, that I was too busy as the Draig-Athar to see what you and my son were doing. But you were good boys being boys, and so I allowed things to progress without interference. Such is the way of druids, and I thought it wise.

But now I see more. Old age has robbed me of my duties and given me time to think and see, and to judge events with wisdom.

Something is terribly wrong with Jason. Something that should never have begun, much less turned into a business. I have already tried to talk to him, but he will not listen. I beg you to help me. You are a full druid now and understand the consequences of his actions. You have studied the same texts he did, and you know the forces he manipulates. But mostly I beg your help because you were once his best friend.

Please help me save my son before he brings disaster upon us all.

In hope,
Tom Boden

Chapter Sixteen

Patrick had a plan. He knew generally what to do, if not the exact details. All he had to do was set it in motion. Which meant he had to start managing the mounting pressures of real life out there in Crimson City. Except, of course, the more time he spent with Xiao Fei, the more it felt like she was real life and the rest was nonsense.

But such a fixation would be irresponsible. With a sigh of regret, he pulled out his cell phone to take charge of his duties. Xiao Fei understood. She leaned back in their tiny booth, cradled her tea in her lap, and closed her eyes. He had turned on his cell phone, but he didn't dial. He was too arrested by the change in her face.

She was meditating. Her face muscles relaxed, her body quieted, and she seemed to shrink into herself—but not in a bad way. It was more like watching a bird unruffle its feathers. In the same way, Xiao Fei became smooth and quiet—and from the deepest well of her spirit, her power began to grow.

Patrick had long since learned how to feel energy, how to sync up with power's ebb and flow. But it had always been the Earth's power—sometimes distorted or blocked, sometimes twisted and aimed in the wrong direction, but always derived from the Earth.

Xiao Fei was different. Her power was her own. Same signature, same frequency as the Earth's, but her power was completely self-contained. She was a tiny little planet unto herself. And when she meditated, as she did now, that power grew exponentially. Her vibration strengthened all around her. The table, the building, the people, and most especially himself, grew healthier, happier, and more whole in her presence. No wonder she was deadly to the demons; she was perfectly attuned to the world they sought to subdue.

His cell started vibrating in his hand. He glanced down, though it was an effort to shift his attention from Xiao Fei. Twenty-four messages. My, he was a popular guy. He sighed, unable to delay any longer. He punched in the number for Peter. The head druid answered on the second ring.

"It's about time—"

"Call everyone," Patrick interrupted. "Tell them to meet at our holy place tonight. Sunset."

"Where the hell are you? I need to know—"

"An IHOP in Redondo. Bring some extra clothes and flip-flops for two people." He gave the necessary directions, then hung up. He didn't even have to tell the man to come get them; he knew Peter would arrive as fast as his Porsche could get him there.

Then he had to face his messages. The first zillion were from Peter. He deleted those without even listening—he'd get those lectures soon enough. Then came a tearful one from his sister. The authorities wouldn't release his parents' bodies, and she didn't understand why. He swallowed and hit delete. Some pains were too sharp to deal with at the moment. He was honoring his parents in the only way he could: by ending the demon invasion.

Next came a message from Hank: "Hey, bud. Me and Slick are handling Pete, but it's ugly. Where are you? I can't watch your back if I can't find it."

Patrick's next message was from his brother. Then his sister again, her voice a bit more frantic as she wondered where he was. Interestingly enough, one followed from the San Bernardino police. They'd like to ask him a few routine questions. *Yeah, right.* Like there was anything routine going on these days.

More from Peter. Then his sister again, truly panicked. She was terrified for him. Apparently everyone assumed he was dead. He needed to call her, but what would he say? That he was alive and hunted by demons? Like that would reassure her. Instead, he opted for a simple text message, one that reassured without revealing too much: HEY, SIS, AM FINE. CAN'T GET HOME. DEMONS EVERYWHERE. LOVE YOU ALL. SWEAR I'LL BE CAREFUL. PATRICK.

He sent the message, then killed his cell. He just wanted to be with Xiao Fei right then. When he looked up, he was startled to see her dark eyes trained on him.

"Who died?" she joked, seeing his face.

He flinched, then said, "My parents. The police aren't releasing the bodies. They probably don't want to advertise that demons hit San Bernadino too."

She stared a moment, then abruptly cursed in Cambodian. "I'm sorry, Patrick. Your face looked pale and I thought . . . Well, I didn't think. I'm sorry."

"That demon attack. I was late to the meeting, and . . ." He took a gulp of coffee. "I couldn't save them."

"Your mother seemed a nice woman. I really enjoyed getting her e-mails. She was so open and honest. She talked about your father. I could tell she loved him a lot, even when she was complaining that he never put his socks in the hamper."

Patrick managed a weak grin. "Yeah, Dad was great in an academic, driven sort of way. I guess that describes both of them," he added after a moment.

"The monks said that death is not an end; it is merely returning home after a long journey."

"Or a short one," Patrick murmured.

Xiao Fei's gaze remained steady. "It is always too short for those who remain on the path."

He looked at her then, really looked at her. Her face was pale and drawn. She'd lost a lot of blood lately, and neither of them had gotten enough sleep. Then Patrick looked deeper. He felt her peace and her strength. Still, he couldn't connect with her warmth, though they'd somehow caught hands across the table.

"Is that how you got through?" he asked. "After the attack in Cambodia?"

Her gaze dropped to their intertwined hands. "I survived."

"I know, but how mentally did you—"

"I *survived*, Patrick. That was my entire focus; that was what got me through. And it's what got me here." She looked back up at him, and he was startled by the ferocity in her face. "And because I live, all my sisters live through me."

"The bloodline continues?"

She nodded.

"So, you don't really believe that other stuff, do you? That bit about 'returning home.'"

She flinched at his question, but he didn't let her

withdraw. He knew he was pushing into a sensitive area, but his grief was driving him.

"I believe in living," she finally said, "and letting the dead care for themselves." She lifted her chin. "It's the only way to keep going."

"No," he murmured. Then he repeated it louder as his conviction grew. "No, that's not enough."

"Patrick—" she began, but he cut her off.

"I believe in meaning. A life, however short, lived with purpose. My parents had a meaningful life. They had their work, and they raised three good children."

"That's great," she began, but he wasn't finished.

"And they sent me to you. That's why I came, Xiao Fei. That's why I searched you out."

"To close the demon gate."

"Yes." Then he shook his head, undercutting his answer. "I'm giving their deaths meaning, and that gives *my* life purpose and focus. It gives *my* life meaning."

She smiled, though the gesture was weak, and drew his hand to her lips. "I'm glad it gives you peace," she murmured, "but don't let it eat you alive."

He frowned. Extending his fingers to caress her lips, then her cheek, he shook his head at her contradiction. "I don't understand."

"Vengeance leads to death—a bitter, angry, withered death."

Was that what he sought—vengeance? He hadn't thought of it in those terms. He hadn't dared touch the part of himself that remembered his parents, that was dealing with their deaths. But with Xiao Fei's hands framing his and her face at the tips of his fingers, he found the strength to delve into that area of his soul.

Hatred boiled through his mind. Fury, rage, and, yes, a bloody drive for vengeance crashed through his thoughts. Part of him reeled back in horror, but the rest of him embraced the ugliness. He wanted to kill the demons. He wanted to rid the entire universe of their presence in the bloodiest, most painfully graphic way possible.

"I want them dead," he said with dark finality.

"If you embrace death, you can never shoulder life. Which is it, druid? Will you heal or destroy?"

His eyes narrowed, and his grip on her fingers tightened. "Which is it, Phoenix Tear? Do you bleed to bring health, or do you drip your poison into vampires and werewolves to end their lives?"

He felt her stiffen. They were joined only through their hands, but he felt her energy shift and her anger flare. "Are you trying to teach me how to fight demons, druid? I think I have much more experience than you."

"You have a *child's* memories, Xiao Fei. What of the woman?"

Her eyes flashed. "I will do what it takes to survive. What of the man?"

"I must end the demon threat on Earth."

Her eyes narrowed. "Of course. But at what cost?"

"Everything I have."

He watched her bite her lip, and a war seemed to spark in her eyes. "Vengeance does not heal, Patrick. I know. The meditations, the prayers—they don't work when I'm filled with anger. I can't even heal my own wounds then."

He frowned, the rational part of his mind latching on to the tremor in her voice. "You must have acted in hate at some point." He thought back through their time together. "The vampire. Stan. Didn't you hate him?"

"I cured him with love for the man before his turning. Without that, my blood . . ." She shook her head. "It won't work without love." She abruptly leaned forward, using their joined hands to tug him closer. "I'm not doing anything more with you, Patrick. Not if it's done in hate."

"Can you embrace the vampires and the were-wolves?" he challenged. "Can you love them as part of Earth?"

She swallowed, her gaze flickering. "Yes," she finally said. "Maybe. But . . ." Her gaze hardened. "Can you give up your vengeance?"

A moment before he hadn't even realized he wanted revenge. Now it seemed too much a part of him to release. "How do you just end it?" he whispered.

She shook her head, her eyes shimmering with tears. "I focus on something else. I replace death with survival."

"I want meaning," he said, only to realize that he was lying. He added, "I want this to end. I want the demons gone."

Xiao Fei looked resigned. "*That's* why we couldn't close the gate, Patrick. It's because you're not focused on the healing."

"But—"

"Listen to me!" she snapped. "I'm just the power source; you shape the flow. Don't forge any connection with the demons. Don't think of them, don't hate them, don't even know them. That just opens the gate wider. It creates ties to them. It allows them to stay in this world."

"But I want to erase them."

"Doesn't matter." Her grip on his hand tightened. "When you think of them, you keep their connection to this world open. You keep the gate from Orcus wide." She leaned forward, her gaze intense. "You have to want something else, Patrick, something that binds Earth together."

"Love," he said. He spoke the word as it popped into his

mind, but he wasn't sure he believed it. His Draig-Uisge training was directly contrary to everything she said.

"Love," she echoed back.

And then Peter burst into the IHOP and ended all conversation but his own.

"We can't count on Joanne and Frank. They're helping dig out refugees from homes that were hit by that first assault. I ordered them to come, but you know she's not going to listen. Scotty's got the plants, and I brought some weapons, but no one—and I mean no one—knows the chant. I can memorize it in seconds and I'll lead, of course, but those others just aren't up to it. And who knows if they'll remember their robes? I told them to bring the cotton ones, you know, but who knows if they can even get to the park? Oh, and flashlights, too, because . . ."

Patrick turned to look at Xiao Fei in the backseat. She had stretched out her legs and seemed to be asleep. Hell, he was halfway there himself; he'd long since tuned out Peter. But still, his mind wouldn't let him relax.

Love? Vengeance? Those words had never held much meaning in his life. He'd studied. He'd worked. He'd even dated and had sex occasionally. And he'd done what he had to do for the other druids. That had always been enough for him; it had kept his mind and his time well occupied.

But now his fists clenched when he saw the devastation wrought by the demons. Fires still lit the horizon to the southeast, washing his vision in red. Images of ripping out demon hearts occupied his mind—except when he looked at Xiao Fei. When he saw her creamy skin, her face smooth in sleep, his heart skipped a beat and his mind faltered. It went blank of everything except her.

"I need to know the exact ritual, Draig-Uisge, in detail. Draig-Uisge. Patrick!"

Patrick jumped. Forcing his attention back to Peter, he saw the Porsche was crawling through surface streets because the freeway was out. At least the streets were clearing. Pete had already told him that the National Guard was responding to the Los Angeles crisis. The military was pouring into the city, which meant most people who hadn't already left were locked tightly in their homes or were congregating at bars and local hot spots. In short, only the die-hards and deluded remained, going about their normal day as if it would all blow over.

He stared out the window at a woman hunched over groceries as she dashed down the sidewalk. How would she fare under demon control? What would happen if he failed tonight?

"Jesus, Patrick, try to pay attention!"

"I'm exhausted, Peter," he shot back. "I don't—"

"You were eating pancakes, goddamnit! During a fucking demon invasion, you were lollygagging about an IHOP like this was a joke or something. You're the goddamned Draig, Patrick. So get your fucking—"

"That's enough, Pete." He kept his voice low, his meaning deadly clear.

Peter slammed on the brakes hard enough that Patrick had to catch himself on the dash. In the back, Xiao Fei rolled off the seat with a Cambodian curse. "Don't you tell me to stop, you goddamned little prick! You work for me! I'm the head fucking druid in all—"

Patrick moved with both speed and a blind rage he barely restrained. Peter's ceremonial knife had been in a bag near his feet; now it was pressed oh, so gently to the fleshy underside of the man's chin.

"I am the Draig-Uisge," Patrick whispered against the head druid's ear. "I work for no one, least of all you. I serve the Earth. You lead other druids to support my task. If you can't do that, then you will be replaced with someone who can."

"Okay, okay. I got it—"

"Do I need to replace you, Pete?"

The man was quivering, making the knife scrape a raw mark in his skin. "N-no! No. Just t-take a breath, okay? We'll all get through this."

"No, Pete," he said softly. "We won't get through this. Not all of us. By tomorrow morning, some of us will be dead. The demons will slice our bellies open and rip out hearts while they're still beating."

The head druid swallowed. His skin had turned a pasty white, and his gaze jumped about. "I . . . We . . . I mean—"

"Do you want to lead that charge, Peter? Do you want to be right out front when we face the demons?"

The man swallowed, too terrified to speak.

"Will you listen to my orders, druid? Will you follow the Draig-Uisge?"

"Yes! Absolutely!" His response was as quick as any soldier's.

Patrick held his position a moment longer, then finally sheathed the blade. A glance at the backseat told him Xiao Fei had watched the whole exchange. She curved her lips in a soft smile of approval, then closed her eyes and relaxed back into sleep.

"Where are we going?" Patrick asked.

"To my office. That's where everyone's meeting."

Patrick shook his head. "Call them back," he said.

"Tell them to gather at the park at sunset—no earlier. We can't risk getting everyone together before that."

Peter's jaw dropped open. "B-b-but how will we prepare? How will they learn the—"

"There is no goddamned preparation! All you have to do is stand in a circle and hold off the demons."

"B-but—"

"Just hold them off however you can. Even if you just impale yourself on their claws." Patrick felt his lips curve in a malicious smile. "You can start with that." Then he settled back in his seat. He dropped Peter's sheathed knife into his lap, though he still clenched the hilt in a tightened fist. "I'm going to take a nap now," he lied. Then he closed his eyes.

Vengeance. Hatred. Love. This was a hell of a time to discover his emotional core.

"That was quite a little talk you had with your friend." Xiao Fei's voice slipped into his thoughts, soothing even as it disturbed him.

"He's not my friend," Patrick mumbled.

"Yeah, actually, I got that. So, what is he?"

Patrick opened his eyes. They were in the department reception area of Peter's UCLA office. The moment they'd arrived, Peter had disappeared into his office to make phone calls. Patrick had stretched out on the floor and shut his eyes, leaving the long couch for Xiao Fei. Except she hadn't lain down. She'd curled into his side and tortured him by slipping her hand beneath his tee and playing with his chest hairs—the ones right below the amulet.

"Pete's the head druid in L.A." He frowned and closed his eyes again. "I mean, the head druid in Southern California." Now that his father was dead.

"But you had a knife on him. You put it—"

"I know what I did."

She was silent a moment. "So, you must be pretty important too." It wasn't a question, so he didn't answer. Then she asked. "You're their muscle, aren't you?"

He opened his eyes a tiny bit, squinting at her. Had she actually asked that with a straight face?

"You know," she continued, "their knuckles, their enforcer." She brightened, and poked him in the ribs. "You're the druid Terminator!"

"You getting bloodthirsty all of a sudden? What happened to 'love thy neighbor'?"

Sobering, she lifted herself up on an elbow and her hair fell in a short curtain behind her chin. "That's what's ahead of you on the path, Patrick. I want to know where you've been."

He rolled his eyes. He tried to cover by closing them, but she must have seen. She grabbed a hunk of chest hair and tugged. "Hey! Ow!" he gasped.

"Talk, Patrick. It's important."

"Why?"

She paused long enough for him to open his eyes again and be struck by her beauty. There she was, her face scrunched up in thought, and he realized she felt solidly, amazingly, totally there. With him. His own personal bright light. And Xiao Fei was the most beautiful sight he'd ever seen.

"Well?" he prompted.

"Well, you made me confess my deep, dark past. It's your turn."

"So you're getting even?"

She shrugged. "Okay."

He laughed. It just burst out of him, and he was so surprised that he tried to kiss her in gratitude.

She pulled back. "Stop avoiding. What is the deal with your name and title and . . . well, everything?"

He sighed. She wasn't going to let this go. "*Draig* means *dragon*. All the . . ." He let his lips curve into a smile. "All the 'druid Terminators' have Draig in front of their name. *Uisge* means water, so my name means water dragon. The one before me was Draig-Teine, a fire dragon, and his father before him was Draig-Athar, an air dragon."

"So this is a hereditary thing, passed from father to son? How'd you become the current Draig?"

Patrick let a long moment pass. "I killed my best friend."

From Patrick Lewis's journal.

June 8, 1992

It is done. I am the new dragon. A water dragon, to be exact, though I don't think I'll ever get used to being called Draig-Uisge. It sounds like a sneeze in a bad French accent.

The ceremony isn't until tomorrow, but I already have the amulet, have already wielded the damn thing, so everything else is moot. Dad has strongly encouraged me to write down what happened.

Jason's dad wrote the official report, of course. It says that Jason died while experimenting with questionable spells. He wrote that I wielded the amulet in an attempt to heal his son, and that my inexperience is what caused me to eventually fail. I have not disagreed with that, since it's essentially true. It's also completely false.

As Draig-Uisge, I have to get in the habit of recording my activities. I have decided always to record the truth here, even if the only ones who read it are future Draigs. Perhaps Jason's story will serve as warning to them. For me, it brings only a dark, overwhelming anger. He was such a god-damned fool.

Here is what happened:

I went to Miracles. It was late and the shop was closed, but Mr. Boden had a key and the code for the alarm. I didn't ask how, but he was Jason's father and the previous Draig; it's not surprising he had it—though he was obviously sick. He suffered from frequent tremors, and his skin was gray and slick with sweat.

I cannot recall exactly what I saw inside the building. I was too involved in feeling the overwhelming power that swirled and eddied around me. It set patches of my skin tingling and raised the hair on the back of my neck. But most of all, it overwhelmed me with a sense of wrongness. Great power, yes, but it was nauseatingly wrong.

Mr. Boden felt it too. It threw off his balance and he often stumbled, steadying himself against the walls as he took deep, gulping breaths. I offered to go on without him, but he refused. I remember that his eyes seemed to glitter in the bright leather-and-chrome waiting room. And his words will haunt me for the rest of my life: "You feel it too, don't you? You know what he . . . That he . . . My son has gone bad."

I knew it was the truth, but I still denied it. I think I'd known for a long time. Since my seventeenth birthday party. But he was my best friend. How could he "go bad"? "We know nothing yet," I lied to Mr. Boden. He didn't argue, but let me lead the way upstairs. We both knew Jason was in his second-floor office. That was where the erratic power was centered.

We climbed the stairs of the big circular staircase. I remember it most specifically because the stairs seemed to weave and pulse, and I rubbed my eyes to try to clear them.

Mr. Boden said Jason was bending space, and when I didn't understand, he sighed and looked very old. "He's using the amulet. He's trying to open a demon gate."

I still couldn't believe it, fool that I was. Jason had been fascinated by that damn demon toy since the day he'd first seen his father with it. He knew he could wield it, even when we were kids, and it became his ambition then to have it. I just never realized what he intended to do with it. He always wanted money, so I figured once he'd bilked enough billion-dollar celebrities, he would be happy. I thought he was using the amulet to heal celebrities, but I was wrong.

Jason was killing demons.

He didn't hear his office door open, and he wasn't looking at us, so we had time to see his work. His profile was to us, his face and body twisted in pain around the amulet as he worked. There was an open dais in front of him, one surrounded by candles and etched with a pentagram. And inside it were dead demons.

There were almost a dozen. Young ones. Old ones. Fat ones. Beautiful ones. The demons looked just like humans, though dressed differently and with oddly colored eyes. I would have thought them human beings, except their energy *felt clearly alien. Not bad, just different—not from Earth.*

But they were all dead. All except for a gorgeous, lavender-eyed woman in the center. She wore a brown suedelike blouse over loose green pants—a strangely stylish outfit—and her eyes were panicked as she opened her mouth in a silent scream. Except it wasn't silent. There was no noise, but there was energy—a loud riot of power pouring forth like blood, draining from her open mouth and into . . . what?

It took a while for me to understand. The scene was unreal, and I still close my eyes and think what I saw could not possibly be true. And yet I know it was. The energy—this demoness's life and power—was pouring into the amulet that Jason held out before him. And from the looks of it, she was only one of many.

I must have said something. The horror of it all was incomprehensible. Whatever I did, Jason heard. He turned in terror until he saw who I was.

In truth, two images still haunt my nights. The first I have already described: that beautiful woman being killed slowly. The second is Jason's face. There was such joyous welcome in his eyes that I cannot reconcile the two images. He was happy to see me—excited, even.

And at that moment, I knew I would have to kill him. How could a druid—how could a man—be so twisted as to think I would celebrate the murder of any life, demonic or otherwise?

He finished what he was doing. I was across the room as fast as I could move, but I was still too slow; the demon woman died. And with a mut-

tered flourish, Jason banished the bodies of the dead back to the demon place—Orcus, he called it.

I screamed. Mr. Boden and I had gone there to speak rationally to him. We went to ascertain the veracity of certain allegations. We went there to give him the opportunity to explain, but I never gave him the chance. He was too pleased with his work, too proud of it to understand my fury. I really heard only one sentence, and even now it still makes my blood boil.

"But the amulet has to be recharged somehow," he said.

That's what he was doing. I have pieced together what he learned from his notes. I have read his scribbles and deductions, and in truth, they're quite brilliant. He learned that the amulet manipulated energy. We all knew that the thing was once used to open windows between Earth and this other place, Orcus. We all knew that, and so the amulet is given to the Draig for protection so that no one will ever dare open the rift between worlds again. So no one will allow the monsters of old to return to torment Earth.

But no one thought about our monsters tormenting them. In the center of this amulet is a dark liquid, a black ichor. It is demon blood that was once bright red in the center, but as the energy drains out of it, as the power was used to heal Jason's celebrity clients, the red became darker—blacker—and more and more useless for a druid looking for power above all things. . . .

He learned to combine the old gate spells with something worse—the power to take demons from their homes and drain them of their life energy. He was killing demons who had not attacked, had not invaded, nor done anything to harm Earth in generations. As far as I could tell, the murdered were simple beings living their lives according to their own customs and culture. Jason caught them, drew them to Earth, then drained their life to recharge his amulet.

Now I come to what I have been striving so hard to admit, what even now makes my hand shake with fury and my skin flush with shame. I cannot explain this conflict within myself. I cannot forget the horror of what I have done, nor the certain knowledge that it had to be done.

I lost control. I could not believe what Jason was doing, and he could not understand my confusion. He pulled the life out of demons to cure rich clients. Of course, I now know from his notes that he inflicted many of those diseases upon his clients and that he felt some guilt for what he did, despite his rationalizations. But truthfully, at the time, none of this entered my thoughts. I was too furious.

He was draining the life out of living souls for the express purpose of increasing his own power. Whether those creatures be human, demon, or even the lowest earthworm, to drain that energy was wrong, completely and utterly wrong.

So I grabbed the amulet. It was the source. It was also Jason's soul, and I think I just wanted to hold it or contain it somehow. I don't know. I grabbed the amulet and felt for the first time the agony that slices through the wielder of that cursed thing. Pain burned through my arm, and yet it was more than pain; it was power—demon power—

that could be twisted and used. Held, controlled, and wielded like a sword.

If it were not for Jason, I think I would have flung the thing away or perhaps fled in fear. The pain burns through the body like dragon fire. It can consume you.

Mr. Boden joined us then. He did not grab hold of the amulet; it was trapped between Jason and me. But he could speak to his son. He said the things that I could not. He reasoned, he challenged, and then he begged.

Jason said nothing. He and I were still struggling with the amulet, both trying to shape the power. And then he began to win. I felt the shift of energy. He had mastered its use, and I was merely a poor imitator. He could have shaped the energy to throw me off, to cast me away from himself and the amulet, but he didn't. I felt the moment he began to draw my power into the jewel, just as he had sucked the life out of the demons. I was fading. My life was draining into the jewel.

I fought back. I believe that Mr. Boden joined in my struggles, but Jason was the master and had lost all reason.

Then, Jason spoke. He thanked me for the gift of my power. My hand and arm were numb, my blood felt drained away, and even my breath rattled in my chest, but he didn't end it. I think, perhaps, he wanted someone to admire what he had accomplished. He would finally have enough energy, he said, to do what he'd always wanted. My recycled soul would protect him when he opened a massive gate into Orcus.

Then he did it. While I gripped the amulet, he

twisted the energy to open a gate. It cut through space and time and reality. Once again, I felt that other energy—the demon power that was that planet: Orcus.

I didn't understand at first. Why pick up more demons when he had not finished me? But it wasn't demon lives he wanted. It wasn't even my poor existence. He wanted the soul of the planet, of the dimension—of Orcus.

He began to draw it in. My strength had allowed him to do this last hideous thing. He ripped a hole in the Earth and began to draw the life out of another planet.

There was nothing I could do. My body was completely numb, my mind equally paralyzed, unable to cope with the shifting currents of power. Then his father struck. It was a chair, I think, made of heavy wood surrounded by plush leather. He struck his own son with it, and in that moment, Jason faltered. Only a short break in concentration, but it was enough for me to wrench back some control.

I could not end the flow; Jason was too strong. But I could twist it, could change it. So I did. I rode the flow of power straight into the amulet, and from there continued the river into Jason. I had not realized until that moment that the power went not into the jewel, but into the wielder. That was what Jason wanted, and that was his downfall.

I twisted from within. I corrupted the flow of power and therefore corrupted him. I twisted it enough to kill him, and then I changed it even more.

Jason deformed before my very eyes. I watched as his body contorted. One side of his chest collapsed; the other ripped open. His face crushed inward, and then he simply dissolved, eaten, I think, by his own power.

It took bare seconds, but I lived every moment as if Jason were me. He died while I watched, and with his death I managed total control of the gate. It closed. It shut. And now I am the new Draig, the new keeper of the demon amulet.

It will not happen again. This I swear as I write these words: such horror will never ever happen again. That is the calling of the Draig—to keep all life safe. Earth life, demon life, all life. And I will sacrifice all in the exercise of that duty.

Today I am Draig-Uisage.

Chapter Seventeen

Patrick watched Xiao Fei's expression flicker at his dramatic statement, but she didn't rush to condemn him. She didn't say anything at all, just waited for him to continue, her gaze steady, her expression bland.

"You don't believe me," he said. "You don't think I really killed him."

"*Are* you lying?" she asked.

"No!"

"Then explain."

He rolled his head away from her, his gaze focusing on a bookcase of journals. One magazine was out of place, the June issue coming before April. On his side, he felt Xiao Fei settle against him, her head a welcome weight against his shoulder. Without conscious thought, he curled his right arm around her, drawing her close.

He turned his face back to her and pressed a kiss to her forehead. His heart swelled. Warmth spread through his body, most especially his lower half. He wanted to make love to her, right there on the dirty reception room floor. He wanted to have her now and keep her forever, and the fierceness of that very emotion surprised him. He would defy anyone who tried to take her from him. Violent images filled his thoughts—pictures of him beating off demons, vampires, and werewolves to protect his mate. It was all very neanderthal, but he couldn't deny the primal thrill it gave him.

He felt her sigh. Her body expanded and contracted beneath his arm, and his T-shirt heated near her mouth. But she didn't demand he confess anymore. In fact, she was conspicuously silent.

"What happens if I don't tell you?" he asked.

"Nothing."

He frowned, sensing a trap. "Nothing, but you'll hate me forever? Nothing, but you'll punish me with angry silence? Nothing, but—"

"Nothing!" She lifted her head, annoyance tightening her features. "You don't owe me anything, Patrick. You want to keep a part of yourself hidden, fine. But don't forget: love is about sharing. It's about joining together. You can't bind together what you hold apart. It's not possible."

He shook his head, half mocking. "Is that what the monks taught you?"

She stared at him. "Yeah, it is. So choose, Patrick. Are we building bridges or walls?"

He growled. It was an actual growl that made his stomach clench and his jaw protrude. It was low and angry, and it made him feel like an animal. And all the while, his mind kept telling him that she was right. That he had asked—was still asking—for a huge amount of faith from her. Telling her his most painful story was the least he could do.

"I'm a killer, Xiao Fei. That's what Draigs do for

druids—we discipline. And in this case, I killed. There was no court of law, no police, no due process. I took my best friend's energy and twisted it so violently that he died. Horribly." Patrick swallowed, stunned that he had spoken so bluntly about something that still haunted his nightmares. "So, you still want to save the world with me, or should I tell Peter the whole thing's off?"

Her voice was matter-of-fact. "The whole thing was never on. I haven't agreed yet."

Patrick covered his eyes with his left arm, a sense of profound defeat stealing over him. It felt as if his soul were shrinking into a tiny, desiccated lump that would blow away in a stiff wind.

Xiao Fei gave him no respite. She saw through his pain and asked, "Want a hair shirt to go with all that self-pity?"

He turned, furious. "What do you want from me, Xiao Fei? And don't say nothing, because we both know that's not true. I know what I want from you—what *the world* wants from you. What do you want from me?"

She lifted up on her elbow to study him. "I don't know," she said softly.

He sighed. "I want to get this damn day over with. I want the gate closed, the demons gone, and—" He stopped abruptly, stunned by what he'd been about to say.

"And . . . ?" she prompted.

"And I want to take you home to meet my mother. I want to show you off to my father, and listen to you talk tea with my sister. I want to see your toothbrush in my bathroom and hear my brother talk enviously about your beautiful breasts." He rolled away from her so that he could sit up and face her fully. "I want you in my life."

She stared at him intently. "Why did you kill your best friend?"

"Because he was killing demons." His words were curt and angry. He didn't miss the irony of the situation. He had destroyed Jason for the very thing he so desperately wanted to do right now—kill demons. "Jason was a faith healer, extorting money from the rich while he used his druidic powers to heal them."

Xiao Fei frowned. "But he was healing them . . ."

"He made them sick in the first place. Then he'd take huge amounts of money to fix what he'd caused."

"Oh," Xiao Fei said.

"Yeah, oh." Patrick rubbed a hand over his face. "His father found out and tried to stop him."

"But as the Draig-Uisge, *you* had to do it?"

Patrick shook his head. How to explain that night? "Jason was Draig then. He poisoned his father for years just so he could get the draig power." He swallowed. "The amulet."

He saw Xiao Fei fit the pieces together. "The demon amulet?" she asked. "That's what he wanted?"

"Yes."

He watched a muscle in her jaw twitch. "And he made that damn thing with sick people just so he could cure them for money." She paused. "What a prick. He was your best friend?"

"Yeah."

She shook her head. "So, Dad finds out and goes to confront him. He pleads with his son to remember all that is good and true and honorable."

Patrick bit back a growl at her amused tone. "You have a problem with that?"

She actually smiled. "It's very American."

"Because you Cambodians don't have a sense of right and wrong?" he drawled.

"In Cambodia, a relative is more likely to congratulate someone for being so smart and then try to wheedle in on the cash."

Patrick drew back in surprise. "That's a very cynical statement."

"I had a very cynical childhood."

"No, you didn't." He didn't know for sure, but he guessed. "You were raised in a monastery. You were taught love and faith and all things good."

"And look where that got me." Xiao Fei leaned forward. "You have a saying here: Only the good die young. But you can't have morals in an immoral world. It makes you too out of step."

"I survived; he's dead," Patrick said. "I was right; he was wrong." He took a deep breath. "Hurting people just to cure them is wrong. Making your own father sick so you can take his amulet is wrong. And killing innocent demons by sucking their life energy into your own soul is very, very wrong." He groaned. Had he just called demons innocent? But Jason's victims *had* been innocent. And a part of Patrick wondered if they weren't invading Los Angeles now because his friend had drained so much of their planet's energy.

If Jason had never used the amulet, *would* Los Angeles now be under attack? Patrick didn't know, but the thought terrified him.

Xiao Fei propped her chin on her fist and came to her own conclusions. "So you killed him. Because what he did was wrong."

Patrick nodded. "Yeah. I was the only one strong enough to stop him. And then, afterward, I was the only one strong enough to wield the amulet."

"To become the next Draig?"

"Yes."

She was silent a moment, studying him. Then she flashed him a smile. "Thanks."

He blinked. "Huh?"

She smiled as she resettled on the floor. "I said, thanks. For telling me what happened."

He gaped at her. "You're welcome."

She closed her eyes, apparently planning on going to sleep, but he couldn't let it end there. "That's it? Thanks. 'Glad to know you're a killer, but it's naptime now'?"

She didn't bother to open her eyes. "What would you like me to say—that you need therapy to deal with murdering your best friend? Well, duh."

"I already went," he snapped.

"Well, then, do it again, because it didn't take," she replied.

He didn't respond. He knew she was right.

She opened her eyes. "Ha! Thought so."

He rolled his eyes. "Xiao Fei—"

"Look, Patrick, you already know everything I'm going to say. Somehow you're going to have to come to terms with being both a killer and a lover. So I'll turn your earlier question around. What do *you* want?"

He stared at her. "I want you to say you'll have sex with me in a sacred grove. That together we'll close the demon gate and end this nightmare once and for all."

She shook her head. "No way." Then her expression softened. "I can't promise about the gate. But I will make love with you there; I will feed you all the power I have in my spirit, based on my love for this Earth. And I will let you, Draig-Uisge, shape that power however you will. Hatred or love, whatever you choose. Because I trust you that much."

He stared at her, and she held his gaze like she was

holding his hands: in tenderness and trust. It took three tries before he could speak past the lump in his throat. "You believe in me that much? Even after what I told you?"

She smiled. "Freaky, huh? But then, you already know I need therapy."

He kissed her. He couldn't move fast enough; he swooped down and locked his mouth on hers. She returned his kiss in full measure. She even opened her mouth to let him explore and plunder, just as she pressed into him with her own touches and desires. It was an awesome kiss, all the sweeter because it had nothing to do with Earth or demons or anything but him thanking her for this most precious gift of her trust.

Peter stomped into the room and clapped his loud, obnoxious hands, reminding Patrick that trust was not enough. "Don't be burning that power early," the druid boomed. When Patrick pulled back and glared, the obnoxious man abruptly sobered. "Er, well, yeah. Um . . ."

Patrick sighed, already starting to stand. "You needed to talk to me?"

"Yeah. About tonight's ritual. I don't—"

"You know, I'm feeling a little hungry," Patrick cut in. He turned back to Xiao Fei. "Do you mind ordering food? Anything you like. Here." He neatly lifted Peter's wallet out of the man's pants pocket. "Use Peter's credit card."

"Hey!" said the academic.

Xiao Fei easily caught the snakeskin billfold, but her expression remained dubious. "Order food? I'll see what I can do, but I don't know what'll be open with—"

"Do what you can. Pete and I are going to talk about druid stuff." Then Patrick strong-armed the man back into his office.

He slammed the door shut, saying, "Settle down, Peter."

Surprisingly enough, Peter did. The man walked silently around his desk, and settled into a large executive chair.

Patrick had enough time finding his own seat to notice the green plants in the office, the comfortable academic atmosphere, and the plush leather chairs. "This isn't a game, Pete. She's skittish enough as it is without your crude sophomoric jokes."

Peter didn't answer; he simply leaned back in his chair and stared hard at Patrick. And for the first time since this had all begun, Patrick remembered that the man was a professional—an academic with his own share of power, and the most skillful druid in Southern California. He was, in fact, a brilliant mathematician and accomplished at a variety of political maneuvers. He'd have to be, having gained his level of power within the academic hierarchy of UCLA. Patrick leaned back in his chair, suddenly wary.

"So, you find my humor sophomoric," Peter said dryly. "That's rich, considering what you're doing."

Patrick frowned. "What do you mean?"

"Come on. Sex with a pretty Asian chick is going to end the demon invasion?" Pete gestured irritably at the spellbook on his desk. It was the one Patrick had given him earlier, explaining the ritual.

Well, Peter had obviously read it. Just as clearly, the man had doubts. Damn, Patrick was getting tired of defending his reasoning.

"I know it sounds far-fetched, but it's not really sex." At Peter's raised eyebrow, he amended, "Well, it is—sort of. The point is, it's already worked once. We closed the gate some, just not all the way."

Peter nodded. "So you said. That's the only reason I'm considering helping you further."

Patrick felt a wave of anger swamp him. "Don't bullshit me, Peter; I'm not in the mood. Tonight had better be all set up."

The head druid suddenly slammed his hand on his desk, his eyes blazing. "I can cancel at any time, you idiot. There are *demons* out there, damn it. And if you think I'm going to put my people at risk just because you want to sleep with that—"

Patrick's hand wasn't quite large enough to wrap around Peter's neck. He knew this because he was leaning across the desk, his right hand squeezing the man's throat hard. Hard enough that the druid's eyes were bulging.

He very slowly released his grip, and as he let Peter breathe again, he spoke very softly. "The spell works. Despite your best efforts to screw this up, you will be hailed as the greatest druid that ever lived because it was on your watch that the demon gate was closed. So get your weapons, set up a perimeter, and let me do the rest."

"That gate wasn't opened with an amulet." The head druid's voice came out scratchy, but with no less power.

"What?"

"It wasn't opened with an amulet. Some asinine research team did it. I don't know how, but it wasn't with an amulet."

Patrick frowned. This went against what he'd assumed. "You're sure?"

"As sure as I can be. I've heard the city government working like mad trying to close it. They may not need you at all."

Patrick released a breath. "Thank God. Do they have a timetable?"

Peter narrowed his eyes, obviously thinking hard. At

last, he shook his head. "I don't know that they've discovered anything useful. I just know an amulet didn't open the gate. You're still our best hope." He sounded like it was killing him to admit it.

"Demons are trying to kill me and Xiao Fei, Peter. Doesn't that tell you we're on to something?"

"Demons are trying to kill everyone," came Peter's response.

Patrick didn't speak. What was the point? The head druid had already made all the phone calls he could; he'd already arranged for the ritual to begin as soon as the moon was up. They'd already done everything they could except wait.

With that thought, he pushed up from his chair and headed for the door. "I'm starved, and I need to meditate before tonight."

"Geez, you're really prepared to do it. Damn, that's cold." Peter's tone stopped Patrick at the door. There was something in it that riveted him. It was part admiration, part revulsion, part horror.

Patrick turned to study the druid more closely. "Of course I'm prepared. I'm the Draig-Uisge."

Peter nodded, but his expression was troubled. "I know you've killed before, but to snuff out the woman you're having sex with while you're doing it . . ." His eyes narrowed. "I wasn't sure you'd be strong enough to do that."

Patrick took a few hasty steps back to the center of the room. "What are you talking about?"

Peter grimaced. "I knew it. Draig-Uisge, my ass—I knew you were too soft for this."

"Explain, Pete. Now."

"She's a Phoenix Tear, right?" The head druid spun in his chair and began typing at his computer. "The only one we've got, right?"

"Yeah, what of it?" But Patrick already knew where this was going. The sick dread it spawned in his belly was enough to make him sit down.

Peter pointed to his screen. "Here it is. From your mother. The e-mail she sent out on the whole history of the Phoenix Tears." He looked back at Patrick, a hand still on the mouse as he scrolled. "The whole sad story."

Patrick leaned over the desk to see the text. He didn't have to read long. His mother had sent him the same letter. "Yeah," he said as he straightened. "What of it?"

"Well, her power's in her blood, right?" Peter abruptly spun his chair to face Patrick fully. "She's going to have to bleed, Draig-Uisge. She's going to have to bleed *a lot.*"

And there it was: the thing Patrick had been avoiding this whole time. Xiao Fei's donated blood might not be enough. In order to access enough power to close the gate, they would need the blood of . . . say, thirty Phoenix Tears, just like they'd had thirty girls in Cambodia. Just as Xiao Fei had been saying all along. Now Pete knew too. But Patrick wasn't willing to accept that. Not yet, at least.

"We already closed the gate some. She bled only a little then."

"How much?" Pete pressed.

"A little. You know, from . . . Well, she was a virgin, so . . ." His voice trailed off in embarrassment.

Peter's eyes widened. "Really? Wow. I wouldn't think a woman that beautiful would—"

"She was raised in a freaking monastery!" Patrick interrupted.

Peter nodded. "Yeah, good point. Well, the breaking of that membrane is supposed to have special meaning—I mean, beyond the obvious. There could have been an extra power boost there."

"That's just male propaganda," Patrick retorted.

Peter shook his head. "The membrane's there for a reason. The body doesn't create things that don't have a purpose."

"Hello? Appendix?"

"Had a purpose. And so does the hymen."

Patrick narrowed his eyes. "As a power source? Come on."

"Yeah. Something like that." Peter fell silent, obviously deep in thought. Patrick, too, keep his mouth shut as he thought through the ramifications. If they'd already used up her extra power boost when he took her virginity, that meant they had only the power of her blood. What if that wasn't enough?

"She's the last of her kind," he said, as much to himself as Pete. "If she dies, there will be no more Phoenix Tears."

"She'll be dead either way," the head druid answered. "You know that, right? She either dies closing the gate or because we fail to close it and the demons find her."

"She doesn't have to die, Pete. We can close the gate without all her blood."

The druid shook his head. "I don't think so. It took thirty of them before—"

"I know, I know. But we're not doing what the Cambodians did. There wasn't our druid power; they didn't have our ritual."

Peter shrugged. "You've got to be prepared for the possibility. You've got to be willing—"

"I know!"

Patrick thought that would be enough to shut the man up, but Peter was not easily swayed. He sprang to his feet, towering over Patrick. "These demons are killing people by the hundreds, and this is just the first assault. They mean to—"

265

"I know!" Patrick snarled.

"One woman's life is a pretty small sacrifice."

Patrick matched the man stare for stare. "It's a huge sacrifice, and I won't do it! Because I won't have to."

"It's what they were born to do, Draig-Uisge. It's their jobs."

"Damn it, we won't need that much blood!" He spun on his heel and stomped out into the reception area.

It was empty. Where was Xiao Fei?

ous to the world as any teen, even though she'd just turned twenty-five. You'd have thought it was just a day like any other in Crimson City.

Xiao Fei scanned the room, sighing in relief when she saw the phoenix persimmon plant at its spot near the window. She followed a trail of dirty clothes to the stereo. Two steps later, she was able to flick the thing off. The sudden silence echoed in her eardrums, and her sister spun around, a knife poised to strike.

"If I were a murderer, I wouldn't have turned off the music."

"Xiao Fei!" Sandy dropped the knife and ran at her full tilt.

Xiao Fei braced herself, then took the body check. In truth, Sandy wasn't all that large. Besides, it felt good to wrap her arms around her sibling one last time.

"I thought I told you to leave the city, brat," she admonished, even as she held her sister close.

"Couldn't. Quarantine. Haven't you been listening to the news?"

Xiao Fei frowned. "What are you talking about?"

"They've closed off the entire city, locked it down. No one in or out except military."

"So you choose to hide by blaring music at a thousand decibels?"

Sandy pulled back. "There have been no attacks here. Who cares about a no-account grad student?"

Xiao Fei touched her sister's sweet moon face. "Innocents die all the time in war." She looked at the persimmon plant. "And you aren't exactly innocent. Not as my sister."

Sandy's eyes widened—no small feat, given how elfin her features were. "What have you done?"

Xiao Fei gestured to the persimmon. "I gave you that

plant, that's what. If any demons find it, they'll kill you on principle."

Sandy grew pale, and her gaze darted between Xiao Fei and the plant. Two breaths later, she laughed. "Oh God, you really had me going. Wow, that's so mean, you witch." She playfully slapped Xiao Fei's arm and crossed to her couch. She tossed clothes and books on the floor with typical flourish, then dropped into the corner against a Big Bird pillow Xiao Fei had made for her as a Christmas present aeons ago.

"So, what's up? What have you been doing during all this? Hey, I'm hungry. Want a sandwich or something?" She pursed her lips. "I got . . . uh . . . peanut butter and jelly, I think. Maybe just peanut butter."

"Sounds great," Xiao Fei said.

Her sister hopped up again, rushed to the kitchen, and began banging cupboards and slamming drawers. Xiao Fei winced at each sound. Her sister had always been exuberant; it was one of her most endearing qualities, but right now . . . She walked over and caught a cupboard door just as Sandy was slapping it closed.

"What—"

"I wasn't joking, *mei mei.*" She used the Chinese term for *little sister.* It wasn't the Cambodian term, but then Sandy was Chinese, so the two of them had adopted that. "They will kill you if they find it."

Sandy swallowed, her entire body stilling. "So . . . let's throw it out. We'll put it down the disposal."

Xiao Fei shook her head. "It's too valuable, and it wouldn't make a difference. Not if they come looking. You've eaten the fruit, remember?"

"Not for years."

"Doesn't matter. You may not have my blood, but something happens the first time you taste it."

Sandy nodded, her eyes shining. "Yeah, I know. I've been studying the components in the fruit. It's got some really bizarre enzymes . . ." Then she was off and running: biochemistry in all its glory. Xiao Fei didn't understand a tenth of what her sister said, but she loved listening anyway. Academic passion was something she respected, even if it was something she didn't share. Unfortunately, she couldn't sit and listen all day.

"I'll take the plant, Sandy, and all your dried fruit. That'll make things somewhat safer for you." And with a little bit of luck, it'd all be over by tomorrow morning.

Of course, the only luck Xiao Fei believed in was the bad kind, so she leaned forward, her gaze firm. It was very big-sisterly. "I want you to lie low, Sandy. Disappear if you can until every demon is gone."

Her sister folded her arms across her small chest, and stuck out her chin. Lord, she looked like a cherub. "You can't have the plant," she said. "You'll be in as much danger as me. More, because you've got the blood thingy."

Xiao Fei grabbed a piece of notebook paper, talking as she wrote. "I'm giving you some information for after everything settles." Her handwriting was barely legible as she scrawled out bank account numbers and her last will and testament. It was one paragraph that identified her, claimed her of sound mind and all that, and gave everything to her sister. "You're going to have to get out of Crimson City, you know. Even after the demons are gone, the veil will be weak. And I don't trust whoever started this whole mess not to start it again."

Sandy looked at the paper. "What the hell is—"

"You'll have to take care of Mom and Dad, too. They're getting up in age even if Dad won't admit it."

"Wait a damn minute—"

Xiao Fei crossed to the window and grabbed the plant. "You've taken good care of this." Then she snatched the tiny notebook beside it, and squinted at the long list of notations. "What's this?"

A long silence followed. It was long enough for Xiao Fei to look up at Sandy to see the girl—the *woman*, she mentally corrected—with a stern expression on her face. Finally, Sandy said, "Is it my turn to speak now?"

"Not if—"

Suddenly, the front door shook on its hinges. "Open up! Damn it, open this door! Xiao Fei! Are you in there? Damn it!"

Xiao Fei frowned at the frantic note in Patrick's voice. Then her eyes widened as she saw the doorknob jiggle. Would he break in? Sandy grimaced and quickly opened the door. She was nearly flattened as Patrick pushed through. He looked frazzled, anxious—and really, really cute.

"Friend of yours?" her sister asked.

Patrick was across the room before Xiao Fei could answer. She barely had time to set down the persimmon before she was enfolded in his arms. He both hugged and frisked her. "Are you okay?" he asked. "Are you hurt? Bleeding? Geez, what were you thinking? It's a damn war out there." He abruptly lifted her face and took possession of her mouth.

Xiao Fei didn't want to stand there making out in front of her little sister. She didn't want to melt into Patrick's arms, either, but she did just that. Their kiss was frantic, possessive, and totally absorbing. To the point that she forgot her little sister was standing right there watching the hot and heavy caress.

At least, she forgot until Patrick broke the kiss to ask very clearly, "Are you all right?"

"She's fine," Sandy answered. Xiao Fei was still a little too breathless. "I'm her sister, Sandy." Patrick tried to speak, but he was cut off as she added, "And I take it you're the reason she's just handed me her last will and testament?"

Patrick's gaze had gone to Xiao Fei, but it leaped back to her sister. "What?" he asked. He turned back to Xiao Fei. "What!"

"Calm down," Xiao Fei said.

"She has quite the flair for the dramatic, doesn't she?" Sandy drawled.

"What?" repeated Patrick.

"I mean, she's always been the quiet one, but every once in a while, I think she likes to stir things up. She comes up with a whammy that just throws everything into chaos."

"I do not!" exclaimed Xiao Fei.

Sandy laughed. "So, your dropping out of grad school wasn't announced in the most dramatic way possible? During Thanksgiving dinner in front of everyone? So you could become an *acupuncturist?*" Sandy turned to Patrick. "I thought Dad would have a coronary right there. Mom dropped the turkey."

"She did not! She just bobbled it."

"Onto the dining room floor."

"What?" Patrick repeated.

"So, sis," Sandy demanded, "no drama this time: Are you about to die?"

"Yes," Xiao Fei said.

Patrick exploded. "No!"

"You're being stupidly optimistic again, Mr. America."

"You're being stupidly pessimistic again, Miss Cambodia."

"Okeydokey," Sandy said, ignoring them both. She

calmly picked up the persimmon with her left hand. Her right hand shoved aside another pile of clothes—clean and neatly folded, this batch—before coming up with a long and sharp pair of scissors. "You're going to tell me everything right now, Xiao Fei, or your plant gets it." Her eyes narrowed. "And don't think I won't!"

"Don't!" Xiao Fei cried.

Patrick, the bastard, actually laughed. But Sandy just stood there, scissors extended around the base of the plant. One snip and it would be dead.

Patrick sobered. "You're not actually going to do it, are you? That's a really valuable plant."

"So, start talking," Sandy shot back.

Patrick sighed and looked at Xiao Fei, who sighed and looked at the plant. "There isn't time to tell you everything, *mei mei*," she said.

"Liar!" Sandy snapped.

"No, actually," Patrick interjected, "we *do* have to go."

Xiao Fei's gaze flew back to Patrick. "What? Why? It's not even three yet."

His thumb caressed her cheek. The gesture was loving, and Xiao Fei found herself pushing more fully into his hand. "There's lots of preparation to do. We've got to meditate, get to the park and set up—I've got an idea how to make a persimmon more powerful. If we mix it with—"

"Helllooo!" Sandy called, her patience obviously worn thin. "Imminent plant death here."

Xiao Fei had had enough. She disentangled from Patrick—not nearly as easily as she should have—and crossed to her sister. She gently took the persimmon plant away from the scissors, then turned to speak calmly and rationally to Sandy.

She burst into tears, instead.

Sandy wrapped her arms around Xiao Fei and held

on. "My god, what's going on?" she said against Xiao Fei's cheek. "You never cry. Except for that time when . . ." Sandy's head lifted as she peered at Patrick. "Oh, dear. You've fallen in love, haven't you?"

Xiao Fei nodded. Somewhere in the background, Patrick exclaimed, "What?" again, but she wasn't listening. Had she really fallen in love? Or was this just pre-death anxiety? Patrick was everything she'd ever fantasized about in a man: smart, powerful, and with a protective streak a mile wide. She felt safe around him. More important, she felt stronger when she was with him, as if his abilities gave her faith that they would survive. That was wrong, of course, but he made her believe despite the odds. But was that love? Did she love him?

Oh God, she did. She was in love. She whimpered.

"And you think the world's going to end because of it," Sandy continued in a soothing tone.

Xiao Fei nodded once more. The gesture was hidden against her sister's collarbone.

"Well . . . it had to happen sometime, you know."

Patrick repeated himself little more forcefully. "What?"

"It's okay," Sandy continued. Then she twisted to pin Patrick with a steely gaze. "You are going to do right by her, aren't you?"

"What?" he answered. "I mean, yes, of course. But . . . what?"

"Oh, wow. The both of you are bumbling idiots, aren't you?" Sandy pulled back from Xiao Fei, her gaze remaining on Patrick. "Look, she's new to this love stuff." Then she frowned. "Exactly who are you?"

"Er, Patrick Lewis."

"He's a botany professor in San Bernardino," Xiao Fei managed.

"And he seems very nice," Sandy soothed. "Just how far have you gone together?"

"W-what?" Patrick stammered.

"Sandy!"

The girl shrugged. "Well, a sister's gotta know these things." She narrowed her eyes at the two of them, one after the other. "It's tonight, isn't it?"

"Uhh . . ." Patrick said.

"Hence the hysterics," Sandy explained. "With the demon attack and everything. Only you, Xiao Fei, would do this now." She shook her head. "My rational, paranoid sister is having sex for the first time in the middle of a war. Who'd've thunk it?"

"What?" Xiao Fei couldn't manage anything more coherent. Her sister had always been able to figure out way more than she was supposed to, which was highly disconcerting. But then again, perhaps that was why she'd come—for the plant, yes, but also in the hope that she'd see Sandy one last time, long enough to get some perspective.

"Look," the girl said to Xiao Fei. She took on a motherly tone. "Don't do it tonight. Wait a bit. You're obviously a little anxious about this love stuff. Take your time. Wait until the demons are gone and things settle down, then go out to dinner and a movie. Afterward set out some candles and stuff. Do it right."

"You don't understand," Xiao Fei murmured.

"Of course I don't," the girl drawled. "*I've* never been in love before." They both knew that Sandy fell in and out of love with alarming frequency.

"No—," Xiao Fei began.

"You're absolutely right," Patrick interrupted, his voice rushed but no less clear. "We'll wait. Once the demons are taken care of, we'll go out to dinner—

someplace nice with linen napkins and twenty different pieces of silverware."

"Exactly," Sandy answered.

"Yeah," Patrick said. Then he grabbed Xiao Fei's arm. "Now that that's settled, we've got to go." He snatched the persimmon off the end table. "I take it you came here for this?"

"Yeah," Xiao Fei answered. "Plus the dried fruit."

"I've only got a couple." Sandy quickly crossed to the kitchen and began banging her way through the cupboards. Patrick took the time to step behind Xiao Fei and wrap her in his arms. Surprised, she leaned gratefully back into his warmth. "Got it!" her sister cried, brandishing a plastic bag of dried fruit.

Xiao Fei held out her hand. "Thanks." She wiggled out of Patrick's hold to wrap her sister in another long hug.

When they separated, her sister's eyes were troubled. "It's not just about love, is it? These demons really are hunting you. Because of your blood?"

Xiao Fei nodded. "But we'll be okay. We're going to disappear tonight." How easily she lied, even with tears blurring her vision. "I'm in danger as long as there are demons."

"Then don't—"

"I'll protect her," Patrick interrupted, stepping forward. "I've got skills and friends." He placed a warm hand on Xiao Fei's shoulder. "Trust me; I'll take care of her."

Sandy looked hard at him; then her gaze dropped back to her sister. "You trust him?" she asked.

Xiao Fei nodded. "With my life."

Sandy abruptly contorted over her couch, presenting her backside while leaning down. A moment later she came back up with her purse. "Right. So where are we going?"

Xiao Fei shook her head. "I trust him with *my* life, not yours."

"But—"

"You're safer away from me. Far, far away."

Her sister huffed, making her ponytail bounce. "I don't care."

"I do."

"But—"

"I can't take you," Patrick interrupted gently. "There isn't room."

Sandy folded her arms. "So, what, I'm supposed to just sit here and worry?"

"You were supposed to get out of L.A." Xiao Fei snapped.

"Yeah, well, that plan's blown."

"She'll be all right," Patrick whispered in Xiao Fei's ear. "The worst will be over tonight."

Sandy's eyes narrowed. "Why? What happens tonight?"

Patrick straightened. The change in his body was so significant that even Xiao Fei twisted to see him more clearly. Gone was the tender and somewhat goofy man of a moment before. In his place stood the Draig-Uisge—confident, military, and obviously deadly. "Trust me," he said.

"Oh . . ." Sandy's voice was a hushed whisper.

"The worst will be over tonight. But you ought to lie low. Just in case."

"And Xiao Fei?" her sister said, obviously awed by the change in him, but still not cowed.

"She'll be with me."

"In danger?"

He shrugged. "No more than she is now." He glanced over at Xiao Fei. "Speaking of which, you put Sandy at risk every moment that we stand here."

Xiao Fei nodded. She knew it was true. "We can go now." She started moving for the door, the persimmon plant clutched to her chest.

"I want a full explanation," Sandy called, her voice trembling slightly. "After this is all over, I want details and answers."

"Of course," Patrick said.

"Love you," Xiao Fei called. Then she ducked out the door before she could change her mind.

Patrick took hold of Xiao Fei's hand as she rushed out of the apartment building. He didn't blame her; it couldn't be easy saying good-bye to a sister face-to-face. And that made him feel really guilty about not saying anything to his own siblings. But right now, he had something more important on his mind.

Heedless of how exposed they were on the street, he tugged Xiao Fei into the doorway of a closed store and turned her face to his.

"Patrick," she said.

"Did you mean it? Did you mean what she said?"

"What are you talking about?" Her gaze slid away. She knew exactly what he was referring to, but she still tried to evade the question.

"Do you love me?" His throat was tight, but he pushed the words through anyway.

"Do *you* love *me?*" she shot back.

"I asked first."

"I don't care."

"Xiao Fei!"

"Yes!" She shoved him away so that his back hit the glass door behind him. "Okay? Yes, I think I'm falling in love with you. How's that for bad timing?"

Something inside him went all soft and warm.

"Well?" she shot back.

He frowned. "Well, what?"

"Well, do you love me back, stupid?"

"I . . ." So many things crowded into his mind: the demons, the druids, tonight's task. "I . . ."

"Never mind," she grumbled. "I can see that you don't."

"That's not true!" he lied. "I . . . I . . ." Xiao Fei turned away from him, but he grabbed her arm to keep her beside him. "I . . . I . . ."

"I heard that part," she snapped. Then her expression softened. "It's okay, Patrick. You don't have to love me, too."

He wanted to say the words. God only knew how much he wanted to say them. He'd already told her he thought she was the love of his life. He'd already said it, so why wouldn't the words come now? "I . . . I can't think," he stammered.

"It's not about thinking, you idiot. It's about feeling." Then she let herself fall back against the brick wall behind her, let her head drop to lean so she could stare up into the sky. "You are so damn American," she said. Then she abruptly extended the heel of her hand, and thunked him on the forehead.

"Ow!"

"Stop thinking, Patrick; what do you *feel?*" she asked.

"Afraid," he said, though that wasn't the word he'd meant to escape his lips. What if he really did have to kill her? What if she really was the love of his life, and he had to choose between her and Earth? "I'm terrified."

She thunked him on the forehead again. "Well, duh—there are demons after us."

"You don't understand, Xiao Fei. I can't say it aloud. Not until tomorrow."

She stared at him. "Okay, I take it back—you're not a damn American; you're a damn guy." She turned and started stomping away, mocking him with every step. " 'I can't say it aloud?' Bullshit!" she shot over her shoulder. "You do love me, you prick. You . . . Oh, shit."

Patrick had been watching the sway of her hips as she stomped away from him, but her abrupt halt jolted him back to awareness. He looked up, then looked around.

There were demons everywhere.

Chapter Nineteen

Oh, shit was right. Xiao Fei was completely exposed, standing at the curb of the street. Patrick was only marginally better protected in the storefront, but that was of little help against the eight demons slowly straightening from behind parked cars.

He reacted as fast as he could, which unfortunately was pathetically slow. He sprang from the door and tackled Xiao Fei. She had already been diving, so their combined momentum threw them into the shadow of a large tree—no real ground cover here—but then he was able to roll them under the carriage of a big truck. They dropped off the sidewalk with a tooth-jarring thud, but at least they were better protected.

It had been the right move. A big flash of searing heat burned the ground where Xiao Fei had been standing. A boom echoed through the air and ground, leaving a crater the size of a basketball in the concrete. Damn, that had been close.

Xiao Fei was squirming beneath him, so Patrick shifted. The truck wasn't going to give them much cover, especially if the bastards had more weapons like those big fireball things. Their only hope was to shoot the demons before the truck blew up above them.

Too bad he didn't have a gun—and how big of an idiot did he feel for that particular oversight? He'd been so worried about Xiao Fei's running off by herself, he'd failed to check the basics. Fortunately, he wasn't completely defenseless. He'd been trying to conserve his strength, but now wasn't the time for prudence. Concentrating hard on the first demon to appear, he prepared to twist the creature's energy so badly that its body would shut down and it would die. But Xiao Fei blew a big hole in the demon's skull first.

Patrick jerked his head sideways to watch her sight another with a big pistol. "Where'd you get a gun?" he asked.

She squeezed the trigger as another demon appeared. It dropped. "Peter had a whole stash of them. Didn't you see?"

Nope. But then he often had tunnel vision when he was with her. He decided to focus on the approaching demons. "I've got the fat one on the right," he muttered.

"How?" He could hear her surprise.

He didn't answer; he just focused. He took hold of the demon's energy and corrupted it. The act made him sick to his stomach. He'd done it only once before, and the effect had been gruesome—to Jason, and to Patrick's own soul. He felt twisted and evil whenever he worked this magic, but it was "us or them" time. He chose "us." Especially since he didn't view these particular demons as innocent victims. They were invading Crimson City, not the other way around.

So he concentrated—hard. The amulet flared against his chest, and he gasped at the burning flash of pain, but at least the power worked. He caught the demon's energy and twisted. It wasn't as quick a death as a bullet between the eyes, but it was more dramatic. The demon in question fell to its knees and began convulsing. Another mental twist by Patrick, and half the creature's chest imploded. The remaining demons stared at their companion, mouths hanging open in shock. Apparently they'd seen gunfire before and were completely unfazed by it. But to see one of their own start foaming at the mouth . . . The monsters became completely unglued.

A horrendous bellow split the air, making Xiao Fei jerk next to Patrick. It was the demons' battle cry—eerie and unnerving—as they rushed the truck. Xiao Fei fired with deafening frequency, but there were just too many of them. Patrick dropped another two, settling for immobilization over murder. He twisted the energy around their knees and legs, making the demons fall on their faces. But though the creatures howled with rage, they kept coming, even if they had to dig their claws in the dirt and crawl.

Thankfully the demons didn't seem to have more of those fireball things. They had knives, swords, and claws, though. Five bad guys still coming. Wait, that didn't compute. Damn, were more showing up? He and Xiao Fei were doomed.

"I'm running out of bullets," she said.

"I'm getting tired" he replied. It was a lie. He'd been cross-eyed tired before they began. "Any suggestions?"

"Run?"

He'd already come to that conclusion, too. But to where? And for how long? He didn't want to rely on the hope that they could outrun these monsters. "Peter's car is around the corner. I brought it. Go first; I'll cover you."

"Bull, druid boy, you've got to concentrate. All I've got to do is aim. You go!"

He didn't have time to argue. He rolled out from under the truck while she squeezed off a few more rounds. Then, when one of the demons started kicking at the truck—okay, some of these guys weren't so bright—Patrick reached underneath and hauled Xiao Fei out by her feet.

She rolled as he pulled, leaping up the moment she cleared the vehicle. Wow. It felt like they had practiced the maneuver a million times. Too bad the demons weren't equally impressed.

He and Xiao Fei took off down the street as the demons let out another unholy roar. A throwing blade thudded into a tree just ahead of Patrick's chest. He hunched his shoulders and pushed Xiao Fei ahead of him. Let the knives hit him; she was the one who would quickly bleed to death.

"Hurry," she gasped.

He didn't waste the time to look behind them; he knew the demons were gaining from the sound of their feet thudding on the pavement. Xiao Fei twisted enough to shoot over her shoulder, but her grimace told him she'd missed.

Patrick put on another burst of speed, but he already knew it was hopeless. There was no way they could outrun trained warrior demons.

Other shots rang out. Someone else was shooting now. Great. The demons must have guns, too—except he sensed that they didn't. Patrick frowned, concentrating enough to feel the negative energy behind him. Where were the demons? Where were the people?

"Don't stop!" a woman screamed. That wasn't Xiao Fei's voice. It was someone else. Her sister?

"Sandy? Get inside!" Xiao Fei bellowed.

Patrick turned to see more than just Sandy. From windows and doorways up and down the street, people were shooting at the demons. He saw Xiao Fei's sister, a couple of security guards, plus a middle-aged guy in a sweatshirt. All four of them were taking potshots at the demons, who were getting peppered from all sides.

That was when he heard the motorcycles: a distant roar that must have been coming for a while, but was now loud enough to overpower the gunfire. Patrick spun, ready to face a new threat, but the three huge choppers that hurtled around the corner weren't ridden by demons. No, and if he wasn't mistaken, that was Hank; Hank's girlfriend, Slick; and Dread. And they all had shotguns.

Dread lived up to his name, blowing the nearest demon into shredded oblivion. Hank and Slick skidded to a stop beside Patrick. "Get on!"

Patrick didn't hesitate. He lifted Xiao Fei up and dropped her on Hank's lap, suffering only a few qualms in the process. Hank would protect her, and he'd probably cop only a couple feels.

"No! Sandy!" Xiao Fei screamed.

With one final shotgun blast from Dread, the last of the demons dropped. Just to be sure, the biker reloaded and shot a few of the ones still on the ground.

Hank bellowed at him, "Save the ammo!"

Xiao Fei was still struggling, but Sandy waved her away. "Go!" she cried. "We're safe here!"

"I'll stay!" Dread called back, maneuvering his bike about the street, checking demon bodies.

Xiao Fei looked like she wanted to argue, but Hank didn't give her the chance. With an impressive spin-skid-roar maneuver, he took off down the street. Patrick climbed up behind Slick, who followed a few seconds later.

"Where are we going?" Patrick bellowed into Slick's ear. The biker just shrugged. Her job was to follow Hank. Fortunately, Patrick soon recognized the area.

They were headed for Hank's third-favorite place in the world: a biker bar with good pool tables. His first two favorite places were strip joints, so the man had obviously decided on some decorum. And actually, Patrick grudgingly admitted, this was a good choice; their bikes fit right in with the other couple dozen parked nearby. And, if he had to guess, there were probably a few more guns inside, with the people needed to use them.

Xiao Fei would be safer in there than just about anywhere in Crimson City.

He was feeling a good deal better by the time he made it into the bar's dark interior. It was a bright afternoon in sunny Southern California, but inside it might as well have been midnight. Especially since every table was filled and, miracle of miracles, the television still worked. Thank God for satellite. Unfortunately, the news was less than happy.

L.A. was quarantined by what looked like every military force known to mankind, the National Guard being the least of it. Patrick saw uniforms from the Air Force, Army, and Navy. He also saw tanks, ballistic missiles, and guys sporting big, big, very big guns. According to one reporter, specially trained troops were moving into

L.A., doing sweeps and taking out pockets of demon resistance, but some of the bad guys were proving remarkably elusive.

"That's because they can shapeshift, you dingbats," drawled Hank over his first beer. He had his arm draped around Slick, belly on the bar, and his free hand digging through a bowl of stale peanuts. Patrick just grinned. Some sights felt right on so many levels, especially as he pulled Xiao Fei into the circle of his arms.

He finally processed what his fellow druid had said. "The demons can *what?*"

Hank nodded. "Yeah, I got a contact at B-Ops. The damn things can look like anybody else. Or some of them can."

"How do we know who they are?" Xiao Fei gasped.

"They shoot at you," Slick answered.

"And they feel different," Patrick said.

Hank rolled his eyes. "Maybe to you, o great Draig-Uisge, but for the rest of us . . ."

Slick slammed down her hand. "If they shoot, we shoot back. Works for the cops; works for us."

Patrick turned back to the news report. There were satellite images of the half destroyed Harbor Freeway, the blackened fields of LAX, and the explosives exchange outside of B-Ops. "I thought they didn't use guns," he said as he stared at a fuzzy image of demons clustered behind a rocket launcher.

"They learned fast. Actually, it seems they've been infiltrating the city for a while, impersonating key people and learning our weaknesses. That first attack took out the docks, the airport, the Times Building, and a bunch of cell towers. They knew what they were doing."

"So, why haven't they completely taken over?" Xiao Fei asked.

The bartender came over, plunked another beer down, and added his two cents. "Because they ain't got the smarts. Sure, they knew how to attack us at first, but now we know they're here. They ain't got the numbers, and they ain't got the smarts. When it comes right down to it, most of them attack with knives."

Nods came from all around. Also, a whole bunch of guns were abruptly revealed strapped to hips, legs, or crisscrossed over chests.

"Nice crowd you got here," Xiao Fei remarked as she looked around. She sounded admiring. "I think I'll have another drink." Since she was drinking soda, Patrick didn't even blink. He was too busy analyzing battle tactics.

Except for the fireball thing, the demons who'd attacked them relied mostly on knives and claws. They were hardy, but not steel-plated. A shotgun blast to the chest took them out as fast as anything else.

He scanned the crowd, thinking hard. Then he looked at Hank. "You trust these guys? You think they want to take out some demon ass?"

"Hell, yes," answered the bartender.

Hank was slower to nod, scanning the crowd, but in the end he agreed. "I think I can control a few of them." He glanced at the bartender. "You know who I want?"

"You got 'em. When and where?"

Hank didn't hesitate. "Sunset. Griffith Park, just off the Ferndell Trail."

"Yeah," Patrick concurred—and off went the bartender, presumably to pass the word.

"So, you're expecting trouble," Xiao Fei commented. "Getting more help. Being more cautious. That's very Asian. Glad to see I'm rubbing off on you."

"It's not 'Asian,'" Patrick retorted, irritation lacing his

tone. "It's prudent." He frowned. "I don't know if the demons will find us, but I damn well am not going into that grove unprepared."

She shrugged. "They'll find us. They do it the same way you find me—you feel me."

He frowned again, even more frustrated. "What do you mean?"

She turned and stared at him. "What do you mean, what do I mean?" She blinked. "Are you saying you can feel the demon energy, but you can't feel mine?"

"No, of course I can feel yours!" he snapped. "It's like a damn sun. You blind me, woman—so much that I can't feel anything else!" His voice was almost a shout, loud enough that when he finished bellowing, the entire bar was silent. Someone had even muted the TV.

Patrick stared around the bar, his face starting to burn with humiliation.

"Oh, man, you got it bad, don't you?" Hank said.

Patrick swung to face his friend, finding an outlet in the leather-clad, muscle-bound tough guy. "No, I do not 'have it bad,' Hank. I do not 'have *it*' at all. What the hell are you thinking? We're fighting a goddamned war here."

Hank blinked, barely hiding a smirk. Beside him, Slick gave a thumbs-up to Xiao Fei.

Patrick gave a grunt of disgust, slammed his empty glass down on the bar, and stomped out. Of course, once outside, there was nowhere for him to go. The sun was up, the sound of helicopters thumped through the air, and a couple of vamps ducked and swerved around treetops trying to hide.

Patrick frowned. No, those weren't vamps. It was full daylight, and these guys were barely dressed. These were demons then. Flying demons.

He dropped down on the curb, feeling defeated. He didn't even know why he felt so awful. Exhaustion? Maybe. Anxiety about tonight? A little. But none of that was unusual. The steady drain of Earth's energy through the portal was giving him a royal headache, but he'd already taken a double dose of painkillers and that was fading. Which meant what?

"So, you're in love and you're not handling it well," drawled Hank, stepping through the bar door. He passed Patrick a beer as he plopped onto the ground beside him. "You intellectual types always make things complicated."

"You don't understand!" Patrick turned to his friend, struggling with words. "Yeah, I feel . . . *everything* for her. She's everything—and more."

Hank shrugged. "What's the problem? Buy her some flowers, get it on, and get it off. If it's really good, get her a ring. Been a while since we've had a good druid wedding."

Patrick groaned and let his head drop into his hands. The helicopter noise was louder now. As was the sudden eruption of gunfire. "She nearly died this afternoon, Hank. We've got demons everywhere searching for her. I can't protect her."

Hank clapped a meaty arm around his shoulders. "That's why you've got us. We've got your back, bro. She'll be fine."

Patrick shook his head. "No, she won't."

"Course she will. We'll do the ritual thingy tonight. Wham, bam, gate's slammed. Then you and her have a nice little wedding, followed by a nice big honeymoon. Nothing could be easier."

"I'm burnt," Patrick groaned. "There's almost no power left in me."

Hank looked surprised. "But you've got enough to close the gate, right? I mean, I thought you weren't the power source anyway. You . . ." He gestured vaguely with his hand. "You shape the patterns, right? *She's* the power source."

"Her blood," he agreed.

"Right. The Cambodian female hemophiliac—how whacked is that?"

If only Hank knew. Patrick felt his body clench so tight that his breath came as a shallow pant. Oh, God, he was about to be sick. He abruptly dived to the side, wrapping himself around the corner of the building as he heaved.

"Damn, man," Hank said from somewhere above his left shoulder, "a little demon blood gets spilled and you—"

"It's not the goddamned blood, you idiot," Patrick growled between gasps. "It's Xiao Fei's blood. That's the power source—her blood."

"Yeah, yeah, I get that," said the other druid.

Patrick straightened, stripping off his shirt to wipe his face. "And do you get that she's a small woman, Hank? Do you get that the last time anyone did this, it took thirty of her kind? Thirty small women to close the gate?"

Hank blinked. "Thirty?" he echoed lamely. "But . . . do we even have thirty of them?" At last, the man understood.

"There's just Xiao Fei and me."

"But . . . you ain't got any juice left. You just said so."

"I know."

"Oh, fuck." Hank looked away from Patrick, his gaze rising to the treetops, where a few dozen demons had just erupted across the skyline, all aiming for the helicopter. They flew fast—damn fast. Too fast for the pilot to compensate. Within seconds the demons swarmed the machine. The thing dipped and swerved and went into a dive. Moments later a booming crash rolled through the streets. A pillar of fire rose up into the air.

"We gotta close that gate, Draig-Uisge," Hank said softly.

Patrick didn't answer. He knew what had to be done.

Hank suddenly refocused his eyes on Patrick. "I've been practicing. I can kinda feel energy. Can I help?"

Patrick closed his eyes to scan his friend. He desperately hoped to find the same type of power inside Hank that he sensed in Xiao Fei, but try as he might, the answer remained the same. He shook his head. "You're honing the same skill I have—to shape energy. What we need is *more*."

"But the Earth's got energy," Hank suggested.

"Less and less every second it bleeds into the demon world."

Hank took a step forward. "But it's still got it, right? It's still got power. Can't you use that?"

Patrick nodded. "Yeah, sure. That's the plan." But his voice lacked conviction, and they both knew it wouldn't work. If things were that easy, they wouldn't need Xiao Fei. It wouldn't have taken the blood of twenty-nine Phoenix Tears in Cambodia to close the last portal.

"Well, sheeeeit." Hank spun away from him, grabbed Patrick's beer, and downed the last of it. Patrick sat beside his friend, and they both stared morosely at the pavement.

"She know?" Hank finally asked.

Patrick nodded.

Hank cursed again. "So, what're you gonna do?"

"Everything I can."

Hank tossed the beer bottle into a rusty garbage can. "Earth comes first, right? I mean, I know you love her and all. Still, Earth comes first. It has to."

Patrick didn't answer. He couldn't say it.

Hank wouldn't let him off so easily. The man twisted to stare him right in the eye. "Earth comes first—right, Draig-Uisge?" he repeated. "I mean, we're the entire planet: billions of people, plus birds and plants and shit. We come first, right?"

Patrick nodded. He had to; it was the truth. "Yeah," he finally said, because Hank wasn't going to release him until he admitted the truth. "Earth comes before Xiao Fei."

"Yes," came a soft female voice from behind him. Both Patrick and Hank twisted to find Xiao Fei standing in the door. "Yes," she repeated, "Earth comes first." Then she spun on her heel and walked out into the open parking lot.

Patrick cursed under his breath and leaped to his feet. "Xiao Fei! Xiao Fei!" he called.

"Shut up," she snapped when he caught up with her. "Just shut up. I know what's important. I was raised in a monastery, remember? All of us Phoenix Tears were raised to live a life of service. I know the score, I can connect the dots. I—"

"What the hell are you talking about?" Patrick grabbed hold of her arm and held her steady. Then he thought better of it and tucked her close. Surprisingly, she let him.

"I'm being American," she grumbled against his naked torso. "I'm speaking in sports and leisure metaphors."

"Of course you are," he murmured. Then he bent down and claimed her lips. The kiss was tender and sweet—or at least it started out that way. Then Xiao Fei wrapped her arms around his neck and tried to inhale him. He wasn't the least bit resistant, and so, within moments, they were wrapped around each other.

A low whistle sounded behind him. It was Slick, not

Hank. Patrick knew because Hank promptly tried to quiet her.

"Don't shush me," Slick snapped. "They should get a room. And what the hell happened to his shirt?"

Patrick broke the kiss, but it was a really hard thing to do. Xiao Fei looked equally reluctant. He stared down into her eyes, seeing tears glitter there. "Xiao Fei—"

"Yeah. Exactly where *is* your shirt?" she asked.

"I, uh . . ."

"He hurled," Hank supplied. Then, to make up for it, he offered Patrick a spare tee he pulled from the compartment on the back of his motorcycle.

Xiao Fei wrinkled her nose. "Really?" She shook her head. "And they say Asians can't hold their liquor."

Given that he'd been drinking soda, Patrick felt particularly wounded by that remark, but he couldn't comment because he was pulling on the too-short tee. When he had it stretched down almost to his belt, he opened his mouth to say something really clever. Xiao Fei beat him to the punch.

"Why'd you bother? We're going to have to get naked soon enough." Then, while his mind and body were still dealing with that, she rolled her eyes. "Don't speak. Just get on the bike and let's go save the planet." Then she gestured to Slick. Within moments, the two women were mounted and had roared away.

Hank stared at Patrick, a dazed expression on his face. "I can't decide if you're the luckiest bastard on the planet or the most cursed."

Patrick looked at his friend, the reality of the situation descending once again. Hank, too, slowly sobered. As they climbed onto his bike, Hank shook his head.

"Yeah," Hank said on a sigh. "Your life sucks."

Chapter Twenty

Life had patterns and rhythms, internal beats that became so ingrained that they usually remained unnoticeable. Even life in a war zone had its own beat, but unlike the Americans who surrounded her in Peter's office reception area, that rhythm was familiar to Xiao Fei.

She slid easily into that constant anxiety that left a body hunched and the eyes restless. The druids who surrounded her were jumpy, like nervous birds, punctuating their talk with unnecessary laughter or abbreviated sentences. They kept trying to reestablish the old rhythm—the safe one—and yet remain vigilant and hyperaware. That mixture too was a rhythm, but it was one that could not be sustained for long.

Patrick, of course, was tending to his own rhythms. After returning to what was now druid central, Patrick had gone into professor mode. He'd taken the plant and fruit she'd gotten from Sandy and disappeared into a lab. An hour later, he'd given her a vial containing a deep red juice.

"Drink this. It'll boost your power," he'd said. "And your blood volume."

She'd downed it without a word. He'd stayed beside her long enough to stroke a tender caress down her cheek, then Peter had demanded his attention. Seems there was some problem with drumming up vamps and werewolves to help tonight.

But that was an hour ago. Whatever the difficulty, Patrick had solved it. Especially since Keeli, the head werewolf, and her vampire friend were now slipping into the room. Xiao Fei heard them apologize to Patrick. Something about the werewolf who had betrayed them being punished. Xiao Fei tuned it out. That was irrelevant now. She barely even acknowledged Pei Ling and crew who were also arriving. Now wasn't time to acknowledge friends.

Patrick must have felt the same way, because moments later she saw him withdraw from the crowd. He sat down to meditate in the opposite corner, a silent statue that exuded power and peace. The part of Xiao Fei that remained a woman longed to sit next to him, to share his quiet and merge with him, but she could not. That was not her function anymore. Not during this war when she was a vessel for power and not a human being at all.

She turned away from Patrick, and ignored the twitters of the others. Everyone was gathering in Peter's front office, because the druid leader had not bothered to tell them to stay away. Which meant, if sensed, they presented a big target to the demons. But Xiao Fei was dampening her power right now, masking her energy signature as best as she could. Hopefully the demons wouldn't pick up on her until it was too late.

In the meantime she sat apart, speaking to no one, watching all but thinking nothing. That was her wartime rhythm: silence, and the slow stripping away of everything that was not duty, responsibility, and sacrifice. That was what she'd learned back in Cambodia, and now she returned to it in America. There was no escape. She was the blood sacrifice. She allowed her mind and body to be consumed by the power in her blood, and in this way she became a Phoenix Tear.

She took off her shirt. A Phoenix needed no clothing. In the background the room went absolutely silent. She ignored it. A Phoenix did not worry about human embarrassments. She pulled her hair away from her face as best she could. It was too short for a ponytail, but she fashioned a headband out of someone's red scarf. That could serve as a tourniquet if things went better than expected.

Next she pulled out a pocketknife to gently, meticulously scrape away the scar tissue at every tattooed tear or curving feather, except one. She started at her wrist, and bit by bit moved up her arm to the beak and eye, neck, spine, even the stretched wing along and between her breasts. When she was finished, the skin was thin but not broken. But the smallest pressure of a fingernail would begin the bloodletting.

In truth, she went too deep on more than one occasion, and then there was the lengthy process of chanting and sealing the wound—but that too served its purpose. It brought awareness of her power to her conscious mind, and settled it into the manipulation of her flesh and blood.

When she finally finished, she started to slide the knife into her jeans pocket, only to remember that she would need to be in a robe or tunic. So she straightened instead, and pulled open her pants.

Someone coughed nervously, but she barely noticed. In Cambodia this process was done by the monks. It was a worshipful moment, meant to reinforce her existence as a vessel for power and not as a woman at all. This act was witnessed and praised. It was only fitting that these druids watch.

She shimmed out of her jeans until she stood naked and proud, a Phoenix Tear in all her splendor. With a steady hand, she held her legs and cut lightly at the skin on the tattooed tears right above her femoral arteries. There were only two tears there—a single large one high on each leg—and no scar tissue at all. A cut at either spot would be deadly, but would also ensure the fastest blood flow.

Now her preparations were complete. There would be more ritual at the sacred grove. She would consume more fruit. She would chant and pray to first clear her thoughts before accentuating her power. But for now, there was little else to do.

For the first time in the last two hours, she allowed her attention to focus outward. She lifted her gaze to see the druids all staring at her, each with a varying degree of shock or horror etched upon his face. But then the crowd parted. Without a sound or apparent signal, people stepped back and away to allow the Draig-Uisge passage. She wanted to smile at Patrick, but the rhythm of the room was too serious, and she was not a woman now who could smile or think or feel.

Patrick held something in his hands—a white druid robe—which he offered her with bowed head. She reached to take it, but he immediately straightened, lifting the fabric high. He meant to dress her, so she extended her arms upward and he settled it reverently upon her.

It was a simple thing: white cotton with a hood, the cut too large for her, the hem trailing all the way to her ankles. It was too ponderous for a Phoenix Tear, and there would be no way for her to easily access her bleeding points. So, when he stepped back, she reopened her pocketknife. She cut away the arms at the shoulders, slit a long vertical line at the neck, and another long slice up each leg. The result looked like a child's first costuming attempt, but at least she would be able to perform her function. Then she handed the knife to the Draig-Uisge. He took it, but with a troubled expression.

"I will manage the bloodletting in all places save one," she said in a quiet voice. But it was so silent in the room that her voice seemed to reverberate in the air.

"Xiao Fei," Patrick said, but she shook her head.

"I am the Phoenix Tear," she replied, then was momentarily shocked by the power invested in her title. As a child, she'd thought it nothing, of no more importance than saying she was a third grader or one of the Ron family. But as an adult, there was a resonance in her words, a meaning and a stateliness in her existence. For the first time in her life, she felt pride in that title, honor in her unique ability.

She straightened her shoulders and tilted her head to expose the long tattooed feather that extended up her neck. "The feather outlines where you can cut—"

"The jugular," he said.

She nodded. He understood.

"I'm not cutting you there." He said it so firmly, so clearly that she knew he believed what he said. He had no intention of letting her bleed to death. But they both knew when it came time to choose, he would do the right thing. She was so surprised that her vision blurred with tears.

She swallowed her self-pity. She was not a woman or a person, she reminded herself. She was a vessel for power, and as such there would be no remorse, only honor for her sacrifice. "Do not fear to do what is necessary, Draig-Uisge. I am prepared. I am a Phoenix Tear." Then she turned to look at all the others in the room, one by one, as their horrified expressions fixated on her neck. "For Earth," she said loudly.

As one, they echoed the words back to her:

"For Earth."

She glanced outside. It was nearing sunset. In truth, they waited for moonrise, not sunset, but either way, it was time to go. "Gather your weapons; sharpen your wits. The time for sacrifice has come," she said.

Patrick grabbed her arm. "There will be no sacrifice."

She slanted him an arch look. "Of course there will be. My blood. Your will." She glanced significantly at the druids around them. "Their witness and *defense*."

She saw his eyes widen, and he looked about him in renewed understanding. Clearly he had been focused on the two of them. That was his function and his duty, but he had forgotten the danger to the ones around them. These brave men and women might die tonight, simply to buy him and her time to complete their task. There *would* be sacrifice. The only question was how much.

Patrick's eyes grew tragic and he opened his mouth to speak, but whatever he would have said was lost as Peter appeared in full regalia. The head druid's entrance was all that it should be for a great hierophant, then was ruined as the man began to pontificate. In the end, neither Patrick nor Xiao Fei stayed to hear it all. After a glance at Hank and Slick, the four slipped out, mounted their motorcycles, and left.

* * *

Xiao Fei looked about the sacred grove and tried not to laugh. Trust Americans to choose a holy grove not more than a hundred feet from a park picnic area complete with garbage cans and wasps' nests. And yet, standing here, she could feel the ancient power pulsing through the ground, whispering through the trees, even singing with the birds and insects that buzzed in the air. This was indeed a holy place, and yet wholly American.

"I love it here," she murmured, walking a slow circle in the clearing. The space was not dominated by one tree, as was the Cambodian site, but was circled by trees both ancient and young, leaving a rough center of peace.

No one had come early to clean the place, so the first thing they all did was walk about and pick up trash, the druids chanting softly with every step.

Xiao Fei turned to Patrick, a question in her eyes. He answered in a hushed whisper. "We bless our site every time we visit, and then we ask for a blessing back."

She watched Hank place a large hand on the bark of a stately oak, his eyes closed in reverence. "How often do you come here?" she whispered.

"Someone comes every night. It is one way we do service to the Earth and the spirits here."

She understood. She also took a moment to perform her own ritual. Kneeling in the center of the space, she performed three kowtows and chanted a prayer of reverence and thanks. When the last kowtow was complete, she stayed on the ground, her face pressed into the grass, and she mentally expanded her awareness.

She connected first with the birds in the trees. Perching on a maple branch with a wren, she felt her heart beat in the small, rapid flutter of one of Earth's tiniest creatures. She grew outward from there. She touched and synchronized with the pulse of the maple, from the highest branch to the tiny roots that burrowed deep into the ground. She knew the insects that crawled in the bark, and greeted the wind and sky that whispered through the branches. And deep down, she expanded into the slowest pulse of the dark stones and the hot tempest of the world's molten core.

She had done this ritual before. Most especially in Cambodia before closing the gate there, but other times as well. It was her deepest meditation, for when she most needed to remember where she came from. She came from the Earth, and from the blessing of the Great One that was in all things.

Slowly, she rose from her prone position until she sat on her knees in the dirt. In Cambodia, the ritual of joining had ended there, and perhaps that was the mistake of the monks. Thanks to Patrick's teaching, she was able to expand her awareness one step further. She knew what she had to do. Not only was she one with nature, but she was joined with the people of Earth—the human and humanlike. Werewolf, vampire, even ghost and nature spirit, all were accepted as part of that which was of Earth—that which strengthened and exploited Earth's gifts, which gave and received from her bounty.

As she rose to her feet in the clearing, she felt herself as one with all. She was Earth: powerful, all enduring, a source of strength and energy to bless aeons of children. And she was dying. Xiao Fei felt the corruption, the pollution, the wounds that ate away at her strength. And she felt the hole that was the demon gate, the sudden and crippling drain of a power trying to sustain not one planet, but two.

It wasn't possible. She was struggling to support her

own children. There was not enough of her to pour into another world as well.

Then came another soul into her awareness. Xiao Fei saw him as a man and yet more than a man. She recognized the water dragon—the Draig-Uisge—that shaped spirit and power. He was solid where she was liquid. He was sinuous strength where she was molten fire. And he was the force that would seal her wound.

"It's time, Xiao Fei. The moon's up, and the grove has welcomed us. The druids protect us." He pressed something into her hand: a phoenix persimmon.

Closing her eyes, she allowed the Earth to direct her actions. She raised the fruit and pressed it to Patrick's lips.

"But . . ." he began. Then, accepting the change, he bowed his head. He allowed her to push the fruit through his lips. She waited in silence as he ate. The blue light that was Patrick chewed and swallowed. Moments later, he seemed to understand. He mimicked her actions, lifting another of the fruits and pressing it to her lips.

She too ate.

"I'm sorry about doing this out in the open," he said. "They've turned their backs. They're watching for demons. . . ."

She pressed her fingers to his lips, silencing his words. Some distant part of Xiao Fei knew she stood in the center of a circle with people all around. She even knew that demons were already massing to strike. They already felt the locus of power that was her—that was the Earth—centering here. But the greater part of her was already merged with the planet. Nothing mattered but she who supported them all. The ones who did or did not watch this lovemaking were merely the tiniest fraction of that bigger reality.

Then Xiao Fei felt it: the phoenix persimmon flowing into her blood and energy. She felt it in her body and in Patrick's. For the Draig-Uisge, there was a surge and a focusing. His energy became brighter, tighter, more like a laser beam than an incandescent light.

"Begin," she whispered.

He flushed, and she felt his hands touch her arm—tentative, trembling, with anxiety in every caress.

"I understand now," she whispered. "I know what you do and why." She was the Earth, powerful and alive even though bleeding energy through a great wound. Patrick was the doctor, the surgeon who sealed and closed and cured. But he was also a man with a man's mind.

What he did required a symbol, a focus to his thoughts. If that symbol for him was in sex, then so be it. It could as easily be in slicing an ax through a demon amulet. In truth, Xiao Fei preferred a man who favored a sexual union to one who needed violence to shape his thoughts.

She reached up and parted her robe, allowing it to slip to the ground at her feet. "I understand," she repeated with a smile.

So began his worship of the Earth, his blessing and reverence and communion with all that was the planet and her. He touched her face first, a soft exploration of cheek and ear, of the line of her jaw and the jut of her chin. His other hand joined the first, touching the opposite side of her face, the curve of her eyebrow, the ticklish drape of her hair. He pulled off her scarf and let it drop to the ground.

Part of her wanted to speak. Words trembled on her lips, but never quite formed. There was something missing in what they did. Something vital that left a hole as gaping as the demon gate. But Xiao Fei didn't know what it was, so how could she express it to him? She remained silent as she gazed into Patrick's eyes and he feathered caresses across her face.

He touched her lips and an electrical current tingled like the precursor to a storm. It centered on her mouth, setting her lips to a gentle burning. The energy was growing.

His eyes followed his caress, and she followed the shift of his gaze. So often the monks had soft gazes and unfocused eyes. Not Patrick. His attention remained laser sharp, and wholly centered on her. She had the feeling he saw everything about her. He would even know if her toes twitched, so total was his attention.

His thumb slipped inside her mouth. She tasted the rough texture of his skin, the hard edge of his nail, and the points where the two joined. The woman inside her body wanted to suck him in, wanted to pull him to her to hurry their joining; her need was already growing. But the part of her that was the Earth kept her steady and quiet. This act was for Patrick. This was his exploration, his worship, his joining. There would be time for her participation, but for now, he was simply growing accustomed to and learning the shape of things to come.

She waited, her breath quickening as he drew near. His thumb continued to stretch and touch—her tongue, her teeth, even the roof of her mouth. And the tingling current that burned in his wake set her entire mouth to a breathless wonder.

He withdrew his hand and a moment later stepped closer. She felt his robe brush against her knees, the press of fabric against her chest, and the near connection of his mouth against hers—but no completion, no true touch. He cursed softly and rapidly stepped back, leaving her bereft.

She might have said something then. The woman in her worried about so many things: men surrounding them, the demons who threatened, and the possibility of the ritual going wrong is a thousand terrible ways. But such worries only took away from her purpose, corrupting her will and her union with the Earth. So she pushed her fears away, and in time they were answered.

Patrick had stepped away to shuck his own robe. In fact, he took the time to lay his and her garments on the ground to form a kind of bower, but she kicked them aside.

"Do not create any barrier between us and Earth. We must touch the Earth and sky. . . ."

"Fire and water," he agreed.

For the first time, she noticed the chalice and the blade on the ground near their feet, and the candles that illuminated the clearing. Above them the sky had turned dark, broken by the twinkling of what stars could be seen past the half-moon and the bright city glow.

Without conscious thought, she opened her arms to the heavens, lifting her face and her chest to the night above. And she felt Patrick's lips on her breast as reward. She also felt the shift and touch of the demon amulet. Patrick no longer wore it as a necklace. He had the chain wrapped around one wrist so that it dangled a few inches below his hand. This way he could grab it easily when it was time, but it also meant that the demon stone brushed against her at odd moments and in unexpected ways.

Her body tightened, and the woman in her gasped. And yet, this burning of the amulet seemed to add to the experience, not detract from it. Pain was part of life, and no power came without cost. Mother Earth was part of her, and Mother Earth accepted the demon amulet. Could Xiao Fei do any less?

So she arched her back even more, giving herself up to Patrick. His mouth teased her breasts. He shaped the soft mounds with his hands, took her nipples in his mouth, and sucked gently, rhythmically. He rolled the peaks around in his mouth and nipped at them to shoot flashes of current through her body.

Thankfully his hands left her breasts to slip around her back; otherwise she would have tumbled to the ground. He supported her, and soon his mouth left her breast, too, tasting a long trail up her chest and chin to her mouth. There he claimed her lips as she had so wanted earlier. He took her mouth with his, and plunged his tongue inside. She clung to him. She tasted him. She teased and stroked and mated mouth to mouth in the most primal of ways. But it was not enough.

Her hands were wrapped around his shoulders, and she leaned shamelessly against him. She had long since lost all strength in her legs, so he was all that supported her. In time, he lost that battle as well. He guided her gently to the ground, then followed her to the sweet earth.

The loamy scent of grass and wood was stronger here, and she inhaled deeply to reinforce her connection with Mother Earth. Patrick, too, took deep breaths, but his face was pressed close to her skin, and she knew he breathed her scent and enjoyed the heat that rose like steam from her body.

"It's not working," he murmured suddenly, an edge of desperation in his voice. "It's not working."

She frowned, trying to separate woman from Earth long enough to understand. "Of course it is," she returned.

"No. I see only you." He pressed his lips against her belly and swirled his tongue in a tiny circle. "I taste only you. I . . ." He choked off the last.

She stroked her fingers through his sandy hair, enjoying the sensation as those cool strands slid across the back of her hand. "Take your time, Patrick. You need not be the Draig-Uisge yet."

He shook his head, then pressed his cheek into her hand. "You don't understand. I cannot see you as Earth. I cannot touch you without knowing you as Xiao Fei."

"All are one," she murmured. "I can be both."

"But—"

"Hush." She drew him up her body. She forced him to rise up past her breasts, though he pressed gentle kisses into her skin as he moved. "Look into my eyes." He did. "What do you see?"

"You."

"You are a druid. Do you not recognize the god in all? The One in everything?"

"Of course."

"Then move from me to the whole."

He shook his head, and his face tightened with worry. "I cannot."

She smiled. "You are thinking again."

"But—"

She pressed her fingers to his lips to stop his words. *"Feel."*

His mouth moved in erotic patterns against her fingertips. "I feel too much," he said. "I feel such fear, Xiao Fei. What if this doesn't work?" He closed his eyes, and she felt him struggle to remain calm. "I have done the hard thing before. I have fought and made difficult choices under the most desperate conditions, but . . . this is different." He opened his eyes. "This is *you*."

She met his gaze, waiting. He needed to take the last step.

It took him a long time, and when he finally understood, his gaze became tragic. "I love you," he said.

"Then love me. And in healing me, you will heal the Earth." So saying, she extended her arm. Before he could stop her, she flicked her thumb against the nearest tear along her wrist. It opened easily, and her blood welled. She felt the power surge with the pain, but it was nothing compared to the Patrick's reaction.

"What are you doing? It isn't time yet!"

"It is exactly the right time," she answered. Then she opened another tear and another and another. All the way up her arm.

"Stop! Xiao Fei, stop!" He grabbed her wrists and wrenched her arms apart. The act brought him on top of her in the most intimate of ways, and she welcomed his weight. "It's not time yet!"

She smiled, feeling the familiar outpouring of energy that came with her blood flow. It welled out of her and dripped into the fertile ground, returning to Mother Earth. "I am Earth," she said to Patrick, reinforcing the symbology he needed. "I am bleeding through the demon gate."

His eyes burned with intensity. She could not identify all the emotions that swirled in the blue depths, but she knew his body was tight with fear. "Xiao Fei," he murmured, the sound echoing with desperation.

"Join with me, Patrick. Heal me."

His expression flattened, and his eyes deadened—not in the way of a man growing cold, but in the way of a man facing an exam. His body hardened and his determination surrounded them in power. He was the Draig-Uisge, and he would accomplish this task.

He adjusted his hips, found her hot center, and thrust. The impact made her arch forward, even as her breath rushed out on a gasp. He was inside her and the sensation was amazing.

She looked up at him, startled to see that his expression had lost its flatness. His eyes were soft, his gaze unfocused. "Xiao Fei," he whispered, clearly agonized. "God, what am I going to do?"

"Isn't it obvious?" she asked.

He frowned a moment, processing her statement. Then, when she moved her hips and made a face, he abruptly burst into laughter—a single rolling sound that strengthened the energy around them. She doubted he felt the difference, but she did, and it was amazing.

Grinning in mischievous delight, she tightened her inner muscles, relishing his gasp. Then she wrapped her legs around him and held him immobile as she did it again.

"Xiao Fei!" he cried. "This isn't about sex."

"Isn't it? It's about joining with the Earth. I am the Earth. What are you?"

He blinked and tried to order his expression into a serious frown, but she tightened her muscles again in an irregular rhythm. Every time she saw his gaze grow abstract, she gripped him. That threw off his concentration, returned him to sensation and the moment, and she felt herself growing wetter and happier with his every frown.

"Stop it!" he finally gasped. "I'm supposed to be healing you. Healing Earth!"

"Kiss me, Patrick," she replied.

He blinked in confusion, but acquiesced. She received a very thorough, very deliberate kiss. And when he pulled back, she nodded in absolute seriousness. "Very nice," she said. Then she flipped them over, straddling him, her knees burrowing into the ground, her breasts jiggling between them, and her blood still sliding down her arm. Then she kissed him.

It was deep, thorough, and wholly unrestrained. Her plan had been to pour her every erotic fantasy into that kiss. She would imagine her fantasy lover in all the myriad possibilities. And yet, as their lips touched, her fantasy man instantly morphed into one surfer druid. He was Patrick, and she needed no other. She kissed him with all the love in her heart, and with this beautiful, sexy, American man she felt the power surge and pulse around them. He was overwhelmed with all she did.

She lifted up to breathe, but only a scant inch. Far enough to capture his slightly dazed eyes with her gaze. "I love you, Patrick," she swore. "Whatever happens, I have such love in my heart for you, I cannot contain it."

He swallowed, looking nervous. There was a power surge, and she suddenly wondered if she had inadvertently destroyed all hope of closing the demon gate. She had just made this union about her and him. But that was how she'd been taught to work: start with the small and grow into the large. She said again, "I lo—"

He surged upward, capturing her lips. And while she was responding to his tongue thrusting into her mouth, he rolled them sideways. They were side by side, facing each other on the ground.

"You are everything to me," he whispered. He began to move again. His thrusts were gentle, a steady slide as he and she began to flow together, Patrick into Xiao Fei and back. His hand caressed her breast, lifting and molding it, pinching the nipple.

Sensation built inside her. Power swirled around them. Fulfillment washed through her.

Xiao Fei was so startled by the abrupt welling of sensation that her breath caught on a cry. She arched into Patrick and shuddered in release. But still he continued to thrust in and out, in and out, the steady wet pulse like a backbeat to the music they made, to all the tingling explosions that zipped and zinged through her system.

"My God," he gasped, though she could barely hear him. "You're like the sun. Your power . . ."

"Join it," she gasped. "Join me."

And so he did. She felt his thighs bunch, his tension, energy, and focus building to fever pitch. His thrusting became erratic, less restrained. And with every push he made between her thighs, her own climax renewed like repeated flashes of light inside her.

He thrust, and his intensity pushed her again onto her back. He thrust, and her legs widened, giving him more access. He thrust, and her entire body convulsed with pleasure.

He thrust, and the miracle began.

Chapter Twenty-one

Patrick could not concentrate. All he could do was feel the incredible pleasure flowing through his body and see the most amazing woman on the planet. Beautiful Xiao Fei shuddered in luscious glory all around him. He saw her with his physical eyes, but he also felt her incredible, glowing light. She was radiant with an energy that surrounded them both, energy that burned like the sun. She was larger than a single person, more amazing than a single entity. She was one person who was also the link to the All. She was a small piece of the whole universe, and yet she was the whole universe in one tiny package.

She awed him, especially as she expanded her light and love to include him, to join with him, to be him, and he, her.

From there it was easy. They were merged, one with the other. Another breath and their awareness expanded. Together they knew the clearing, the plants and the birds, the dirt and the air. They knew the demons attacked all around, and felt the brave death of one of the youngest druids. That young man expanded out from himself, touching them before stretching somewhere Patrick couldn't follow.

Patrick wanted to linger, wanted to explore this amazing oneness with all. He knew, too, that he could help his brothers in the clearing: druids, bikers—even werewolves and vampires had come, joining in the battle. But he had his own task, and his time was growing short. Xiao Fei tugged his soul wider, larger, and he knew better than to resist. Together they expanded, becoming Earth and sky, sun and moon. And together they bled into the other planet.

Orcus, the demons' home planet. He felt the nexus where Earth and Orcus intertwined, and he felt the Earth pouring her energy into that dark world just as Xiao Fei poured her lifeblood into the ground.

He would seal her wound. He would seal the Earth's wound. He applied all of his power and skill to this effect, only to be disappointed. Nothing shifted; nothing changed. What was wrong? Entwined with his consciousness, Xiao Fei echoed his confusion.

He knew the answer. Almost before the question was phrased, he knew what he had to do—but his mind and heart rebelled. He hid the answer from Xiao Fei. If she hated werewolves and vampires, how would she react to this?

But he'd forgotten how embedded they were in each other. She was part of him, so she too struggled with his sudden understanding. She too knew what they had to do. They had to embrace Orcus. They had to know the demon planet and all it contained. Not only did they have to know it, but they had to love and embrace it.

They had to be one with it just as surely as they embraced all that was Earth.

The thought was repellent. These were the creatures who had brutally murdered his parents. They had ripped Cambodia apart and murdered all the monks and Phoenix Tears there. The images of Xiao Fei's experiences flashed in both their minds, merging with his own horrible memories.

Anger surged through him. Hatred, fury, bloodlust. He wished for destruction and death, the end of Orcus and the devastation of all demonkind.

But in that way, the nexus between the worlds widened. The ground buckled as the two planets were assaulted. The air boiled, for Patrick's fury created tidal waves of reaction in both worlds. For every evil he visited upon Orcus, an equal horror emerged on Earth. He could not harm one without devastating the other. Because all were one.

He didn't know which of them understood the truth first—Xiao Fei or him. It didn't matter. They both needed to stop. They both had to step past their anger and the fear. It was as she'd said. They had to . . .

Love.

A tiny ray of it whispered through his soul, lightening the darkness in his heart. It was Xiao Fei, focused on him, expressing her feelings. Patrick answered with his own love for her, his joy at their union, at the beauty of her wonderful presence. Theirs was a love that strengthened the more it was reciprocated, a love that was all-embracing and eternal. And most important, it was a love that healed.

Together, they turned their emotion outward, allowing their hearts to soothe what had been hurt, to calm that which boiled—on Earth and on Orcus. But their love was first and foremost for each other and the creatures of Earth—that was where it all had to begin.

Patrick knew what had to happen next. He understood, but he didn't act. It took Xiao Fei to open her heart first. She was the power; he was the one to shape and mold her. She shone brilliant with love. He took that energy, added his own, and shaped it into a force that healed. Together, they expanded that love to embrace both worlds. They accepted all, demon and human alike. And as the two worlds healed, they began to separate. The two worlds' existences grew stronger, and they naturally pulled apart.

The gate was closing!

Patrick could feel that all was becoming right again. He could sense that the rift narrowed, that soon all would be as before. And then . . .

A hand gripped his at the exact point where he held the amulet—a human hand, that of someone trapped on Orcus. It was a human woman, filled with terror and confusion and a dark hatred that coiled within her like a snake. In desperation, she grabbed onto all that was Earth and wrapped long fingers around the amulet.

Patrick tried to jerk away. It wasn't a conscious decision; with such love welling about him, the sudden presence of this darkness was like a blight on all that he and Xiao Fei did. But the human woman would not let go, and her despair reached him.

His other hand left Xiao Fei and reached for the amulet. His grip extended beyond the artifact to the new woman's hand, then to her wrist and forearm. With a single heave, he pulled her through from Orcus to the Earth.

The force of his motion ripped through him. He tumbled away from Xiao Fei and felt the amulet's chain uncoil from his wrist. The strange woman was there on the ground, too, her hand still clutching the amulet. Patrick's grip slackened as he stabilized himself. The amulet fell from his fingers as the woman gained her feet and ran, taking it with her.

"No!" he screamed, but she didn't slow. His body felt numb and empty with the loss of power; then fuller awareness intruded with a painful crash. He was no longer large and whole and all-embracing. He was just Patrick, sprawling naked on the dirty ground, while around him . . .

Heat seared past his head, blistering his shoulder before hitting the ground with explosive force. Dirt showered and stung his face while sound finally returned. He heard gunfire, explosions, and screams—some bellowed in anger; others sobbed in terror. And he heard a single whimper close by.

"Xiao Fei!"

The air cleared of smoke enough for him to find her. He scanned her body even as he scrambled to protect her. She was covered in blood and dirt, but her chest moved as she breathed, and her gaze was alert. She, too, was crawling forward, and as she moved, he saw that her wounds were sealed. She no longer bled.

"What happened?" she gasped.

"That woman . . ." He glanced around. He thought he saw her sprinting out of the melee, her body hunched, her speed almost inhuman as she dodged and jumped and finally disappeared. She didn't fade into the smoke; she faded out of existence. "Oh shit." With the amulet on her wrist and the eddies of power that swirled in the grove, that woman had just winked into the nowhere land between Earth and Orcus.

"The gate was closed!" Xiao Fei rasped.

"It still is!" he said, praying it was true. But was it? It had been. But something had changed when that woman came through.

He frowned, trying to focus despite the battle that raged all around. He could feel with his druid senses, could know more about the battle and the world from those than he ever could from his eyes.

Demons still surrounded the park, but the change in the gate disoriented them. They no longer worked as a coordinated unit, but railed and screamed and attacked without solidarity. The humans, vampires, and werewolves weren't nearly as confused. They picked their targets carefully, and one by one the demons fell.

"The gate . . ." Xiao Fei repeated in a whisper.

From somewhere to his right, a figure stumbled forward. It was Peter, a bloody knife gripped in his hand, and he dropped to his knees beside Patrick. "Is it done?" he rasped. Xiao Fei shifted to Patrick's other side.

Patrick closed his eyes and concentrated. The gate was closed. The worlds were separate again, but by only the thinnest margin. When the woman ran through, she'd torn the veil; she'd disrupted the energy—and her anger still kept the worlds dangerously close.

"Is it done?" Peter demanded again.

Patrick nodded, then shook his head. "It can be reopened easily. The veil is too thin."

Peter cursed with impressive venom. "We need more power," he said, turning to Xiao Fei. "I knew we would have to use all of her." And he raised his knife.

"Wait!" Patrick cried, but he was too slow. Xiao Fei reacted as well, but equally late. She protected her face and neck, but Peter was aiming for a different target. His knife tore into the tattooed tear on her left thigh.

Bright blood spurted upward before falling to soak

the ground. Lots of it, in a pulsing stream. Then Peter shifted the knife to Patrick.

"Finish it!" he bellowed. "Earth is more important than this one woman. Finish it!"

Patrick lunged forward, but not for vengeance. Peter and his knife were in the way, so he shoved the man aside with one powerful heave. Pete landed hard on the ground, far enough away for Patrick to close his hands around his beloved's wound.

"Close it, Xiao Fei!" Patrick screamed as he desperately searched the ground for something to stop her bleeding. His eyes fell on her scarf, but he couldn't reach it. And Peter suddenly reappeared in his line of sight.

"Do your duty, Draig-Uisge! Heal Earth," the druid demanded.

"She *is* Earth!" That wasn't exactly accurate anymore, but he hadn't the breath to explain. Especially as Peter gripped his shoulders and looked madly into his eyes.

"Don't waste her sacrifice. Save Ear—" But that was the last thing Peter said, for something ripped him apart from behind. Demons had breached the defensive perimeter. Three of them. And they were roaring forward.

Patrick barely spared them a glance. His focus remained on Xiao Fei, praying some defenders still remained. But the demons were heading for Xiao Fei, sensing she was the center of the rapidly dwindling energy they needed to reopen the gate.

Patrick turned and pushed Peter's body at the nearest demon just as a shotgun blast boomed through the air. The demon's head exploded in a bloody mass, and Hank appeared from out of the smoke. More shotgun blasts followed in rapid succession as he took care of the other attackers.

Then he grinned like a giddy schoolboy and gave a single thumbs up at Patrick.

Suddenly, Hank's chest contorted. He twisted grotesquely, blood and gore erupting from his entire left side before he dropped dead to the ground. Behind him stood . . . Jason, smiling evilly.

Patrick stared. He had no thought beyond a silent scream. *Jason* stood there. His dead former best friend was right in front of him. The man Patrick had twisted and contorted and killed ten years ago was very much alive.

He looked down at Hank's mangled body. There hadn't been a corpse ten years ago; Jason had just disappeared, eaten by his own corrupted energy. Or so Patrick had thought. Apparently not. Somehow, the man had survived. Not only had he survived, but thrived. He looked strong and healthy, dressed in stylish leather that perfectly matched his dark hair and even darker eyes. And power surrounded him like an electrical storm. It churned and coiled in the air between them, and Patrick knew it would take the slightest effort—the merest thought on Jason's part—to blow this whole park to oblivion.

"Give me the amulet," Jason said, his voice strangely compelling.

Patrick gestured vaguely off to the side. "Gone. Some woman."

"Damn. You never could get anything right."

Patrick just stared. Some part of him understood that he was facing a deadly threat; he knew that a battle still raged around him. Yet most of his attention remained fixed behind him on Xiao Fei. She was dying. And he couldn't help her, not without turning his back on this newest threat. Not without risking that Jason—the not-dead-Jason—would finish what Peter had started.

"Go away, Jason. There's nothing for you here."

"Oh, but there is. There's you." Jason stepped forward, and Patrick felt his hair lift as the crackling energy intensified. "Don't you want to know how I survived? How you failed to kill me?"

Patrick shrugged, his thoughts scrambling. How could he get rid of Jason as fast as possible? He had no weapon. Geez, he was standing naked in the middle of a field. His own energy was nearly gone, and he didn't even have the amulet to boost what little remained. All he had was his tenuous connection to Xiao Fei that told him her time was running out.

His only hope was to keep Jason talking and pray that somebody else shot him—soon. Unfortunately, Jason was human. He was standing and talking calmly to the Draig-Uisge. If anyone saw him, they would think he was a good guy.

"I went to Orcus, you bastard," Jason said. His energy crackled hotter, sending tiny pinpricks of pain through Patrick's skin. "You sent me to that demon hell to die."

"You were killing people."

"Demons!" Hatred boiled in the word.

Patrick threw up his hands in disgust. "So you masterminded an Earth invasion? You bring these bastards here to destroy both planets for revenge?"

Jason sneered. "Oh, I didn't mastermind this. I just came along for the ride when I heard it was happening." He shook his head, and Patrick saw oblivion in the man's eyes. It was more than disgust, more than horror—it was a black, all-consuming and total loathing of everything. "No, I was busy with another plan entirely."

"Which was . . . ?" Damn, where was everybody? One glance around told Patrick that the battle still raged. Demons continued to ravage, defenders continued to kill, all was death and chaos. Except for here, where Jason calmly listed his accomplishments. How strange that the man seemed just like he'd been as a teen: a braggart. Brilliant, powerful, and a bit sadistic, but he still needed an audience.

"Can't you feel it?" Jason asked. His energy surged again. Dark, ugly, and angry, it poisoned the air. "Power. Lots and lots of limitless power. To do with as I want, whatever I want."

"Why?"

Jason blinked, but he didn't stop talking. "I didn't need the amulet on Orcus. Going through changed me somehow. I was so damn sick at first. Dying, you bastard. Then I discovered I didn't need the amulet."

The energy continued to crackle along Patrick's skin, but each needle-prick of pain seemed to burrow deeper now. Jason's energy was slipping inside him somehow, syncing up and sliding in. It was an awful sensation—like black oil seeping into his soul—and he tried to shore up his mental defenses against it.

No go. As Jason continued to reminisce, the evil man's energy steadily infiltrated and corrupted Patrick's own.

"I could absorb energy without the trinket. Sure, it helps. And I'll get it back, by the way, don't think I won't. But I don't need it to take what I want."

The assault began: Jason began stealing Patrick's energy, Patrick's life force. He just sucked it away, draining it steadily while Patrick fought and struggled to stay himself, independent and separate from this psycho. But he had just opened himself to all that was—Orcus, Earth, Xiao Fei. They were intertwined. He couldn't close down what he'd just worked so hard to open. The transition just didn't work that fast.

And as Jason drew Patrick in, he drew in all the other

power as well. He was sucking in the life force of two entire planets.

"Why?" Patrick rasped. "What do you want?"

No answer. Jason was busy now. He had to manage the power flow. His concentration was fierce, his power unbelievable—and growing by the second. The energy flowed through Patrick to Jason. Patrick tried to direct the flow, to shape it somehow, but the stream was too fast, the current too strong. No man could stop it once the flow had begun.

Love.

The word whispered through Patrick's thoughts, the sound so soft it was a miracle he heard it at all. It came from Xiao Fei. She might have been sending him the thought for a while, but he only now heard it.

Love.

Yes, he loved her. She was dying. It was her last good-bye, not only to him, but to the world, because—thanks to Jason—both planets were now doomed to die.

"I'm not going to take it all, you know," Jason said. His voice trembled with strain. "I've got to live somewhere, don't I? I'll take just enough."

"Enough for what?" Patrick asked.

"Whatever I want."

No reason then, Patrick realized. Jason had no purpose beyond greed, no thought except of more power. Patrick felt himself drop to his knees, his body unable to support the current. Damn, how much could a man want?

Love. Again Xiao Fei's word slipped into his thoughts. He heard it, accepted it, and tried to dismiss it. He was battling for two worlds here. He had to maintain his focus. But her love was too bright to ignore, too insistent to forget.

"I love you, too," he whispered. He meant the words

324

for Xiao Fei. He sent the thought to her mentally even as he whispered it. And in that moment, the current changed. The moment he embraced her—even in his thoughts—was the moment the power shifted in nature. It warmed, it surged, it became more alive.

He heard Jason grunt with effort.

Love opens.

Patrick frowned. Xiao Fei was telling him something. Why didn't he understand?

Open.

Open what? Open Jason! Understanding rippled through him. Jason was just one man. He held and shaped the energy he stole; he didn't become it. It circled him, it surrounded him, but it didn't suffuse him because he was too small to hold it. No wonder Jason hated with such fury. That kept him closed to the energy. It kept him separate.

But if he was filled with love, if he had to open to what he did . . .

Patrick began to work. Amazing, how simple it was, how easy once he'd been shown the way. He began with the small and worked outward. He loved Xiao Fei. With his whole heart, he loved her. He loved the Earth and Orcus. Mentally, he embraced all that lived. He began with the plants and animals, the fish and the birds. He expanded to people—human, werewolf, vampire, demon—all were embraced. Human, werewolf, vampire, demon . . .

And villain.

He remembered Jason the boy. He remembered his friend's torn socks, ripped too-small jeans, and cocky grin. He recalled the boy's missing mother, distracted father, and the yearning for something else, something more. Love, though neither child knew it then. Jason had wanted love. And so Patrick gave it to him. He pushed the thought into the current. Better yet, he poured the emotion into the power of two planets and surrounded Jason with it. Love—eternal and all embracing. Love—complete and filling. Love—the power to open even the hardest hearts and the most closed mind. Patrick loved Jason as completely as he loved Xiao Fei. And with that love, he brought this entire horrible mistake to an end.

Jason screamed in agony. Patrick suffered, too. His love made him open to it. He experienced his friend's pain as if it were his own. He sensed it as Jason's soul opened to the love that surrounded him. It was a tiny crack at first, the smallest softening to the most overwhelming of wonders. And as Jason opened his spirit, Jason let the power in. He absorbed all the energy of the people he had killed, the souls he had taken, and the life force of two planets. All of it poured into him.

It was too much. No physical mass could contain it all. Jason's mouth stretched wide, his chest began to pulse and expand, and his body heaved. Patrick extended a hand, not knowing what he could do, but offering nonetheless.

It was too late. Behind him, he heard Xiao Fei scream. "Take cover!"

Before him, Jason convulsed. He gasped. And then he exploded.

There was no doubt of his death this time. Patrick felt the man's body explode. In his mind's eye, he saw Jason's spirit, too—bloated and diffuse—as it threw off all the energy it had taken. Power poured out in wave after wave. And Patrick knew what to do. It was easy, in fact. It was how he had first learned to see the energy, to feel the waves.

He surfed. He stepped upon an imaginary board and rode the waves of power. He entered that zen state of perfect acceptance, perfect unity with all that was. There was no ownership. How could one own the ocean or the power of two planets? You could only step onto a tiny piece of wood and enjoy the ride. If only he could share it with . . .

Xiao Fei was there. As soon as he had the thought, she appeared beside him, standing precariously on the board he navigated through the currents. He held her tight, laughing at the glory of it all, and feeling her love embrace and support them both. He returned it full-force, amazed that no matter how much energy he gave to her, she returned it magnified ten-fold. But then that was the power of love: it grew stronger the more it was shared.

Without Jason to hold it, the ocean of power returned to its natural state. The energy flowed back to each planet. Orcus took its own, and Earth held what belonged here. Patrick's job was to surf to the rough spots and use his will to smooth out the difficult separations. He and Xiao Fei did it together, laughing whenever the waves got rough.

And so, the veil that had been torn asunder began to knit. The forces that knotted the planets together began to unravel.

It was almost done. The balance was nearly restored.

Then Xiao Fei trembled and fell away.

In Patrick's mind, she simply lost her footing and slipped off the board. In reality, he knew she had lost too much blood. The link to her dying body was fading.

He could save her. He knew what to do. But he couldn't both knit her body and surf the energy. He couldn't seal the veil if he was shaping her healing.

He had to choose: Earth or Xiao Fei? A planet or the love of his life?

Indecision made him shake on the board. His footing began to slip. Then he jumped off.

He landed naked on his knees in the grove. Battle sounds still buffeted him from all sides, but his thoughts were on Xiao Fei. He saw her immediately. She was on the ground, blood still seeping from her leg, her skin a transparent gray. He scrambled forward, a scream on his lips.

"Xiao Fei!"

She opened her eyes. "Did you finish it?" she whispered. "Is it done?"

"Yes," he lied. In truth, he didn't know. It was nearly done. The energy ought to settle as it should, even without him there to direct it.

"Finish it," she ordered. "I've got a little power left. Use it . . ."

He didn't know how she knew the truth. Their hearts were so intertwined, she probably read it from him. But it didn't matter. He had abandoned the larger power to protect the smaller. He couldn't seal the veil if he tried. So he used her power not to save the Earth, but to surround her with love. He shaped the energy as she had taught him. He focused first on her thigh. Cell by cell, he painstakingly reknit the pulsing artery in her leg. As he worked, he had to fight the surge of each heartbeat, the blood that would rip open what he'd just put together. But the pressure was lessening, her blood loss severe.

Pushing away his fear, Patrick focused on her all his power, whatever energy he possessed, and all his skill. Breathless seconds later the artery closed. But he didn't believe it. He spent long moments making sure the vessel was sealed and the skin whole. Too much was at stake. Only after his sixth pass over the area did he finally allow himself to breathe. At last, the dreadful wound was closed.

He expanded his awareness to her full body, and realized he had taken too much time; she'd long since lost consciousness, her body slack and cold against him. But she was alive. Her heart still pumped what little blood was left through collapsing veins. There was hope.

He shifted his attention and searched out all her other little wounds. He closed the nick at her neck, a half dozen tiny cuts along her face and body, even a long, raw scrape on her knee. But it wasn't enough; she was still dying, and the terror of that thought would not release him. He knew that his fear interfered with his work. Love energy healed; fear corrupted and destroyed. That was what Xiai Fei had taught him. He'd done all he could anyway, and yet it caused a physical pain when he separated their minds.

The world was silent. That was his first thought. He heard no birds, no gunfire. Even the wind and trees were quiet. He blinked and tried to focus his eyes.

It was night, but several lanterns gave enough light to see people standing in a silent circle around him. One of the druids saw that he was aware, and silently offered him his robe. Patrick used it to cover Xiao Fei.

"She needs blood," he said, his voice raw in his throat. "Help me get her to a hospital."

"An ambulance is on its way," said the man.

Patrick nodded as a vampire pushed through the crowd. "The gate feels . . . different," the vamp said.

Patrick didn't answer. He was looking at Xiao Fei's skin. Even in the gentle glow of the lanterns, he could see the fine tracery of her veins, stark blue in her transparent flesh.

A hand gripped his shoulder. "Draig-Uisge! Did we succeed? Is the gate closed?" a voice asked.

He shook his head, his misery overwhelming. "I . . . don't know." All around him, the crowd muttered or cursed in anger. Patrick tried to care. God knew, part of him was horrified by what he'd done. Had he sacrificed the world to save one woman? Had he just betrayed the people who'd fought and died to protect him while he poured everything he had into Xiao Fei?

Try as he might, he couldn't regret his actions. And yet, he couldn't look into their eyes either. He couldn't speak as all. He simply wrapped himself around Xiao Fei and closed his eyes.

Chapter Twenty-two

Xiao Fei opened scratchy eyes and groaned. The light was too thick, and her head felt too bright. Were her eyes really open?

She blinked. Okay, they *were* open, but she really didn't want them to be. So she closed them again.

Fuzzy. Tired. Important.
Important? Mission. Mission: important.
Wake up!
Xiao Fei swam upward from the warm abyss of floating nothingness. Reality wasn't an improvement, but it did seem vital in some obscure way.

She opened her eyes. No, she blinked her eyes many, many times. What she was seeing couldn't possibly be real.

"Xiao Fei. How are you feeling?"

Sweet heaven, it was real. There was Patrick, looking like he'd fought a rooster in a pigsty, then slept in the mud.

"Xiao Fei?" her beloved asked.

"Water," she croaked.

He moved and pushed a straw into her mouth. She frowned but obligingly sucked. Tepid water flowed into her and tasted amazingly good. She took a few gulps, then pulled away. He set the cup to the side while she continued to frown at him. He wore a mud-and-blood–streaked white T-shirt that was too short on his lanky frame. And what was that smell?

"Water," she said.

He froze. "You want more?"

"No," she gasped. "For you. To wash."

He stared at her. Then he suddenly burst into laughter. It shook his frame and reverberated off the walls. In fact, he laughed so hard he had to brace himself on the bedside table.

Xiao Fei tried to lift up. She wanted to see when he actually collapsed on the floor, but her head was too heavy. And she was suddenly thirsty again. "Water," she croaked. "To drink."

It set Patrick off on another laughing fit. Fortunately, the door opened and someone else walked in. Xiao Fei turned to see Slick and a very big guy enter the room— her hospital room, she now realized. But something was wrong. They were dressed in basic jeans and tees, but Slick's eyes were rimmed in red and swollen. And her companion wasn't right. He was the druid named Dread, but it should be . . .

Hank. Hank was dead. He'd died protecting her and Patrick from demons. She remembered now. "Slick . . ."

"Well, I guess you're alive then, if he's laughing," Dread boomed, while Slick made it to the bedside. Without a word, the woman lifted the water cup and gently pushed the straw inside Xiao Fei's mouth.

Patrick sobered and touched Slick's shoulder. "You didn't have to come—"

"She wanted to report," Dread said from the other side of the bed.

"And bring you some clothes." Slick gestured to a plastic bag in Dread's hand. Then she looked down at Xiao Fei. "You're okay, right? They said you were, but there was so much blood."

"She'll be fine," Patrick said as he gave the woman a hug. She returned it in full measure, despite the dirt.

"Lots of people are fine, too," Slick said. "The remaining demons are on the run. B-Ops and others are chasing. But as for us . . ."

Dread continued when Slick faltered. "Seven druids dead, lots of wounded. But everyone's getting treatment—vamps and werewolves too." Dread glanced at her. "Your Chinese friend is doing fine."

Xiao Fei blinked. "Pei Ling? That's good."

Dread nodded. "Spry little guy."

Xiao Fei smiled. Only the massive Dread could call Pei Ling little. "But Hank," she whispered. "He saved our lives."

Slick pulled away from Patrick, wiping her eyes. "It's okay. He always wanted to go out a hero."

"I'm so sorry."

Slick touched Xiao Fei's hand and squeezed. She tried to return it, but Slick drew back too fast. Then Slick moved away so Patrick could move close again.

"How much do you remember?" he asked. She almost lost his question. He stroked her cheek in a caress that made her close her eyes to appreciate it better.

"Does she know?" Dread asked.

Xiao Fei's eyes sprang open. Did she know what? She remembered druids. A ritual. The gate. She frowned. "Something happened. The gate . . . Is it closed?"

"Yes," Patrick answered.

"Not for long," groused Dread. Patrick silenced him with a dark look. Meanwhile, Xiao Fei tried to concentrate. Everything was so fuzzy.

"I remember Jason. And surfing . . ."

"The gate is closed," Patrick repeated firmly. Xiao Fei wasn't listening; she was trying to feel for demons. She should be getting information. She should be sensing something, but when she tried, she came up with nothing.

"I can't feel anything," she said.

"You're paralyzed?" Slick gasped.

"No," Xiao Fei explained. "I can't feel the gate. I can't feel the Earth's energy at all."

"Has that ever happened before?" Patrick's voice was soothing and calm. She focused on its gentle cadence, on his warmth against her cheek, and his very solid presence where she gripped his hand. She didn't even remember clasping that, but they were joined in such a way nonetheless.

"Once before," she finally said. "In Cambodia. After . . ."

"After you closed the gate there."

"Yeah."

He stroked her palm. "But it came back, right? It was probably from the blood loss."

And the trauma, she finished silently. "I didn't want it to come back then. But . . ."

"It's okay. They poured a whole lot of other people's blood into you. As you recover, you'll probably get your power back."

She nodded, reassured. She'd often thought of her abilities as a curse. But while hemophilia was no picnic, it was her curse, and she felt "off" without the energy of her strange blood. She took a deep breath, mentally calming herself. The others waited for her to relax, and for that she was grateful. Until she remembered the purpose of this little discussion. "The gate. A woman ran through it? She—"

"Don't worry about that now." Patrick's voice was firm, but Xiao Fei ignored him. Of course she was worried about the gate. Extremely worried, now that she remembered Pete and his knife. She'd been dying, but there'd been so much power. Oceans of it.

"What happened?"

"You lost too much blood and started drifting in and out of consciousness. Without you to hold the connection, I couldn't shape the energy anymore." He leaned forward, his gaze strong, his touch against her cheek gentle. "The gate closed. The veil's just very thin right now. But it'll strengthen with time."

"Assuming the demons don't re-open it before then," Dread repeated.

"But they're not going to," said Slick. Her voice was strong and angry. "They're on the run with nowhere to hide."

"The whole city's looking for a little payback," Dread said with a nod. "We'll get them all soon enough."

Xiao Fei's gaze returned to Patrick. His face was calm, his eyes almost serene. "Could you have finished it? Could you have sealed the veil for good?"

He shook his head. "Not without you. Never without you."

"But . . ." Her words were cut off as he pressed a kiss to her lips. It was tender, and it heated her lips and her body as nothing else could. She hadn't even realized she was cold until he touched his mouth to hers. Then he slowly pulled back.

"Marry me, Xiao Fei."

She blinked. "What?"

"I love you. I can't live without you."

"But . . ." She frowned, trying to keep up. "What about the demons?"

"They're not invited."

She smiled. She couldn't help it.

"Well?" asked Dread. "Answer him!"

Xiao Fei grinned. Suddenly, everything felt right. None of it made any sense, but it all felt absolutely and totally right. She didn't care about gates or demons or any of the fears that had perpetually dogged her thoughts; for the first time ever, they were completely irrelevant. Patrick loved her, and she loved him. That was all that mattered.

"Yes," she said.

"Yes?" asked Dread.

"Yes!" echoed Slick.

"On one condition," interrupted Xiao Fei quickly. Patrick abruptly stilled. "You have to go shower now; then come back and make love to me until my eyes roll back in my head in ecstasy."

"Wow, that's a pretty tall order. I'm not sure I'm up to the task."

She leaned forward, pretending to want a kiss. He stretched nearer, only to be surprised when she reached her real target—her hand slipped down between the bed and his belly and found his long, hard length. "I think you're up to the task," she said.

"God, I love you so much," he said on a groan.

"I love you, too."

The morning light filtered slowly through the broken branches and across charred remains of the battlefield.

Barely thirty-six hours had passed since the fight, but Patrick felt as if it were all happening again, right in his head. He remembered the screams, watched again as Hank was gutted from behind, tasted the bitter air from Xiao Fei's blood spilling into the ground.

But Xiao Fei was fine. She'd been released from the hospital yesterday and now looked better than ever, especially bathed in the rosy tones of sunrise. Like him, she stood in silence, her body and spirit completely still.

"How do you get past it?" he asked her. "How do you . . ."

"Live to fight another day?" She slid her arm around his waist and tucked herself tight to his side. "You just do."

He walked to a half-broken branch. The tree wasn't going to be able to repair it, and so he pulled it off and tossed it into a nearby garbage can. "The amulet's still out there, you know. I have to find it." He began to clean.

Xiao Fei joined him in his task, spreading out mulch to cover bloodstains and gore. But when they both reached for the same shell casing, she shifted direction and grabbed his hand instead. "Do you?" she asked. "Do you really have to find that thing?"

He frowned. "You know how powerful it is."

"Yeah, but you can't sense it now—you're too weak."

He shook his head. "It's not because I'm too weak that I can't sense it." He sighed and sat wearily down on a tree stump. "We were using the amulet; it was working the energy. When she took it from me—that woman— she took the energy too. She . . ." How to explain? "She disappeared, Xiao Fei. Not into Earth. She's trapped somewhere between Earth and Orcus."

"Oh no," Xiao Fei whispered.

"It's not that bad. It'll feel like nothing to her, like no time at all. And eventually, she'll reappear on Earth."

"Not Orcus?"

He shook his head. "I don't think so. She's human. Her energies should reassert themselves and take her back where she belongs: here."

"But, when?"

Patrick sighed. That was the problem exactly. "I don't know. Could be five minutes, could be months."

She pressed her fingers to his lips. "So we have time to rest."

He nodded. It was time they needed—not only to rest, but to attend funerals and sanctify a new druid leader. He pressed a kiss into her palm, then turned away to pick up the shotgun shell. It could have been from any of a number of guns, but in his mind's eye, he saw Hank shooting the three demons. He saw Hank saving their lives before he was brutally murdered. Then other faces whipped through his mind: Pete, Jason—his parents as well, and a dozen other victims.

"You can't keep torturing yourself," Xiao Fei said, interrupting his thoughts. "We closed the gate, Patrick. It's time to rebuild."

He swallowed, startled to realize how trapped he could be in this grove, in the events of the last few days. "I don't know if I can go back, Xiao Fei. I don't know if I can go to San Bernadino, drive by my parents' empty home, and just pick up where I left off."

"You can't," she agreed, her voice tender. "But you can go on. We'll do it together. We'll help each other."

As she spoke, Slick came into the grove. She carried a seedling of an olive tree—for Hank and for peace. The real service would be in a few days, but for now, this was the healing they all needed. Patrick and Xiao Fei watched as Slick planted. "May it grow strong in this land and in our hearts," the woman said as she poured water onto the roots.

Patrick added his own silent blessing. But when it was over, his mind continued to spin, continued to worry. "I'll have to find that woman. She's going to be disoriented. She won't understand—"

"Not now," whispered Xiao Fei. "Not yet." Then she pressed a kiss to his lips. Her mouth was warm, her touch a balm, and just like that, he found the strength to go on. With her help, he could release the past and look to the future.

He lingered as long as he could over their kiss, but at last drew away. Taking her hand, the two walked together to the car. Slick joined them. She would come along to San Bernadino and be part of the ceremony that made Patrick the next Druid leader. She was also going to be a bridesmaid at their wedding.

There was a bright future spread before him. Did he have the strength to face it, to grasp it with both hands and hold on? Patrick glanced down at Xiao Fei just as she looked up and smiled at him. Of course he did. With her he'd faced the end of the world. What could be worse than that?

"You know," said Xiao Fei, "I'm the last of the Phoenix Tears. It's my solemn duty to reestablish the line." She gave him an impulsive hug, and brightened his world. "We're going to have babies, Patrick. Lots and lots and lots of babies!"

CRIMSON CITY

Don't miss any of this fabulous series!

CRIMSON CITY
Liz Maverick

A TASTE OF CRIMSON
Marjorie M. Liu

THROUGH A CRIMSON VEIL
Patti O'Shea

A DARKER CRIMSON
Carolyn Jewel

SEDUCED BY CRIMSON
Jade Lee

CRIMSON ROGUE
Liz Maverick
April 2006

Hungry Tigress
JADE LEE

Joanna Crane joined China's Boxer Rebellion because of the emptiness inside her. But when the rebels—anti-foreigner bandits with a taste for white flesh—turn out worse than their ruthless Qin enemies, her only hope is a Shaolin master with fists of steel and eyes like ice.

He has no wish to harm the meddling American, so, when she learns his secret, Joanna's captor determines to stash her at a Taoist temple. True, the sect is persecuted throughout the land, but he sees no harm in seeking divinity through love. What he does not see is that he and Joanna are already students, their hearts are on the path to Heaven, and salvation lies in a kiss, a touch, and sating the…*Hungry Tigress*.
